AN ELUSIVE HEART

"Will you dance with me, Julianna?" Carlton asked, his gray eyes beseeching her intently.

"Yes, of course I will," she breathed, uncertain if she had spoken loudly enough to be heard. He smiled, faintly again, as he had when she had first seen him at the entrance to the rooms. He then offered his arm and led her out onto the floor.

"Are you all right?" he asked, turning her to look at him. "You're very pale."

"How else should I appear," she asked, "given the circumstances?"

He frowned slightly as he led her to a place on the floor in preparation for the waltz. Only vaguely was Julianna aware that all about her other couples were arranging themselves to make up the numbers. Her heart, her mind, her eyes, were, for the moment, all for Carlton.

He began speaking, and it was as though her mind was inside his own. "I love you," he began quietly, looking into her eyes. "Whatever you choose tonight, it will not change that love. I will always love you. But tonight you must choose. Tomorrow, I must marry. But I beg you will choose me, Julianna. Choose me, choose my love for you and my determination to spend the rest of my life proving that you can trust me."

Julianna averted her gaze, not wanting to think or to choose.

ZEBRA'S REGENCY ROMANCES
DAZZLE AND DELIGHT

A BEGUILING INTRIGUE   (4441, $3.99)
by Olivia Sumner

Pretty as a picture Justine Riggs cared nothing for propriety. She dressed as a boy, sat on her horse like a jockey, and pondered the stars like a scientist. But when she tried to best the handsome Quenton Fletcher, Marquess of Devon, by proving that she was the better equestrian, he would try to prove Justine's antics were pure folly. The game he had in mind was seduction—never imagining that he might lose his heart in the process!

AN INCONVENIENT ENGAGEMENT   (4442, $3.99)
by Joy Reed

Rebecca Wentworth was furious when she saw her betrothed waltzing with another. So she decides to make him jealous by flirting with the handsomest man at the ball, John Collinwood, Earl of Stanford. The "wicked" nobleman knew exactly what the enticing miss was up to—and he was only too happy to play along. But as Rebecca gazed into his magnificent eyes, her errant fiancé was soon utterly forgotten!

SCANDAL'S LADY   (4472, $3.99)
by Mary Kingsley

Cassandra was shocked to learn that the new Earl of Lynton was her childhood friend, Nicholas St. John. After years at sea and mixed feelings Nicholas had come home to take the family title. And although Cassandra knew her place as a governess, she could not help the thrill that went through her each time he was near. Nicholas was pleased to find that his old friend Cassandra was his new next door neighbor, but after being near her, he wondered if mere friendship would be enough . . .

HIS LORDSHIP'S REWARD   (4473, $3.99)
by Carola Dunn

As the daughter of a seasoned soldier, Fanny Ingram was accustomed to the vagaries of military life and cared not a whit about matters of rank and social standing. So she certainly never foresaw her *tendre* for handsome Viscount Roworth of Kent with whom she was forced to share lodgings, while he carried out his clandestine activities on behalf of the British Army. And though good sense told Roworth to keep his distance, he couldn't stop from taking Fanny in his arms for a kiss that made all hearts equal!

Available wherever paperbacks are sold, or order direct from the Publisher. Send cover price plus 50¢ per copy for mailing and handling to Penguin USA, P.O. Box 999, c/o Dept. 17109, Bergenfield, NJ 07621. Residents of New York and Tennessee must include sales tax. DO NOT SEND CASH.

The Elusive Bride

Valerie King

ZEBRA BOOKS
KENSINGTON PUBLISHING CORP.

ZEBRA BOOKS are published by

Kensington Publishing Corp.
475 Park Avenue South
New York, NY 10016

First Printing: June, 1994

Printed in the United States of America

To Charlene, a friend for every season

Beauty is truth—truth is beauty.

John Keats

Chapter One

Lord Carlton stood on the threshold of the Angel Inn, looking outward at the gray sky, at the snow banked all about the edges and corners of the stableyard, at the stone cobbles made dark by snowmelt. A chill March Yorkshire wind, stealing brazenly through the inn's wide, stone-arched gate, bit at his cheeks and reminded him yet again that he was in the north of England, instead of the friendly south, and that he had come on a most hated mission—marriage.

An *arranged* marriage.

Snow had greeted his arrival to the north, a blight to his first journey to Yorkshire in many years and a reminder of why he never traveled beyond Nottinghamshire if he could help it. His closest friend and companion, Edward Fitzpaine, had accompanied him for the strict purpose of supporting him during the wedding ceremony, but had succeeded in adding to the difficulties of the trip. As a budding poet, Edward had insisted that a trip across the wild moorland of the Hambleton Hills beginning at Thirsk and ending at the village of Redmere tucked on the west side of the Vale of Pickering was most decidedly in order. After all, Sutton— some nine hundred feet higher in elevation than Thirsk— was not to be missed. His poet's heart and eye must have a view of the York Plain and the Pennines, a panorama which could only be witnessed from Sutton atop the Hambleton Hills.

Lord Carlton had wanted to travel northeast from York to Malton and into the Vale of Pickering—a much less harrowing journey, especially at the end of March, when the weather could still be unpredictable.

But Edward would have none of that! He had not come all this distance—over two hundred miles from London—to miss seeing what had long been one of his objects.

When Lord Carlton had suggested the possibility that once he was safely wed, Edward could spend the rest of his life at Sutton if he so wished for it, his friend had eyed him with hostility and countered with the notion that Carlton hadn't the bottom for such a trip.

Of a practical turn, Carlton pointed out that however-much he would ordinarily accept such a blatant challenge to his pride and dignity, of the moment his largest concern was reaching the village of Redmere in a timely manner. He wished to do so—without mishap from traveling lesser maintained roads and losing a wheel or breaking a pole—so that his marriage to a young lady, completely unknown to him, might have at least some small chance of enjoying a propitious beginning.

In Ferrybridge, however, Edward enlisted the aid of a retired postboy who said he had ridden from Thirsk to Sproxton for years and that he knew the way as well as he knew his left foot—which, he had seen fit to add, had been maimed in the Battle of Salamanca many years ago. Lord Carlton had wondered at the time if this was somehow an ill-omen. But Edward, always willing to seek the brightest side of a dark cloud, merely shoved him into his traveling chariot and told him to stop being so henhearted.

So Sutton it was, along with a heavy snowfall, fog, and a cold wind that howled over the carriage like a pack of wolves. Poor Edward did not have his view from Sutton after all, but the aging postboy had been as good as his word and had delivered them safely to Sproxton and the village of Redmere three miles south, without the smallest mishap.

An unforgiving, barren land, he mused, as he watched a bluenosed stableboy, hugging his arms, race from the gate to the stables. *Unforgiving and barren, probably not unlike my future wife.*

The truth was, the bridegroom had not wished to arrive at all! But here he was, standing beneath a leaden sky, his heart heavier than the clouds above, taking a last breath of cold freedom into his lungs before ordering the horses put to. Shortly, he would complete the last leg of his journey—a mile or so to Marish Hall, Lord Redmere's home—and a few feet more, *down the aisle* into the yawning chasm of wedded bliss.

He would never have married at all, he thought, save that if he wasn't wed by his birthdate in late April, he would forfeit his title and estates to a most unworthy, weak-willed cousin. His absurd relation was a veritable pink of the ton who, in Carlton's opinion, should have been drowned at birth, for a more useless fellow he had never known.

The viscount had always supposed he would have been married by now. He certainly had never had the least intention of letting the years drift by and ram him into a corner of desperation. He had always believed love would arrive at an opportune moment and spare him the natural discomforts a marriage of convenience would undoubtedly afford him.

But the years had drifted by, love had eluded him completely, and this marriage—set into motion by his informed grandmama—was all that he had been able to contrive after ten years of being a man about town. In less than an hour, he would be joined in matrimony to a veritable stranger, to a chit just barely turned nineteen, and his heart as far away from her as it could possibly be.

Providence, deliver me, he murmured, his breath streaming away from him in a soft vapor of mist.

An unearthly quiet surrounded him suddenly as he stepped off the threshold of the inn and pulled the door shut behind him. He had never known such silence before—the perpetual wind had stopped most unexpectedly, the habitually bustling stables in front of him were oddly still, and even from the kitchens behind, the murmurings, squabblings, and laughter of the inmates within had all but disappeared.

Just as quickly as the quiet had intruded, so then did a sudden, long gust of wind sweep abruptly through the stone gate and pierce his chest, the snowy cold ringing in his bones. He shivered for a moment, flicking his head backward in an attempt to shake off a chill as he puffed out another breath of vapor from his lungs. He was about to utter an oath when suddenly a young woman appeared, riding hard on horseback, a dark green hooded cape tied beneath her chin and soaring out behind her as though she was a kestrel in flight. Quickly bringing her horse to a walk, she passed by him, her cheeks pink with cold.

Good God! What sort of phantom had arrived?

She was by far the prettiest female he had ever seen. But who was she? Was she running from someone? he wondered. He knew a powerful impulse to discover from whom and why.

She in turn glanced curiously at him, a questioning frown between pretty brows as she guided her chestnut mare to a halt near the stables where she called to one of the stableboys by name. She dismounted her horse, rapping her gently on the rump. The mare, her coat steaming from her exertion and the cold, needed no encouragement to take herself into a place promising warmth and hay.

Carlton stared unblinking at the young woman, feeling as though he had been struck senseless by a powerful Olympian spell—his limbs would not obey his command to move, his mouth had fallen rudely agape, and even his heart beat a fast, demanding cadence in his ears.

Who was she?

Even though he was about to marry, he had to know. Was this *Providence*? He had uttered the prayer, hadn't he? Was his request to be answered in so stunning a manner, on a river of wind?

When she turned to look at him again, a second sensation assailed him, as though he had just been kicked hard in the stomach. Her direct gaze as she watched him, the poise she exhibited in her every movement, and the intelligence in her eyes bespoke a lady of quality of exceptional abilities. His skin prickled in anticipation of making her acquaintance and he forgot for the moment that in less than an hour he would be joined in matrimony to Julianna Redmere.

He bowed to her very slowly and deliberately. When he straightened he was not surprised that she approached him. She would not have been the first to have been entranced by his careful manners or his practiced countenance.

The closer she drew, time seemed to slow, permitting him the wondrous privilege of scrutinizing her beauty of face and form. She was clearly a diamond of the first water, her skin as smooth and delicate in appearance as fresh cream.

He knew a desire to draw near her, to touch her cheeks, to determine for himself if her complexion was as soft as it appeared. Her face was oval in shape, her cheekbones high and beautifully rounded, her nose straight, her lips a moderate perfection. Arched brows were still drawn together in a concerned frown over quite possibly her best feature—large, sparkling green eyes.

He watched her lips move. They must be forming words, he thought, but he couldn't yet hear them. He was too caught up by the sight of her rosy lips to be able to actually *hear* her speak. How many young men had ignored her maidenly protests and kissed her anyway?

He ought to listen to her now, though, lest she come to think he was addled. He opened his ears. Her voice reached him through a continuing daze of sentiments as he regarded her. The timbre which rose from her swan's throat was a warm blend of the strings of the viola and a soft feminine sound which seemed to penetrate his chest and envelop his heart. What was she saying?

"Sir?" he heard her query at last. "Can you not hear me? Are you unable to perceive my questions?"

"Of course I can," he responded with a half smile. "I just

wasn't ready to hear you. Your beauty, miss, has deafened me."

Then she smiled, a giggle catching in her throat. "But how absurd you are! How can something you see with your eyes affect your hearing?" A glimpse of even, white teeth confirmed his opinion that she was in every respect a deuced lovely female.

"I don't know," he said honestly. "But for a moment, I felt completely lost, and though I saw your lips move, your voice was shy of my ears. I am, however, in complete command of my senses now, so pray tell me, how may I serve you?"

Her smile diminished in stages as she glanced nervously about her, up to the windows of the first floor and then behind her to the stables, before speaking again.

"Are you perchance Lord Carlton?" her resonant voice whispered. "I must know. Pray forgive my impertinence, but I am aware that you are foreign to Yorkshire, at least, to the Vale of Pickering, for I have lived here all my life and know everyone from miles about. Carlton is expected to arrive. Are you he?" She pulled her forest green velvet cloak more tightly about her neck, shivering slightly as the cold wind lifted the garment high about her shoulders only to set it down with a heavy thud against her white satin gown. The hood, secured close about her face, fell slightly askew and several red curls escaped from the confines of her cape. She brushed them away from her green eyes with a sweep of her hand, resettled the hood, and smiled faintly by way of encouragement.

His mind was all confusion. Magnificent red hair, perfect teeth, the visage of an angel. What had she asked him? Was he Carlton? Of the moment, he did not know who he was.

When at last he spoke, it was not to answer her question. "Won't you come in out of the cold?" he asked instead.

As he stepped aside, opening the door carefully and gesturing for her to precede him, she hesitated for only a moment. She then brushed quickly past him and entered the hallway leading to the taproom.

Who was she?

Yorkshire! Of all places to find a goddess! Perhaps even love, if *Providence* indeed had had a hand in her timely arrival.

As he heard the rustle of her skirts and saw the dappled water and mud stains all about the hem of what he could perceive was an expensive, pearl-strewn white gown, the cool air of the hallway suddenly felt like a blast from a kiln. Awareness licked at him like hot flames.

Suddenly, he knew precisely who she was.

Hell and damnation!

His bride!

Julianna Redmere!

The young lady before him could be none other!

She fit perfectly the description given to him by two of his acquaintances, each of whom had seen her at the Harrogate Assemblies the year prior. The white gown reinforced the truth of her identity. He had always believed his friends had exaggerated her beauty for the sake of his sensibilities—what man in his situation would not fear he would soon be marrying a platter-faced ape-leader? It had never occurred to him that both gentlemen were actually relaying their opinions honestly.

Now he was looking at his bride for himself and could see, if anything, they had failed to convey her beauty in even a particle of its perfection.

However . . .

He drew in his breath, because however much he might be a connoisseur of beauty in the feminine form, appreciation did not rule him in this moment, but rather a sort of blinding rage which emanated from the striking and sudden belief that he was being toyed with.

Why was she here, when scarcely half an hour remained before the commencement of their nuptials? She had fairly ruined her bridal gown in the process of stealing away to the Angel Inn and, as soon as her absence was noticed, would cause a scandal to rain down upon his head. Did she expect him to be pleased to have his bride water-stained and muddied as she joined him, before her mother's host of guests, in matrimony? He could do little more at this juncture than eye her with suspicion and hostility. After all, she had completely disrupted his enjoyment of his last hour as a bachelor.

All his former pleasure in viewing her physical beauty dissipated like chaff in the wind. She could have been a goddess, indeed, and he still would have resented her presence.

And worse. Was this how the future Lady Carlton meant to conduct herself once they were wed? Would she be forever casting a rub into his contentment and amusements? He wouldn't have it, not by half!

When they reached the empty taproom, she turned to face him squarely. "Are you Carlton?" she asked again, pushing back the hood of her cloak to reveal a mountain of red curls laced with pearls and crowned with a garland of small, artificial white roses.

He blinked several times at her. Now why was it that the mere sight of her hair sent his uncharitable thoughts flying about disjointedly in his brain until they all but disappeared?

He couldn't say.

All he knew was that he could not remember having seen such glorious red hair. It was glossy, thick, and by the manner in which it was coiffed, very long. A sudden image of her hair dangling about creamy white shoulders slipped traitorously into his mind, of his fingers becoming entangled in the web of her tresses, his lips pressed against the mass, first in one place, then another, perhaps touching her shoulder . . .

He shook his head by way of attempting to clear the unwelcome vision from his brain.

"Oh, I see," she said, surprising him, the frown again creasing her brow. Apparently she had thought this shake of his head to be his answer. "Are you acquainted with Carlton, then?" she pressed him. "Are you perchance his friend, Mr. Edward Fitzpaine?"

"Yes," he responded promptly.

Now what the devil had caused him to tell such a whisker, and where would it lead him? He had the chill feeling he had just committed a grave error and that he ought to correct it at once, but such was his state of mind in finding his bride at this inn just prior to their wedding that instead he remained silent and waited for her to speak.

Chapter Two

Lord Carlton watched his bride carefully as her slender fingers glided along the gold-embroidered edge of her dark green cloak front. He believed the crease between her brows was clear evidence that she was weighing a heavy matter in her mind. How oddly fragile she appeared as she traced the embroidery with her fingers, her gaze dancing from any number of objects near the wood floor of the taproom, from the tips of his black leather top boots, to the spindly legs of a stool by the stairs, to the yellow-and-white cat curled up on the windowseat in front of the bow window, to the scuffed wooden bar. All the while, she chewed ever so slightly on her lower lip.

Finally she spoke, her brow clearing. "Would you spare a moment alone with me, sir? I have a matter of great import to put to you, and since I have heard you described as a man of sense, I would value your opinion. Indeed, I find myself in a desperate quandry and in need of—of advice."

"Are you sure you can trust me?" he queried, blatantly extending a hint to her that she ought not to.

"Whether I can truly trust you, I cannot say. You have a candid manner of speaking which I admire and which lends itself to *trust*, but only you know to a certainty whether I can offer my confidences to you without worry or fear. For the moment, I rely on your reputation alone for making my decision. Will you come into the parlour with me? I shan't detain you long, I promise."

She offered her arm by way of encouragement. The cloak fell back, revealing a pretty puffed sleeve of tulle and the snowy skin of her arm leading to a well-shaped wrist and hand. How could he do other than take her arm and avail himself of her invitation?

When she looked up at him and smiled so very sweetly, any remaining anger at her unlooked-for arrival deserted him. Whatever her faults might be, he would forgive her, and as soon as she had revealed the nature of her *quandry,* he would, in turn, tell her the truth about his identity. Until then, he decided he would enjoy this moment of hearing what his betrothed might have to say to a mere, harmless, *sensible* Mr. Edward Fitzpaine.

"I am at your service, Miss Redmere."

He drew her into the clean, whitewashed parlour, where she began a slow, almost thoughtful progress across the tidy chamber. How prettily she moved, swaying gently, so light upon her feet. The curtains of blue gingham were drawn away from the window, permitting the subdued, cloudy light to bathe her cloak of forest green. She paused for a moment before a square table of highly polished oak which sat in the very center of the room, straight-legged, flat-footed, and proud on the worn but gleaming Angel Inn floor. She reached out, rather sadly, it seemed to Carlton, as he continued to watch her, and touched a dried stalk of pink heather, a mound of which filled a brass tub in the middle of the table.

She sighed, and completed the distance to the fireplace which glowed with a thick layering of coals. Near the hearth was a settle and over the mantel hung a coaching print by James Pollard. Only when she lifted her hands to warm them at the fire did she speak. "So you know who I am."

With the practice of a man who had slain the hearts of a score of pretty young females over the course of a dozen London Seasons, he responded, "I would be a perfect simpleton not to have known the beautiful Miss Redmere upon first glance." He closed the door easily behind him with a careful kick of his booted foot.

"Oh, pray, do not attempt to flirt with me, Mr. Fitzpaine," Julianna countered with devastating frankness, looking back at him. "I haven't the heart for it, though I must confess, you seem a most obliging gentleman, besides being perhaps the handsomest man I have ever met. Still, if you would attend me most assiduously, I would be immensely grateful."

"Did I appear to be flirting?" he queried, placing a hand at his breast as though she had wounded him. "What sort of man would I be to go about flirting with the betrothed of my bosom beau?"

She smiled, her green eyes dancing with amusement. "A confirmed rake!" she answered forthrightly. "As I have been warned an hundred times by Mama's friends and acquaintances."

He was caught.

That much he admitted to himself without reservation. Caught by her candor, by her beauty, by her good sense. And she was his bride. How very much suddenly he wished it otherwise, for what fun he might have had pursuing such a disarming creature—instead of just marrying her!

"I don't know whether to be angry with your mother's friends or to applaud at least one of them who has warned you most sensibly of the dangers any young, unprotected female might experience unawares." He had answered in a lighthearted manner, intending primarily upon sustaining the wonderful green glints of light shining from her eyes. But for some reason, his words returned the frown to her brow and her shoulders dropped a notch as she whirled and sank to the settle beside the glowing fireplace. Her gaze became fixed upon her muddied white slippers.

"What is it?" he queried, crossing the room to seat himself beside her and adopting his most concerned expression.

"I shan't detain you long," she said, untying the strings of her cloak and pushing it away from her shoulders. The enchanting décolleté of her gown naturally drew his gaze toward the soft mounds of her bosom. Strands of pearls, entwined in gentle ropes of a beautiful white gauze, decorated the length of the bodice, ending where the delicate puffed sleeves of tulle began. He repressed a sigh, and only with the strongest of efforts was he able to return his gaze to her face.

Her lower lip trembled as she continued, "Only tell me this, for I have been given to understand that your friendship with Lord Carlton is of long standing—does, does his lordship wish for this marriage? I know it must seem an odd question to ask and at such an eleventh hour, but I have heard such things of late as to cause me to wonder if—well, I have begun to think he may not wish for a wife at all."

Carlton leaned back against the shiny horsehair cushions of the settle and watched her profile. "Of course he wishes for the marriage," he said, intending to reassure her. "Why would he have come if he did not want to marry?"

Julianna glanced sharply at him. "You answer too easily, Mr. Fitzpaine," she said simply. "I'm afraid you have now convinced me what I suspect is true."

"Do you tell me I have lied to you?"

"No," she answered slowly. "But I do think you are coming it a bit too strong."

He smiled. "I suppose you are right. But do you realize what an awkward position you place me in as Carlton's *friend*?"

"Oh, I see," she responded. "Yes, of course I do. How silly of me. I won't trespass further on your kindness. Would you be so good as to fetch his lordship for me? I realize now that I ought to address this matter to him directly. I was only hoping for your impressions lest, given the lateness of the hour, he should be unwilling to speak the nature of his heart to me." He could see tears sparkling on the ends of her lashes. "It is merely that I fear I may soon be entering a marriage that would neither give comfort to his heart nor joy to mine."

He knew a most profound desire, quite inexplicable, to take her in his arms and comfort her with a kiss or two. Then she laughed, and retrieving an embroidered white kerchief from the pocket of her cloak, said, "You will now think I am the silliest goose that ever lived—a veritable watering pot."

As she began to touch the kerchief to the corners of her eyes, Lord Carlton discerned that for some reason his bride did not really wish to speak to her bridegroom at all. This left him with the alternative of prolonging the interview if he wished for it. And of the moment he found to his surprise he wished for nothing more!

It wasn't that he wanted to hurt her or to embarrass her by his pretenses, only that being with her and receiving her confidences was a sensation akin to paradise. Some part of him, some deep hitherto unknown part of him, reveled in the quiet intimacy of the moment, and he determined he would do nothing that might jeopardize these few minutes with her.

At the same time, he was fully aware that the longer he maintained her belief he was Edward Fitzpaine, the harder it would be for her ever to trust him again once she learned his identity. Yet for all that, he simply had to know what she intended to say without her being cognizant of who he really was. He wanted to see the expression in her eyes when she spoke further of her dilemma, her worries, of what she had heard of late. He longed to see the truth of her sentiments exposed without the dampening effect *Lord Carlton's* presence would undoubtedly inspire.

Therefore, he said nothing, but instead gently wrested the kerchief from her hand and slowly began dabbing at the several teardrops which only now tipped from her eyes and rolled down her cheeks.

Having completed the task of ridding her face of teardrops, he pressed the damp kerchief back into her hand. "You spoke of having heard gossip regarding his lordship. I would suppose, then, that the tattlemongers have been busily employed since the posting of the banns. Is this so?"

She let out a great breath of air, apparently grateful that he had decided not to *fetch his lordship* after all.

"Yes," she nodded emphatically. "You cannot imagine all that I have heard! His escapades—in the manner they have been related to me—are horrifying in the extreme. But beyond this, it is even rumored he still keeps a—a—fancy-piece." She lowered her gaze as a blush crept steadily up her cheeks. For all her mature beauty of person, for all her sense and directness, in this moment she seemed very young.

Lord Carlton felt his anger return to him. "A fancy-piece?" he asked, stunned that anyone would have said something so vile to his betrothed, or within her hearing. Who would have been so cruel as to have told Julianna that the man she was about to marry was dallying in the Cyprian Corps?

Any of a dozen, he thought cynically.

Of course it wasn't true, not even in the remotest sense. Contrary to the wretched tales told of his conduct, he had never in his life supported a mistress. Any of his friends who had done so had soon found themselves in the basket before the cat could lick her ear, for these women were ravenous, their central ambitions relating more to the acquisition of wealth and fine jewels than anything of a noble nature. But the very thought that he had been maligned to Julianna sickened him, and he found he was able at last to comprehend something of the source of her distress and what had driven her to seek him out at the Angel.

"I hear he is very much in love with his mistress," she whispered, nodding again, her gaze firmly pinned to her lap.

Lord Carlton felt his eyes burning beneath their lids. He was looking at Julianna's red locks, but not seeing them at all. He thought of the ropes of gossip which drew all of Mayfair together into a tight knot of excited misery. He wondered how many fine young women, with whom he might before-times have found love, had been turned away from him by more scrupulous mothers who had heard and *believed* all the gossip spoken of him. In his heart, he knew there might easily have been a score of them, and this knowledge increased the burning sensation upon his eyes.

Julianna ceased to exist entirely in the heat of his angry thoughts. The truth came to him that he had been deprived of love, of real love, because of the Tabbies, and rage consumed him.

He looked beyond Julianna into the thick coal fire, feeling his hands ball up into tight fists. His jaw ached as he ground his teeth together.

The Tabbies!

How he despised them, one and all!

How he would revel in taking revenge on them.

If only he could.

Revenge.

Revenge could be sweet. He had heard so a hundred times. But how? How to do it?

"Tell me, Miss Redmere," he said at last, his gaze shifting to the artificial white roses wreathed among her red curls. "What precisely has been said about my very good friend— that is, besides the matter of his *mistress?*"

She blinked several times and with her kerchief laced through her fingers she folded her hands upon her lap. He thought she appeared more like an obedient schoolgirl than a young woman about to be married. "That he is a libertine of no mean order, a rakehell who has no true regard for or respect for the ladies of his acquaintance, a man who flaunts his mistress wherever he goes, pretending all the while that she is not his mistress."

He reflected for a moment on the various ladies of his acquaintance and wondered to which of them the Tabbies had been referring. In the end, he supposed his name had somehow become linked with Charlotte Garston, a widow with whom he enjoyed flirting. But she was not in any manner his mistress. Where would such a rumor have gotten started? "Do you believe all that is said of your betrothed?" he asked, watching her carefully.

She was silent apace, then turned to look at Carlton. "Though I have never before met his lordship," she answered firmly, "and therefore cannot have had the occasion to determine his character for myself, I have the highest regard for those who have spoken so unkindly about him. Both are veritable pillars of tonnish society and have never given me reason to doubt either their motives or the accuracy of the tidings they were imparting. Besides, Mama would not have invited them to my wedding had she not deeply approved of them."

"I see," he responded gravely, his heart weighed down with disappointment. Was this, then, the extent of Julianna's ability to judge those about her, to discern truth from lies? "Tell me, did these fashionable ladies whom you esteem approach you directly, or did you merely chance to hear such unwelcome news as you were, let us say, passing by?"

Julianna sighed heavily. "There is a tapestry suspended from the ceiling of the blue drawing room which separates that room from a very cold antechamber. Marish Hall is quite ancient and draughty beyond speaking. We have many such tapestries designed to keep the cold air in one chamber from transgressing the warmth of another."

"And you were standing behind such a tapestry and chanced to overhear the gossip?" he asked, beginning to wonder if she was just like all the rest. He found himself growing increasingly irritated.

"I was walking by, if that signifies a jot. Naturally, when I heard Carlton's name, I could not help but pause in my steps."

"Naturally," he said.

"Does it seem childish to you that I felt compelled to stop and listen?"

"Only a very a little," he responded, trying to smile but feeling as though somehow his cheeks had become frozen in his anger.

"I can see that you don't approve, but I was fairly starved for news of Lord Carlton. You cannot imagine what it is to be betrothed to someone with whom you aren't even remotely acquainted."

"I can very well imagine," he responded ironically.

She turned toward him slightly and beseeched him. "You must understand, I could not bear to see my husband live out such an existence as has been suggested he now does— keeping a dozen mistresses and the like. I believe I would go mad with jealousy."

"A dozen mistresses?" he responded. He could not help but smile in earnest at this absurd remark, and queried, "All at one time? Surely even for his lordship this would be a great hardship, not to mention an inconvenience of no mean order!"

She giggled in return, her green eyes dancing with merriment. "Well, perhaps not a dozen. But pray tell me, Mr. Fitzpaine, since you know him best, does Carlton wish for this marriage? From all that I have heard, I would suppose he wishes himself rather well out of it. Perhaps he would prefer to marry the woman of whom I have heard so much—his mistress. Tell me his mind; then I shall know what to do."

"But would knowing his mind be sufficient if you already believed his character to be so very bad?"

"I don't know," she responded, her voice full of anguish. "I don't know what to think or what to do."

"What do you intend to do if I tell you he has no wish to marry you?"

"I will put an end to our engagement."

"And relinquish your chance to become a peeress?"

She sighed again, but if he thought she was expressing regret, he was soon set straight. "Mama is a peeress and has found little contentment in her lot. I have never placed great store by the supposed advantages of rank."

"Yet your mother pushed for this match. I know she did."

"I believe she was persuaded by my grandmother to pursue Carlton. You see, my Nanna and his grandmama are famous friends. As for Mama, she has her own particular reasons for wishing me to enter a marriage of convenience."

"I see," he responded, wondering what these reasons might be. He continued down another path. "You know that Carlton must wed by the end of April in order to secure his title and fortune. If you did end your betrothal to him, you would be placing him at a severe disadvantage with respect to his father's will. Have you considered as much?"

"Yes," she answered with a slow nod of her head. "I have. But if he means to continue, once we are married, as though he is not married, I believe there must be a hundred ladies who might wish to become leg-shackled to him with less concern than I for—that is, for marital happiness."

"You are very young," he said with a chuckle.

She tilted her head slightly. "Do you think it is too much to ask to be happy in one's choice of a husband or wife?"

He was knocked a little out of stride by her question. "For a long time," he responded carefully, "I believed there was no higher virtue. But given my peculiar circumstances—"

She interrupted him, "—You refer to your lack of fortune?"

"Er, yes. Precisely so. At any rate, given my *lack of fortune*, love, marriage, the contentment of finding oneself in the midst of a growing family has eluded me. Having reached the age of thirty, I no longer—"

Again she interrupted him. "—You are only thirty? I thought I had once heard you were several years older than Carlton."

He gestured with a careless wave of his hand. "I was speaking generally. As it happens, I am three-and-thirty, though I believe once you attain your majority, age begins to carry less significance than it does in one's youth."

"Oh, I quite agree," she responded with a smile. "My friend Lizzie is nearly seven-and-twenty and quite my dearest, most beloved confidante. There seem to be no years between us. But I am rambling. Pray, continue."

"As I recall," he said, "you were asking if it was possible for one to be content in marriage. I believe now it occurs only in the rarest of cases. And if I am not much mistaken, I daresay your opinion does not differ too greatly from mine, else you would not have agreed to marry Carlton without knowing him."

"My mother convinced me I had the greatest chance of happiness the *less* I knew of my intended husband."

He was greatly surprised. "Indeed?"

"You cannot be unaware that my father does not reside with my mother."

"Oh, I see. The voice of experience, as it were. I suppose that does explain a lot."

"Quite so."

He touched his fingers lightly against his brow and said, "I believe I will now tell you what you desire to know— about Carlton, that is, and his disposition toward marrying you."

"Yes, please, and hold nothing from me, I beg you," she responded eagerly.

"As you wish," he answered quietly. "It saddens me to say that from Highgate to York, his lordship was one long complaint about having to marry you. But do not suppose he rejects *you*—how could he when he has never even met you?—merely he rejects the matrimonial state, devoid, as he supposed it would be, of love." He eyed her thoughtfully for a moment, then attempted to provoke her with, "That and the fact that you are so young. He complained bitterly that you had not had the advantage of even one London Season."

If he had expected her to rise to the fly, he was mistaken. She seemed strangely downcast and he found himself longing to know why. "What is the matter?" he queried. "I thought you would be relieved to have your suspicions confirmed. Are you disappointed?"

"Only a very little, for reasons I am loath to explain. But

I assure you, you have helped me settle matters in my mind, and for that I am grateful."

As he looked at her, he was struck yet again by her beauty and her innocence. He appreciated her candor and comprehended fully her disinclination to marry, given the circumstances as she saw them. What he could not forgive in her was that she chose to believe the wicked lies the gossips told of him, not to mention the fact that she even *esteemed* these same gabblemongers.

Perhaps, then, he was well out of it.

He was about to break his silence at last and tell her who he really was when suddenly inspiration struck. He now saw an avenue of revenge broaden before him, one so simple, so perfect, so sweet, that he chose to set down the path without a moment's hesitation. He began by gently possessing himself of her hand and pressing a kiss upon her fingers which were still laced with the handkerchief.

So he was a rake, was he?

Then he would be the rake the Tabbies had said he was, only this time he would seduce an innocent, one he could see by the way she swallowed very hard as he kissed her hand a second time, who was not disinclined toward him.

And when he had seduced her, after taking her to Paris— yes, Paris would do quite well—he would cast her aside and marry any of a number of women, one of those to whom Julianna had already alluded, who would grasp at the chance of becoming the next Lady Carlton regardless of the wickedness of his former conduct.

The image of the beautiful Charlotte Garston came sharply to mind. Yes, perhaps Mrs. Garston would do. She was of an easy temper and had cast out sufficient lures to him to convince him his attentions would be welcomed by her. She would make him an unexceptionable wife and would not blink twice at the scandal he meant now to create. Hadn't she told him only a fortnight past, after rapping him flirtatiously on the arm with her fan, that *she had been in love with him for years?*

But could he convince Julianna to elope with him?

He took her chin gently in his hand and tilted her face toward him. "Tell me why you seem so sad, Miss Redmere. Did you somehow, in your very young, schoolgirlish daydreams, suppose you would find love with Lord Carlton?"

She did not seem in the least disconcerted by his touch but searched his eyes steadily for a long moment. He heard the smallest sigh escape her pretty lips. "Would you think me very foolish if I said yes?"

"Perhaps a little," he returned quietly, tilting his head ever so slightly and leaning toward her in slow stages. Even as young as she was, he knew she could not mistake his intentions.

"Oh, dear," she murmured, her gaze drifting to his lips.

"I am beginning to think Carlton was the fool," he said, in a low whisper. He was so close to her now he could smell the faint scent of lavender in her hair. His gaze was drawn to her lips. Would she permit him to kiss her? She gave no evidence of turning away.

Suddenly, he felt her hand on his chest. "Do you mean to kiss me, Mr. Fitzpaine?" she queried breathlessly.

Lord Carlton had been resisted before, but today he would not be refused. He would begin his campaign against her heart and against his society—here, now, with this kiss.

"Yes, I mean to kiss you," he said quietly. "Quite thoroughly, too." And before she could protest further, he placed his lips fully upon hers, releasing her chin from his tender grasp and slipping his arms about her. He held her tightly to him. He felt her struggle for only a moment, and greatly to his surprise, she not only acquiesced to his assault but slipped her arms about his neck and returned kiss for kiss.

Oh, yes, he thought with wild satisfaction, the young, innocent Miss Redmere could be quite easily seduced. Once he had her in Paris, he would coldly suggest she return to her mama, like a good little girl, give her sufficient funds to take a packet back to England, and the Tabbies be damned. Let it fall on their heads that one of their own was ruined beyond repair. A little note to the *Morning Post* to the effect would set all of London ablaze with gossip.

And then, he would wed Mrs. Garston, claim his rightful inheritance, and march into his future.

Chapter Three

Julianna had never been kissed.

She had dreamed of being kissed, had listened surreptitiously to the scullery maids speak of their adventures, had discussed the possibility with her dearest friend, Lizzie, a hundred times, but she had never been kissed.

And why she was permitting Mr. Fitzpaine—her betrothed's most constant companion—to violate her lips even now, was entirely beyond her comprehension. It was the wickedest thing she had ever done in her entire existence!

She suspected the knowledge that Carlton did not wish for the marriage was her primary motive, or perhaps equally so, all the terrible gossip she had heard about him.

But even as she savored the soft, sensual sweetness of Mr. Fitzpaine's lips, she knew the truth—from the moment she had dismounted her horse and looked into the stranger's eyes, she had been smitten with the worst *tendre* she had ever known and had felt a sudden and profound desire to be kissed by him.

Was it possible to love so quickly, so easily?

Her mother had warned her about such sentiments. What had she told her? That they were like brief, quick flames that burst to life only to die—oh, she didn't care! All she knew was that to be held in Mr. Fitzpaine's arms was an experience beyond every schoolgirl dream she had ever cherished.

Her thoughts began spiraling upward in a cloud of pure

enchantment. Hitherto, the world had been something she viewed as a dispassionate spectator, the people around her objects of conversation, flirtation, and sometimes dislike. But to be surrounded by a man's arms, to be caught up breathless by the touch of his lips, to feel as though she did not know where her body ended and his began—these were sensations she knew would change her forever. If only she could remain in this blissful state, how happy she would be!

The sound of laughter in the hallway outside the parlour, which drifted away toward the innyard, brought Julianna abruptly to her senses. She pulled away from Mr. Fitzpaine with a cry of astonishment. She rose to her feet, took a step backward, and drawing the kerchief at last through her fingers, exclaimed, "Oh, dear! I am as bad as—why, I vow I am as bad as Carlton himself, by all accounts! Mr. Fitzpaine, I do beg your pardon. I oughtn't to have permitted you to kiss me in that truly astounding fashion. I suppose it was just the pique from knowing my betrothed does not want to wed me that led me to such hoydenish conduct. Will you ever forgive me?"

The gentleman before her opened his eyes wide. "Forgive you?" he began with a laugh, remaining seated on the settle. He lifted a hand in protest and continued, "It is I alone who ought to apologize. I should never have taken such wretched advantage of you. Will *you* forgive *me*?"

Julianna smiled, and drawing near him again, touched his cheek with her hand. "Why couldn't you have been Carlton?" she queried softly, looking down into his eyes. "Perhaps all would have been well, then, for I vow you kiss delightfully!"

"Do I?" he responded, eyeing her with considerable amusement shining in his gray eyes.

She smiled shyly. "Yes, very well, indeed, though I've little doubt you weren't in the least need of assurances on that score."

When he continued to look back at her, holding her gaze steadfastly, she felt a wondrous trembling begin in her heart and travel langorously to the tips of her fingers and toes. What was he thinking? she wondered. Was he experiencing even the smallest *tendre* for her, or was he just a gentleman who enjoyed kissing? She knew many of that sort, but somehow she hoped Mr. Fitzpaine was not one of them.

She had spoken truthfully when she'd told Mr. Fitzpaine that he was quite the handsomest man she had ever seen. His hair was coal black and brushed in an easy, attractive manner she believed was known as *à la cherubim*. The sweetness of the name, rather than describing a heavenly creature, rather gave Mr. Fitzpaine a daring appearance. She believed Byron wore his hair in the same manner and immediately the image of the *Corsair* came sharply to mind, of adventure and love, of danger.

He could be the *Corsair*, she thought, for there was a wild look about Mr. Fitzpaine, in the loose black curls which touched his white neckcloth, in the sharpness and directness of his gray eyes, in the firm line of his jaw. At the same time, he was clearly a man of fashion. His neckcloth was tied with great care in a clever design she found unfamiliar. His shirt-points were well starched and of a precise, medium height, his black coat and black pantaloons she had known at first glance were of the finest cut and quality.

She watched him take her hand, a hand which was still strangely caressing his cheek as though it had a will of its own. When he kissed the inside of her wrist, she nearly swooned. "Oh, dear," she murmured again, fear striking a sharp chord within her, reminding her of the proprieties. "I think I ought to go. I will only say again, I wish you had been Carlton, for I believe had you been, everything would have turned out so differently."

She then laughed and pulled her hand from his grasp. "You see what a silly schoolgirl I am, for you have turned my head with only a couple of harmless kisses."

"I wish I were Carlton," he said, retrieving her hand again as she started to move away from him. His touch forced her to turn back. "But alas, I am not. I am one of those in the most wretched of circumstances—a fine education, a family of impeccable lineage, and not a farthing to call my own, save a quarterly allowance left to me by a kind uncle. Were I Carlton, I would drop to my knees before you and insist you take my name. But since I am not—" he broke off, his gray eyes taking on an extremely intense expression.

"—What?" she queried breathlessly. Oddly enough, given the look on his face, she knew a sudden urgency to run from him, to race from the parlour as though she was in some sort of danger she could not as yet fathom. Her heart began pounding in her breast. What was it he had started to say? Why did her instincts tell her to flee? And more important, why did she not obey them?

Perhaps it was because she was enjoying so very much the feel of his warm clasp as he continued to hold her hand. So instead of running, she merely sighed.

"You will think I've gone mad," he said in a low voice.

"No, I won't," she responded, anxious to know his thoughts.

He smiled and placed a quick kiss upon her fingers. "I've had the most shocking idea, one that I ought to keep from you, but for some reason I feel compelled to lay the matter before you. Yet I will give you the opportunity of refusing to hear it. You have but to say the word and I will remain silent."

Julianna could not have refused if her life had depended upon it. Curiosity had taken strong hold of her. "Pray tell me, Mr. Fitzpaine," she laughed. "Or I shall perish from never knowing why your eyes seem to be burning."

He leaned toward her slightly and whispered, "What if I took you to London—to your father—now. We could leave in the time it would take to have the horses put to. It would be hours before anyone knew of our departure, and I," he paused, placing another kiss on her fingers, "and I would have the extreme pleasure of your company the entire way. Do I frighten you if I tell you nothing would delight me more?"

"I am not frightened—well, perhaps only a very little," Julianna returned, feeling dizzy with sentiments she did not entirely comprehend. "But I believe you were right in the first place, Mr. Fitzpaine, *you have gone mad.* I couldn't possibly go. Not with Mama's home full of guests, and what of Carlton?"

"Do you intend to marry him, then?"

"Of course not! You could not think I would permit you to kiss me in one breath, then marry him in the next."

"I have known many ladies who have done worse."

"Don't be absurd. Who would behave so improperly?"

"More than you might imagine," he said. "But this is hardly to the point. I am thinking only of this—that if you return to your home, you might be forced to march down the aisle whether you wished for it or not? Could you bear the hysteria which would likely ensue upon such an announcement as, *'I cannot marry Lord Carlton today'?*"

Julianna felt her resolve to return home shrink within her. She had not considered the logical results of ending her engagement with Carlton, especially when the principal rooms of Marish Hall were full to overflowing with her mother's friends.

And just how would her mother respond to her decision?

She pondered the many occasions upon which she had tried to broach the difficult subject with her parent, but Lady Redmere had been inaccessible. Her thoughts were all for preparing her home to receive and make comfortable so many guests as well as for striving to transform her wintry stone mansion into a spring paradise. She had literally emptied her succession houses of every bloom—daffodils, pansies, roses, pots of moorland heather—and had littered the floors, sconces, and banisters with ropes, vases, and bouquets of flowers all entwined with ferns. White gauze and ribbons had been hung from the chandeliers, had been draped across archways from room to room, had been pinned to the linen skirts of tables. How easy would it be, given the mountain of

Lady Redmere's efforts, to simply say, *"I cannot marry Lord Carlton today?"*

It would be utterly impossible.

Even if her mother could contrive to comprehend her sentiments, what chance was there that she wouldn't still insist that her daughter fulfill her part of the bargain anyway?

All these thoughts swarmed over Julianna until she simply crumpled up and sank back down beside Mr. Fitzpaine, resuming her place on the settle. "Mama would very likely burn pastilles every day and night for the next six months—and I cannot abide the smell of ambergris. It comes from whales, you know. Oh, dear! Oh, dear! The tears! I might be able to bear her recriminations, her rantings, even her anger. But I know she would cry, and, my dear Mr. Fitzpaine, I don't think I could bear her tears. I am very grateful you opened my eyes to the difficulties I would face were I now to return to my home and attempt to appeal to my mother. But the alternative, to go to London with you—wouldn't we create a terrible scandal?"

"Is it true your father refused to make the journey north, that not only does he not attend your nuptials, but is even as we speak comfortably ensconced in his London townhouse?"

"Yes. He and Mama had a dreadful quarrel a month ago and he refused to come home."

"Then it is all but settled. You must trust me in this. We will travel discreetly, there will be no scandal, and your father will know what to do once I deliver you safely to his doorstep." He again possessed himself of her hand. Smoothing his own over hers in a comforting manner, he added, "I promise I will take excellent care of you on the journey."

Julianna looked at his hand and felt warm all the way to her heart. "But what of Carlton?" she queried. "Perhaps I ought to speak to him now—to explain everything to him—my reasons for not wanting to wed him. I could suggest to him what I have already suggested to you, that he marry someone else with less exalted expectations."

He placed another kiss upon her hand and said quietly, "Do not bother your head about Carlton." She would have protested, but he lifted a hand, effectually silencing her. "Trust me, Miss Redmere—"

"—Oh, do call me Julianna—or Jilly, if you like. After all, you have kissed me, and 'Miss Redmere' does seem a trifle absurd now—especially if we are to travel together. Besides, I fully expect we shall soon become fast friends."

"Jilly," he cooed, leaning toward her and looking deeply into her eyes. "What a pretty nickname. What a pretty young woman."

Because of his nearness, Julianna felt a rush of sentiment rise up so sharply within her breast that she gasped a little. It seemed the most reasonable response in the world simply to lift her face to him. She was certain he wanted to kiss her again, and given the warmth flowing in her veins, she was more than happy to accommodate him. She closed her eyes. She could feel his breath on her cheek. His lips touched her skin and she turned toward his touch just in case he doubted her willingness, but no sweet lips reached hers.

Instead, she felt his hand firmly beneath her chin, but he pressed his cheek against hers. "I must not importune you, Julianna," he whispered deeply into her ear. "You are far too lovely to be kissing again and again without the direst of consequences ensuing."

She could hardly breathe. The words he had spoken were exciting in the extreme. But beyond that, his breath in her ear drove a flurry of chills racing down her neck and all down her side!

He drew back from her and held her gaze, his hand still holding her chin. "If I am to travel beside you for some two hundred miles, I must be the very soul of propriety. Perhaps once I have you safely in your father's house—but it hurts me even now to think of the future when I can so ill afford a wife! Oh, but enough of that or I shall succumb to despair.

I have only one object now, to deliver you to Berkeley Square. I shall speak with Carlton at once. I shan't be above five minutes, I promise. Only tell me again you wish to go with me."

Julianna looked blankly at Mr. Fitzpaine. She knew he had asked her to say something to him, but she found herself so bemused that she couldn't find the necessary words. Her senses were reeling. Her heart raced in her breast as though it was a mail coach desperate to arrive at its next destination. She had thought no finer sensation existed than the feel of Mr. Fitzpaine's lips on her own, but merciful heavens, when he had breathed his speech into her ear, she had thought he had poured fire into it! She was still shivering with a strange sort of exhilaration she could not put a name to.

She tried to speak, to reassure him of her intention of going with him, but she found herself mute. All she could do was nod in what surely must have seemed like a completely doltish manner.

"You look very worried, my dear," he said, giving her hand a squeeze. "Carlton will not resist me, on that you may depend. If only you could have heard him for the last five miles of the journey here, you would know I speak the truth."

"I believe you," she finally uttered.

At last he seemed satisfied with her response and a few seconds more saw him quitting the chamber. Only when the door closed upon his back did she finally begin to breathe again. She had not even been aware she was holding her breath until he was gone.

She bit her lip and giggled, feeling very silly, yet happier than she had in ages.

Goodness gracious, whatever was happening to her?

She had come to the Angel to speak with Carlton, to discover his heart, and now she was planning an elopement—of sorts—with his good friend.

If only she had met Mr. Fitzpaine at one of the Harrogate Assemblies. She would most assuredly have danced two dances with him, he would have begged her to take supper with him, and the next day he would have called upon her at her aunt's house in Harrogate, and—and . . .

Was she falling in love with Mr. Fitzpaine? She was certainly caught up in the grips of a most forceful *tendre*. But was this love?

Tears of fright suddenly smarted her eyes and she turned toward the fireplace. Above the mantel, the Pollard print depicted a burgundy-and-black mail coach in full flight.

Her mother's warnings rose from deep within her mind. She was never to love a man too much in *just that way*, her mother had told her.

"What way?" Jilly had queried, confused.

"When you are older, you will know. It is like a *tendre*, only a great deal worse, and completely devoid of meaning. Such absurd emotions have been the cause of all my worrisome troubles with your father. I loved him in *that way*, and now I am the unhappiest of women."

Lady Redmere had burst into tears after her brief, fairly incomprehensible explanations, and nothing more on the subject had been said. It was her mother's misery which had at last prompted Jilly to agree to marry Carlton. She had not wanted to initially. Only her mother's insistence that an arranged marriage was more likely to produce a happy result than being caught in the throes of a violent passion had persuaded her to accept Carlton's proposals.

Yet how devastated her mother would be once she learned of her daughter's wretched behavior!

For the longest moment, Julianna knew a profound urge to retrace her steps to the stables, mount her chestnut mare, and gallop back to Marish Hall.

But to what purpose? To be forced into marriage with a libertine?

Julianna leaned back into the settle, resting her head on its winged back. She could never marry Carlton now. Never. He would have to find someone else to rescue his title and fortune.

If only she had been able to end the betrothal earlier.
If only.
There was nothing for it, however.
She was going to London with Mr. Fitzpaine.
And that was that.

Chapter Four

Mr. Fitzpaine looked up from a worn copy of the *Gentleman's Magazine*—a periodical fully two years old—and lifted a surprised brow. "You intend to elope to London with your betrothed, all the while pretending you are me?" He was reclining on the bed, his long, lean frame taking up the whole of its length, his legs crossed at the ankles.

Only a few minutes prior he had chanced to glance at his pocketwatch and noticed that it was clearly time to be going to Marish Hall. Carlton had appeared but two seconds later and with a wild look in his eye had begun relating the most bizarre tidings that his bride, Julianna Redmere, was belowstairs and that he was intent upon eloping with her.

Really, it was all quite astonishing.

"Yes, she believes I am you," Lord Carlton responded. "It was a simple mistake made early in our conversation and one I perpetuated when I learned the gabblemongers had sullied my reputation thoroughly to her." He went to the table by the door and hastily scribbled a note to his waiting bride. Holding it up to Mr. Fitzpaine, he said, "This is a note to Julianna from you—that is, from me. In it I state that you intend to explain the situation to her mother, to reassure her that her daughter is safe and that Julianna wished to go to London. What I want *you* to do, in fact, is go to Lady Redmere, and tell her instead that I took Julianna to Gretna Green—"

"—Set the pack off on the wrong scent, eh?"

"Just so," he responded. He then smiled broadly, "Edward, I would give a monkey to see their faces when the truth is known."

"And to think only a half hour ago, you were complaining bitterly about having to marry at all, and now you are intent upon eloping with your bride. Quite singular! But however did you manage to persuade her?"

"My charm, of course," he stated facetiously. "Oh, but Edward, she is quite beautiful, and perhaps might even have made an unexceptionable wife. But this will be much better, I'm sure of it."

At that, Edward sat up very straight. "I don't understand. And why do you look like the cat who has got the mouse? What is it you mean to do? I take it, then, you are not marrying her out of hand?"

"If you must know, I am not marrying her at all. If you must know, I intend to take her to Paris."

"Paris?" he cried, shocked. "And she has agreed to go?"

"Not yet, but I hope to convince her of her love for me by the time we reach, let us say, the Peacock at Islington?"

Edward frowned, slowly closing the magazine now resting on his lap. "I don't like the sound of it. How do you think it possible such a gently nurtured young woman as I have heard Miss Redmere to be would agree to such a wild scheme?"

Lord Carlton again smiled, dropping down before the bed and pulling a large portmanteau from underneath it. "What a sapskull you are, my dearest Edward. I kissed her a moment ago and she agreed to journey to London with me. I suspect if I kiss her again, she'll naturally wish to accompany me to Paris."

Edward smoothed out a dog-eared corner of one of the inside pages. "I don't like to mention it, Stephen, but Miss Redmere is not an opera-dancer. You will not easily be forgiven any indiscretions such a flight as you propose will undoubtedly entail. Are you prepared to face the scorn of your peers?"

"Haven't I already?" he countered harshly. "Don't look so surprised. Julianna expressed her disinclination to marry me because she believes me to be, how innocently did she put it? Let me think. Ah, yes, because I am a rakehell, a libertine of no mean order, and because I flaunt my mistress all over London."

Edward blinked at him. "Have you a mistress? I didn't know. You were always so opposed to dabbling in the petticoat line. I had no idea."

"There, you see! Even you are willing to believe—why are you laughing?—oh, do stop making sport of me!"

"How could you have a mistress," Edward responded reasonably, "when you spend nearly every waking hour in my company? No respectable courtesan would tolerate such conduct in her quarry."

Lord Carlton slapped the portmanteau down on the bed and with his hands on his hips smiled fondly upon his excellent friend. "I shall miss you, Edward. I daresay my current expedition, including the Paris sojourn, will require no fewer than three weeks to accomplish, and after that I expect to be banished to the Continent for a year or two."

"Do you mean to return to London afterward? What of Miss Redmere?"

"I shall return to London, but only for as long as it requires to send a notice to the *Morning Post* of my adventures, to fault the Tabbies for their hideous involvement in my affairs since times out of mind, then to find Mrs. Garston and see if she will have me, which I have no doubt whatsoever she will. I do have my inheritance to consider. As for Julianna, I really don't give a fig what becomes of her." He then set about emptying the chest of drawers beside the door of his various articles of clothing and shaving gear and tossing them into the open valise. When he was done, he commanded his friend, "Be a good fellow and fetch my coats, vests, breeches, and pantaloons. I need to have the horses put to. Don't forget my slippers and boots, either!"

"You should have brought your valet, since I am not trained in such a trying mode of service," Edward responded, eyeing the portmanteau with mock misgiving.

"You have only to throw my clothes in there. I don't care if they're crumpled beyond repair." He then hurried to the door, bethought himself of stealing his friend's calling-cards, and after slipping the silver case into the pocket of his coat, bid Edward *adieu.* "Remember," he added. "Tell Lady Redmere we went to Gretna. Tell her that I simply couldn't bear the thought of facing so many well-wishers. No, I suppose that won't fadge. Oh, the devil take it! Tell her whatever you like." Then he was gone.

Mr. Fitzpaine frowned, and after pulling a wrinkled blue coat from the wardrobe near the bed, he looked at the door, raised his voice, and pretended to call after his friend. "You'll have to send a servant for your valise! I refuse to carry it downstairs!"

The door opened suddenly, startling Mr. Fitzpaine. Carlton stuck his head in and said, "I shall send up a servant for my baggage. And Edward, thank you."

The door snapped shut. "You're welcome," Mr. Fitzpaine said to the empty air. "I think. Good God—an elopement to Paris—with a complete innocent!"

When he had finished his task, he moved to the window and stared out at the snow-laden countryside. Hills and moorland to the north rose up into the sky. He wished he could stay for the several weeks he had originally planned. The moors had been calling to him for months and very soon would be free of snow and ice. He had reached an impasse in his poetry and had wanted the solace of a wild country to reawaken inspiration in his heart.

Instead of disappearing into the north country, now he had to seek out Lady Redmere with tidings which he knew would do nothing less than strike horror into her soul. A daughter marrying over the anvil at Gretna Green in Scotland was every mother's nightmare, of that he was certain. To tell her even this much would be a wretched business, but what of the truth?

And what of this scheme of Carlton's? Did he really understand his friend to say he meant to strip Miss Redmere of her innocence, then throw her upon London society without the smallest concern for her reputation?

He clasped his hands tightly behind his back. He knew Carlton, and unless something or *someone* interfered with his scheme, Miss Redmere would soon be in the devil's own fix.

A scratching on the door announced the arrival of the promised servant. After seeing the portmanteau dispatched, Edward returned to stand by the window. A few minutes later, he watched Carlton's coach emerge through the gates of the inn and head to the north, toward the road to Thirsk. He watched until other stone buildings along the High Street obscured his view.

What will the end of this be? he wondered, as he began making preparations to carry out Carlton's request. Moving to stand before the mirror mounted slightly askew above the chest of drawers, he tugged gently upon the folds of his neckcloth. How was he supposed to tell Lady Redmere her daughter had eloped, whether to Gretna or to Paris?

Lady Redmere.

His thoughts suddenly slipped around a bend in the highway as he wondered if she was still as beautiful as ever.

"But where could she possibly be?" Lady Redmere cried, her nerves fairly prickling the surface of her skin. She was waiting in her bedchamber for further word of her daughter and was seated in an overstuffed winged chair of apricot velvet. She addressed her handsome Cicisbeo. "James, she simply can't have left the Hall, yet her abigail has searched everywhere—all the upper chambers including the attics, the lower chambers and principal rooms, the buttery, the scullery, the gardens, even the snow-covered yew maze. The poor child's teeth were chattering when she told me that Jilly was not to be found."

The viscountess held an embroidered kerchief in one hand and tugged at it over and over with the other. Her constant companion did not seem to be moved by her speech and she wondered if he had heard a single word she had directed toward him. "Are you listening to me, James?" she queried.

Still, no response. Her dear captain had attached himself yet again, to the looking-glass.

Captain Beck was a tall, attractive gentleman, well proportioned, lithe in appearance except for a slight paunch, and a great favorite with the ladies. He possessed droopy brown eyes, the cast of which he cultivated in hopes of one day attaining to Byron's fascinating *underlook*. Any London hostess, with the smallest pretension to fashion, included him in her drawing room upon every possible occasion. He was considered an expert in decorum, manners, and dancing, and Lady Redmere had thought herself beyond fortunate to have acquired his devotion. If she occasionally wondered what had prompted him to attach himself to her when so many other, higher-ranked ladies had bid for his attentions, she had but to return to her own mirror to find the answer.

At forty years of age, Lady Redmere could not have been happier with her appearance than most women were at thirty. Jilly resembled her in nearly every respect, and it had been greatly to her ladyship's credit to have had one gentleman only last year in Harrogate beg Julianna's *elder sister* to dance with him. Lady Redmere had found herself blushing with pleasure, her heart warmed by the sincere compliment, even more so when, after revealing the fact that she was indeed Jilly's mother, the gentleman seemed not only astonished but embarrassed. He quickly begged pardon for his lack of perception and she had just as quickly taken his arm, insisted they go down the dance together regardless of his error, then made him promise to continue in his ways, for he had most assuredly made her the happiest of women.

The dance had been exquisite, for he was a kind man, quite eligible in every respect, and had she been widowed— instead of merely *estranged* from her husband—she believed he was the very sort of gentleman she might have encouraged to seek her hand. He had also seemed much struck with her and gravely disappointed to learn of the existence of a *Lord Redmere*. That he had disappeared from the Harrogate Assembly Rooms shortly afterward both distressed her yet eased her mind. She wondered, even now, whether or not, had he pressed his affections upon her, she could have resisted his advances.

The truth was, she was very lonely.

But what use was it to repine?

No use at all.

Shaking off such useless reflections, she returned her attention to the captain, who still gave no evidence of having heard her. He was entirely caught up by his reflection in a tall, gilt-framed mirror near the window. Using a cleanly plucked white chicken feather, he was busy fluffing his exceedingly curly black hair—of questionable color!—and paused in his efforts only to shift the mirror closer to the windows in order to take the best advantage of the midday March light.

He shook his head several times, back and forth, very much in the negative, and exclaimed, "I shouldn't have permitted *your man* to cut my hair. He hasn't the finesse, the artistry requisite for the task—a most delicate pair of hands is required. Do you recall the hairdresser in Brighton last summer—*mon Dieu,* but he was *formidable!*" He clicked his tongue. "Had I only the blunt, I should have paid him handsomely to travel with us. But here I am, at your daughter's wedding, and I appear as though I've been receiving electrical treatments!"

"Oh, do hush, James!" she cried. "You may not credit it, but I have a greater concern of the moment than the state of your hair."

He turned around abruptly, an expression of shock evident in the lift of his thick, arched brows. "Whatever could that be?" he queried, astonished.

"You have not been attending to me, have you? I suspected as much."

"I suppose I have not. But now I am deeply distressed, for I can see that you are overset. Whatever is amiss? No, do not tell me, let me guess. Did the pearl buttons not arrive for your gown? And we took such care to select them."

She lifted her arm and turned it slightly toward him to reveal the very buttons of which he spoke, stitched in a long row upon her sleeve of light blue silk. "Yes, of course they arrived," she chided. "Two days ago by post from York. I told you all about it at dinner that night. James, I vow you never attend to a word I say."

"Don't be absurd," he cooed. "You know I live only to console you and soothe you in your frettings." He slowly began turning back toward the mirror, however, as though drawn toward it of a will not his own. "So tell me, what is troubling you, my pet?"

"I tell you again, Julianna is missing! At least, her maid has searched everywhere for her and cannot find her."

"Oh—oh that! Well, yes, I did hear you say something of the sort, but really, I think you have taken a pet over a trifle. It is not like you, Millicent. But let me assure you that your concern is unwarranted. After all, you couldn't precisely have a wedding without a bride, now, could you?"

Lady Redmere set her elbow on the arm of her chair, and propped her chin up in her hand. "You have completely relieved my mind," she answered facetiously. She watched Captain Beck begin picking at his curls again, and sighed in exasperation. "Whatever am I to do with you?"

His attention, however, had already drifted away from her

concerns. He said, "Really, this new oil is quite impossible. I can't abide the fragrance. Do you think the manufacturer added ambergris? It comes from whales, you know. Doesn't it seem odd that a substance belonging to a rather large ocean creature would be used to perfume an oil? I find it rather disgusting. Flowers, yes, but fish?" Upon that he whirled about and approached Lady Redmere, bending his head near her nose for her inspection. "Tell me what you think? Am I not correct? Is this not ambergris?"

Lady Redmere rolled her eyes, but obliged her exceedingly vain companion by leaning toward his head and sniffing twice. "Almond, perhaps, but not ambergris," she responded.

"A nut?" he asked, dumbfounded and grievously displeased. "I am wearing the oil of a nut on my hair?"

"Oh, do set aside your concerns over your hair for just a moment. Tell me what I am to do, James. If Julianna does not appear quite soon, how will I explain her absence to the fifty guests milling about my drawing rooms—nonetheless to Carlton when he arrives?" She glanced at her favorite ormolu clock settled on the mantlepiece near her chair, and gasped, "Good heavens! He should be here at any moment, if he is not already. Whatever am I to do?"

Her anguished query did not appear to elicit even the smallest response from her Cicisbeo, since he was already headed back to the looking-glass, where he proceeded to examine his thickening stomach carefully, swelling his chest a trifle and turning his head to the left in order to better view his profile. He had a cleft chin, and as his mother had told Lady Redmere a score of times since her beloved son had singled her out with his attentions, the deep cleft meant he had been kissed by the angels.

Lady Redmere sighed. She rather thought the good captain had been kissed by Narcissus instead.

James Beck was a peculiar mixture of absurdities. He had been granted a face and figure which could have charmed a dozen heiresses to balance his relative lack of fortune; instead his vanity superceded even that of Beau Brummell, who in her opinion was quite the most self-consumed man she had ever known. Captain Beck—he professed to having served in His Majesty's Royal Army for a full month before selling out—was nearly forty to a day. In the past year, after Redmere had flaunted his mistress beneath her nose and she had retired to live her life exclusively within the upper circles of York society, Beck had attached himself to her.

Most thought theirs an affair of the heart, but her closest friends knew the truth—he was nothing more than a balm she carried with her for her poor, shattered nerves. He had never so much as kissed her, save the theatrical salutes he placed upon the back of her wrist when they were in company. True, he did attend her morning toilette, but since he always spent the entire process studying every line, crevice, and unwanted spot on his own face in the mirror, she had never felt her modesty or her womanliness in the least danger of ravishment.

She sighed yet again, heavily, and leaned forward in her chair, looking down the years, her forehead crumpling into a painful frown.

Redmere had ravished her.

She swallowed hard at the tight feeling in her chest which accompanied the memory. Her fingers tingled with thoughts of how delightfully strong he could be. Her cheeks grew warm and her limbs began to ache. She missed him, as she had every day for the past year; she missed his touch and the sound of his bellowing voice, the firmness of his arm as he would draw her quickly into an embrace, then crush his lips upon hers.

Then, his name had become inexorably linked with Charlotte Garston's.

"Oh, dear," she murmured into the quiet air of her bedchamber.

Captain Beck twirled a curl about his white quill, then met her gaze in the mirror. He clucked his tongue again. "There,

there, my dearest Millicent." He turned away, somewhat grudgingly, from the looking-glass, the quill still stuck in his black curls, and crossed the room yet again to drop to his knees beside the arm of her chair. "I know it must seem hopeless to you, but I assure you, all will be well. Once we are returned to London, I can purchase my former macassar oil and my curls will be as they were. You won't then be distressed by the sight of them. Why are you laughing?"

"You are so absurd, James, but I do adore you. Indeed, I do."

"Of course you do, now why the tears? Oh! Are you still fretting over Jilly's absence? I'm sure there is some perfectly reasonable explanation as to why she cannot be found."

Lady Redmere stared at him. "Give me one, then," she demanded with a half-smile, wondering what clever insight he would put forth.

He chortled, rising to his feet. "Well, I didn't say that I could come up with a reasonable explanation, only that I thought there might be one." He was again riveted to his reflection, and approached the looking-glass, this time, assuming a sideways posture and pulling in his stomach. "I must return to London soon and pay Jackson a visit." He lifted a fist and punched at the air three times in quick succession. "A round or two with the gentleman and I shan't have the least need for this rickety Cumberland corset. Have you heard it creaking? I can't abide the sound. I vow it makes me feel as though I'm sixty instead of two-and-thirty." He again punched at the air.

"Two-and-thirty!" Lady Redmere cried.

"Well, I feel as though I'm not a day over thirty, which I believe is all that matters, and don't look at me as though I've completely taken leave of my senses. Age creeps up on one only when one welcomes it, and I don't! After all—"

A scratching on the door interrupted his speech.

"See to it, would you, James? Perhaps Burton has received word from the servants searching the outbuildings."

"Can't abide your butler, Millie. He hasn't a particle of sense about him."

"Well, that is the pot calling the kettle black."

"Eh?" he queried, crossing the room. "I don't think I take your meaning."

"I daresay you don't," she responded, wide-eyed, trying not to smile.

Burton appeared and began his speech. "M'lady—" But when he caught sight of the quill sticking out of the captain's curls, his mouth fell agape.

"What are you staring at, man!" the captain cried, lifting an offended, arched brow. "Why do you look at me in that terrifyingly stupid manner?"

Lady Redmere enlightened him. "Your quill, James."

"Oh, is that all?" he said, lifting his second brow. As he plucked the quill from his hair and turned away, he began muttering, "Provincial nodcock. Always the same with these rustics. No manners at all. And not a particle of sense about 'em."

The viscountess bade the butler ignore her swain's ill-temper, then asked, "Have you found her?"

"No, m'lady," he said. "The servants have not yet returned from searching the estate, but that is not the reason I'm here. It would seem that Mr. Edward Fitzpaine, having just arrived, begs a private audience with you."

"Then Carlton is here?" she asked, leaning forward.

"No, m'lady. Mr. Fitzpaine arrived alone."

For the first time since being made aware that to all appearances her daughter had vanished, Lady Redmere became truly uneasy. It was one thing for Jilly to have secreted herself in some forgotten part of the sprawling, ancient stone mansion—perhaps in response to a quite forgivable onset of wedding nerves—but it was another for Carlton to have failed to appear to marry his bride. Her mouth became suddenly dry as she rose to her feet and with trembling knees, said, "Pray show him to the study. I shall join him presently." As the butler bowed and turned to go, she added, "And, Burton, do not hesitate to inform me at once the moment the servants have returned with news of Julianna."

"Of course, m'lady."

Chapter Five

Lord Carlton's well-sprung traveling chariot climbed the gentle rise toward the moors, slowly and carefully as the postillion made sure of the road. Spring was sneaking into the Vale of Pickering in stages and was gradually making the same ascent up the Hambleton Hills. Patches of green peeked through the recent snow and occasionally the early stiff leaves of daffodils appeared like upright swords among the snowdrifts.

For now, however, snow crusted the rocky hillsides, hiding the pretty gorse and heather, giving a strong impression of a desolate land even to Julianna, who loved the North Moors passionately.

She was looking out the side window of the coach, the slope of the road forcing her to recline her head against the comfortable squabs. She thought of the many lengthy walks she had enjoyed in the summer across the moors, discovering secret valleys bedecked with yellow daffodils, resilient, pungent ferns, and hidden gills. Once she had happened upon a doe with her fawn drinking from a brook and felt as though she had arrived in paradise. Her presence had startled them, of course, and they had darted away like shooting stars, arching in their long-legged leaps over boulders and rotting logs. They were gone so quickly that only their prints in the grasses around the rock-strewn rivulet gave evidence of their presence, otherwise she might have doubted she had even seen them.

Her childhood had been in many ways idyllic. Summers were full of long walks—alone or with her robust nurse and playmates through the months of June and July, then August and September with her parents, once they had returned from their summer sojourn in Brighton.

The fall brought freezing temperatures to the constant winds of the moors. Her father would disappear for the whole of the hunting season, heading south to join his friends in Quorn country while she and her mother prepared for Christmas and enjoyed a whole round of wonderful, gossipy visits with all the notable families residing in the Vale. Trips to York, when the weather permitted, to shop for a warm, velvet gown, to purchase fabric for her bedchamber, or ribbons, silks, and artificial flowers with which to decorate her bonnets were the highest peaks of enjoyment for her. Then her father would return, a man she adored beyond speaking, Christmas would finally arrive, and he would shower her with gifts he had repeatedly told her he most certainly had not purchased.

She looked up at the sky, a piercing sensation hurting her chest as she thought of her Papá. In all her nineteen years, only the last one had been truly painful—when her mother had returned early and unexpectedly from the London Season without her father, without an explanation, without her habitual mantle of happiness which kept Marish Hall, even on the rainiest of days, sparkling with sunshine.

Through the window of the carriage, she continued to look at the sky, trying to set aside the pain her parents' recent quarrel had forced upon her. Though still gray and angry in appearance, the clouds above appeared to be thinning. She didn't think it would snow for some time, if at all, and they would likely reach Thirsk without mishap.

When the rise was completed, and the moors achieved, a familiar wind pressed against the side of the coach, prompting Mr. Fitzpaine to speak. "Is it always so?" he queried, glancing down at her. "This shrill, demanding wind of yours?"

"A *lazy* wind," she replied, with a teasing smile.

"There is nothing lazy about this wind," he returned emphatically.

"On the contrary," she returned. "If you stand facing it, taking it deep in the chest, the wind is so lazy it will not even bother to go around you. It simply shoots straight through— quite *lazy*, don't you think?"

Mr. Fitzpaine laughed. "I had never thought of it that way, but you are very right. Though since it snowed on our journey from Thirsk to the Vale of Pickering, I daresay the little flakes served to buffet the wind, for it seems much stronger than I remember from yesterday." He paused for a moment, then, in a gentle voice, asked, "Are you regretting having agreed to my scheme, Jilly?"

Julianna heard him clearly, but she did not immediately respond. Her gaze was fixed to the passing snow-laden York-shire moorland. Occasionally, gorse and rock appeared beside shallow drifts of snow, and as the road dipped, the hint of a gill, and a snow-shrouded pine tree, beckoned to the mysteries waiting to be discovered among the rolling flats of the land.

Jilly clasped her hands tightly upon her lap, giving consideration to Mr. Fitzpaine's question. She realized she had not looked at him once since having taken up her seat beside him. She supposed that was why he posed the question he did. Certainly everything about her demeanor, her silence, the taut line of her being must lead him to conclude she was regretting her decision.

But she realized regret was far from what she was feeling.

"On the contrary," she breathed at last, finding that speaking seemed to release the odd constraint she felt. "I find myself utterly astonished at how—" she paused, unclasping her hands and lifting one palm up in an effort to collect the true state of her thoughts, "—at how sublime my feelings are. I am more alert to everything I see and hear than I have ever before experienced. If the truth be known, I do not regret going with you at all. Indeed, I am content beyond words to be gone. If I have any fear of error, it is in the contentment I feel. Is it wrong to be enjoying this sensation of freedom so very much? Oh, I know I must sound as though I am mad as Bedlam."

Only then did she turn to look at him, leaning her head against the squabs again and letting the easy jolts of the finely sprung traveling chariot rock her gently.

She found herself looking into contemplative gray eyes as he held her gaze. He seemed to be searching her face for some clue to her speech and she could not help but wonder what he was thinking.

She withheld a deep sigh as she looked at him. Goodness, but he was an elegant creature! He wore a thick black woolen double-caped greatcoat, the white of his neckcloth in sharp contrast to the dark wool, the points of his shirt pressed against his cheeks. She was struck yet again by how handsome he was and felt what was fast becoming a familiar surge of affection for him which washed over her heart like water traveling swiftly over rocks in a cool Yorkshire gill.

Was she tumbling in love with her betrothed's nearest and dearest friend?

She remembered the kiss she had not only permitted him to take from her but in which she had become completely engrossed. She averted her gaze, fearing suddenly that he might comprehend the nature of her thoughts. However much it might be considered perfectly natural for a man to desire to kiss a lady, wouldn't she seem somehow less than proper in his eyes if he suspected she wished to be kissed again?

Feeling the scrutiny of his gaze upon her, she turned and saw that an intriguing smile of amusement touched his lips.

What was it she had been told of Mr. Fitzpaine? What did she really know of him? She tried to recall the snippets of gossip regarding Carlton's friend. Formerly, all her attention when listening to others on the subject of her betrothal had been for news of her bridegroom. For the longest time she had so hungered for knowledge of Carlton in order that she might better know how to make him a good wife that she could scarcely now bring to mind more than a sentence or two about the man beside her.

He had been termed a man of sense, and for the most part he appeared to be just as he was reputed.

But what else? While he remained silent, yet still watching her with a smile on his lips as though he knew what she was thinking, she searched every tiny pocket of her mind, hoping for enlightenment.

Mr. Fitzpaine. A memory finally strode forth. She could even hear Lady Catterick's smooth, nasal voice drift to her from the past. *Mr. Fitzpaine is a man of sense, and perhaps for that reason I have never quite understood his connection to Carlton. Fitzpaine is a gentleman. He has kind, blue eyes, even teeth, and the gentle manners of an archbishop. Carlton would do well to imitate his friend.*

Blue eyes.

Julianna felt very peculiar suddenly as she blinked once at Mr. Fitzpaine. She was looking into gray eyes and could not keep from leaning toward him to examine the gray shards which composed the iris of his eyes. Her heart felt as though it simply melted fearfully away within her bosom. She found it difficult to breathe.

Was it possible she had made a terrible mistake? Could she have been bamboozled by a stranger at an inn and—and kidnapped?

"What is wrong?" Mr. Fitzpaine asked abruptly, interrupting the truly frightening realm of her thoughts. "I can see by your expression you're afraid. Tell me at once! What is it?"

"Your eyes, sir," she responded, in a small, tight voice.

He smiled faintly. "You do not like them? I have been told upon more than one occasion they were *very fine.*"

"Your eyes are supposed to be blue, sir—not gray!" she countered.

"Blue?" he queried, clearly astonished. "I can't imagine

anyone thinking my eyes were blue," he continued. "Not by half. Unless, of course, one views the color of my eyes in the sunlight, then I believe it could be construed a shade of blue, but not to signify. Who told you as much?"

"Lady Catterick. *'Kind, blue eyes'* were her exact words. I could not be mistaken in that."

"Ah, that would explain it, then. Have you ever seen Lady Catterick's spectacles? Each lens like that of a telescope."

Julianna let out a long, deep sigh of relief. "How very true," she returned, remembering she had once been startled by the sight of that good lady's eyeglasses. Whatever fright had possessed her now drained quickly away in the face of Mr. Fitzpaine's quite reasonable explanation. She laughed at her own absurdity and continued. "Do you know I feel very silly, for it occurred to me just now, when I was looking at you and trying to remember all that I heard about you, that since we were not properly introduced, you could be anyone you wished to be, and I would have no means of knowing otherwise."

"I hadn't thought of that," he responded easily, also with a laugh. "I suppose for all you know, I could be Carlton himself."

"That would be quite impossible!" she cried, throwing up a hand of protest. "In no respect do you fit the portrait all of society draws of his lordship. You simply could not be Carlton." She saw a keen, angry light flash in the grayness of his eyes, and she knew she had offended him.

"I am his friend, Julianna, and I feel I must reproach you for having taken so completely to heart the numerous false reports which abound regarding him. You've no notion the piece of work made over his every move. I tell you this, he does not sneeze without it being reported as a slur upon some lady's character or other."

Julianna shifted her gaze to the postillion's back, hunched over the lead horse, his left leg covered with a metal brace to protect it from the carriage pole. She did not know how to answer Mr. Fitzpaine. "I honor you for your loyalty, Mr.

Fitzpaine, but perhaps Carlton should have taken greater care where and how he sneezed. You may protest all you wish, but even if I *were* to discount most of what I have heard, I cannot as easily dismiss those who conveyed such unhappy opinions. Ladies of honorable character do not make up stories, and Mama's friends are honorable."

"You are certain of that?"

"Of course," she replied, again turning toward him.

His nostrils flared as he looked away from her, his gaze for the moment darting out the window. "You base your opinions too thoroughly on connection and relationship."

"I have spoken my mind too freely," she conceded. "And I do beg your pardon, for I can see that I have wounded your sensibilities."

"My what?" he cried, looking back at her with amused astonishment.

"Your sensibilities," she countered, cocking her head. "It is very clear to me that you hold Carlton in the highest regard, that you value his constant friendship above all things, and I have violated your most noble *sensibilities*. I am sorry, Mr. Fitzpaine, indeed, I am. It is a most profound and undesirable fault I possess of speaking a deal too forthrightly. But setting aside my inclination to take to heart the opinions of those I cherish, I might not have held his lordship in such low esteem if he had been a more considerate correspondent. You see, to all the letters I sent him in hopes of establishing some measure of rapport with my future husband, he responded with only one."

"Only one?" Mr. Fitzpaine asked quietly, in what seemed to Julianna a small voice.

"Only one," she reiterated. "So you see now that I might have some cause, as a young lady with *sensibilities* of my own, to be inclined to view Carlton in not an entirely happy light."

These last words had a strangely calming effect upon Mr. Fitzpaine, all evidence of his ill-temper disappearing entirely,

"One letter," he stated again. "Then it is not to be wondered at that you despise him."

"Oh, I don't despise him, pray do not think me so bad. How could I, when I really don't know him at all."

"Well, in my opinion, Carlton was an unforgivable brute to have treated you with such contemptuous indifference. I will admit he erred in this case, grievously so. But then, I can't be too angry with him, since his lack of proper attention to you has been entirely to my advantage. He is left to kick his heels in Redmere while I am given the delight of traveling with you."

"Let us not quarrel, then," she said, placing a hand on his arm. "Now that I have a moment to reflect, I daresay you would have found me in the boughs had you maligned one of my friends to me."

He looked at her hand and covered it with his own, returning the pressure gently.

Julianna felt relieved. She had not spoken kindly in light of Mr. Fitzpaine's considerable affection for his friend.

She watched him reach into the pocket of his coat and withdraw a slim silver case. Snapping it open, he presented her with one of his cards. "Lest you doubt my identity again," he said with a teasing smile.

The card read, *The Honorable Mr. Edward Fitzpaine.*

He returned the case to his pocket and again took her hand in his. "Now tell me," he commanded, placing a kiss on her fingers, his eyes appearing warm and inviting. "Are you in truth *Miss Redmere?*"

She sighed, caught by the light in his eyes. Again her heart responded to him, to his words, to the sound of his voice, to his manners, all affecting her like the careful dance of skilled fingers upon the strings of a harp. She felt musical when touched by him, alive, joyous, ready to sing and dance. She again knew a profound desire to be kissed by him.

"You're so very pretty," he whispered, his words barely audible above the continuous roll of the wheels rolling relentlessly forward and the horses' hooves pounding into the crusty snow. "But are you Miss Redmere? The truth, now!"

Julianna felt her heart straining toward the man beside her. "I daresay it is now time for me to confess," she responded in a whisper, taking his lead. "You were right to question my identity, for I am not Julianna Redmere at all."

"You are not?" he queried, again kissing her fingers only this time, so slowly that she nearly forgot what she meant to say next.

"Who are you, then?" he prompted her, his lips moving tenderly over each finger.

She swallowed hard and continued, "I am an actress, of course. The moment I saw you I knew that if I was clever enough, I could persuade you to take me to London. And that is just what I have done, for here we are."

"Yes, here we are," he said, his gray eyes regarding her with an almost wicked expression as he kissed her little finger quite languidly, not once but three times.

"Oh, dear," she murmured.

"If I were a wealthy man," he added in a whisper, "I would help you become a very famous actress, too."

"You would?" she asked, not really listening to his words, but feeling quite lost in the sensation of his warm lips on her finger.

"Indeed, yes. I should have all of London worshipping at your feet, and then perhaps I would take you to Europe, to Paris, to Rome, and let audiences there admire your beauty and your abilities on the stage."

Again she swallowed. She knew somewhere in the driftings of her mind that he was being quite absurd in what he said, but the tone of his deep voice, kept so low in his whisperings, along with the feel of his lips upon her little finger, so mesmerized her that she responded without thinking. "I would go anywhere with you, Mr. Fitzpaine. Anywhere."

But her words for some reason broke the spell of the moment. Mr. Fitzpaine paused in his kisses and Julianna became aware of what she had said. She then quickly retraced her words and added, "If I were an actress, that is."

"Do you now tell me you are not?"

"Alas," she responded. "I dislike telling you as much, but I am in truth Miss Redmere, and as for acting, my friend Lizzie will tell you I have no such abilities at all. We have attempted several plays—particularly during the long winter months—but whenever I try to portray my characters, I succeed only at setting everyone in stitches."

He stopped kissing her fingers, and taking her hand more fully into his clasp, held it against his cheek. Even though the carriage was cold, his skin was very warm. "I wish to know something," he said, his gray eyes narrowed slightly. "When I gave you my opinion earlier that Carlton did not wish for this marriage at all, you were very sad. Why was that? If you only corresponded with him once, were you cherishing false hopes of him?"

Julianna rested her head against the squabs again, tilting her head so that she might continue to look into his eyes while she considered how best to answer him.

He still held her hand against his cheek and she wished for just the briefest moment that she could curl up next to him and rest her head on his shoulder, burrowing snugly into his thick woolen coat. She rather thought it likely that she would fit well against him.

The warmth which flowed over her at these thoughts forced her to look away from him. She knew she was feeling too much for a man who was a veritable stranger and wished she could do something to stop the sensations which were quickly taking command of not only her senses but of her good sense as well. They weren't yet five miles from the Angel and already all she could think about was being held in a comfortable embrace by Mr. Fitzpaine again.

With great effort, however, she set aside these disturbing thoughts and turned her attention to giving answer to his original question. Had she cherished false hopes of Carlton?

Finally, she responded. "In all these weeks, I knew it was an unhappy circumstance that Carlton saw fit to write only one letter, but I found it so appealing that I believe I pinned all my hopes on it. As you probably already know, he has a quite errant mode of expressing his opinions—opinions which I must say are not so very different from my own. I was entranced by the portrait he painted of the life he wished to share with his wife—his admitted love of adventure, his desire to visit distant and exotic parts of the world—the Colonies, the Levant, the Cape of Good Hope, even China. I felt as though he had somehow divined all my secret thoughts and dreams and set them to paper."

He interrupted her in a strangely insistent manner. "I am curious, Julianna, did you express any of this in your correspondence to him?"

"No," she responded. "Shortly afterward, I received a letter from my friend Lizzie, who felt compelled to relay to me that she had just heard a rumor that Carlton was keeping a mistress."

A heavy silence weighted the air between them. "I see," he said after a long pause.

"I wanted to write to him, but I was so hurt by Lizzie's news that I did not know what to do."

"Believing gossip again, Jilly? I am come to think that is your real flaw. Is Lizzie a gabblemonger?"

"On the contrary. She is forever rejecting gossip."

"Then why would she send you such a tale?"

"In her letter, she told me that she had heard of his mistress while in company with Lady Hertford."

"Lady Hertford?" he cried, astonished.

Only then did Julianna look at him. He seemed very surprised. "Do you know her?"

"Yes, of course. She is the very best of women. I cannot understand why she would have passed on such an untruth."

"Mr. Fitzpaine, is it possible your loyalty to Carlton has affected your judgment? Perhaps you do not know him as well as you think."

He smiled crookedly, an inexplicable smile, but one which

lent such an adorable aspect to his face that she felt her heart melt within her all over again.

"I know him better than you could ever imagine. We have been friends since childhood. Indeed, from the cradle, I think." Before she had time to ask how long their respective mothers had been such close friends, he added, "I will say only this, Carlton was a fool not to have written you more than once. So his letter pleased you, did it?" he queried, gazing into her eyes, leaning toward her slowly.

"Exceedingly so," she responded breathlessly.

"He should have taken greater care of your heart and your affections, Jilly."

"Yes," she whispered, as his lips drifted lightly over her cheek.

"I can't kiss you," he whispered in return. "I won't, though I want to more than anything."

Julianna felt tears sting her eyes. "Please?" she murmured, surprised she was being so brazen.

His every movement ceased as though her plea had paralyzed him. She could not even hear him breathing.

After a long, tense moment, he said hoarsely, "I'm sorry, Julianna."

She did not know precisely what prompted her, perhaps because tears had begun to sting her eyes, but she slipped her head deeply into his shoulder, just as she had wanted to do earlier. Taking the thick collar of his greatcoat in hand, she held him close.

For a moment he remained very still, as though uncertain what he ought to do. Finally, he let out a sigh and encircled her with his arms very tightly. He whispered words into her hair which, though she wasn't entirely certain what he had said, sounded very much like, "Whatever am I to do with you?"

Chapter Six

"How do you go on, Mr. Fitzpaine?" Lady Redmere queried politely from the doorway of her husband's study. "It has been ages since we last met." She entered the book-lined room tentatively, offering the tall, handsome young man her hand. Her knees still trembled as she glanced quickly about the study, somehow hoping that Burton had been mistaken and Lord Carlton would now pop magically from behind the red velvet drapes flanking the tall Elizabethan window, or from behind the gold silk-damask winged chair by the fireplace, or even from beneath the writing table of gleaming satinwood situated behind the sofa of midnight blue velvet. But no such happy apparition appeared to ease her motherly concerns.

"Very well, thank you," Mr. Fitzpaine responded, crossing the room and possessing himself of her hand. She was drawn back to his face by the warmth of his clasp and by the kind, gentle tone in his voice. She had met Edward Fitzpaine only a very few times in society, and combined with her absence during the course of the entire year past, she believed she had not actually seen him in three, possibly four, years. She was a little surprised at the admiration in his blue eyes, and in spite of her anxiety, she could not help but be pleased that he held her hand far longer than was considered necessary.

He bowed precisely, slowly, and quite elegantly over her

beringed fingers before turning his attention to her Cicisbeo. He bowed to Captain Beck and asked politely after his health. But the captain did not at first respond to Mr. Fitzpaine's courtesies. His gaze, though initially directed toward the younger man, had become fixed upon the tall man's black locks, which Lady Redmere noted were groomed to perfection. When Beck did speak, it was to ignore every societal dictum as he took two steps forward, his hands clasped tightly behind his back, and demanded to know, "Macassar oil?"

Mr. Fitzpaine's brows rose sharply. "I beg your pardon?" he queried, obviously stunned.

Captain Beck waved a hand in a series of small impatient circles toward Mr. Fitzpaine's head. "Do you perchance use macassar oil? And if you do, I don't suppose your valet would lend me a dram or two . . . I'm afraid I left London with the most atrocious oil in my possession, and as you can see, my hair is a positive riot of indiscretion!"

"A riot of *indiscretion?*" Mr. Fitzpaine repeated, blinking slowly. Lady Redmere thought she saw the faintest twitch of his lips and found herself intrigued.

"Indeed, yes," Captain Beck returned firmly.

If Mr. Fitzpaine was either offended or amused, only a second twitch of his lips revealed a clue to his sentiments. He was, however, a gentleman, and responded, "You will have to forgive me, Captain Beck, but I do not use oil on my hair at all."

"No oil!" he cried, dumbfounded. "It's not possible! I vow you've not a single strand rebelling from the whole."

"I take that as a compliment, but if you don't mind very much, sir, I would greatly appreciate a few moments' private speech with her ladyship. I have come on a mission of some import."

Captain Beck was not attending to him, however. He had chanced to glance to his left and had caught sight of himself in the reflection of a highly polished chest of drawers whose gleaming mahogany surface revealed that yet another curl had collapsed. He moved quickly into position before the elegant piece of furniture and one moment more saw him remove his quill from the inside pocket of his black coat and commence the delicate process of reshaping every strand of hair on his head.

Lady Redmere rescued Mr. Fitzpaine from what she could see was a veritable avalanche of astonishment. "Do not pay the least heed to my swain," she whispered with a smile, looping her arm about his and drawing him toward the sofa of dark blue velvet. "As you can see, he will be unable to attend a word you might say in his presence for several minutes more. Won't you sit down and tell me what has gone awry, for my butler has informed me that Carlton is not with you."

"No, ma'am, he is not," Mr. Fitzpaine responded, waiting until she had seated herself opposite him in an oversized winged chair before sitting down.

Mr. Fitzpaine inclined his head surreptitiously toward Captain Beck. "Are you certain I may speak freely," he whispered. "What I have to tell you is of an extremely delicate nature."

Since Beck was now dropping down drawer by drawer in hopes of finding the most polished piece of wood for his purposes—and would soon be on his knees if he continued as he was—Lady Redmere shrugged her shoulders. "Decide for yourself, Mr. Fitzpaine. But do you really think your mission here is in the least danger of either my dear captain's interference or his intelligence?"

For the first time since his arrival, she saw the younger man smile, and felt a little easier because of it. He had fine, even teeth, and a genuineness to his expression that caused her instantly to trust him. He was tall and broad-shouldered, though quite lean and long-legged. His hair, which Beck so admired, was cut short and brushed neatly à la Brutus. She wondered how old he was and by careful calculation—using his first appearance among the beau monde as her guide— determined he must be three-and-thirty. His eyes, she decided, were his best feature, being a vivid blue, almond-shaped, and set off to extreme advantage by straight brows which arched downward only at the very tips—a quite striking angle.

He has a wise appearance, she thought, biting her lower lip ever so slightly and wondering why he was not married. Then she remembered that he was one of so many younger sons who were left quite impoverished, poor man!

He turned his clear blue eyes upon her, took a breath, then released it with a concerned huff. "Are you made of stern stuff, madame?" he queried, a frown marring his brow.

"I—I don't know," she stammered, fear suddenly striking at her heart. Where was Jilly? Why had Carlton not come with Mr. Fitzpaine? "I suppose I am to some extent. I have never succumbed to a fit of the spasms, if that is what you mean. You are not here to tell me that Lord Carlton is breaking his engagement to my daughter, are you?"

He leaned forward and placed a hand on each of his knees. "For the first time in my life, I am failing to side with my friend," he began somberly. "But after grave consideration, I feel I must reveal all to you. Prepare yourself, madame, for the worst. The truth is, Carlton has eloped with your daughter and is even now heading south to London."

Lady Redmere blinked very slowly. She had heard him. Of course she had heard him. Every word. But somehow his speech seemed to be making a strange, disjointed progress from her ears to her brain. *Carlton. Eloped. Daughter.*

"I don't understand," she responded at last, shaking her head numbly. "Why would—why would Carlton *elope* with Jilly when, were they both here now, our good reverend, Mr. Aysgarth, would be joining them in wedlock? You make no sense at all, Mr. Fitzpaine."

"What Carlton's purposes are once he reaches London, I cannot say, but I believe his intent is then to continue on with her to Paris—with no one awares—and *without* benefit of matrimony. His instructions to me were to tell you he was taking Miss Redmere to Gretna Green. I suppose that is when I began to realize we were in the devil of a fix."

Lady Redmere squeezed her eyes shut very tightly and pressed a hand to her temple. "I feel very dizzy," she responded. "First, I thought you had come to tell me Carlton wished to be rid of Julianna. Now you are hinting at something so horrible, I cannot even conceive of it. Are you saying he wishes to hurt my darling Jilly, to create a scandal of the most wretched sort which will ruin her in the eyes of the world forever? But why? What has she done, or what have I done, to have so aroused his wrath? Did Redmere somehow incur his grievous displeasure? Mr. Fitzpaine, you must be joking, but if you are, I tell you now, it is the cruelest joke in the world!" She felt tears begin to trickle down her cheek. She did not even know she had started crying.

He rose quickly from the sofa and drew a nearby Empire chair forward so that he could sit close to her. Taking his kerchief from the pocket of his coat, he tucked it gently into her hand.

"I am so sorry," he said, speaking in a low, quiet voice. "I should have stopped him, but until a moment ago, I don't think I truly realized the horrific nature of the crime he was about to commit. I knew I needed to warn you of his actions, but will you ever forgive me for not having thrust a spoke in his plans before he had got his carriage beyond the gates?"

Lady Redmere was trying desperately not to give way to the sobs which were causing her chest to rise and fall in silent horror. Tears still ran down her face, and her nose had begun to run most untidily. "I must think," she whispered. "I mustn't cry. Why do I have the most terrifying feeling I am going mad?"

"How else would any woman feel in such a circumstance?" he said soothingly, taking one of her hands in his and stroking it tenderly over and over. "Do not think I mean to leave you. You have but to tell me what you want me to do, and I will be your most obedient servant."

Lady Redmere looked down at her lap, and saw that it

was dotted with her tears. There was nothing for it now. She
had to blow her nose and did so quite soundly. She wondered distractedly just how terrible a breach of manners it
was to blow one's nose in front of a gentleman when one had
just been told one's daughter had eloped.

Eloped!

"What sort of monster is Carlton become?" she asked.
"Of late, I had begun hearing rumors of his conduct, that he
is a hopeless rakehell, a seducer of virgins. I had always
believed such reports were rooted in vicious, unfounded
gossip. Now I don't know what to believe. But never in my
wildest imaginings would I have thought he would snatch
Jilly from the bosom of her family and ruin her!"

Merciful heavens, there was no worse scandal than an
elopement—save murder perhaps, and even then . . . ! A
thought suddenly flew into her brain, like a gust of wind
through an open window. "Whyever did Jilly go with him?"
she asked. "Really, Mr. Fitzpaine, the more I think on it, the
more I find myself utterly confounded. Why would she have
agreed to elope with Carlton when they would soon be man
and wife anyway? She can't possibly know that he means to
do her harm."

Mr. Fitzpaine shook his head. "She knows nothing of his
true intentions. The fact is, she believes she is traveling with
me."

"You?" Lady Redmere cried, utterly astounded.

"Yes. Though I don't pretend to comprehend the whole
of Carlton's scheme, it appears he lied to her about his
identity and persuaded her—posing as one Edward Fitzpaine—to flee with him to your husband's home in London.
I daresay she would never have agreed to go had she known
her traveling companion was Carlton himself. It would seem
over the course of the past few weeks she has come to dread
his reputation."

"The whole thing is so bizarre. Julianna never said a word
to me of her *dread*. Yet how sinister of Carlton to deceive
her!"

"I quite agree, which is why I am here. When Carlton approached me about his scheme, there was a look in his eye that disturbed me, a sort of quiet rage which I found to be most unlike him. I believe when he learned from your daughter's own lips the extent of the tattlemongering being reported of him even in your own house, he became quite enraged, losing as it were his ability—one hopes only temporarily—to judge the rightness of his conduct. His whole plan appears to be centered upon a wish to avenge himself on those who had so thoroughly maligned his character to his prospective bride on the day of his nuptials. Julianna, it would seem, had come to the inn in order to determine for herself both his character and whether or not he truly wished to marry her. I believe he decided then and there to create a real scandal—with Julianna none the wiser." He squeezed Lady Redmere's hand and continued, "I have known Carlton these many years and more. I have never known him to behave less than honorably toward the women of his acquaintance in all situations. I am convinced he will come about before it is too late!"

"But why must he suddenly now go off half-cocked—and with my poor Julianna?"

"I don't know precisely, though I do beg you to consider how trying it has been for him to be the most sought after matrimonial prize in London—and that for so many years."

"I find it difficult to feel a great deal of sympathy for him in this moment, as you may very well imagine!"

"Wouldn't you agree, however, that the gossip which you and your daughter have been subjected to was prompted by a strong measure of jealousy on the part of those ladies whose advances Carlton has rejected? You must agree, it is not an uncommon occurrence for a lady to discredit a man when he has not, er, *come up to scratch?*"

"Yes," she responded slowly. "Though I am reluctant to agree with you on a notion which can only place my sex in the poorest of lights, I believe you have the right of it. So you think he has been slandered by one or more unhappy females?"

"I believe so. In his defense, let me say that I am here not only because I believe what he has done is wrong, but also because I esteem him enormously. I only wish you and your daughter had had an opportunity to become better acquainted with him before the marriage settlements were signed. You would know then that I am speaking the truth to you."

"Your loyalty does you great honor, Mr. Fitzpaine."

"Carlton has been an excellent friend to me, and a man in my circumstances needs quite excellent friends. The least I can do is try to help him out of this coil before he injures himself and your daughter beyond repair."

As she wiped away a stray tear which had been anxious to join the others on her lap, Lady Redmere felt a calmness descend over her troubled spirit. "We must find them, then," she stated simply.

"With discreet inquiries along the Great North Road, I have little doubt I can discover their whereabouts."

"I imagine they are well on their way to York by now."

"Yes, I believe so. Even though Carlton and I journeyed here by way of Easingwold and Thirsk—"

"—You crossed the Hambleton Hills in a snowstorm?" she asked, dumbfounded.

Mr. Fitzpaine appeared quite sheepish for a moment as he lowered his head and explained, "I have wished for the longest time to see the Yorkshire Plain from Sutton."

"Ah, yes, of course," she responded, remembering that Mr. Fitzpaine had published a book of poetry recently and therefore was permitted some foolishness for the sake of the Muse. "Your *poet's heart*, no doubt?"

"Carlton was opposed to the trek, of course, but in Ferrybridge, we chanced upon a clever fellow who said he knew the route as thoroughly as he knew his lame foot."

"His lame foot? How curious."

"Indeed, but he proved to have been telling the truth, and

saw us safely arrived at the Angel Inn late yesterday after-noon."

Lady Redmere smiled faintly and then sighed. Though for a brief moment, Mr. Fitzpaine's anecdote had diverted her unhappy mind from her present difficulties, her thoughts were drawn back quickly to her daughter's amazing flight. She frowned and shook her head. She could feel her lip quivering as she spoke. "I see now that Julianna tried to tell me of her distress, her unhappiness, but I wouldn't listen to her. I was too enrapt in wedding preparations. I wish I had attended to her. Oh, my poor, darling daughter!" More tears flowed down her cheeks.

"There, there," Mr. Fitzpaine reassured her. "It will not do to be wishing for what ought to have been instead of what is. We must look to the future—and be quick about it—if we hope to accomplish our purpose."

Lady Redmere again blew her nose and thanked Mr. Fitzpaine for being so completely sensible.

She turned around and began, "James, please summon my abigail and—goodness, where has he gone?" Captain Beck was nowhere to be seen. She rose and shrugged her shoulders, adding, "I don't know why I keep him around."

"I rather suspect he enjoys considerable beneficence at your hand," Mr. Fitzpaine suggested, also rising to his feet.

"Do you suppose that I give him money, as many do?" she queried, looking up at him. She was not at all offended by the nature of his remark, since it was frequently suggested to her. When he remained silent, she smiled and said, "It is nothing of the sort. Though he lacks a fortune, he is not entirely bereft of funds and generally pays every bill of fare when we travel."

"Indeed?" Mr. Fitzpaine responded, obviously surprised. "I had thought—at least, I recall having once heard he hadn't a feather to fly with. I do beg your pardon if I have offended you."

"You haven't," she said, moving toward the door. "I suspect you, too, have been subjected to unwelcome gossip.

He might not be sufficiently well-shod to keep a wife, but he can certainly purchase enough macassar oil to keep himself content."

Mr. Fitzpaine laughed. Lady Redmere looked up at him and said, "I do thank you for being a friend to me and for revealing Carlton's secret when it must have gone sorely against the grain to do so. I know with what vows of honor you gentlemen are bound to one another, so I do not proffer my gratitude lightly. Would you consider traveling with the captain and myself? My coach is quite commodious and well-sprung. Even sitting forward, you would not find yourself made uncomfortable. Besides, as you make inquiries at all the towns and villages along the way, I will want to be present—at least, near enough to hear the earliest communications regarding the whereabouts of my daughter."

"I believe your scheme has considerable merit, and I will accept your kind invitation." He paused, frowning slightly before continuing. "Though I dislike causing you further distress, have you considered yet what you mean to do with your guests or what you will tell them?"

At that, Lady Redmere felt the blood drain from her face. She had lifted her hand to open the door to the hallway, but upon hearing his query, she drew her hand back abruptly from the handle as though it was too hot to touch. "Merciful heavens!" she cried. "I hadn't thought of that! Whatever am I to do?"

At that moment, the butler returned with news which only confirmed Mr. Fitzpaine's history—Julianna's mare was gone, and not an hour past, one of the laborers admitted to having seen her flying across the snowy moorland toward the village. "There can be no mistake, m'lady," the butler added, his face pinched with worry. "She was wearing a white gown and her green cloak. I daresay we shall have other reports soon."

"Pray don't fret, Burton. Mr. Fitzpaine has come with news of Julianna. She is quite safe, and we are discussing what must needs be done next. Pray inform the staff that—

oh, dear." She glanced up at Mr. Fitzpaine hopefully, not
knowing how to proceed.

He did not fail her. "Perhaps you ought to explain everything to Burton," he responded, drawing her back into the
study and bidding the butler to follow after him. When the
door was closed, he added, "He will undoubtedly know best
what to tell your servants."

"Of course," Lady Redmere responded. Within a few
minutes, she was able to relay to her most trusted retainer
the wretched events which had brought her daughter's wedding to such an abrupt end. He calmly accepted what was
told to him and responded politely that he thought the servants and the guests ought to be informed that Miss Redmere had decided not to wed Carlton after all and was
closeted in her bedchamber—with only her abigail to wait
upon her—due to the onset of a most horrendous headache.

For several minutes, Lady Redmere remained silent, giving herself to consider this very simple suggestion. When she
had arranged it all in her mind satisfactorily, she agreed to
it. Of course it was likely to become known within a day or
two that Julianna was not in her bedchamber at all, but was
in truth traveling south to London, but the tale would give
her sufficient time to find her daughter before her elopement
became generally known.

When Burton headed back to the nether regions to perform his duties and Mr. Fitzpaine returned to the Angel to
pack his belongings where he would await her ladyship's
traveling coach, Lady Redmere quit the study, squared her
shoulders, and prepared to face her many friends and acquaintances.

To her incredulous guests, Lady Redmere told Burton's
tale. Carlton, she added, had seen fit to return to London.
She then saw to everyone's comfort, promising the enjoyment of a fine dinner as though her daughter had been
married after all.

Although the fifty guests—most of whom resided in the
Vale of Pickering and would return to their respective homes

on the morrow—were properly shocked, scarcely a one did not blame poor Julianna Redmere for jilting her roguish bridegroom at the eleventh hour.

After an hour and a half had passed in company with her guests, Lady Redmere feigned a sudden, violent headache and gave every evidence of retiring to her bedchamber for the duration of the festivities.

Chapter Seven

"All is arranged."

Julianna glanced up from a scalding, but quite welcome, cup of tea, and smiled at the sight of Mr. Fitzpaine shaking snowflakes from his black woolen greatcoat as he hung it on a peg by the door.

"You've found a chaperone for me, then?" she queried. She was only now, after sitting for some few minutes in the warm parlour of the Slubbers Inn at Thirsk, no longer shivering from the cold. The journey across the Hambleton Hills had been accomplished without mishap and the snow had only begun to fall once the carriage had begun its descent from the hills into the Plain of York.

"A rather dubious one, I fear, but a chaperone nonetheless."

"Whatever do you mean?" Julianna asked, taking another sip of tea which burnt the tip of her tongue. She withheld a cry of pain, rubbing her tongue on the inside of her teeth instead.

"Your new maid is all of three-and-twenty, and I strongly suspect the true shade of her hair is not the hue of overripe carrots!"

"Oh, dear," Julianna responded with a laugh. "She will have to do, I suppose. I daresay there were not a dozen females or so clamoring to travel to London today."

"No," he responded. "Not by half, I fear. But this particular female has been pining to remove to the Metropolis for some time. It would seem," here he paused, and while giving a straightening tug on his waistcoat, finished with, *"Artemis Brown* has designs upon Drury Lane."

Julianna let out a trill of laughter. *"Artemis Brown!* Do not tell me *Artemis* is her Christian name."

"No. The landlady called her Molly—er, Milkmaid Molly, I think—not at all suitable for the stage." As he approached the table, he added, "The pair of you no doubt will have a great deal to discuss about your respective future careers."

Again Julianna laughed. "No doubt." She was silent for a moment, then said, "I do thank you, Mr. Fitzpaine."

He stamped his feet several times, and satisfied that his glossy black top boots were free of snow, moved forward to seat himself opposite her.

She lifted her cup to her lips, then bethought her earlier experience. Without risking a second burn, she resettled the traitorous brew back on its saucer.

"Hot, eh?"

She smiled in return, liking very much the warmth in his gray eyes as he answered her smile with one of his own. They had scarcely conversed during the remainder of the trip across the hills. For the longest time she had stayed curled up next to him, his arms holding her tightly as the carriage rose and fell, one side of a gentle hillock meeting the next, the road dipping and rising gradually. He had been very much the gentleman, and now, as she savored the fragrant steam rising from her cup, she looked at him, wishing ever so much he had been her betrothed instead of Carlton. She knew he had restrained himself only with the greatest of efforts in refusing to surrender to his desire to kiss her again. She did not know which she could have wanted more, however, for while it was wonderful to be in the company of a man who could show such restraint, she had desired to feel his lips on hers so much that her heart had simply ached for miles afterward. Restraint was a noble virtue, but she strongly suspected that the first person to champion such a virtue had perhaps never been properly kissed.

She lowered her gaze to the clear, hot amber liquid, her fingers now able to touch the side of the ceramic teacup without being burnt, and wondered what her mother would think of her if she knew how thoroughly Mr. Fitzpaine had kissed her. Her chest grew tight suddenly as she remembered her mother's insistent warnings—against taking seriously the passionate sensations one might experience with a handsome man who had known many adventures.

Was Mr. Fitzpaine a man who had known adventures? He had certainly kissed her as though he knew his business well. She brought the cup to her lips, and with great care took an infinitessimal sip.

She winced slightly.

"Still a bit too hot?" he asked softly.

She nodded, feeling shy suddenly because of the nature of her thoughts. She met his gaze only briefly, then returned to looking into her cup.

Mr. Fitzpaine was Carlton's friend and had been—even as Fitzpaine had said—companions from the cradle. Surely, the man opposite her was not an innocent. She glanced back at him and saw that he was watching her closely.

"Dare I guess your thoughts?" he asked quietly.

She blinked several times and shook her head slowly from side to side, afterward smiling. "I am trying to draw your character," she said at last.

"You seem to be quite worried. Have I given you cause to be concerned?"

"Oh, no, on the contrary," she gushed. "You've been wonderful and so very considerate. I have no concerns on that score. It is just that—well, as closely as you are connected with Carlton, do you find that your interests are the same? Or are you very different from him?"

She watched as he transferred his gaze to an ancient spinning wheel mounted on the wall opposite the fireplace. He grew very serious for a long moment, before finally responding. "Carlton has been known to spend Sunday evenings lost in reading the poetry of John Milton, and every now and again as I would sit scratching out another tiresome couplet, he would read to me knowing I would appreciate the sound of the poet's written voice. Though Lady Cowper would gladly provide him vouchers for Almack's—it has been a full eight years since he vowed never again to cross the portals of that particular establishment—he refused to attend because of the busy work of the gabblemongers. I attend Almack's because I refuse to relinquish my hope that love might find my heart someday, but I believe Carlton gave up hope many years ago. His lordship does not frequent the East End hells, as the gossips would have everyone believe, and I should know, because I am with him six nights out of seven. He attends only his club and mine—White's, if you do not already know—and though he enjoys staking a wager on a dozen absurdities and delights in seeing his name written down in the proprietor's book—I have never seen him lose more than one or two hundred pounds of an evening, and that quite infrequently. His tastes run to reform in politics—he is a friend to Byron, however disgraced his lordship has been also by a great deal of unwanted gossip. He visited Leigh Hunt in prison and took him wine and bread and every other manner of comfort he could contrive, and encouraged me a dozen times to write essays for the *Examiner*—which have been published, I might add. He loves to ride and hunt, as do I. Swimming is a favorite pastime for both of us when the weather permits. Neither of us can abide Bath, though Brighton has brought a few not unhappy memories. The Prince Regent counts Carlton among his friends, though they differ in political emphasis, and I believe he enjoys the music at the Pavilion as much as I do—Prinney has a brass band which can play virtually any piece of music. Really, it is quite remarkable.

"From all of this you may draw something of my character, something of Carlton's, too, I think, as well as how many activities we share in common."

"You are not describing a man I recognize in the least," she said, stunned. "Why did no one tell me these things?"

At that, he turned to her, a smile warming his face again. "Perhaps you should have corresponded with me, Julianna. I could have told you all you desired to know. If I had, there is not the smallest doubt in my mind that you would now be married to Lord Carlton, instead of journeying to London with me."

She responded, "I am coming to esteem Carlton more than I thought possible because I am seeing him through your eyes, but I hope I do not offend you when I say that I am at this moment exceedingly grateful I did *not* correspond with you after all."

He smiled what seemed to her a smile of satisfaction and reached his hand across the table to touch her arm. "At this moment, I place a curse on all my pens, since they had the audacity to pose a threat to my becoming acquainted with you."

"You are the most absurd man I have ever known," Julianna responded, placing her hand over his and repressing a deep sigh of contentment.

"Oh, my poor dear," Lady Catterick exclaimed, entering her hostess's bedchamber in a rush of amethyst silk skirts draped with Brussels lace. "I cannot begin to conceive of the agony you are enduring. Poor, poor Millicent." She strode toward Lady Redmere with all the subtlety of a typhoon and before the viscountess's abigail could do ought but utter a surprised squeak, she had wrested from that servant's hands a kerchief soaked in lavender water. "Aren't you burning pastilles? I find nothing effects a cure upon the headache better than the pungent smell of ambergris."

Captain Beck, who was stationed beside the window, his arms folded across his chest in protest of Lady Catterick's arrival, exclaimed, "Ambergris comes from whales. I can't abide the stuff."

"Well it doesn't matter what country a perfume comes from," Lady Catterick returned in her smoothly nasal voice. "Wales or New South Wales, what difference does it make? The only question one must ask is whether or not it relieves the horrific pain of the headache, which it does. Where is your ambergris, Millicent? I shall tend to you and nurse you until I see your color vastly improved—though I must say, your cheeks are rather pink. How—how very surprising! My complexion, so delicate, turns a profound, chalky white when I am afflicted with the headache. Of course, no one suffers quite as I do."

Lady Redmere squinted and groaned as her new nurse began her ministrations.

Lady Catterick was one of the *ton*'s leading hostesses and had been an acquaintance of Lady Redmere's from the time the ladies had shared a "come-out" season some two-and-twenty years earlier. Lady Catterick had always been myopic, tall, thin, and positively relentless in her pursuit of scandal. She was most noted for the fine array of black wigs she wore to obscure her thinning hair. The charm of her personality, however, was less exact, and Lady Redmere had always believed her friend's success among the *haut* ton had been due primarily to the fact that her passion for gossip made her an ideal partner at the dinner table.

In a sickroom, she was less useful, and to Lady Redmere's dismay, Lady Catterick's first effort was to drench the kerchief with even more lavender water so that rivulets began seeping into Lady Redmere's hair and onto the apricot velvet chaise-longue on which she was disposed. Slipping her own hands into her hair, and dispersing the trickles of water, Lady Redmere responded, "Your—your sensibilities are spoken of in every drawing room, Eliza," she began hurriedly. "Even Princess Esterhazy wrote as much to me not two months ago. But I fear the lavender water is having an ill effect upon me."

"You need your pastilles," Lady Catterick returned

quickly. "Only tell me where your little china chimney is and I will see to it. Where's your ambergris?"

"Alas, I burned the last of it a sennight past, and with all the plans for the—the—" She began weeping distractedly and effectively brought Lady Catterick to her knees beside the chaise longue, where she took Lady Redmere's hand in hers. Petting it gently, she said, "You meant to say 'wedding,' didn't you, dearest? And oh, everyone, upon arriving, exclaimed over the ferns and daffodils all tied up in pretty bows and decorating the banister and the doorframes. Wherever did you get so many roses at this time of year?"

"My—my succession houses," Lady Redmere wailed. "I stripped them bare of every bloom and greenery all for—for nought! Whatever is to become of my darling Jilly? To have rejected her bridegroom on the very precipice of her nuptials—I shan't be able to bear the recriminations which are likely to fall on my head for permitting her to enter into such an engagement."

"You can't blame yourself, my dear. Julianna was always such a headstrong, selfish child."

Lady Redmere felt her temper shoot straight up to the ceiling upon hearing such an unjust criticism of her offspring. It was only with the strongest of efforts that she kept her tongue still. Fortunately, Captain Beck intervened.

"You dare to speak unkindly of Jilly when a sweeter child was never born?" he cried. "You, who gave birth to seven of the nastiest creatures who ever roamed a drawing room? Why, Edgar alone, with all his spots, not to mention his tendency to make sport of every other person present, ought to put you to shame! I never heard such an absurdity in all my life! You, criticizing Millicent's child? Pure humbug!"

"James!" Lady Redmere cried. "How very kind of you to champion my unhappy Julianna, but Lady Catterick is right. Jilly is behaving very badly and I have consigned her to her chambers, where she may sit alone for the remainder of the year, if necessary, until she comes to her senses and is ready to apologize to his lordship. If you must know, Eliza—I beg you will tell no one of this—Mr. Fitzpaine was here—"

"—No," the tall gossip breathed.

"You may well stare. It would seem Julianna sent a missive to Carlton at the Angel, breaking off the engagement—and not one word to me, mind! Carlton then persuaded Mr. Fitzpaine to call upon me and request confirmation. Only then did I proceed to confront my dear daughter. But I found her prostrate upon her bed, her face swollen beyond recognition from hysterics, her voice quivering with distress as she conveyed the dreaded tidings to me—she had broken with Carlton forever. She would not marry a rake—those were her very words!" She drew in a deep breath before continuing her tale. "Mr. Fitzpaine received the news somberly and afterward informed me that Carlton meant to leave immediately—north to visit that author—dear me, what is his name—"

"You mean Scott?" Lady Catterick suggested. "Sir Walter Scott? The author of *Waverley*?"

"That is the man," Lady Redmere said, nodding and squinting and pressing a hand to each temple. "The very one. Mr. Fitzpaine, whom I have come to realize is the most charming man, said he would undoubtedly follow. Whatever did I do to deserve such a wretched year—first, that Garston woman—"

"—Oh, do not mention that woman's name," Lady Catterick breathed. "You know, I begin to think Julianna has shown a great deal of sense, for did you know, Millicent, that Charlotte Garston is none other than Carlton's professed mistress?"

At that, Lady Redmere sat bolt upright, and cried out, "What? Carlton's mistress? You cannot—you cannot—you cannot—be—serious—oh . . ."

Lady Redmere felt herself floating as though she was lying on the softest cloud imaginable. She felt nothing, no pain, no worries, only a peace beyond reason. She could not remember ever having felt so content, so happy. She wanted to stay upon this cloud forever.

Suddenly, a vile odor rushed toward her like a wind bearing the disgusting smell of a chicken coop. She felt nauseated and began to cough. What was that in her face? "Stop," she murmured.

"She's coming 'round," she heard Lady Catterick say from a great distance. "That's it, Millicent, take a deep breath."

"Let me be. Do go away, you wretched simpleton." She opened her eyes and blinked. She found herself staring into Lady Catterick's thin, worried face.

"Feeling better?" Lady Catterick cooed. "My poor dear. I would never have mentioned that woman's name to you had I known you would go off like that."

"I feel very sick, Eliza. Will you please see to my unhappy guests tonight? And tomorrow perhaps I can rise from my sickbed and bid everyone *adieu*." She glanced hopefully at her friend, then, licking her lips, queried, "I know I shouldn't ask, but are you sure Carlton is keeping the widow Garston?"

"It is spoken of in every credible drawing room in Mayfair. Perhaps I should have told you sooner, but I was afraid it would likely spoil your enjoyment of your daughter's wedding. The point seemed moot. You do not mind very much, do you—that is, that I kept this *on-dits* from your ears?"

"On the contrary," Lady Redmere sniffed, taking Lady Catterick's vinaigrette from her hand and holding it bravely beneath her own nose. "It was kind of you to want to spare me pain. It would explain everything. I expect Jilly knew of Mrs. Garston, but because of my own circumstances, did not have the courage to tell me. I can now forgive her completely for refusing to wed Carlton, if it is true." She then burst into tears which were as real as her headache had been false. The only trouble was, now she had the headache indeed, and could not imagine how she was to endure the journey south through Malton to York.

Lady Catterick's parting words assured Lady Redmere that her guests would be attended to. Once the door closed upon the older woman, Lady Redmere pushed aside the cashmere shawl draped over her legs and was on her feet in an instant. "Is all in readiness?" she asked, feeling the blood rush to her head and a steady pounding resound through her skull.

"Yes, our baggages have been stowed in the boot and the horses are ready. Burton has seen to everything—most discreetly."

Within half an hour, yet a full three hours since Lady Redmere learned of the dreaded elopement, she and her maid, Polly, along with Captain Beck, were ensconced in Lady Redmere's large coach—visible from the north windows of the manor—and heading toward the village. Once there, they would take up Mr. Fitzpaine and begin a steady progress toward Malton and the Great North Road.

From her first-floor bedchamber, Lady Catterick stared through her window at the departure of a large, lumbering coach. Beside her stood Mrs. Whenby and Mrs. Bulmer, her dearest friends. She slipped her hand between the thin muslin drapes and shifting them aside ever so slightly, whispered conspiratorially to her two companions, "There, you see? What did I tell you? A coach laden with passengers. Notice how low the wheels sink into the snow. I daresay, were we to inquire of the servants as to the whereabouts of Lady Redmere and Captain Beck and perhaps even Julianna, we would receive nervous answers."

"I don't believe it," Mrs. Whenby countered in her birdlike voice. "Why would they leave at such an hour?" She was a short woman, with a thin frame, a small nose, and round, protruding, blue eyes.

"In pursuit of Miss Redmere, of course," Lady Catterick responded.

"What?" her friends cried in unison.

Mrs. Bulmer gestured with a plump arm to the door behind her. In a commanding voice, she argued, "But Miss Redmere is laid flat upon her bed even as we speak. I was told as much not fifteen minutes past by her maid—and she did not seem in the least embarrassed in her responses. I believe she spoke the truth to me. Besides, why would Miss Redmere have gone anywhere after ending, at such an absurd hour, her betrothal to Carlton?"

At that, Lady Catterick lifted a victorious eyebrow and whispered, "Follow me, if you disbelieve me. I shall put an end to your doubts even now."

She and her two compatriots stole quickly down the long hall in the east wing until they arrived before Julianna's bedchamber door.

"But you cannot, Eliza," Mrs. Whenby whispered in her bird's voice. Her cheeks were quite pink and her round, bulging blue eyes were rounder and more protruding than ever. "How very improper." She then giggled.

"Oh, indeed, yes," Mrs. Bulmer pronounced, with a deeper chortle than Mrs. Whenby's. She glanced up the hall and down the hall, and seeing that no one was about, barked a command: "Give it a shove, Eliza, and be quick about it."

Lady Catterick wasted no time.

She quickly turned the ornate brass handle and pushed the heavy carved door open.

Julianna's chambers were lit brightly from light streaming through windows flanked by dark green velvet drapes. The mahogany bed was neatly made up in a matching spread of green velvet. Tasseled, plumped pillows, artfully arranged, confirmed Lady Catterick's tale.

"Oh," Mrs. Whenby cooed ecstatically.

"Oh, yes," Mrs. Bulmer agreed, in her deep voice.

"Oh, yes, indeed," Lady Catterick breathed through her nose.

As one, the ladies turned and sped quickly to the next door across the hall, the very bedchamber Lady Catterick had quit but recently and in which Lady Redmere ought to be resting.

"I spoke with her not half an hour ago," Lady Catterick said. She nodded to each of her friends and threw the door wide. A sweep of apricot furnishings sat silent in the empty chamber, the bed also neatly made up.

"Oh," Mrs. Whenby cooed, a little more ecstatically than before.

"Oh, yes," Mrs. Bulmer agreed, her massive bosom shuddering eloquently.

"Oh, yes, indeed," Lady Catterick breathed slowly, again through her nose.

As one, yet again, the ladies whirled about, silk skirts rushing into one another, as they continued down the hall two doors more.

"The captain's quarters," Lady Catterick announced. She paused for a long moment and with a flourish threw this last door wide.

The aqua-and-peach chamber, decorated *à la chinoise* in black lacquer and gilt, was glaring in its emptiness.

"Oh-h-h!" Mrs. Whenby cried, in a trill of pure excitement.

"Oh, yes, yes, yes!" Mrs. Bulmer agreed most emphatically.

"Oh, yes! Indeed, yes!" Lady Catterick breathed at her most nasal, regarding her dearest friends through eyes dreamily misted with societal ectasy.

Finally, again as one, all three ladies giggled and in unison whispered, *"A scandal!"*

Chapter Eight

"I prefer to stop at this inn, if you would not mind terribly, Mr. Fitzpaine," Julianna said, opening her eyes very wide and hoping that her meaning would be translated quickly to her escort. Her hands were knotted together, not from the cold, but from distress.

She watched Mr. Fitzpaine glance dubiously at the ramshackle establishment a hundred yards ahead and grimaced. "I doubt that the service will prove all that you desire. There must be a dozen far more agreeable inns in York. This is only the first since Easingwold. Are you very certain you wish to stay here?"

Milkmaid Molly chimed in, her voice as loud and as piercing as it had been for the past twenty-four miles. "Oh, the Potter's Wheel! I know the mort wat tends the cattle 'ere. He's evuh so nice though without 'is wits. He used to 'ave a brother wat was a fav'rite wi' all the ladies—serving wenches, I means—but he left York to join His Majesty's Navy. Last wat wuz 'eard of 'im, he were livin' in America. Had a pig farm, methinks. Quite respectable. La, but I'm so empty in my squeeze-box that I feel like to swoon. I might even 'ave need of yor vin-aye-gritt, Miss Redmere."

When she elbowed Julianna in the ribs in a hard, albeit purely friendly manner, Jilly turned back to Mr. Fitzpaine and begged him with a silent, *please*. Molly's ample form, her common manners, and her loud voice had finally taken their toll. She would suspend all comfort for the sole prospect of getting rid of Molly, if only for the evening.

"This inn will do quite nicely," Mr. Fitzpaine responded quickly. "It seems I find I'm a trifle empty in my *squeeze-box* as well."

Julianna tried to smile at him, but her faltering attempt only made Mr. Fitzpaine laugh as he ordered the postillion to pull through the gates of the Potter's Wheel Inn.

Julianna was grateful to be in York at last, not only because she would soon be free of Molly's tiresome society, but because night was nearly upon the northern city and she was fairly fagged to death. The day's trials had been severe, taking a toll upon her sensibilities in the same way riding a horse for hours on end tended to wear thin the threads of her riding habit.

Arriving in York was in some ways like arriving home. She knew the sprawling city well, from the Minster rising high above all the other buildings and visible from the Hambleton Hills, to the imposing gates, to the ancient walls. The Romans founded York in the first century A.D., so its history was an exciting and noble one. But by far her favorite haunt was a locale called the Shambles, in which dozens of shops were located among the narrowest of streets. Some of her brideclothes awaited her there and she wished she was able to somehow fetch them, for she was becoming decidedly uncomfortable in her muddied wedding gown. Already she had been the object of numerous impertinent stares.

Mr. Fitzpaine addressed her in a quiet voice, interrupting her thoughts. "One advantage of staying the night here," he said, "is that I daresay neither of us will chance unpropitiously upon an acquaintance."

However discreet the choice of his words, Milkmaid Molly was not slow to take up his meaning.

"Be ye elopin'?" she cried ecstatically. "I knew, oh, I knew it! I told Silly Sally—that's wat we calls her, as she is always pullin' a face or playin' off a trick on one or t'other of us—I was tellin' Sally I thought t'were likely you wuz 'eadin' toward Gretna. She were watchin' the coach from the first-floor window, and when she sawr us turn south—she pulled a face wat nearly set me off—just to show me how wrong I wuz. But I knew ye wuz elopin' cuz ladies don't travel proper-like without maids and baggage. I only wish Sally were 'ere. Her daylights would fairly pop from 'er 'ead with the tale I could tell her now!"

"Oh, the carriage has stopped at last," Julianna remarked, ignoring Molly's comment about their supposed elopement. The journey from Thirsk through Easingwold to York had been a mere four and twenty miles, but just past Easingwold they had lost a wheel and suffered a delay of three hours.

Merciful heavens!

Three hours!

The longest three hours of her entire existence!

After listening to Molly's full, theatrical voice for so long a time, her nerves were near to shattering like a goblet of fine, thin glass perched precariously on the edge of a table. "Where could the hostler be?" she continued, fearing that Molly would begin speaking again. "How very odd. Molly, open the door and let down the steps. My brick has gone quite cold and I find I am chilled to the bone. I wish to go inside at once, if you please."

"Oh, yes, ma'am! Of course, ma'am! Right away, ma'am!"

Each time the girl uttered an exclamation, Julianna winced. But her movements were far from the swiftness she promised. Molly—taking great pains to rise to her newly elevated position as lady's maid to *Mrs. Fitzpaine*—began to slowly tie her hood about her neck and afterward equally as carefully began gathering her slim belongings with all the éclat of a princess. She finally opened the door and let down the steps. A stableboy with a dull look in his eyes and carrying a lantern appeared and offered Molly his hand, which she took with affected graciousness.

Once Molly was safely landed, Julianna took the boy's hand and stepped down from the coach. She found that the crunch of icy snow beneath her half-boots was the most welcome sound in the world. The young man smiled crookedly upon her, his expression one of simplistic purity, as he told her she was very pretty and added, "It be that hard to travel in a coach fer hours, eh? 'Specially with Molly. She tawks awful sharp!"

"Indeed, yes," Julianna said with a sigh.

Molly stood behind the boy and rolled her eyes and pointed to her head by way of indicating the young man's mental ability. She was about to speak, but Julianna could bear no more and silenced her with a quick command. "Pray go before us and bespeak a private parlour from the landlord for, er, Miss Red—that is, for Mr. and Mrs. Fitzpaine."

"Indeed I will, *ma'am*," Molly replied with emphasis. "And he will give you the best parlour, make no mistake! You may rely on Milkmaid Molly! You know why they call me Milkmaid Molly, don't you?"

"Yes," Julianna returned with a sigh. "Because you could bring the cows trotting home with a single long bellowing call clear from the barn door!" Molly had repeated the origin of her nickname a dozen times.

"Right you are!" Molly bellowed happily in return, and leaped for the door.

Julianna stood in the snow for a long moment, staring at the bright beacon of orange hair which appeared the moment Molly opened the door to the inn and threw back the hood of her brown cloak. *"Land-lord!"* she called out, as though hailing a ship across a wide stretch of sea.

"Pluck up, Julianna," Mr. Fitzpaine whispered in her ear. After directing the stableboy to see to the horses and carriage for the night, he slipped an arm about Julianna's shoulder and gave her a comforting squeeze.

"I don't think I can bear another mile with that creature," she returned quietly, as the sounds of the horses and carriage being drawn away echoed off the stone wall of the inn in front of her. "Oh, Mr. Fitzpaine, I know you will not like my

saying so, but I had by far rather marry Carlton than endure
another shrieking anecdote about Pegleg Meg or Wooden
Willy."

Mr. Fitzpaine laughed and bade her enter the inn. "I'll see
what I can contrive though I rather thought it clever of
Wooden Willy that he could make his teeth sound like rattling bones when he clacked them together."

At that, Julianna laughed and felt some of the journey's
tensions relax from her shoulders. But when she reached the
threshold of the inn, she found her contentment short lived.

"Oh, dear," she murmured. "Did I actually beg you to
stop here?" The paneled walls were rough with wear, as was
the wood floor. Splinters rose from the planking and tufts of
hay crusted with mud had been tracked well down the hall.

"Try to think of it this way," Mr. Fitzpaine encouraged
her. "If we have any good fortune at all, the plague will strike
us within these walls and we will both die sudden deaths, and
therefore be spared any more of Molly's delightful recount-
ings."

Julianna looked up at him and replied with mock gravity,
"There you would be out, I'm sure. I've little doubt that
were we to die here, Molly would likely perish as well. And
we would soon discover, far from being in Paradise, that the
ancient Greek legends were true, that there really is an
underworld and a River Styx and that Milkmaid Molly has
just been promoted to barge-woman!"

He laughed outright, continuing to chuckle as they progressed down the narrow hall. After a moment he whispered,
"You are quite morbid for one so young."

"That from a man who speaks of the plague," she countered readily, also in a whisper.

If there was any mystery as to the location of the parlour
within the sagging inn, Julianna was soon informed of its
whereabouts when Molly appeared at the far end of the
narrow corridor. She stood in the middle of a bright puddle
of light which glowed from a chamber to her right, and cried
out in rustic wonder, "Ye won't believe yer daylights!"

Julianna withheld a shudder at the sound of her maid's voice and with much trepidation approached the doorway of what she soon found to be a clean, warm chamber, illuminated by three branches of candles. She was completely astonished. The parlour was exquisite, almost beyond belief! It was decorated in the Egyptian style—of all things!—with a delicacy of taste equal to many of the finer homes in the Vale of Pickering. Given the dilapidated and even somewhat unkempt appearance of the inn, she couldn't credit her eyes.

The walls of the chamber were painted a pale yellow and both the rich draperies hanging criss-crossed over a large Elizabethan window and the mahogany sofa with lotus-shaped feet and arms were of expensive royal blue silk-damask. Even if the fabric was a trifle weary with age, both the drapes and sofa had clearly been kept in excellent condition. In front of the sofa were two matching footstools in the curved console style.

A highly polished mahogany dining table bearing pillar-and-claw supports graced the center of the chamber and was adorned by four beech scrollback parlour chairs, painted black and gilt. A small mahogany writing table, sporting charming lyre-shaped legs, sat next to the window. Directly across from the writing desk, a curved sideboard decorated with Egyptian caryatids completed the ensemble.

Near the sofa, a warm fire beamed strongly from the fireplace, and above the mantel was a painting that fairly took Julianna's breath away.

Mr. Fitzpaine's gaze had traveled in a similar direction. "Good God!" he cried. "That is a Turner."

"Indeed, I believe you are right!" Julianna responded, stepping into the room, her attention held spellbound by the sight of the bold watercolor. The majestic York Minster— the largest cathedral in all of England—awash with a brilliant sunset blazing against thunderous Yorkshire clouds, bespoke the famous painter's unmistakable hand.

A woman's raspy voice called out. "I've had more than one tell me so." Julianna turned around and glanced toward

Molly. For the first time she noticed that an elderly woman, diminuitive with age, stood near her abigail—the inn's landlady.

"Oh," Julianna remarked, surprised. "I do beg your pardon. I did not see you before."

"You'll not be the first to say as much to me, not that I mind, not by half." She had kind blue eyes and Julianna liked her immediately. The landlady's gaze drifted toward the painting. "The man what give this to me—I believe out of sympathy for the recent death of my husband—winked when he told me 'is name was *John Constable*."

As one, both Julianna and Mr. Fitzpaine gestured toward the painting and exclaimed, "That is not a Constable!"

Julianna turned surprised eyes upon her supposed husband and queried, "You are familiar with his landscapes?"

"Yes, as I see you know Turner's works."

"Indeed," she nodded, feeling pleased that they obviously shared a common interest.

"You are both welcome to the Potter's Wheel," the landlady said, advancing into the room. "My name is Mrs. Rose. It is quite lovely to have you here. The Quality don't frequent my inn as much as I would like. Not but what I don't blame them. The hotel isn't what it was in days gone by, when my husband were alive. I've only one serving girl, and of course, Bibbel. You met my son, did you?"

Mr. Fitzpaine moved forward and bowed to the lady, treating her with a respect her gray, tightly bound hair, her starched, immaculate apron, and her composure commanded. "Yes, he seemed quite eager to care for the horses."

"He loves the cattle, he does," she said, clasping her hands proudly in front of her and smiling with affection. "A bit of a slow top, though, as you could see, I'm sure. I only wish you and your wife had happened along in a month or two. My garden is covered with daffodils, hundreds of them. This late snow took us a bit by surprise. But if you're heading south, I expect spring will meet you along the way, if not in whole, then in bits. Be ye hungry? I've a bit of roast beef, a few vegetables, ham, perhaps a couple of partridges—would that be suiting to you?"

"Very much so," Julianna responded.

The old woman turned to Mr. Fitzpaine. "And you've the look of a Madeira man. I've a bottle or two put aside. Are ye wishful?"

"I am. Very," Mr. Fitzpaine responded. "Indeed, thank you."

"Lemonade for you, Mrs. Fitzpaine," she admonished Julianna, her tone brooking no argument.

When she left the chamber, she returned two seconds later. "You there!" she commanded Molly. "The kitchen, if you please. Were you thinking to remain where you were least wanted and of no use at all?"

"No, ma'am," Molly cried submissively. With a flurry of her brown cloak, she stretched out her neck obediently toward the landlady, and followed quickly behind.

Julianna sank into a chair by the table and heaved a thankful sigh. "I have never been so grateful to a woman in all my life. I had begun to believe Molly would be with us forever. What are we going to do with her?"

"I am almost tempted to leave her here at the Potter's Wheel, but our good landlady does not deserve such cow-handed treatment. Therefore I can only conceive of one solution—we must hire a second post-chaise."

"What an excellent notion!" Julianna responded brightly, clapping her hands together. But after a moment's consideration, she could feel her cheeks begin to burn as she addressed a quite delicate matter. "But—but hiring a second chaise will be quite dear, won't it? I mean—" she broke off, unable to look at Mr. Fitzpaine. She pressed her hands upon her cheeks, wishing she could force from them what she knew to be their sudden reddish hue.

"Whatever is the matter, Julianna?" he queried.

She turned back to him, ignoring her discomfiture, and looked him straight in the eye. "I don't like to mention it, Mr. Fitzpaine, but it is commonly known that—that—"

"—That I am not precisely well-shod?"

"Well, yes," Julianna breathed, grateful to have been so readily understood.

Mr. Fitzpaine drew near to her, and giving a tug on one of her red curls, said, "By a stroke of great good fortune, of which we both are in desperate need, I am in funds of the moment. Before leaving London, I had a considerable streak of luck at White's, and I can see no better use for such questionably gotten gains than to hire a chaise for Molly. So you see, not only can I stand the nonsense, but I am content beyond words to put it to such gainful effect. Besides, I greatly fear that another league in her company and I should be unable to restrain myself from strangling the child."

Julianna giggled. "If," she responded with a teasing smile, "murder would be the result of frugality in this particular instance, then I heartily recommend you follow your inclination and hire a second coach."

He slipped his hand in hers. "I am sorry, Julianna," he said softly, giving her hand a squeeze. "Had I known the vexation you would endure with Molly at your side, I would never have contracted her services—er, such as they are!"

Hearing her name spoken so tenderly brought a rush of affection swirling about Julianna's heart. She returned the pressure of his fingers and said, "You were thinking only of my honor, and for that I will always be grateful."

For some reason he seemed nonplussed by her response, and she was about to ask why he was troubled when Mrs. Rose arrived bearing a tray of Madeira and lemonade. While the landlady poured out their glasses, Julianna untied her green velvet cloak and draped it over one of the black-and-gilt scrollback chairs. She looked down at the skirts of her gown and the sight of her stained hem reminded her that her flight from the village of Redmere had left her bereft of proper traveling garments—she did not even possess a night-gown. When she saw that Mrs. Rose eyed her skirts curi-ously, she came to the firm conclusion that she could not continue the remainder of the journey with only her wedding-clothes to wear. There was not the smallest doubt in her mind that traveling in her white satin gown would continue to provoke much unwanted interest and speculation. However romantical the notion had been to flee a marriage her bridegroom did not want, doing so in a stained, white satin gown held nothing of beauty or romance.

She glanced toward Mr. Fitzpaine, wondering if he had noticed Mrs. Rose's expression, but he was taking a glass of wine from the lady, apparently oblivious to everything save the bouquet of the wine. She had several dresses awaiting her at a shop in the Shambles—if only she could get to her dressmaker's before leaving York. The trouble was, if she was recognized by anyone, her journey might meet an untimely end.

Perhaps Molly could go . . .

When Mrs. Rose quit the chamber, Julianna followed after her—much to Mr. Fitzpaine's surprise. The landlady listened to her request and nodded approvingly. "Bibbel knows the Shambles well. He may not be quick-witted, but once he knows his way, he never forgets. He'll see that Molly gets to your shop in good time tomorrow morning."

When she further requested two chambers, as well as a bed set up in her room for her abigail, she felt secure that every detail had been attended to and returned to the parlour with a lighter heart.

At first, she had intended to tell Mr. Fitzpaine about her clothes, but knowing it would be an excellent surprise for him to see her on the morrow gowned properly for traveling, she limited her revelations to the news that she had made arrangements for their rooms for the night.

"I'm sorry," he cried. "It didn't occur to me that that task had remained undone. Forgive me, Julianna. I should have seen to it myself."

"What nonsense!" she returned. "It is not precisely the most fatiguing of errands to secure a bedchamber. Besides, Mrs. Rose is most obliging and kindhearted. She did not even blink when I requested *two* chambers."

He sipped his wine, then swirled the Madeira around in his glass. He seemed much struck by her answer and smiled. "Are you certain you are only nineteen years of age?" he queried.

Julianna smiled in response, feeling that somehow she had garnered his respect in that moment. Picking up her glass of lemonade, she moved to stand beside the fireplace. A polished brass andiron—a relic of former prosperity—fronted a warm blaze of coals. On the hearth sat a partially filled coal skuttle, a bellows, and a poker. She knew a childlike instinct to pick up the poker and begin thrashing the coals to see the red embers fly about. She giggled, and when he asked why she was laughing, she responded, "Now I will prove my age to you." She then recounted her impulse.

How surprised she was when he immediately set his glass on the table, moved to kneel before the fireplace, picked up the poker, and disturbed as many of the coals as he could without causing any of them to flee the hearth.

"So what have you just proved to me, Mr. Fitzpaine?" she asked, looking down at him and feeling as she had the first moment she saw him—as though a violent *tendre* had taken complete possession of her senses.

He replaced the poker and stood up to face her. "That our respective ages have no bearing upon our friendship and that you must call me by my Christian name. Or better yet, the name my closest friends call me—Edward."

"Edward it is," she responded, taking a deep breath.

Looking into his gray eyes brought a dozen warm sentiments flooding her heart yet again. She approved heartily of him, of the fact he broke up the coals, that he recognized the Turner watercolor, that he was willing to risk society's disapproval in order to help her reach her father and avoid a disastrous marriage, that he could tease her about Molly by speaking of plagues and the like, that he was not shocked when she countered with truly wretched comments about the River Styx and Molly being a barge-woman. She approved of the tender light in his eyes as he watched her, of his many kindnesses on their trip south, of his intention to hire a second vehicle. If she could have begged the heavens to send her a gentleman who answered her every girlish daydream, Mr. Fitzpaine—Edward—would have been the answer to her prayer.

Her heart swelled with pleasure in her breast. Goodness gracious, but her sentiments sang strongly for this poet. The way her breathing became labored when he was near, the manner in which her thoughts rarely ran cohesively together when she looked into his eyes, the trembling which frequently afflicted her knees when he looked at her as he was now, as though he wished to kiss her—merciful heavens, it was far too much to comprehend. She knew full well that her feelings were running too high for Edward. She should try to temper her thoughts and her responses to his closeness. But how?

She looked away from him, from the intensity of his own gaze and cloaked thoughts, and directed her gaze out the window. The cloudy skies above York had made for a dark night and all that was visible in the street was a cast-shadow of yellow light on the snow outside, a reflection of the candle-light which kept the parlour in a steady glow. Traffic had all but disappeared from the moonless, drifted roads. Who wanted to be about on such a night when a warm fire would call every sensible man home to his hearth?

Thoughts of the comforts of one's home and hearth brought Marish Hall and her mother sharply to mind along with the truth that were the *beau monde* to learn she had spent the night in an inn with Mr. Fitzpaine, she would likely be ruined forever.

She thought of her beloved mama and how much she had wished for her marriage to Carlton. She knew her mother would be devastated by her elopement, and perhaps even now was nearing Gretna Green to see if she could find her only daughter.

Her throat began to constrict as she pondered the horrific nature of her flight with Mr. Fitzpaine and how sad and disappointed her mother must be feeling even now. Perhaps she, too, had stopped at an inn along the way, seeking shelter from the cold, dark night. Perhaps she had retired to her bedchamber and was even now crying into her pillow at thoughts of her errant, ungrateful daughter.

Chapter Nine

"Good God," Captain Beck cried, his astonishment giving a strange lift to his droopy brown eyes. "If you mean to tell me they are spending the night alone under the same roof, then by morning Julianna will be lost forever. Oh, Millicent, I can't begin to conceive of the terrible scandal that must follow! You must cast her off! From this moment on, you must treat Jilly as though she is dead to the world. She can no longer be your child."

Lady Redmere was seated at a table in the parlour of an inn whose name kept escaping her. It was the Crown and Bear, or some other large animal. Or was it the Castle and Bear? She could never keep the name straight! Good Captain Beck stood beside her, an arm draped over the back of her chair. She lifted an arched brow as she turned her head around to address her absurd Cicisbeo. "I asked for comfort from you, James," she stated with a shake of her head. "Not a death-knell."

Captain Beck blinked his eyes, bewildered. "Have I said something wrong?" he queried, sliding his arm off her chair, and taking up his seat beside her. "Perhaps I ought to try again?"

"I'm afraid if you do, you'll risk sending me to an early grave."

"Well, I wouldn't want to do that," he responded sincerely.

Lady Redmere could only chuckle. "I shall be grateful to you then if you refrain from trying to *console* me." She sipped her tea and not for the first time grimaced at the taste of the watery brew. She thought it likely the landlord's rather grim-faced wife had laid down a strict rule that three tea leaves only were allowed in the preparation of a proper cup of tea. She stared into the tepid water, and could not help but wonder whether the liquid was indeed amber, or if the candlelight was merely making it appear so.

Whatever the case, she did not look for an extreme attendance to her comforts at the—now, where were they? Oh, yes, it finally came to her—the Elephant and Crown, near Nessgate, in York. She had wanted to put up at Etteridge's Hotel, the finest inn available to the nobility and gentry visiting the large northern city, but Etteridge's was full to overflowing, as was the Black Swan in Coney Street, the York Tavern in St. Helen's Square, the George, the White Horse in Coppergate, the White Swan, the Robin Hood, and the Pack Horse in Micklegate. Come to think of it, it now struck her as quite odd that during a less hospitable season, as it now was, so many inns would be full!

She wondered suddenly if there was some reason why they had been refused shelter at all the other inns and it occurred to her that upon arriving at last at the Elephant and Crown—with nightfall hard upon the city—Mr. Fitzpaine had told a whisker and introduced Captain Beck as her brother!

Lady Redmere then cupped a hand over her mouth and gasped. So innocent had been her own thoughts and intentions, so purposeful were her own actions in trying to help her daughter to avoid a scandal, that until this moment, it had not occurred to her that she was creating a scandal of her own by traveling with two unmarried men with only her abigail to lend her countenance.

"Merciful heavens!" she cried. "However did I come to be so birdwitted?"

"I can't say, really," Captain Beck returned.

She merely looked blankly at him for a long moment, then requested politely that he order supper, since Mr. Fitzpaine, who was searching the town for news of Jilly, would undoubtedly be returning any moment. When he left the small, cosy parlour, she glanced about her and thought that in the same way her cup was spare of tea, the parlour was equally spare of furniture. A small cottage sideboard in the Gothic style adorned the wall opposite a small window—a window, she noted, which was deepset and bare of curtains. The walls were white, the dining table at which she was sitting was straight-legged, and the chairs an oddity in that they were carved and painted to simulate bamboo. The chairs put her forcibly in mind of the Pavilion at Brighton. She could not conceive how such chairs had made their way so far north and that to an inn as unwelcoming in its decor as its tea was devoid of flavor! And what on earth did an elephant have to do with a crown, she could not imagine!

The only adornment to be found on any of the walls was a row of worn pegs near the door used for cloaks, pelisses, and greatcoats. A decidedly poor chamber, she thought, but not poorer, perhaps, than the state of her spirits as her reflections again turned to her daughter's elopement.

She sighed, setting her cup aside, and in a most unladylike manner propped her elbow on the table and dropped her weary chin in her hand.

The moment the snow had begun drifting down upon the horse's ears past Malton, she felt certain their expedition was doomed, particularly since it was likely—if pressed—Carlton would hire a sporting vehicle, bundle up his victim, and take the ribbons himself in an effort to reach London, Dover, then Paris in good order. He was a notable whip, a fair Nonpareil, as Captain Beck had so kindly pointed out to her no less than three times in the past hour. He could easily have taken his prize anywhere in the Kingdom by now.

She had only herself to blame. How utterly foolish she had been to have agreed to such an outlandish marriage, when even Redmere told her she was being a silly goosecap and would only find herself and Jilly in the basket if she continued down this road.

The mere fact he had chosen to express himself in such a manner, calling her a *"silly goosecap,"* had firmed her resolve to see the ghastly betrothal to a conclusion.

To Carlton's credit, however, everything had been polite and orderly from the moment terms had been agreed upon and the lengthy marriage settlements signed. She had received two letters from him, both gentlemanly and sensible. He had promised to make Julianna what he hoped would be an unexceptionable husband.

As for seeing her daughter wed to the viscount, she had pushed for the match because it had the best advantage of all—that *love* was not present to confuse either party.

It was infatuation which had been her own undoing, of that she was convinced. She should never have wed Redmere. Theirs had been a marriage replete with conflict—well, at least in the past year it had—and she wanted, as every mother had from the beginning of time, something different and better for her child. No, not for Julianna to suffer the wretched trials of being so madly, so hopelessly in love that she would be *aux anges* one moment, then cast in despair the next. Of course, she could number on one hand the times she had truly been cast in despair prior to last season. But what did that matter? After all, last season had fully made up for nineteen years of general happiness.

Last season, she had suffered enough vexation for an entire lifetime!

No, Julianna would not have to suffer as she had suffered, and she had been fully persuaded that in time, she would *learn* to love Carlton.

And now Carlton, whose true character had been revealed, had Jilly in his clutches.

The door opened suddenly and Mr. Fitzpaine entered the parlour, his appearance as immaculate as always. Except for slightly wilted shirtpoints, he did not look as though he had been traveling all afternoon or as though he had been scouring the city for news of Julianna for the past hour. He crossed the room and she could see that not a single flake of snow clung to either his top boots or to the hem of his greatcoat—at least, not to her eye. Really, he was amazing.

He stopped abruptly, however, turned his head slowly, and spied an errant snowflake halfway down the sleeve of his coat. With an easy flick of his thumb and forefinger, he dislodged the traitor, then progressed the remainder of the way to her table.

Once there, he bowed graciously to her and stated, "No one has seen them. I returned to every inn from which we originally sought shelter and a few more, less worthy of notice, but not one person I spoke to recalled having seen your daughter's cloak or coppery hair or her white gown. I can only conclude Carlton has pressed on and is even now in Ferrybridge."

"Is it possible you missed one of York's inns? I know there is one near the road leading to Easingwold."

"The Potter's Wheel. I inquired there, and although the hostler did not seem to have all his wits about him, he clearly stated he had not seen a young lady with red hair, wearing a green cloak. He seemed most emphatic and gave me no reason to doubt him, despite the limits of his mental abilities."

"We should have crossed the Hambleton Hills as you suggested," she said. "But I despise that trek. The road is uneven and undulates in parts. I feel quite sick just thinking about it. But now that we cannot find them in York, I wish I had had the courage to follow your advice."

He smiled, and softened his voice a trifle. "Don't fret so. For your sake, I am glad we did not attempt the journey to Thirsk. Besides, I have every confidence, with a little diligence, we shall find Julianna."

Captain Beck, who had returned from his mission of ordering dinner, appeared in the doorway. "You are mistaken, Mr. Fitzpaine," he said, his voice full of gloom. "I have a terrible prescience. I believe she is buried in a snowdrift and

is dead. I am sure of it. I—I feel it somehow in my heart."
He thumped his chest three times with his fist, then sighed
heavily.

Lady Redmere covered her mouth and nose with her
hands to keep from laughing. The captain, his expression
one of agonized sadness, stood in the doorway, mouth
drooping, eyes drooping, one hand on his hip, one foot
forward, shaking his head gravely. He looked as though he
belonged on the stage, opposite Kean, perhaps, in one of
Shakespeare's darker plays.

From the beginning, Beck had been a bearer of doom and
destruction. Every turn in the road had brought a groan
issuing from his weak stomach and a wish the coach had
wings. Every glimpse of a lady in green culled forth a distem-
pered shriek.

He looked at her now and clicked his tongue. "There,
there, my dearest Millicent," he said to her in a quavering
voice, as he crossed the room to stand beside her. "I know
it is more than you can bear, but I am here to support you."
He placed a gentle arm about her shoulders and gave her a
small hug, followed by another long sigh. "Carlton should be
hung by the neck and his stomach flayed open for the blackbirds to feed on."

Lady Redmere could not suppress her laughter this time
and was able to diminish the effect only by covering her face
fully with her hands. She dared not exchange a glance with
Mr. Fitzpaine, who had remained standing beside the dining
table opposite her. She had already come to know that she
shared a similar sense of the absurd with him. If she met his
gaze, she was certain she would lose her countenance entirely.

"Yes, my dear," Captain Beck said, patting her shoulder.
"Give full vent to your anguish. You will feel all the better
for it, I'm persuaded of it! I've been thinking, you should
have a bust of Julianna made up for the family vault. Everyone can come 'round to admire her beauty. Perhaps Mr.
Fitzpaine could compose a poem in her honor—'Ode to a

Dead Traveling Lady'—no, that sounds a bit harsh. Perhaps, 'To a Lady Who Traveled the Wrong Road.' What do you think, Fitzpaine? I haven't the turn for language you do."

Lady Redmere uncovered her eyes in order to see how Mr. Fitzpaine would respond to Beck's suggestions. The poet was clearly dumbfounded, his blue eyes opened wide in stunned fascination. His expression of amazement only made her laugh harder still.

"I should prefer," Mr. Fitzpaine returned quietly, "To defer any such effort until I was certain it was needed."

Lady Redmere could not imagine what Captain Beck would say to this and she shifted her gaze, still peeping from between her fingers, to her Cicisbeo. He nodded gravely. "Very sensible. No use wasting your words if she ain't dead!"

Lady Redmere now wept with laughter, uncovering her face to wipe her tears with the palms of her hands. "James, my dear, you are such a comfort," she cried, when she could steal a breath between chortles. "I cannot imagine what I would do were I on my deathbed and you were not nearby to—to usher me into the next world!"

"Don't even think of it, dearest," he said, his lip quivering. "Oh, my! I am suddenly feeling queasy. Millicent, what would I do if you suddenly stuck your spoon in the wall?"

This was too much for Lady Redmere, who collapsed in whoops on the table in front of her. Mr. Fitzpaine bit hard into his lower lip, turned abruptly away from the table, then moved quickly to stand facing the deepset window.

"I am completely overcome," Captain Beck announced. "You must forgive me, but to see you so distressed—I can't bear it!" And with that, he hurried from the parlour.

Lady Redmere lifted herself with some effort from the table to sit upright. She drew a handkerchief from her beaded reticule and began dabbing at her cheeks. For several minutes she continued chuckling and squeaking out trills of laughter. She had nearly composed herself when Mr. Fitzpaine chanced to turn around and reveal that he had also been weeping with laughter. She was immediately in whoops again, laughing until her sides ached and the tears would no longer flow.

At last, when her laughter had subsided, he rejoined her at the table, taking a seat opposite her.

But when she took a glance at her cup of tea, her giggles returned. "Whatever you do," she said, trying to restrain herself with a squeak, "don't bother ordering tea unless you are particularly fond of—of steaming water!"

He looked into her half-empty cup and feining Captain Beck's familiar astonished expression, and droopy eyes, exclaimed, "Is that tea?"

"No, pray don't," she cried, holding her cheeks which had begun to ache. "Or I shall be off again."

She looked up at the oak-beam ceiling, blackened from the fireplace and sagging with age, and shook her head. "I know you must be wondering why I keep such a simpleton about me."

"The thought had crossed my mind."

She chuckled again and wiped another tear from her cheek, only to giggle all over again. "I don't know why. But I think its because he is—is such a comfort."

She lowered her gaze and looked directly into his eyes, and they both fell into a fit of whooping which subsided only after several minutes.

Finally, she could breathe easily again and happened to look down at the kerchief in her hand. She realized suddenly it was the cambric handkerchief Jilly had embroidered for her at the age of ten—a single stalk of violet heather, bound by a green ribbon.

"Oh, dear," she murmured, her face feeling pinched suddenly as she touched the kerchief affectionately. "Do you think she is dead, Mr. Fitzpaine? As absurd as Captain Beck may be, he could be right."

Mr. Fitzpaine exchanged his chair opposite her for one beside her. Covering her hand with his own, he said, "You must never listen to such nonsense, particularly when your daughter is in Carlton's hands. Howevermuch he might be misguided by a profound desire for revenge of the moment, he is not seeking his own death, and certainly not your daughter's. He is a careful and accomplished traveler."

"And what of her virtue?" she asked.

"I know you will not credit it, Lady Redmere, but at heart Carlton is a good man, sometimes even a great man, and I have every confidence that he will neither inflict harm on your daughter nor permit harm to touch her. He will come 'round, and he will leave off this madcap scheme—I promise you!"

"Even if he wished to do so, how will harm not befall her when they have already journeyed together for a whole day unchaperoned, and now will be spending a—a *night* together! Beck was right in this, he has compromised her. Thoroughly."

"I don't know how all will be settled. But when Carlton comes to his senses—as I am convinced he will—he is sure to find a way out of this coil."

Lady Redmere fell silent, her heart heavy with concern. Her gaze dropped to Mr. Fitzpaine's hand, which still covered hers in a most agreeable manner. She was strangely comforted by his touch, and without thinking, began tracing the line of his York tan gloves with the tip of her finger. She sighed, wishing she had been more observant with her daughter, that she might have recognized how unhappy Jilly was before it was too late. Her conscience smote her as she began to consider her daughter's conduct over the past several weeks.

"Oh, dear," she murmured aloud again. Her distress prompted Mr. Fitzpaine to slip his free hand into hers in a warm clasp. She was still too engrossed in her thoughts to think anything other of this action than that Mr. Fitzpaine was being remarkably kind and understanding.

For herself, she continued quite absently to trace the clean seams of his gloves with her finger, her mind bending back into the past as she recalled the several times she brushed her daughter away, as she might have a puppy from her skirts. She realized now Jilly had wanted to speak to her of her misgivings several times, but each time she had done little more than bark at her or burst into tears.

"I don't mean to intrude, Mama, when you are so busy," Julianna had said to her, not a fortnight past. "But I wish to speak to you of—of Carlton."

She had not even looked at her daughter but had snapped in return, "I am doing everything I can to make your wedding the most delightful event of your life. You might have a little compassion upon my poor nerves. I have only just learned there is not enough white soup for all the guests you insisted must attend—"

"—But I never insisted. You forget, I wanted only Papa and you—"

Lady Redmere had thrown her head on her arms and sobbed, "Now you blame me!"

She had heard the sound of Julianna's footsteps fade from the study into the hallway, then disappear entirely.

She shook her head quickly, clearing the horrid memory from her mind. Lifting her gaze, she looked into Mr. Fitzpaine's kind blue eyes. "It is all my fault," she said. "I see that now. Jilly kept trying to tell me how unhappy she was, and I insisted on a large attendance for her nuptials, and at such a late hour we were not able to properly stock the buttery, and a hard frost had killed all the daffodils in the vale which I had planned on using to decorate the entrance hall and the stairs. I had wanted her to walk down the stairs—theatrical, I know, but you know how pretty Jilly is—"

"—I have never seen her," he interrupted gently. "But if her beauty even approaches your own, then I can perfectly understand your wishing to enhance the ceremony in order to display the daughter of your heart."

"You have not seen her?" she asked. "Well, of course you have not. I keep forgetting she has not had a proper London Season."

"She would most certainly have cut a dash."

"Do you think so?"

"When we were nearing Malton, you were describing her to me and how much you looked alike. I can only conceive that if she is half as pretty as you, your townhouse would be overrun with suitors. Why do you demur and shake your head? Do you not know how beautiful you are?"

"Oh, my," Lady Redmere murmured on a sigh. Thoughts of Julianna deserted her completely in the light of Mr. Fitzpaine's prettily spoken compliment. It had been some time since a gentleman—and no less significant, one who was several years her junior—had expressed his appreciation for her beauty that the force of it was like a fresh summer breeze rushing across a quick-flowing gill. "How delightfully you speak, Mr. Fitzpaine. And I do thank you."

She wasn't sure, but she rather thought a blush of pleasure touched his quite handsome cheeks as he slowly withdrew his hands from about her own.

Chapter Ten

"Julianna," Lord Carlton said quietly, drawing her away from her reverie. "What is wrong? Why are you crying?"

Giving her head a quick shake, Julianna wiped tears from her cheeks, unaware she had even shed them. "Oh, I am sorry," she responded instantly. "I don't know how I came to be weeping. I was thinking of my mother and wondering what her thoughts might be at this moment. I only know that were I a parent and had my child disappeared at the very hour she should have been saying her vows, I would be feeling utterly desolate."

He stepped toward her and parted his lips slightly as if to speak, but remained silent. He was looking down at her and began stroking her cheek with the back of his finger.

She was caught again, as she always seemed to be, by his closeness. What was it about him, she wondered, that caused her heart first to skip a beat, then to begin racing madly forward like a light gig, drawn by prime 'uns over an even road? She placed her hand over his, pressing his fingers into the soft warmth of her cheek.

"Julianna," he whispered. "I don't want you to be sad, or to regret your flight."

"Edward," she responded, savoring his name on her lips, "I'm not sad, and I don't regret leaving my home. Truly. Especially when you are so kind to me."

"Oh, Jilly," he responded, half-smiling. "I know I

shouldn't, but I can't seem to help myself." He leaned forward as though to kiss her, but the door opened quite suddenly as a young serving girl entered the pale yellow chamber. Julianna felt a blush suffuse her face and she stepped quickly away from Edward.

Though the young girl could not keep from smiling shyly at the *tête-à-tête* she had interrupted, she kept her eyes averted and began busily laying the covers. A few minutes more, as Julianna and Edward waited by the mantel, her bustling activity saw the glow of the fire washing its golden light over china plates edged in blue, over the sparkle of goblets, and over silver cutlery all resting upon fine white linen. The girl then quit the parlour but was soon replaced by Mrs. Rose, who rolled in a cart laden with the evening meal. She placed all the dishes on the sideboard of mahogany and was about to begin serving her guests when Edward surprised both *his bride* and the landlady by begging her to permit him to serve *Mrs. Fitzpaine*.

Mrs. Rose nodded with a smile of approval wrinkling her kind face and shining from her blue eyes. She picked up her gray wool skirts and swished from the parlour on light feet.

Edward then picked up Julianna's plate and took it to the sideboard, offering her only a wink by way of explaining why he had chosen to wait upon her.

As she remained by the fireplace for a moment, she regarded his back, wondering what sort of man this was who would wish to serve his lady. Somehow, the gesture made him more dear to her than ever.

Was she his lady? She wanted ever so much to be, but was his heart equally inclined toward her, or were his touches, the words he spoke to her, his tender gestures, merely the practice of many years being a man about town? Was he, as her innocent heart feared, merely as accomplished a flirt as Carlton was reputed to be?

Whatever the truth might prove to be, of the moment she wanted only to enjoy his attentions—and perhaps to be clothed in something other than a crumpled, stained white satin gown. And worse, her hair was a shambles. After so many hours of traveling, her curls had become tangled and several errant strands hung past her shoulders and down her back.

While Edward was turned away from her, Julianna seated herself at the table in one of the black-and-gilt chairs and seized the opportunity to separate some of her tangles. In the process, however, a string of pearls became hopelessly caught up in one of her tresses, and the faster she tried to get it unstuck, the more firmly the pearls entrenched themselves in her hair. To have given a hard tug would have seen the pearls bouncing all over the floor.

"Oh, dear," she murmured, without realizing she had spoken aloud.

He half-turned toward her with a slice of roast beef carefully held between a large fork and a knife. Glancing up from his labors, the beef suspended in mid-air, he queried, "Is something amiss? Oh, I see. Well, we can't have that, can we?"

"Perhaps I ought to send for Molly," she suggested, trying without success to keep from smiling.

He laid the beef gently down on one of the plates. "I had by far rather leap from Roulston Scar," he countered readily, clicking his tongue at her then laughing.

He rounded the table and extended his hand to her. She took it, rising from her chair, and permitted him to lead her to the sofa by the fire.

He began gently working the pearls from the prison of her tangles and she found herself wishing that more of the pearls and at least some of the artificial roses had also become tangled in her hair that she might be able to keep him next to her a little longer.

"You've the loveliest hair I have ever seen," he said quietly. "Why did no one tell me of your *crowning glory*? I believe such knowledge would have made a considerable difference, you know."

"A considerable difference?" Julianna queried. "In what way? I don't take your meaning."

He did not answer her right away, but she felt him pause in his delicate movements before speaking. When he did respond, he leaned quite close to her ear and whispered, "Had I known, I should have been able to persuade Carlton that he was wedding a Celtic warrior woman and undoubtedly, instead of dragging his heels from London to York, he would have driven his own curricle, springing his horses the entire way, in order to hasten to his wedding day."

Julianna had felt his breath on her cheek and so close to her ear that shivers coursed all down her side, leaving her with so profound a sensation of pleasure that she all but gasped. She turned her face slightly toward him and noticed the line of his handsome features sharpened wondrously by the yellow glow from the fire. "You are being absurd again," she whispered in return. His lips were very near her cheek because she had turned toward him, and she realized that if she but moved barely an inch more, he would be able to kiss her. The mere possibility of kissing Edward again brought another wicked shiver tumbling over her.

But to kiss him again! Merciful heavens, she must not!

She started to turn away from him, fearing the strong sentiments which moment by moment were taking complete possession of her, but he caught her chin lightly with two fingers, holding her captive as he forced her to look at him.

"And you are by far too pretty for words. I know I should not say this to you, Julianna, but I have the most profound desire to kiss you again." His eyes shifted to move slowly and deliberately to her lips.

How peculiar she felt, two rivers converging within her breast as he gazed upon her lips, one of great desire, the other of hope that she had at last found love. She tried to take in a breath but found the task impossible. She couldn't breathe, she couldn't think. Would he kiss her?

Somewhere in the deepest reaches of her mind where her natural common sense had always held sway over her impulses, she heard a sharp warning that she was treading on dangerous ground. At least the warning started out very sharp and clear, but by the time it progressed near the rivers entwining within her heart, the warning grew muffled and indistinct, like a voice shouting beside a thundering waterfall.

A weak battle took place in her mind. Three times she told herself she should not encourage Edward by engaging in a second kiss, and each time the river swept her under and submerged her warning conscience.

She lifted her face to him by way of invitation. He drew so close to her that she could feel his breath on her parted lips. She closed her eyes and waited. She felt the two fingers on her chin become a full, warm palm. She sighed and waited a little more.

But no kiss followed.

"I cannot," Edward breathed, his lips sweeping over hers and brushing them ever so lightly.

She followed after him, hungering for his. "Yes, you can," she whispered. But the quickness of her words, spoken in response to the potent feelings raging about in her chest, snapped her to a less lethargic state. "I—I mean no, of course you cannot. It would be most improper."

She thought she saw his gray eyes dance a little as he responded with a half-smile. "I want to kiss you, Julianna, but I will not take such wretched advantage of our, er, *predicament*."

Now why, she wondered, did she want to tell Edward he could take advantage of their predicament if he wished to do so? She wanted to say as much, but her common sense began asserting itself in firm stages so that as he returned to disengaging the string of pearls from her hair, the floodwaters in her breast began in equal stages to recede. Her heartbeat slowed down, she found it much easier to breathe, and her thoughts grew more rational.

"Our supper is growing cold," she said. "Perhaps you ought to leave this task until after we eat."

"I shan't move until I have these pearls free. Ah, there! No, don't rise just yet." To her surprise, he began quickly searching for pins in her once-elegant coiffure. The strip of artificial white roses came off next, followed by three narrow white ribbons which had traversed the path of the pearls several times. She did not argue with his efforts, in part because she found herself growing rather fatigued from the day's activities and in part from the sense that his wish to make her more comfortable was kindly meant.

With all the pins removed, he gently tugged on her locks and drew the mass of her thick curled hair to her shoulders and pulled it to cascade down her back.

"Just as I thought," he said, continuing to pull at her hair in long, downward strokes, until it was settled softly about her shoulders. "Magnificent. Does that feel better?"

"Oh, much," she responded.

He gathered up the collection of pins, ribbons, and roses and set it in a pile on the sofa. He then took her hand and led her back to the table, where he seated her with great care and consideration.

Within a few minutes, she was sipping her lemonade and enjoying what proved to be a remarkably flavorful meal of roast beef, potatoes, peas, stuffed partridges, slices of ham, jellies, creams, and turbot in lobster sauce.

The journey had sparked her appetite and she ate what he served her with great relish.

Several times as she conversed with him, she knew a strong disappointment that he had not kissed her. He'd said the journey to London would require at least four more days, and she could not help but wonder if sometime during that time he would relent and kiss her again. The truly wicked thought came to her, just before she took another sip of lemonade and smiled at Edward over the rim of her glass, that if the opportunity arose, she might just kiss him herself and be done with it.

Goodness, she thought ruefully—whatever was happening to her that she had begun plotting to actually kiss a man?

Was it the beginnings of love, or of something her mama had warned her about at least a score of times—a dreaded *tendre*, designed to deceive her every rational thought and ruin her life forever?

Chapter Eleven

On the following morning, Lord Carlton stood alone in the taproom of the Potter's Wheel Inn, tapping his cane upon the scuffed wood planks of the floor, waiting. He felt accountably irritable—it had been four hours since he had been informed, at eight o'clock, while in the midst of shaving, that his supposed bride was suffering from the headache and would require a dose of laudanum before she would be able to continue on their journey.

He still could not credit that four hours had been required to procure laudanum from an apothecary and for its beneficial effects to be enjoyed.

And worse. For with the clock nearing the noon hour, he had been told Julianna was sufficiently recovered, Milkmaid Molly had packed her frayed bandbox, and the pair of them would be descending shortly, if he would be so good as to have the carriage brought 'round.

But fifteen minutes had passed since he had requested Bibbel to prepare both carriages, and he was irritated. After all, keeping the horses standing was a condition not at all beneficial to either their health or their performance, particularly when the snow was still banked solid against the inn-yard walls.

The tapping of his cane droned in his ears as he glanced first toward the empty stairwell to his left and then to the front door of the inn, where light shone through several

rectangular glass panes. In truth, he did not know whether
to be exasperated with Julianna or grateful that for the entire
morning he had been separated from her company. When
he was near her, as he had discovered several times last
night, his intention of seducing her seemed to become
strangely turned about. Twice he could have kissed her but
didn't. Yes, once the serving girl had interrupted a hopeful
moment, but the second time, he had restrained himself
when it would have been immensely to his advantage to have
crushed his lips upon hers.

And she was so very willing!

What a sapskull he had been!

For the life of him, he could not explain his conduct.

The clouds of the day before had partially broken up and
throughout the morning billowy fragments drifted over the
brilliant blue sky in patches of white and gray. When the sun
shone, the snow sparkled against the stone buildings of York
like diamond shards imbedded in rock. Then a cloud would
pass by and drop a dullness upon the city, a dullness which
had become quite unnerving to Carlton, particularly in his
agitated state.

The odd thing was, he didn't know quite why he felt
prickly and nervous, except that all morning he had been
thinking of Julianna. He ought to have been thrilled at the
progress he was making in the seduction of his virgin bride.
She had seemed as eager to kiss him last night as she had
shown herself enamored of his embrace when they had first
met. Regardless of his intentions toward her, he was still
merely mortal and had found her conversation charming,
her beauty of person bewitching, and her forthright manners
a delight. When he had held her thick hair in his hands,
untangling the pearls and pins and flowers from her tresses,
it was all he could do to keep from burying his face in the
fragrant mass. The delightful essence of lavender had
greeted his senses the moment he'd begun unpinning the
pearls.

And precisely how he had kept from kissing her he would

never know. Julianna's parted lips, the smell of lavender emanating from her rich curls, and the tenderness of her expression with her eyelids closed had almost been more than he could bear. As it was he had permitted himself to brush her lips with his own and break the spell that had swirled up about them both.

He laughed lightly at his own folly, striking the side of one gleaming Hessian boot with the solid tip of his walking stick. He still could not believe he had actually said to her, *"Why did no one tell me of your crowning glory? I believe such knowledge would have made a considerable difference, you know."*

It apalled him that for a moment he had actually forgotten his false identity, yet it had been easy enough to overcome this slip, only because she was completely turned away from him. What if she had seen the momentarily stunned expression on his face or in his eyes? All might have been lost. Once she discovered the truth of his identity, he would lose every chance of seeing his scheme through to the end. As long as that trust remained solid, he knew he would conquer her.

A cloud drifted across the bright sky, darkening the cold entrance hall of the inn. He shuddered, pulling his black greatcoat more firmly down on each shoulder. He found himself again irritated that his quarry was keeping him kicking his heels when she had promised to descend the stairs. He drew a watch from the pocket of his blue coat and saw that he had now been waiting a full twenty minutes. His mood was quickly becoming as stormy as the gray cloud blotting out the brilliant sun. He would have to instruct Julianna at the earliest moment on the necessity of not keeping the horses standing about in the wind, the rain, or the snow, and certainly to have enough consideration for him to be ready when she said she would be ready—especially after a four-hour delay!

When a small clock on the wall sounded the hour, his choler reached its peak and he bolted for the stairs, preparing to mount them two at a time and pound on *Miss Redmere's* door, if need be.

Where was the chit?

But just as his hand touched the banister, her voice floated down to him in all its lovely low resonance. "You must forgive me, Edward, but at the very last moment, a button popped from my gown and Molly must have spent ten minutes securing a needle and thread. I do apologize, a hundred times. I hope the horses have not suffered?"

Lord Carlton's reproach dissipated on the tip of his tongue as he heard her apologies, and when he took in the full length of her, his mouth fell agape, his anger melting away at the sight of the vision before him.

Was this Jilly?

She was begowned in exquisite traveling garb, a bonnet trimmed with white fur, a dark blue pelisse of fine merino wool, and a large, elegant muff. It seemed somehow extraordinarily appropriate that the cloud out of doors moved on, permitting the sun again to shine, the diamonds in the snow again to gleam brightly, and the light through the glass in the door to touch Julianna's face as she descended the stairs.

How had she possibly achieved such a striking transformation when he knew for a fact she had left the village of Redmere with nothing more than a green velvet cloak on her back, stained white satin slippers on her feet, and a white gown, muddied about the hem?

"Julianna! What is that?" he cried stupidly, gesturing toward her muff as the warm winter light bathed her face.

"A muff," she responded, smiling happily as she lifted the furry white cylinder for his inspection. It was made of rabbit fur dotted with tufts of ermine. "Do you like it?"

"Yes, of course I do. It is exquisite. What I believe I meant to ask was, wherever did you get it—and the rest of your costume?"

Julianna responded, "I have a confession to make—I did not have the headache this morning."

"You didn't?" he queried, sliding his hand back down the banister and permitting her to descend the remainder of the stairs.

"No," she said, giving her head a shake as she slowly set pretty half-boots of calfskin upon the next step and the next. She reached the planked floors of the inn and twirled around in a happy circle for him. Her blue pelisse spun out into a conelike shape, revealing a silk traveling gown beneath made up of a small block-print fabric of colorful summer flowers on a wide border-hem of dark blue silk. Over her curls—save for several red wisps scattered across her forehead—rested an adorable poke bonnet of matching ruche blue silk, trimmed about the edge with a soft, furry strip of white rabbit. She had tied a blue silk bow beneath her ear. She looked innocent, youthful, and adorable, and to his amazement, all his irritation vanished completely.

"I arranged yesterday with Mrs. Rose to have her son lead Molly to my dressmaker's in the Shambles and return with the remainder of my bridesclothes. I would have told you last night, but I wanted to see your expression this morning, to surprise you. I daresay, Lord Carlton would not have cared for such an interruption to our honeymoon above half, but you are of such a kind, governable temperament that I believed you would not mind a delay in our journey for such an excellent reason. But now you must speak your mind honestly to me. Have I made you terribly angry? Would you have preferred I continued to travel in my wedding gown?"

"Of course not," he responded, stepping off the bottom stair and stroking the soft white fur of her muff. "I should be a complete gudgeon to be other than grateful for your foresight. It did occur to me more than once since leaving Redmere that your lack of baggage as well as your odd attire would provoke comment and speculation. So I thank you."

She chided him lightly. "But you did not seem so pleased when I began descending the stairs. No, do not even attempt to pitch me the smallest bit of gammon, for there was thunder on your face and in your eyes. Am I forgiven?"

"I was only angry that we have kept the horses standing."

"As well you should be, and again, I am very sorry."

He heard her apology only vaguely, and though he knew

he ought to be directing his booted feet toward the stable-yard, he could do nought but remain where he was, staring down into Julianna's beautiful face, drinking in the pleasure the sight of her emerald eyes always seemed to bring him, and longing to again assault her quite kissable lips. If Milkmaid Molly had not been present, he thought he might have thrown caution to the wind, braved the furry brim of Miss Redmere's poke bonnet, and forced a kiss upon her.

When he heard Milkmaid Molly murmuring her hope that Bibbel would not be upset, the spell seemed to break and he quickly led both ladies to the two waiting carriages. A moment later, after the last of Julianna's portmanteaux were stowed in the boot, they were bowling down the street. The snow had begun melting into the stones, darkening the streets and sending a spray of water flying from the wheels as they drove away from the inn.

For the first few minutes of the journey, as the carriages wended their way through York, Lord Carlton studiously avoided both looking at Julianna and conversing with her. He was attempting to comprehend the whole of his sentiments toward her. His initial scheme to persuade her to accompany him to London and then to Paris in order to create a scandal of enormous proportions had become increasingly swallowed up by how he felt when he was with her.

He felt like a halfling still wet behind the ears. Hadn't he acquired enough town bronze to master every situation, particularly those involving young ladies? Why, then, was his desire to take Julianna in his arms overriding every sensible thought, every careful aspect to a perfectly simple scheme, and dominating every moment of his waking hours?

He glanced at her, at the smoothness of her complexion, at the perfect profile, at the twinkle in her green eyes as she caught his gaze, smiled, then returned to looking out the window. There was no artifice in her, there were no demure attempts to gain his interest or approval; she was just Jilly. When he wished to be silent, she made no effort to engage him in conversation, but seemed to understand. And when she did respond to his inquiries, she was ready, polite, and agreeable, just as he hoped he was with her. Once, yesterday, she had kindly laid a hand on his arm and responded to one of a dozen questions he had put to her regarding her childhood, "I can't give you an answer just yet. Perhaps later, when we have rested at another inn."

He had taken the hint readily, permitting her a stretch of solitude, and thought how very much he had appreciated her lack of dissimulation. She had not wanted to speak and had gently told him as much. Her company was so very easy—a quality he could not remember having experienced before with any other woman of his acquaintance.

He could not help but wonder if she felt as he did, and so as the coach passed from York onto the road leading to Tadcaster, he hinted that she must find him a dreadful bore.

"What?" she responded, surprised. "Oh, you mean because there have been many times you have directed your gaze out the window and indicated strongly you wished for a moment of quiet—just as you did a moment ago? We have nearly two hundred miles to travel, Edward, and I certainly don't expect you to entertain me the entire distance with clever anecdotes or remarkable comments upon the state of the weather. Of course, please be assured I shan't feel obliged to see to your amusements the entire distance, either."

She smiled so prettily and he quickly returned to staring out the window, a habit he realized he was rapidly developing whenever he felt in danger of being enchanted by her.

He heard her giggle and murmur, "There, you see!" She did not sound in the least offended or distressed.

Damn! He liked her very much!

Tadcaster, nine miles from York, was reached without mishap, the horses exchanged in a trice, a cup of tea handed up to Julianna by one of the serving girls at the Angel, and the coaches were rolling again.

After Tadcaster, the road began to change, undulating

almost continuously. To his question "Are you feeling ill?" Julianna sighed with immense satisfaction.

"Not by half!" she responded eagerly. "And far from feeling poorly, I adore this delightful sensation of falling. I wish it would go on forever. I feel as though I'm on Papa's yacht."

"You've sailed, then?" he queried.

"Once, with my parents, when I was very little and enjoyed a summer holiday near Brighton, I believe. It was marvelous, and Papa seemed quite proud of my abilities. Poor Mama was below deck, stretched out upon her bed, her abigail tending her constantly. She never went sailing again, and though I begged for it, I was very soon returned with Nurse to York."

"How very unfortunate for you," he offered kindly.

She giggled again. "Oh, yes. Papa was quite a monster to send me north to my home, to my friends, and with my dear Nurse, just when the moors were in their most glorious season, the heather in bloom for miles and miles about, and the gills fastly flowing with water. Nurse and I would tramp about the moors for hours. If we had been permitted, I think we would have been gone for *days* at a time. I shouldn't have minded sleeping out under the stars—with sufficient covers, of course."

"Oh, of course," he responded. He stared at her and wondered and stared a little more. "Did you ever travel west to Cumberland?"

"To the Lake District? Where the poets haunt every village, lake, and old abandoned quarry? But then, of course, you would have gone there."

"Why is that?"

"You are a poet, silly!" she responded.

He laughed, hoping he sounded easy and lighthearted. He had forgotten for the moment that he was a poet. He countered quickly. "But you didn't answer my question. Have you been to Cumbria?"

"You will be disappointed to know that except for my trip

to Brighton, Harrogate is the extent of my traveling—and London twice, once when I was eleven, I think, and again when I was fourteen."

"No. Impossible," he countered. "How have you borne it when a perfect nodcock can see that you were made for adventures?"

The smile drifted from her face and a sigh first filled her lungs then emptied them so completely that her shoulders fell.

"What have I said?" he queried.

"I am such a silly schoolgirl that I had hoped when I was married to Carlton he would want to take me to all the places he spoke of in his letter."

"He meant to frighten you with such nonsense—China and the like, and I seem to recall a fort in the Americas— Fort Ross, established by the Russians. I'm sure he did not believe he would please you by speaking of foreign parts. In fact, I'm certain of it."

Julianna turned to look at him, her brows raised in surprise. "How did you know of Fort Ross?" she asked, a frown beginning to crumple her brow. "Edward, did Carlton show his correspondence to you before he sent it? I know yesterday I mentioned several of the details of his only letter to me, but I know I did not tell you of Fort Ross. If he *did* show you the letter, I do not hesitate to tell you how displeased and hurt I am. Truly, he must have despised me to have cared so little for our privacy."

To this charge, Lord Carlton placed his hand upon her arm, and said, "I do him a grave disservice in taking you away from him without benefit of introduction. Whatever his sentiments might have been after signing the marriage settlements, they would most assuredly have altered completely upon meeting you. As for the letter, he did not show it to me—it was improperly sealed. I had been given the task of sending it off and I could not resist reading it over. So you may now despise me instead."

"Oh, dear," she returned. "You place me in a most awkward position, for now that I have berated Carlton's actions, I most surely ought to reprove you for yours, but I find I can't. I am too well disposed toward you."

Hoping he did not sound as relieved as he felt, he responded, "You have a generous heart and you are right—you should reprove me. My conduct was wholly unbecoming a gentleman."

She then smiled and was about to respond when her attention was caught by the change in the road. The undulations had ceased and she directed her gaze out the window. "It is very level through here," she said. "We must be near Towton Field—the Battle of the Roses, you know."

"Yes," he responded, grateful she had shifted her attention away from him. He turned away from her as well, also glancing out the window. He had completely blundered into that one, but why had he felt it imperative to rescue *Carlton*'s reputation? It would not be to his advantage to encourage any well-wishes toward her former betrothed. He needed her to trust him completely as Edward Fitzpaine, and what better way to do so than to show *Carlton* as a monster? Next time, he promised himself, he would do better!

Chapter Twelve

Within another hour, the coaches lumbered into Ferry-bridge, where Carlton bespoke a light, early dinner at the Greyhound Inn, providing an opportunity for a brief respite in preparation for the remaining fifteen miles of their journey. The land from Ferrybridge to Doncaster, through Barnsdale Forest, was more rugged than the previous twenty miles, and a restorative meal was in order.

When he introduced himself as Mr. Fitzpaine, he was startled to have the landlord open his eyes wide and cry, "Well, what do you think of that? There was a Mr. Fitzpaine—very much of your cut—here in this taproom not two hours past and traveling with his sister, who had the prettiest red—hair—"

The man's voice trailed off as he glanced from Carlton to Julianna, who stood several feet behind the viscount. She was just then removing her bonnet of blue silk and white fur, revealing her exquisite coppery tresses. Her curls were sadly flattened, and the sight of them caused her to bite her lower lip in exasperation as she peered into a nearby looking-glass. As far as Carlton could discern, she seemed to be completely oblivious to the landlord's tale.

"You were saying?" Carlton queried politely. "A man? Fitzpaine? Must be my cousin. We are having a sort of race to London. I don't suppose he asked after us?"

"Well, that he did, sir. A very tall gentleman, well set up, quite proper and courteous."

"That would be my cousin. And we are a full two hours behind him, did you say?"

"Two hours, almost three, mebbee, though I'll bet you don't like hearin' as much."

Carlton winked and nodded toward Julianna. "My *wife* would have to stop at every little shop in York and then again at Tadcaster. We hired a second coach to transport all her fripperies along with her maid. Quite tiresome, but there you are!"

"Aye, but she's a pretty lass."

"Yes, she is and that!" Carlton agreed. "Have you a private parlour, perchance? But pray, say nothing of my cousin. One word about *him* and Mrs. Fitzpaine flies into the boughs. Can't abide him. We've been friends forever, you see."

The landlord nodded knowingly. "Wimmen," he sighed. "I married a fishwife, I did. But I got a passel of sturdy boys to the bargain—they run the horses to Tadcaster, Aberford, and Peckfield Bar—so I've no regrets. A parlour it is, my good sir."

"Thank you, and remember, not a word."

"Mum for that!" he agreed, with a wink and a nod.

After Milkmaid Molly was settled in the kitchens, Carlton ordered dinner for himself and Julianna, a fine repast comprising of ham, broccoli, oysters, steaming fresh-baked bread, butter, and East India Madeira. Usually, the hour would have prompted a much larger, more complete meal, but Carlton knew well the remaining road ahead and suggested to Jilly that she take care with regard to how much she ate. "I don't know how long it has been since you journeyed from Ferrybridge to Doncaster, but we will be passing through some rather stiff hills in and out of Wentbridge and Barnsdale Forest. The road in several places is quite dangerous—"

"—Yes," Julianna breathed, savoring a slice of ham, her green eyes sparkling. "I know. I can hardly wait!"

"Indeed?" he queried, a little astonished as he watched her beg the servant to place three more oysters on her plate.

"You needn't fear that I shall cast up my accounts— though I hope you will forgive me for speaking so boldly on a truly reprehensible subject—but I have never suffered from carriage sickness, and if I could have ordered my life as I wished in every particular, I would have insisted that three times per sennight I was allowed to drive a curricle-and-four quite madly up and down that truly exciting decline just this side of Wentbridge."

Lord Carlton had lifted a fork laden with ham and broc-coli to his lips, but he paused in his efforts to assuage his hunger, looking at Julianna as though for the first time. He was watching her spread butter on a slice of bread, but he no longer saw her seated at a table at all, but driving the curricle of which she had spoken, her bonnet long since disappeared in the reckless nature of her jaunt, her red hair streaming out in glorious waves behind her, excitement shining from her green eyes and glowing on her pink cheeks. His heart thrilled to the vision in his mind. He could teach her to handle the ribbons, if she wished for it, and somehow he knew she would like it above all things.

He finally took his bite of broccoli and ham, ignoring the rich flavor of the food and instead giving thought to the many ladies he had known over the years—those he had danced with at Almack's—before he had vowed never to attend again!—flirted with at Vauxhall Gardens, and dallied with in many of the larger country houses throughout the south of England. It had always been part and parcel of a lady's presentation to appear docile and subservient—what man would knowingly leg-shackle himself to a fishwife?

But how completely bored he had been by such women, though he had not comprehended as much until this very moment, when Julianna took a proper mouthful of the Madeira—there was no Mrs. Rose present to prevent her!—

instead of a ladylike sip, and speared another oyster with her fork. He smiled at her, thinking it was quite pleasant to have a lady attending to her meal with great appetite, rather then trying to flutter her lashes at him.

She looked up at him suddenly, her eyes wide. She saw that he had scarcely eaten a bite and a mischievous light began dancing on her face. "Do not tell me you haven't the bottom for the next portion of our journey?"

He smiled broadly in return, but said nothing. Instead, he, too, speared an oyster, spread a quantity of the mushy broccoli across the back of his fork, and set to his meal as well. Hearing her laugh in response was worth it all.

He thought oddly that he would always remember her like this, quite fondly, in fact, as she made short work of her dinner this the second day of their flight to London, running away from—well, running from Carlton.

How odd. He did not feel like Carlton of the moment, rather like some mysterious man her presence was culling forth. Where would it all end? he wondered. He suddenly felt another strong, urgent prescience that he ought to tell her the truth, but the thought that he would thereby ruin the easy camaraderie his false identity had created between them ended any inclination to do other than drink half his own glass of Madeira in one long, satisfying swig.

A half hour later saw the two coaches returned to the Great North Road and heading toward Wentbridge.

Julianna had thoroughly enjoyed the repast shared at the Greyhound Inn. Edward had been charming and handsome and a good sport to have endured her teasing. Indeed, he had seemed to delight in it.

Her heart was full of the pleasure of his company, but she knew her quickened pulse—which kept her senses alert and alive—had very little to do with him. Instead, her thoughts were all for the most exciting portion of the journey south— the quick descent and subsequent climb just before reaching the village of Wentbridge.

She did not try to converse with Edward, since she was

certain she could not have listened to one word in two, and by his silence, she knew he comprehended something of her sentiments.

As one mile overtook the next, and the object of her interest drew closer and closer, only once did he speak, and that was to say, "You haven't long to wait, Julianna—we are nearly arrived!"

"Indeed, yes," she breathed.

Finally the moment came, the postboy assumed a more daring, more poised position over the lead horse, and the descent began.

Julianna pressed the soles of her half-boots against the wall of the coach directly in front of her and took a deep breath. The well-sprung chaise gathered speed, quickly dropping into the gray-green shadows of the trees as it descended the hill. Her heart pounded furiously in her breast as she closed her eyes and let the sensation of falling sweep over her. She could hear the rhythmic straining of the horses against the harness, the traces jingling faster and faster.

A tingling sensation traveled up her neck and into her face. She felt wondrously dizzy, wishing the experience would go on forever. A few seconds more and the horses reached the bottom of the hill. She heard the postboy cry out to his horses, speeding them on, because the rise opposite was the true object of the dangerous descent—the faster they pushed down one side of the hill, the easier it would be to achieve the hard rise of the next.

Barreling across the shallow bottom of the hill, Julianna sighed with pure happiness, her stomach careening about wildly. The ascent followed, and for a few seconds more it seemed as though they would arrive at the very top without the least difficulty. But some thirty feet short of the crest, the momentum of the carriage faltered against the weight of gravity, and the horses struggled fiercely to take the equipage forward, each snorting in hard bursts.

But at last the job was done, the pinnacle reached, and the horses evened out their strides.

"What perfection!" Julianna exclaimed.

"You do enjoy it, don't you?" Edward stated, laughing.

"Yes," Julianna breathed ecstatically. "Do I shock you?" she asked, turning toward him.

"No, not precisely. But it has been my considerable experience that most young women, given the frightening aspect of the descent, would be more likely to faint in my arms than to brace themselves and actually take pleasure in the experience of being plummeted into a narrow gorge."

"Perhaps they *wished* to be in your arms, Edward," Julianna teased. "And don't bother trying to convince me otherwise, for you would be speaking mere humbug! Of course, now that I think on it, I don't wonder if I haven't made a grievous mistake. Even Lizzie said that I ought to avail myself of every maidenly opportunity possible to capture the attention of a man I favoured."

"So, am I to apprehend that you *favour* me? No, pray do not answer me, for I can see by the twinkle in your eye you are not in the least serious. Only tell me of this *Lizzie* of yours. Did you leave her behind at Marish Hall? She sounds just the sort of woman who could have supported you with your mother and perhaps even averted our flight."

Explaining Elizabeth Holt's absence at her wedding was a simple matter, but one which caused Julianna to blush. "My dear friend is—is increasing, and very near her time," she said, shifting her gaze away from Mr. Fitzpaine. "Naturally, she could not attend my nuptials. But you are right—I, too, am persuaded that had she been with me at any time prior to the date of my wedding, she could have helped Mama comprehend the seriousness of my distress."

He sought her hand from the depths of her white muff, and retrieving it, held her fingers in a gentle clasp. "I wish I had known you weeks, months, nay, years prior to your becoming betrothed to Carlton. Then I could have helped you in Lizzie's stead."

"Years, Edward?" she asked, teasing him again, and returning to look into his intense gray eyes. "I am only just

turned nineteen. You would have then known me when I
was scarcely more than a child."

"I could still have been your friend," he suggested.

"And how frequently does a man of seven-and-twenty
befriend a schoolroom chit of thirteen or fourteen?"

He frowned, his lips twitching in amusement. "You are
making this difficult, you know."

"What?" she asked, lifting her brows in mock bewilderment. She knew very well he was flirting with her.

"Such an innocent," he returned facetiously. He then
lifted her fingers to his lips and placed a kiss upon them.

She repressed a deep sigh of contentment, her heart swelling with affection for the man beside her. How odd that the
mere touch of his lips should cause her to feel nearly as
exhilarated as she had moments ago, when the coach was
descending rapidly down the hill. When he a placed a slow,
lingering kiss upon the curved back of her hand, even the
dizziness associated with the recent adventure assailed her.
She looked at him in complete wonder, her hand still held
captive by the touch of his lips and supported firmly by his
hand beneath hers. She watched his profile only vaguely
aware of the passing landscape—a blur of trees, dappled
light, and shrubs—all rushing beyond his face. The movement beyond brought the curves of his features sharply into
view as he continued to kiss her hand.

She knew a strong impulse to stroke lightly the line of his
cheek with the back of her free hand. She could not comprehend the source of the impulse save that something about
being very near Edward seemed to arouse a quite overpow-
ering instinct to touch him, as though in doing so her mind
would touch his and her soul would know the warmth of his
soul.

These thoughts followed one another as surely as one
village followed the next along the Great North Road. She
had never been in love before, but if this wasn't love, then
she was entirely incapable of explaining why she lifted her

free hand, surrendering to her initial impulse, and let the back of her fingers rest for a moment on his cheek.

He did not look at her, but assaulted her hand more fervently than before. She let the back of her fingers drift down the angled curve of his cheek, into the hollow beside his starched white shirtpoint, and downward to trace the folds of his tidy white neckcloth around his neck and beneath his chin.

For a brief moment, her fingers touched a smooth, small round object tucked into the folds of his cravat. She discovered that it was an exquisite diamond pin—a rather large one. She wondered if Carlton had given him the expensive piece of jewelry as a gift, perhaps. If he had, she could well comprehend Edward's remarkable loyalty to the man.

She did not stop the movement of her hand, but with one finger, she traveled back to his jawline and just barely touched the side of his lips. He was still besieging her hand. At the touch of her finger, she watched his lips withdraw from her hand ever so slightly as a sigh escaped him. But the moment the sigh departed him, he was again kissing her fingers, this time slowly and tenderly.

Sliding along the seat, she closed the small distance between them, so that she could feel the length of his leg against her thigh. Was it improper? Her thoughts became fragmented, and somewhere in the swirl of her emotions, she knew she was no longer thinking rationally. Yet even though she was unable to think clearly, still her mind drove her forward. Her attention became fixed wholly upon Edward's quite handsome profile, upon his closed eyelids as he kissed her hand, upon the tender place beside his lips which had begun to beckon to her own. Her gaze was fixed firmly to the spot, where the shadow of his black beard was only now, so late in the day, giving evidence that the hour was waning. She wondered if his skin would be rough against her lips or smooth. Somehow in the vague press of her mind, she needed to know. Her entire happiness now depended upon it, she was sure of it!

It was just that ever since he had refrained from kissing her at the Potter's Wheel, she had felt unaccountably deprived of something that belonged only to her.

Very simply, she wanted him to kiss her, and if he would not, then she would kiss him.

She braced herself by placing her hand upon his shoulder. With a sigh she leaned toward him and kissed him, just beside his lips. She could feel that the furry brim of her blue silk bonnet was pressing into his black hair. She closed her eyes and savored the smell of his shaving soap and a little of the Madeira he had enjoyed at dinner. She heard him groan and felt the pressure of his lips upon her fingers become insistent, demanding.

Was he struggling to keep from kissing her?

Somehow she knew he was. He had already refrained twice.

She would encourage him a little.

She shifted the smallest bit and let her lips touch not just his skin but the side of lips as well. She kissed him once. And again. A slight bump in the road caused her to bounce and separated her touch from his. Only then did he open his eyes. Only then did he stop kissing her hand. Only then did he turn toward her.

How full of meaning and intent were his gray eyes as he looked deeply into hers. He would kiss her now. He had the look of it writ in every line of his face. He gave a hard tug on the blue silk ribbons of her bonnet and when the bow fell apart, he gave another tug on the smooth fabric and separated the bands entirely. He then carefully removed the bonnet from her red curls.

He did not speak and she did not want him to. She feared that the very sound of his voice, or hers, would break the taut thread of tension which held them together in a most vulnerable, sweet, yet silent communion. He placed his hand upon the side of her face, sliding his fingers into her hair and at the same time forcing her back against the squabs.

THE ELUSIVE BRIDE   139

He stroked her cheek with his thumb several times, a tense movement that caused her chest to constrict, as he continued to look deeply into her eyes. He was very close to her now, his lips parted, an almost worried expression on his face.

"Edward," she whispered, wanting to say his name aloud, to soothe him, to make the worried lines disappear.

Instead, the sound of his name seemed to fret him even more, as his gaze drifted over her face, her brow, her eyes, the line of her cheek, her chin, her nose, to rest finally upon her lips. "Julianna," he whispered, invoking her name as well.

Would he kiss her? Or as before, would he refuse out of honor's sake?

Fearing he would again surrender to scruples she believed wholly unnecessary, given her sentiments for him, she slipped an arm about his neck and pulled him toward her. He needed no further encouragement, but swept his arm about her waist and kissed her full upon the lips, holding her hard against him.

Julianna's heart sang at the feel of his embrace. All former dizziness returned to her in the most delightful manner as she returned the pressure of his embrace and threaded her fingers into his hair at the base of his neck. He was hurting her lips in the most pleasurable manner. Over and over he kissed her, breathing her name across her lips only to kiss her hard yet again.

She had never known so much sweet pleasure could exist in the embrace of a man. The feel of his kisses began to change, becoming gentler as he drifted his lips over hers, the sensation causing her to feel very detached from her body as though in the act of permitting, even encouraging, Edward's kisses, she had become part of him. Kissing was a joining of sorts, she thought, and a beginning.

The first kiss had been a surprise and a response to only an initial impression that she had met her ideal.

But this second kiss meant everything to Jilly. I am giving

my heart, she thought, fully, completely, without the smallest hesitation.

He drew away from her, creating the smallest space he could without releasing her yet affording him the ability to look into her eyes. "Julianna," he began softly. "I believe I've fallen quite profoundly in love with you. I didn't think it was possible in so short a time to feel so very much, but it began the moment you flew through the gate of the Angel Inn upon your beautiful chestnut mare, your cloak flying out behind you. Only tell me you are not indifferent to me."

"Not indifferent?" she queried, wanting to laugh at the absurdity of his concern but she couldn't. She could only look deeply into his eyes, see her love reflected, and shudder out a long sigh. "I love you, with every particle of my poor girlish heart."

"We shall have a life like none other before us, full of adventures and love and a hundred kisses every day."

Upon this last promise, he kissed her again and once more the clarity of Julianna's thoughts began to separate, images of a future with Edward Fitzpaine blending with the softness of his lips, the strength of his arm about her waist as he held her tightly to him, the incredible feel of his thigh pressing into hers. She felt safe with him and knew that he had spoken the truth—theirs would be a life like none other before.

A few minutes more, the kiss ended and Julianna snuggled deeply into Edward's shoulder, her heart content, her hopes high, her spirits soaring. She turned her heart toward the future and thought it was somehow just that she was an heiress, since her beloved Edward was quite without proper means of support. He would spend his days composing his poetry and she would lean over his shoulder and places kisses upon his ear—but only once in a while, since she would not wish to disturb the Muse, at least, not too often.

She giggled and snuggled more closely still, her arm wrapped about his, her unneeded muff cast aside.

How beautiful, how wondrous her future appeared to her. She dozed for a mile or so, her dreams full to overflowing with visions of a simple wedding, and being addressed by friends and family afterward as Julianna Fitzpaine.

Chapter Thirteen

"What do you mean, *which Mr. Fitzpaine?*" Lady Catterick cried, giving a tug on her black wig as she frowned the landlord down.

When the balding man before her began scratching his head and frowning at her in return, she continued, "You are speaking nonsensically, man. Where is your wife? I'd rather speak to a woman than try to gain a sensible answer from a man!"

"Yes, where is your wife?" Mrs. Whenby queried in her bird's voice. "We are acquainted with Mr. Fitzpaine and wish to hear what your wife has to say of him."

Mrs. Bulmer, her pudgy hands clasped in front of her, scowled fiercely at the landlord. "Your wife, if you please," she commanded.

But the landlord was not so easily badgered and returned easily, "I would fetch her for yer ladyships, but the missus went to Doncaster, where her good mother resides, and will not be returning until Wednesday next. You may take chambers until then, if it be pleasing to you."

"None of your insolence!" Lady Catterick snapped. "I suppose I have no choice but to ask you again, what did you mean when you asked, *which Mr. Fitzpaine?*"

"It were a joke," he replied, all the humor having long since deserted his eyes. "About an hour ago, a Mr. Fitzpaine, his wife, and her maid boarded two coaches and headed south. Aye, but she were lovely, her with a pretty blue bonnet and red hair." He sighed appreciatively before continuing, "But two hours before they arrived, the other Mr. Fitzpaine stopped to change horses. I was given to understand by the second Mr. Fitzpaine—that is, *the* Mr. Fitzpaine what arrived at a later hour—that the first Mr. Fitzpaine was his cousin. The one who arrived first also traveled with a lady with red hair—his sister, methinks. Now that I recount it, I doubt but what you don't think me quite addled. But there it is—the latter Mr. Fitzpaine said that he and his cousin were having a sort of race to London. Why are ye all starin' at me like I've got a brick loose in me chimney?"

Lady Catterick glanced at her friends and saw that they were in a state of shock, not unlike herself. Mrs. Whenby's protruding eyes now gave her a nearly apoplectic appearance, and Mrs. Bulmer's perpetually frowning lips had fallen unattractively agape. Neither could speak.

Lady Catterick returned her attention to the landlord. "Describe both gentlemen to me." When he seemed resistant, she sighed impatiently and whispered, "It will be worth two sovereigns to you."

At that, the landlord opened his budget quite freely and in great detail described both parties to Lady Catterick. After pressing the sovereigns into his hand, she ushered her amazed friends back to her traveling coach. Once inside, Mrs. Whenby seated herself to Lady Catterick's right and Mrs. Bulmer to her left, all facing forward as the horses again stretched their necks and legs toward Doncaster.

The ladies eyed one another back and forth, around and around, until all three were giggling and clapping their hands. "A scandal!" each cried in turn, until the very ceiling of the black coach reverberated with their joint glee.

After a time, Lady Catterick became thoughtful, ignoring Mrs. Whenby's speculations on precisely what had happened and why Lord Carlton was masquerading as Mr. Fitzpaine and pretending to be Edward Fitzpaine's cousin. It was some time before she could arrange everything in her

mind, but when the coach began the dangerous descent
outside of Wentbridge and started to gather speed, she announced, "We will hurry to London, traveling all night, if we
must. Lord Redmere will want to know what scandal is
brewing where his wife and daughter are both concerned,
and of course we will be in possession of the finest *on-dits* of
the decade! To London, and the best season ever!"

"Oh, yes! On to London!" Mrs. Whenby chirped.

"Oh, yes, yes! Indeed, yes!" Mrs. Bulmer boomed. "On to
the Metropolis!"

Faster and faster the coach sped, the horses driving forward, on and on.

All three ladies sat abreast, their feet planted into the
carriage wall opposite them, which kept each from flying
forward off the seat and crashing through the window. Lady
Catterick, who sat in the middle, glanced at her friends in
turn. They both seemed quite happy. Of course, this was
their favorite part of the journey—they loved the dangerous
feel of the drop to the bottom of the hill. When she had
instructed the postboy to spring 'em, he had not believed she
meant what she said. But she reassured him in her firm
manner with, "Do it, or you'll not see your *douceur* at Robin
Hood's Well."

"Yes, my lady," he had responded, stunned. "If you want
me to spring 'em, that I will!"

He was as good as his word, and as the coach reached its
peak speed just before the road began to level out, as one the
ladies again cried in unison, "A scandal!"

The road curved, rose, and fell as it marked the remainder
of the way to Wentbridge. How quickly they were traveling,
Julianna thought. The quiet cottage-strewn hamlet, through
which the River Went lazily drifted, appeared then disappeared with several blinks of the eye as the postboy pressed
his horses on.

Only rarely was snow sighted again, and green dominated

the surrounding countryside of woods and hills, just as Mrs.
Rose had promised it would. Spring was meeting them along
the way.

The sun slanted its rays across Barnsdale Bar, where five
road ends met, where the Pontefract, Castleford, and Leeds
coaches left the Great North Road. The old toll-house was
a square, solid building, backed by a glorious old wood. The
gatekeeper let their coach fly through, recognizing the livery
of their postboy who, on his return trip, would settle up with
him.

Julianna remained tucked beside Edward until they arrived at Robin Hood's Well. She was sorry to have their
quiet intimacy disturbed, but as she stepped down from the
coach she was grateful to stretch her legs, and looked forward in a very private moment of rubbing some of the
numbness from her limbs.

Mr. Fitzpaine appeared in the doorway of the coach.
Glancing up at the sky and to the west, where the sun was
settling behind the hills, he said, "We should make Doncaster shortly after dark, I should think."

"But are we in any particular haste?" Julianna queried,
smiling appeallingly at him. "Must we press on to Doncaster? I confess I am completely enamored of Robin Hood's
Well. The loveliest dell, Edward, and a beautiful park so
close at hand. Mama says deer can still be found there.
Besides, Doncaster is so large and noisy."

"And Robin Hood's Well is not?" he cried. "I have been
given to understand that something like thirty coaches pass
through the village every day, not to mention the luggage
and fish wagons that wend their way from York to London."

Julianna looked about her, seeing the New Inn across the
street, where a gentleman's coach had just arrived and a
wagon was leaving. A horn sounded from up the street and
the Royal Mails suddenly came into view. "The moors are
like this," she whispered. "The wind makes just this sort of
constant bustling sound. How much I love it! I know I must
seem a complete oddity to you, but can we stay?"

The postboy began dismounting and Mr. Fitzpaine said, "A complete oddity and an adorable one, but we ought to continue on." He leaped lightly down and offered his arm to her. "A cup of tea, if you like, then we must be off."

When he tried to lead her into the inn, she held him back and said, "If you are certain the landlord in Ferrybridge described Mama and Lord Carlton to you—though I don't see how it is possible—"

"—We were delayed twice, if you remember. Once this morning, when you so wisely procured your gowns from your dressmaker, and the previous day when the wheel came off just past Easingwold."

She gave a small cry of astonishment. "I had completely forgotten about yesterday! Goodness, Edward, have we been traveling together only two days? It seems as though I have known you forever."

"It does seem quite impossible," he responded, gently touching her cheek with his gloved finger, apparently oblivious to the sounds of yet another wagon approaching the inn along with the curses of its exasperated driver.

Julianna looked up into his face and sighed deeply. The noise of the coaches, and the jostle of horse-keepers and servants all attending to the mail coach and the wagon driver, seemed to disappear into a delightful distant cacophony, like the faint rumble of thunder over distant hills. She saw only Edward, his gray eyes and firm, handsome features. She knew a terrible longing, as she had several times since being kissed by him so recently, to again touch his face, to embrace his broad shoulders, to be held close to him. His expression softened suddenly, as his gaze drifted over her features in what seemed a wondrously loving manner. "So you wish to stay where our country's most famous thief once plundered the countryside," he said softly.

"Yes," she murmured, sighing again. "If we could linger a day or two, I would insist upon taking a long walk across the old Roman ridge. It leads to Sherwood Forest, you know.

I've little doubt with a trifle earnest investigation we could discover remnants of his treetop home."

"A house in the trees? A man of simple tastes."

"Or of meagre pocketbook."

"I doubt if Maid Marion would have cared overly much for the draught in such an abode, not to mention the continual plague of rats."

"Were you always such an exceedingly romantic fellow?"

He laughed. "Always."

"And you, a poet!" she cried.

"A poet?" he countered. "Can only tolerate the stuff of a Sunday evening. Although, Edward——" he began coughing quite unaccountably the moment she drew back from him, surprised.

"Can only tolerate poetry!" she cried. "And you with a volume published and another very soon to be!"

"I was only teasing you," he returned. His color seemed strangely high as he glanced toward the postboy, who was awaiting his orders. "Go inside, Jilly, if you like. I must let the postillion know what we are about."

"Then we are staying the night?" she asked eagerly.

"Yes, if you wish for it," he said.

"Indeed, I do," she returned happily.

He pinched her chin before turning away from her and approaching the postboy. Though Edward had bidden her enter the inn, she decided instead to wait for him. He had become very dear to her, she thought wistfully, as she watched him conversing with the postillion.

She was unspeakably happy, she realized, and she truly could not have been happier, save perhaps if they had been man and wife. Her whole being became flooded with a sweet sensation she could only conclude was nothing less than *love*.

Real love.

Not just a *tendre*, but love.

Was it possible?

When she looked back at Edward, who was now approaching her as the coach disappeared behind him through the gates of the inn, she knew it was true. In the incredible space of just a little over a day, she had tumbled quite violently in love with the Honorable Edward Fitzpaine.

Chapter Fourteen

Lady Redmere looked at Mr. Fitzpaine with growing fondness. He was seated opposite her in her traveling coach, his eyes closed—not for sleep, but for another purpose—as the horses drew the conveyance steadily onward toward Doncaster. The day was quickly waning, the shadows of trees bordering the highway stretching far across the road. The trials of traveling, usually so severe upon her, had been considerably relieved by Mr. Fitzpaine's attentiveness to her every need. She realized she had not been so content in ages and that she owed her present happiness exclusively to him.

While his lids were shut and he awaited the approach of another vehicle lumbering along the Great North Road from the opposite direction, she let her gaze linger over his features—over his clipped black hair to his brows, which arched attractively at the very tips, to his straight nose, to the firm hollow of his cheeks, which slanted from high cheekbones in clean lines to his lips, to his jaw, which matched the angle of his cheeks. She thought yet again that he was quite a handsome man. It struck her not for the first time how odd it was—even though he lacked a fortune—that he had not persuaded one of London's many charming heiresses to marry him. He could easily have done so—she hadn't the smallest doubt on that head.

Of course, he was a man of considerable principle, and

though he had not said as much, she strongly suspected he would wed only if he fell deeply in love.

Was he tumbling in love with her, she wondered for the hundredth time since arising from her bed that morning. He gave every indication that he was, and she sighed again, uncertain why such a hopeless notion as love between herself and Mr. Fitzpaine should please her so very much. All she knew was that her contentment knew no bounds.

Yet she should not be content at all, she admonished herself, particularly since inquiries at the various villages at which they had stopped during the course of the day in order to discover news of her daughter had revealed not the smallest indication Julianna had passed that way. She should therefore be deeply concerned, but of the moment she was unable to generate anything more than a faint pang of worry over the whereabouts of her daughter.

The truth was, her attention had become wholly fixed upon Mr. Fitzpaine and the game they were playing.

When a carriage finally approached from the opposite direction, he opened his eyes and stated, "Most assuredly a gig—possibly a Stanhope."

"Precisely!" Lady Redmere cried, clapping her hands as a light Stanhope whirled easily by, heading north. "But how do you know them all?" she queried. "You have not made a mistaken in the past eleven vehicles. You are quite astonishing!"

"I believe in part I know because I possess that typically masculine failing of adoring vehicles of any kind. But my real ability must be accounted to my unfortunately limited circumstances—you cannot imagine how frequently I ride sitting forward. Therefore I am in the habit of *hearing* a vehicle approach instead of seeing it. Practice has made me an authority of sorts on the sounds carriages make on the road."

"And this one?" she asked, lifting her brows. Surely he would not guess the nature of the oncoming lumbering transport.

"A wagon," he responded promptly. "And quite heavily laden, I would think. Do but listen to how loudly the stones grind and crunch beneath its large wheels."

Lady Redmere closed her eyes and heard the sound. "I see how it is, now," she returned. "Let me try." She waited for a moment until the next vehicle came within the range of her hearing. "It—it must be a curricle!" she exclaimed, opening her eyes with a blink and staring hard out the window. "Oh," she groaned, as a post-chaise with yellow panels on the doors shot by. "A yellow bounder! How very lowering."

"Try again," Mr. Fitzpaine encouraged her.

Captain Beck, who was seated beside Lady Redmere, whined, "I don't see how you can abide closing your eyes. The very moment I do so, my stomach turns over twice. And pray, tell your maid to stop kicking me."

"Oh, I have not, Captain, I assure you!" Polly cried.

"Of course you have not," Lady Redmere reassured her abigail immediately. "Do not pay the least heed to Beck's complaints while on the road. I never do. He frets until he imagines every manner of imagined insult and sickness."

"I don't hesitate to say, Millie," the captain countered, "that I take it very unkind in you that you must take up Polly's part instead of my own. She has kicked me a dozen times since Wentbridge. A dozen!" He eyed the abigail situated opposite him with evident hostility.

"Oh, do hush, James," Lady Redmere returned, again closing her eyes. "I can't concentrate if you are forever kicking up a dust over trifles."

"Kicking up a dust, indeed," he muttered. "It's Polly who's been doing all the kicking. No one ever attends to me!"

"Hush!" Lady Redmere cried. She then lifted her head high, straining to hear the sounds of the next carriage. Soon the breakneck gallop of horses' hooves on crushed stones sounded, looming louder and louder. Now she could hear the harnesses jingling and a coachman calling to his team. As the horses—there were certainly more than two—approached her window, she could even hear their breathing and snorting as they pounded forward. How deafening was the sound of the wheels—large wheels—as they ground into the stones.

"The mails!" she cried, opening her eyes with a start and just in time to watch the burgundy-and-black coach rush by. A myriad of faces appeared for a moment within the frame of her own glass side-window, then disappeared into a cloud of dust. Realizing she was right, she literally bounced up and down on her seat, clapping her hands.

"Do have a care!" Captain Beck cried out irritably. He patted the top his head and again whined, "I hit the ceiling when you bounded upward! Damn, but I think you've done it now. My curls are flat."

"I do beg your pardon, James," she responded. "But what do you think of my having guessed the last coach correctly?"

Captain Beck blinked at her. "I don't like to mention it, Millicent, but you could have easily seen it coming from where you sit!"

"But I had my eyes closed!" she exclaimed.

"You did?" he asked, surprised. "Were you sleeping?"

Lady Redmere looked at her swain and sighed. "Yes, I was," she responded hopelessly.

"Ah, well, that explains everything," the captain responded cryptically.

Mr. Fitzpaine intruded, ignoring Captain Beck. "Not so difficult, then, is it?" he queried, reclaiming Lady Redmere's attention. "I suppose now, however, you will not think so highly of my abilities."

"On the contrary," Lady Redmere assured him. "I would never have believed you could discern a barouche from a phaeton. Truly, Mr. Fitzpaine, you are remarkable."

His expression seemed to soften with her praise, and he

sighed with apparent satisfaction. "So long as you think so, I am content."

Lady Redmere looked into his wondrous blue eyes and without thinking responded, "So am I." She immediately felt a blush burn her cheeks and hastily added, "Er, that is—I find your company quite agreeable. My, how quickly the day has passed. We should be in Doncaster very soon, where I will be more than *content* to spend the night." She turned to Captain Beck and queried, "Don't you agree we should stay in Doncaster, and not press on?"

But Captain Beck did not hear her. He was nodding and moving his head about in the strangest manner as he stared at her abigail's throat. She could now see that poor Polly was nearly apoplectic with irritation. She did not at first comprehend why until her maid suddenly reached up behind her neck, unclasped her shiny gold locket, and thrust it toward the captain. "When you are finished with it," she cried, "you may return it to me."

Captain Beck looked at her with lazy brown eyes, oblivious to her scorn. "Why, thank you very much," he responded, taking the locket without hestitation. "I forgive you now for kicking me. That last bounce of her ladyship's displaced several of my curls—I am sure of it!"

Lady Redmere frowned at him. "James?" she queried, nonplussed, "whyever do you want my maid's jewelry?"

But Captain Beck did not give her answer. Instead, he held the locket at a distance and taking his quill from his coat pocket kept his gaze fixed to the locket and began picking at the curls atop his head.

Lady Redmere gasped and covered her mouth. He was using the miniscule locket as a looking-glass! She knew she oughtn't to look at Mr. Fitzpaine, for he would surely laugh outright at her absurd Cicisbeo, but she seemed drawn toward him like a magnet. Their eyes met for a brief moment, whereupon Mr. Fitzpaine looked sharply out the window, biting down hard on his lower lip.

That was more than the viscountess could bear, and she

immediately burst into a tremolo of laughter. Her maid eyed her curiously for a moment, then her lips began to quiver as well until she, too, joined her mistress. Polly's laughter was Mr. Fitzpaine's undoing, whereupon he joined the ladies, much to the captain's astonishment.

"What is so amusing?" he queried innocently. "Did something escape me?"

"Yes," Lady Redmere answered succinctly. "Completely."

"Ah," the captain responded, apparently finding nothing in the least ungratifying about her comment. When he resumed staring into the small locket and shifting his head around birdlike in an effort to check all the curls on his head, the three witnesses of his folly laughed all over again.

After a time, the sounds of their amusement drifted gently away, the coach sailed on toward Doncaster, and only then did Lady Redmere's thoughts truly turn toward her daughter. Where was Jilly? she wondered. By now it had become apparent that either the hapless couple had chosen an alternate route, or her coach had somehow managed to pass the Carlton's traveling chariot. But how could that be, unless some accident had overtaken them—a broken trace or pole, perhaps, or a lame horse. Or it was possible, though she did not at all enjoy the notion, that Carlton had purposely held her back in some lesser frequented village or inn and was taking complete advantage—oh, dear, but she could not think of that! She would go mad if she did!

Instead, she turned to look out the window at the Yorkshire countryside. They were now nearly five-and-thirty miles from York. At how many inns had Mr. Fitzpaine inquired for word of her daughter or Carlton? A dozen, two score? At Tadcaster, they had paused in their journey at the Angel, the White Horse, and the Rose and Crown, which were all coaching houses. Mr. Fitzpaine had even had the audacity to peer within the Wellington—a London coach bearing eleven passengers—believing it was possible they might have taken one of the highflyer's to the Metropolis. The coaches were so quick and traveled all night; they would certainly have had the advantage of outstripping their pursuers—only Carlton would have no way of knowing he was being pursued.

But Mr. Fitzpaine's efforts were of little avail. Julianna was not to be found in Tadcaster.

The journey from Tadcaster to Ferrybridge was always one of her least favorites. The stretch of road was irregular and undulated continuously, leaving her stomach rather queasy. Julianna had always enjoyed the dips and swells, but for herself, she had felt nearly as bad as when she had gone yachting with Redmere for the first and last time.

She wondered if Mr. Fitzpaine enjoyed sailing.

Mr. Fitzpaine then insisted upon stopping at the Old Fox in Brotherton, in order to procure her a cup of tea, as well as to inquire about Jilly.

Dear Mr. Fitzpaine.

He was so very kind to her, attentive to her every need, while Beck! Well, he was about as useful as a deep well without a bucket! And worse! He had actually disappeared for half an hour, delaying their rush to find Julianna, and was found by her abigail emerging from the kitchens of the Old Fox with a vague explanation that he had been wondering how many London coaches departed from the Old Fox daily. Lady Redmere had tried to explain that the Old Fox was not a coaching house, but was a drover's house, accommodating Scottish drovers who brought their cattle down from Scotland, but Captain Beck had become quite cross and had said he had no opinion of an inn which did not have a post office.

"Were you trying to post a letter, then?" she had queried, a little surprised.

"No!" the captain had returned sharply. "Why would I wish to do that? When could I possibly have had time to write one word, nonetheless an entire letter?" He then clambered irritably back into the coach, and stared blankly out the window.

If Lady Redmere had not known better, she would have thought by Beck's odd behavior that he was indeed attempting to send a letter, but to whom and why, and why he would need to be so secretive, she could not imagine.

She then thought it likely he had merely become bilious from their travels and his general irritability had affected his reasoning capacity as well.

At Ferrybridge, Mr. Fitzpaine had stopped first at the Golden Lion, which was a house frequented primarily by heavy luggage wagons. The inn shipped and received goods which came upriver from Hull by boat. It was an unlikely stop, and Jilly was not to be found, but Mr. Fitzpaine was determined to be thorough in his search.

Nor was there sign of Julianna at the pretty Swan Inn near the bridge, nor at the great rambling Angel, with its multitude of buildings and endless amount of stabling and housing for chaises and coaches, not to mention shelter for postboys and horse-keepers. As for the Greyhound—where they paused for nuncheon—Julianna's red hair had not been sighted. Lady Redmere could only conclude that somehow they had gotten ahead of their quarry.

"Or do you think Carlton has sequestered her somewhere?" she asked of Mr. Fitzpaine, as they approached the third coaching house found in the village.

"No, I don't," he pronounced after a long pause, a frown between his brows. "I know he meant to go to London. I'm sure of it. He had no reason to take her to Gretna Green, since he did not intend to marry her, and every reason to take her south. He is sufficiently well known in the Kingdom that somewhere in his travels, were he to leave the Great North Road, he would be bound to encounter an acquaintance. Anyone who could recognize him would also be able to ruin his schemes. No, I am convinced he is traveling south, and as quickly as he can. But you know what the roads are—a broken pole, a lame horse, and there you are! An hour, a day, completely lost!"

Leaving Ferrybridge, the road had gradually risen, passing through the heart of fox-hunting country. Afterward, the land grew more rugged and the horses strained against their collars time and again. This stretch of road was always a trial for Lady Redmere, but Mr. Fitzpaine's presence made the whole of it easier to bear than ever before. Even the terrible descent preceding Wentbridge, which usually sent her stomach reeling and brought on the headache, had scarcely had any effect upon her. Truly it was remarkable. Of course, when the steep decline of the hill caused her to slide from her seat and fairly land in Mr. Fitzpaine's strong arms, she certainly had no reason to be frightened, and any illness she might have been experiencing magically disappeared.

At Wentbridge, Mr. Fitzpaine found nothing of Julianna or Carlton at the Old Blue Bell Inn, which at one time had been a harbour of poachers and footpads.

Past Wentbridge, the road grew exceedingly rough all the way to Robin Hood's Well—a place reputedly frequented by its namesake in days gone by. But her daughter had not been sighted at either of the two inns found in this hamlet sequestered in a charming dell.

Beyond Robin Hood's Well, Mr. Fitzpaine did not bother pausing the horses at the Red House, since it was a very minor coaching inn servicing primarily the crossroads.

After the Red House, the road grew dead-level, and it was at this point that she and Mr. Fitzpaine had begun playing their coach game.

She was drawn back from her review of all the inns which had seen nothing of her daughter by Mr. Fitzpaine begging her to close her eyes and name the next coach.

She did so happily, though not without at least one small pang of guilt that while she was enjoying herself hugely, her daughter was being plunged deeper and deeper into a dreadful scandal.

Still, she could not keep from smiling, her heart swelling with pride at her growing abilities. "A landau and four!" she called out happily, opening her eyes and determining for herself that she had indeed named the carriage correctly.

Chapter Fifteen

Later that evening in Doncaster, Lady Redmere sat in a tall settle at the Red Lion Inn, opposite her Cicisbeo, and watched her dear captain yawn a third time. His mouth actually grew wider than during his previous two efforts. She was tempted beyond rational thought to send him to bed, but she couldn't for the simple reason that she was afraid to.

Having traveled all day in Mr. Fitzpaine's company, she knew her heart was in a vulnerable state.

She glanced down at her feet, where Mr. Fitzpaine half-reclined, reading to her from a volume of Milton, an elbow propped onto the vacant space beside her knees. She thought he ought not to be situated so close to her, in part because he looked so dashing with the golden light of the fire glowing on his black hair, upon the fine curve of his cheekline, and on his lips. Merciful heavens, but he seemed to grow more handsome with each passing hour.

Captain Beck's voice intruded. "I do so enjoy a good reading," he said, wiping another stream of yawning tears from his eyes as he slouched farther down into the tall winged chair he inhabited. He was very near the brightly burning fire, which accounted for much of his sleepiness. He stretched his long legs out in front of him and added with another yawn, "You've a terribly fine voice, Mr. Fitzpaine. Pray continue."

Lady Redmere found herself alarmed. When had Mr.

Fitzpaine stopped reading? She did not know. How could she have not known? She glanced down at him and he lifted his gaze from his book, now lying closed upon his leg, an inscrutable expression on his face.

"Yes, pray continue," she whispered.

He glanced back at Captain Beck, and satisfied that his eyes were now closed, he rose to a kneeling position and took one of her hands in his. "I don't want to read, my lady, except perhaps the answers written in your touch and in your eyes. No, do not demur, do not pull your hand from mine. Only tell me you feel nothing for me and I will retire at once and leave you in peace." She stopped trying to disengage her hand and whimpered slightly as he turned her hand over, kissing first the inside of her wrist and then the very center of her palm.

Lady Redmere felt positively weak to her knees and found herself struggling for breath. All day long he had sat opposite her in the traveling coach, smiling upon her, entertaining her, and working a very odd sort of magic with her heart. Never for a single moment did he cease to be the gentleman he was, nor did he cross the bounds of propriety, which was in itself part of the magic for her. The guessing game—so childlike in its abiltity to amuse—had only increased her enjoyment of his company.

He was so different from Redmere, as sweet, gentle, and considerate as her husband was brusque, brutal, and self-absorbed. The truth was, she had never known anyone quite like Mr. Fitzpaine before.

Throughout the course of the day, he had engaged her in conversation, wishing to know where she had spent her childhood, where her favorite hidden haunts were, and upon how many trees she had scarred lovingly the initials of her young beaux. Perhaps this question had been fortunate, for it set her mind running quickly back to her wedding vows. Once married, she had actually dragged Redmere into the home wood behind Marish Hall, and made him scratch their

TAKE ADVANTAGE OF THIS SPECIAL OFFER,
AVAILABLE *ONLY* TO
ZEBRA REGENCY ROMANCE READERS.

You are a reader who enjoys the very special kind of love story that can only be found in Zebra Regency Romances. You adore the fashionable English settings, the sparkling wit, the captivating intrigue, and the heart-stirring romance that are the hallmarks of each Zebra Regency Romance novel.

Now, you can have these delightful novels delivered right to your door each month and never have to worry about missing a new book. Zebra has made arrangements through its Home Subscription Service for you to preview the three latest Zebra Regency Romances as soon as they are published.

3 **FREE** REGENCIES TO GET STARTED!

To get your subscription started, we will send your first 3 books ABSOLUTELY FREE, as our introductory gift to you. NO OBLIGATION. We're sure that you will enjoy these books so much that you will want to read more of the very best romantic fiction published today.

SUBSCRIBERS SAVE EACH MONTH

Zebra Regency Home Subscribers will save money each month as they enjoy their latest Regencies. As a subscriber you will receive the 3 newest titles to preview FREE for ten days. Each shipment will be at least a $11.97 value (publisher's price). But home subscribers will be billed only $9.90 for all three books. You'll save over $2.00 each month. Of course, if you're not satisfied with any book, just return it for full credit.

FREE HOME DELIVERY

Zebra Home Subscribers get free home delivery. There are never any postage, shipping or handling charges. No hidden charges. What's more, there is no minimum number to buy and you can cancel your subscription at any time. No obligation and no questions asked.

TO GET YOUR 3 FREE BOOKS
ILL OUT AND MAIL THE COUPON BELOW

. . . .

3 FREE BOOKS

Mail to: Zebra Regency Home Subscription Service
120 Brighton Road
P.O. Box 5214
Clifton, New Jersey 07015-5214

YES Start my Regency Romance Home Subscription and send me my 3 FREE BOOKS as my introductory gift. Then each month, I'll receive the 3 newest Zebra Regency Romances to preview FREE for ten days. I understand that if I'm not satisfied, I may return them and owe nothing. Otherwise, I'll pay the low members' price of just $9.93 for all 3 books and save over $2.00 off the publisher's price (a $11.97 value). There are no shipping, handling or other hidden charges. I may cancel my subscription at any time and there is no minimum number to buy. In any case, the 3 FREE books are mine to keep regardless of what I decide.

NAME _____

ADDRESS _____ APT NO. _____

CITY _____ STATE _____ ZIP _____

TELEPHONE ( )

SIGNATURE _____

(if under 18 parent or guardian must sign)

RG0694

Terms and prices subject to change. Orders subject to acceptance by Zebra Home Subscription Service, Inc.

GET
3 FREE
REGENCY
ROMANCE
NOVELS—
A $11.97
VALUE!

ZEBRA HOME SUBSCRIPTION SERVICE, INC.
120 BRIGHTON ROAD
P.O. BOX 5214
CLIFTON, NEW JERSEY 07015-5214

names into the ancient oak which also bore the names of her mother and father and her father's parents.

"Redmere only," she had responded quietly, looking away from Mr. Fitzpaine. At the time, she had been exceedingly overset, and he had not intruded upon her thoughts for another hour.

Now, Mr. Fitzpaine was situated beside her and she could scarcely breathe, since he was just then placing his lips softly on the tender skin at the base of her thumb. "You shouldn't be kissing me," she added.

He looked up at her. "I'm not kissing you," he said, with a twinkle in his eye. "Though I wish I were. By heaven and earth, I wish I were. Of the moment, I am merely enjoying the taste, the soft contour, the sweetness of your hand."

"Oh," Lady Redmere sighed. She leaned forward in her seat and touched his hair with her hand. "You are a very dear and gentle man, Mr. Fitzpaine. But this must not be. It is very wrong, and well you know it."

He leaned toward her in a mock menacing manner, and whispered, "If it is because you fear Beck will call me out, I promise you, I am equally skilled in swords or pistols—though I do believe he might best me in a bout of fisticuffs."

Lady Redmere stroked his cheek with her hand. "You are by far the most absurd, the most delightful creature I have ever known. Only do stop teasing me, for you must know I like it above all things."

"Then your heart is not impervious to my careful assaults," he returned.

"My heart is overturned," she responded simply.

He was very close to her, close enough to take her in his arms and kiss her. Lady Redmere knew she should move away from him, lean back, and return to a place of safety, but she felt fixed by the very strength of his adoration of her. He drew nearer still, his lips so very close to hers. She closed her eyes, she felt the touch of his lips upon hers, then suddenly a loud snort erupted from the direction of the winged chair opposite her.

Fear of being caught in mischief as well as the fact of
having been startled by Captain Beck's sudden snore sent
Lady Redmere thumping backward into the cushion of the
settle. Even Mr. Fitzpaine had been sufficiently jolted by
Beck's eruption to lean away from her, a fist against his
forehead.

"Good God," he cried. "I thought a gun had been fired!"

By now, Captain Beck had fallen into a gentle, persistent
rumbling, for which Lady Redmere found herself extremely
grateful. She was not precisely certain, but she thought it
likely that a man would have some difficulty continuing to
make pretty love to a lady with the rise and fall of snoring
providing the only ambience.

She therefore took the opportunity to rise to her feet and
hurry from the parlour with a hastily bidden goodnight,
ignoring Mr. Fitzpaine's plea that she stay for just a moment
longer.

Once in her chamber, after awakening her dozing abigail
from her slumbers, she promised herself that never again
would she permit herself to be in a compromising situation
with Mr. Fitzpaine. Whatever indiscretions her husband had
committed over the past year, she had promised herself that
she would not fall victim to a hopeless love affair which in
her opinion could never possibly enjoy a happy ending.

But more than that, she thought sadly, she did not think
she could bear the prospect of falling in love with another
man, then watching his love turn flat and cold, his head
turned by the next pretty woman who might chance to pass
by and cast out a lure to him.

Once was quite enough for her.

Mr. Fitzpaine remained on the floor, his elbow propped up
on the settle Lady Redmere had so recently occupied. The
shiny, smooth horsehair fabric was still warm from her
body's touch, and he felt as though his heart would melt in
him for the love which abounded for a woman nearly seven

years his senior. He could not remember, even in his salad days, having tumbled so hard or so quickly for a woman.

He could not precisely explain to himself what it was about her that had so captured his fancy—she was not exceptionally intelligent, though at times she presented a keen insight which served to astonish and please him; she was, however, quite beautiful, and if her daughter were half so pretty, he imagined Carlton would very soon find himself in the basket rather than see his careful schemes come to fruition.

He hoped so, at any rate, for the mother did not deserve to have such a wretched scandal brought down on her lovely head. But beyond this, there was a sweetness to Lady Redmere's disposition, as well as an adorable liveliness; they were like small strokes of lightning to his deprived soul. If only she weren't married.

Here, reality sent its own bolt of lightning to jostle his fantasies. Even had she been free, what could he have offered her? He was penniless except for the miniscule royalties he received from his published volumes of verse.

Ironically, only a few months earlier, he had finally become content with his lot, having decided to expend every energy he possessed on the composition of his poetry. He had lived too many years in a form of decadent despair which had characterized his life for so long—love eluding him persistently. He had held fast to his associations from Cambridge, written radical essays, wished he could have spent a year in gaol, along with Leigh Hunt and others, but contented himself by merely visiting them. There he had met Carlton and formed a friendship as unlikely as it had become fast. It was Carlton who had made it possible for him to publish his poetry and thereby begin earning a living.

At one time he had contemplated joining Southey and Coleridge in their scheme to set up a colony in America based on the highest principles of equality, freedom, and the casting off of the bonds of property. But Southey and Coleridge had quarreled, and Coleridge had begun a career as lecturer and essayist. So much for idealism and pantisocracy.

No, Carlton had befriended him, and almost as patron to artist, permitted him residence during the summer at his county seat in Hampshire. There he had courted the Muse among summer's bounty, and argued politics, poetry, and Napoleon's finer qualities with any of the guests who'd chanced to pass through during the course of the sunny months. He'd beaten Carlton at billiards three games out of four, boxed, fenced, and practiced shooting with him.

He had clearly seen the downward trend of Carlton's existence, especially over the past two years, but he would never have believed that events would come to such a critical pass as this.

Good God! Carlton had stolen his own bride.

And here he was, trying to win the affections of a married woman!

Good God—had all of creation suddenly turned upside down?

Chapter Sixteen

"He nearly kissed her!" Lady Catterick whispered. "If that feather-headed gudgeon had not erupted with a snort, he would have! I am persuaded of it!"

Lady Catterick's breath fogged the bottom diamond-paned window of the parlour as she informed her co-conspirators of what was going forward. Supported by Mrs. Bulmer, she stood on a rain barrel, her gloved hands clutching the paint-chipped windowsill as she peered into the cozy chamber.

She continued, "But it is just as I thought—Millicent did not return. A pretty scandal, this!"

She tried to descend, but Mrs. Bulmer, whose grip proved quite powerful, held her knees locked in place. She gave her leg a shake, and bending downward, cried out in a low voice, "Henrietta, pray let go of me! I am coming down."

"Thank heavens for that," Mrs. Bulmer returned, releasing Lady Catterick's leg and offering up her hand for support instead. "It is so cold that my knees are banging together. Well, what do you make of the whole of it, Eliza? Is it an *affair de coeur*? A *tendre*?"

"My, it is cold, isn't it?" Lady Catterick responded, noticing for the first time that the temperature had dropped sharply. As her half-boots touched the cobbled stones of the innyard, she addressed Lady Bulmer's question. "A *tendre*, assuredly, and more, if Redmere does not very soon take his wife in hand."

Mrs. Whenby stood nearby, her arms folded tightly across her chest. "And to think I believed the scandal was merely in appearances," she chirped, her teeth chattering. "But are you certain Mr. Fitzpaine intended to kiss Lady Redmere?"

"There can be no two opinions on that score," Lady Catterick replied firmly. "Millicent leaned toward him, her eyes closed, her expression quite—quite feverish. No, he meant to kiss her, and she was equally as willing." She shivered and touched her fingers to her face. "Goodness, it is so cold I can't even feel my nose. Well, it would seem we have a mission of no small import to accomplish upon reaching London."

Her companions nodded in agreement, following in step behind her as she walked toward her postboy, who was gawking brazenly at the ladies. "Are you for pressing on to Barnby Moor?" Lady Catterick asked.

"If you be wishful, my lady," he responded, glancing toward the window in complete wonderment, then back to the ladies. Clearly, he had never before witnessed the extent to which ladies of quality might go when uncovering the seeds of scandal. "But ye'll be needing the postboy what covers that stretch of road. I'll fetch him for you, if you like."

"Excellent. Also, we stand in strong need of hot bricks, hot tea, and a dram of brandy. We mean to travel through the night." She glanced back at her companions and saw as much determination in their eyes as was in her own heart. Scandal was one thing, the ruination of a marriage because of Millicent Redmere's stupidity quite another!

The postboy assisted the ladies to clamber aboard the traveling coach, then led the entire equipage to the innyard, where the horses were changed and a new postillion hired.

Once all three ladies were properly settled, once thick carriage rugs were tucked neatly about cold laps, legs, and feet, and once hot tea and brandy had been passed 'round from a waiting servant, Lady Catterick clicked her tongue. "I suppose we could have foreseen how it would be with Carlton," she began. "I have little doubt he stole his bride away in hopes somehow of serving the *haut* ton a bad turn. Why, of late I have had only but to open my mouth and he was on his high ropes. We even brangled at the opera not a sennight before his wedding! And I merely asked him if he thought he would enjoy Mrs. Garston's company as much once he was married to Miss Redmere—"

"—Oh, dear, Eliza! Tell me you didn't!" Mrs. Whenby cried, astonished, but smiling appreciatively all the same.

"And you never breathed a word to either of us!" Mrs. Bulmer complained. "I don't hesitate to say, I find it quite wicked in you!"

"Wicked?" Lady Catterick queried, surprised. "I have never known you to disapprove when I have tried to provoke Carlton."

Mrs. Bulmer's massive bosom shook as she tried not to laugh. "Oh, not that you tried to provoke his lordship— wicked that you did not tell us beforetimes!"

"Oh, of course!" Lady Catterick exclaimed. "How silly of me!"

All three ladies chortled together.

Taking a sip of her tea, which had been cooled with a hearty measure of brandy, Lady Catterick continued, "At any rate, I would never have predicted this! Mr. Fitzpaine—a poet of little consequence and no fortune—making pretty love to Lady Redmere—in Doncaster, of all places. Incredible!"

"She was always a bit of simpleton," Mrs. Whenby said.

"Birdwitted," Mrs. Bulmer stated.

"The silliest goose," Lady Catterick agreed. "Imagine! She believed all this time that the Garston had won Redmere's affections when anyone with even half their wits about 'em could see that he was, is, and has always been head-over-ears in love with his wife!"

"She would have listened to you, Eliza," Mrs. Whenby said, giving evidence of a conscience. "One word from any of us, really, and she would have discounted the whole of what was being said about her husband and Charlotte Garston. Sometimes I wonder if we aren't cruel to keep alive these absurd untruths by passing them from one ear to the next. I believe now that I should have said something to her."

"What? And ruin a year's fine sport among the drawing rooms of Mayfair?" Lady Catterick cried, astonished that her companion could say anything so absurd. "Never set about trying to correct a simpleton's deficiencies—that is what I always say! Besides, look what delights Millicent's disbelief in her husband have wrought. She has all but succumbed to Fitzpaine's caresses. I suppose, however, it was Providence that kept Captain Beck in the same chamber. It was his snoring that disrupted the tender scene." She giggled. "Really, it was quite amusing, and not at all romantic. Poor Mr. Fitzpaine. He nearly jumped from his skin when Beck first rumbled out a snore. Lord, but men can be such horrid creatures! Catterick snores to wake the dead. I can hear him from my chamber across the hall!"

"Vile!" Mrs. Whenby cried.

"Cretinous!" Mrs. Bulmer boomed.

"*Cretinous?*" Mrs. Whenby queried. "Is there such a word? Even if there isn't, there certainly ought to be, for it describes most of the brutes to perfection."

After they all laughed together yet again, Lady Catterick summed up the day's adventure. "And to think I almost refused Millicent's invitation to witness the marriage of her daughter. I nearly refused because I couldn't abide the notion of traveling north at the cold edge of spring. But oh, my—how my heart has been warmed by all that has transpired."

When the teacups were returned to the servant, the bricks tucked beneath the ladies' feet, and the door closed upon their amazement and laughter, the new postboy put the horses in motion. The coach disappeared into the night, leaving the Red Lion quickly behind.

* * *

Early the next morning, Lord Carlton lay flat on his back, stretched out upon his bed, and stared up at a whitewashed ceiling. The room was filled with a gray light, dawn just breaking to the east. In his left hand he held his pocketwatch. Already, traffic from the street below had begun to bombard his window. The horns of a variety of carriages had begun sounding a good hour earlier, and had increased steadily since the sun's light had begun tearing the blackness away from the small hamlet.

He had not slept well, even though the accommodations at the Robin Hood Inn were quite comfortable. His restless sleep had been due entirely to his growing dilemma where Julianna was concerned. Glancing at his watch, he could see that he had now been awake two full hours, and during that time he had examined his sentiments from every possible vantage point at least a dozen times. Still, he did not know how to proceed.

Even had he been a less perceptive man, he could not have mistaken that his betrothed had tumbled quite violently in love with him. Affection shone in her exquisite green eyes, dictated every word she spoke to him, and prompted her to query politely what was troubling him.

How sweetly she had asked him last night, after a light supper, "Whatever is the matter, Edward?"

His name was Stephen.

That was what was the matter, at least in part.

Only he couldn't tell her. Yet what surprised him most was how strongly he wanted to. He didn't understand himself. His heart kept whispering to him to reveal the truth to her. But always another part of him refused to obey. His mind told him that he needed to keep his heart detached from her completely if he hoped to achieve his end.

Therefore, he had not remained with her for very long after supper. He had professed a profound fatigue, and when he'd led her upstairs to her bedchamber door, he'd merely saluted her fingers before saying goodnight.

How disappointed she had seemed.

How worried.

The last glimpse of her had been of a furrowed brow over anxious green eyes.

It couldn't be helped. The kiss they had shared just past Wentbridge, besides having been one of the most passionate he had ever experienced in his entire existence—good God, he had wanted to go on kissing her forever!—had sent off warning bells in his head. More than one halfling had been led astray by a warm kiss or two, and oddly enough, once caught up in the pleasure of holding her in his arms, he felt as though it was he who was being led down the garden path, instead of Julianna.

But what did he feel toward her? He wasn't certain, and no matter how fiercely he struggled to come to a conclusion, he could not seem to sort it all out. For one thing, whatever he would decide while apart from her seemed to metamorphose the moment he drew near her. If he determined in his mind that he would not kiss her, when she but drew close to him, all he could think about was kissing her—and twice thus far he had succumbed against his will to assaulting her sweet lips. On the other hand, if he decided he would kiss her—for the truly wicked reason he meant to seduce her— he had but to come within three feet of her and every scurrilous intention fled him replaced most strangely by a desire to protect her.

Perhaps it was her age.

She was only nineteen, after all, and to bring his scheme to fruition, he would be taking advantage of a complete innocent. Why, the chit had not even had the advantage of a London Season by which to gain sufficient wisdom to fend off the inappropriate advances of a libertine.

He would have been easier in his mind, then, if she had been a trifle older.

Yet her age could not account for why he felt so much at

ease in her company. If anything, he should have been bored with a young woman eleven years his junior. Ordinarily, the prattling of young ladies just come out set his teeth on edge. But not Julianna. Her opinions were incisive and relatively mature, her conversation involved subjects ranging from art, to books, to politics, and her expressed values truly did ressemble his own.

In the face of these facts, only one thing surprised him—why was he still intent upon doing her harm? Common sense—which flowed strongly in his blood—kept warning him to avert his absurd scheme; he could only hurt himself by hurting Julianna, and most assuredly she, of all people, did not deserve such wretched treatment.

But the moment he would decide to set aside his intended elopement to Paris, without benefit of matrimony, something Julianna would say—relating a remark of Lady Catterick's, for instance—would again put him forcibly in mind of how piqued he was with her belief in the *on-dits* and of just how angry he was that up to this point the gossips had fairly ruled his life. His former rage would again flow over him, oversetting his ability to reason, and his heart would again be set on doing Julianna Redmere a great deal of mischief.

No, he would continue as planned, and within a sennight he would be in Paris, his scheme nearing its just conclusion.

Chapter Seventeen

Three days later, her heart heavy, Julianna lifted her eyes from her muff of green silk and was surprised to see the spire of the church at Highgate Hill come into view. How quickly time had passed. Imagine having arrived at Highgate already.

London was now but a breath away.

She felt a lump rise in her throat and with only the strongest effort did she keep tears from forming in her eyes.

How promising everything had seemed at Robin Hood's Well.

Now all was changed, but why?

What had happened?

She was thoroughly bemused as she glanced toward Edward. He was, as he had been so much of the time during the past several days, looking out the window, his expression inscrutable, distant, removed.

She swallowed the lump in her throat and began reviewing all that had gone before in hopes this time of ascertaining where she had erred in her conduct with him. And erred she must have, because his conduct toward her had altered so completely.

She knew when it had begun, of course—the day after he had kissed her near Wentbridge. She had been awakened the following morning at Robin Hood's Well by a sharp rapping on her door. A sleepy-eyed Molly had opened the door to Edward and learned that he had decided sometime during the night that they must now travel with all possible speed to London—resting only for a few hours each night.

At first, his decision hadn't troubled her in the least. How much better to arrive quickly in London in order to seek her father's counsel and at the very least to officially end her betrothal to Lord Carlton by sending a notice to the *Morning Post*. Indeed, she was happy to be traveling at a spanking pace.

But as each hour succeeded the one before, and as each night gave way to a new morning, she soon realized something was terribly amiss. Gone was most of her easy camaraderie with Edward, gone were most of their shared amusements and conversation, gone was even the smallest prospect he would kiss her again.

But why?

And the closer the coach drew to the Metropolis, the more an insidious anxiety had begun working in her heart.

When she had first noticed that she was uneasy and fretful, she had tried to tell herself it was merely a fit of nerves at the thought of confronting her father with the dreadful news that she had abandoned Carlton at the altar. After all, she had had so little contact with her papa over the last year that she simply had no way of knowing whether he would be furious or compassionate with her.

But as each mile claimed the next, as Barnby Moor gave way to Scarthing Moor, as Newark disappeared and bustling Grantham appeared, she came to understand that a great measure of her growing uneasiness was due to the simple fact that Edward was fairly ignoring her.

He continued to be as kind and as gentle as always. But more often than not, he directed his gaze out the window— just as he did now—and when she attempted to engage him in conversation, his responses were less than generous.

On the third day, she had, of course, provided him with at least half a dozen opportunities by which he might possess her lips—lifting her face to him whenever she could—but he seemed content merely to chuckle at her eagerness, pinch her chin, and bid her behave herself.

Between Grantham and Witham Common, she had given over trying to engage his interest. He seemed imperturbable in the extreme. To have continued in her persuasions would have caused her to feel foolish beyond permission, and she ended the day by asking politely if she had somehow offended him.

He had begged her to believe she could never offend him.

At Stamford, on the fourth day, she approached the strain between them from an entirely different direction and hinted that she was a very great heiress and could certainly support a comfortable household if any particular gentleman of her acquaintance had a fear on that score.

Edward had seemed quite nonplussed and had stared at her for a hard moment before responding politely, "Then you have the advantage of me."

Her heart had sunk at his words, at the confusion in his eyes, at his reluctance to open his heart to her.

As though regretting his words, his conversation the entire distance to Alwalton had been a partial retrieval of her confidances. He had even begged pardon for having hurt her because, as he said, he could see that she was overset by his reference to the inequality of their fortunes.

She had searched his gray eyes and found herself unable to believe him entirely. For the first time she wondered if she had misjudged his character somehow. This was not the man in whose company she had taken such enormous delight on the first and second days of their flight together. This was a man who, after having kissed her so thoroughly near Wentbridge, seemed to have decided he had made some grave error in pressing his advances upon her. But why?

Alconbury Hill, Eaton, and Biggleswade had sustained her belief that all was not well. To her three carefully worded and quite gentle inquiries along this line, he had insisted—most politely—she was very much mistaken, all was quite well.

But she knew better.

Her greatest fear was that he felt he could not marry her because he was poor and she was wealthy.

On the fifth day, she had wanted to confront him at Stevenage about his lack of fortune, but since her previous attempt had failed dismally, she was unable to brook the difficult subject a second time.

Nor could she at Hatfield. Though she opened her mouth several times, intending to reassure him that she didn't give a fig that he was an impoverished poet, something either in his demeanor, as he kept his gaze fixed upon the green countryside while the coach whirled its way toward London, or in the elusive expression of his eyes, when he did look at her, kept her lips clamped shut.

By the time they reached Barnet, so very near the Metropolis, she was searching every pocket of her brain trying to determine what had happened to disrupt the passionate tenderness which had hitherto characterized their relationship. But she could think of nothing she might have done or said to have caused such an unhappy change in her dear poet.

The closer the coach drew to Highgate Hill, the more she became determined to find a way of provoking Edward to speak his mind, his heart, if she possibly could. She had no way of knowing what he was thinking, but because she suspected the worst—that he meant to leave her the moment he saw her returned to her father in London—butterflies of the meanest kind had begun assaulting her stomach and insisting upon action.

But how difficult it was to find the words.

The coach was now threading its way through Highgate. She wanted to speak, but her heart had begun hammering in her breast. She strove to compose herself, letting her gaze drift over the isolated hilltop village. The bustling street, crammed with stage wagons and coaches, did not diminish the charm of High Street, lined with cottages sporting delightful red roofs, and shops that bordered a tiny village green.

She would wait to speak until the brief stops and starts which characterized their progress through Highgate gave way to the more even descent toward Islington.

She knew she was procrastinating, but she so feared hearing that kissing her had meant nothing to him that her mouth had become dry and cottony.

The postillion at last guided the post-chaise through the village at Highgate and began the descent. As the midday sunshine bathed the carriage windows with light and warmth, Julianna stole another glance at Edward's quiet, thoughtful profile. The pounding in her heart grew stronger and drove upward to the top of her head. The time had come to speak. She could wait no longer. She wanted more than anything to assure Edward that he could trust her to understand whatever his concerns or thoughts might be, but she was afraid.

What if he had no feelings for her at all?

"Edward," she said quietly, bracing herself for the descent into Islington by placing a foot against the opposite wall of the coach. "Will you not look at me?"

Finally, he turned slowly to meet her gaze, and she knew the moment had come for the truth. She was not surprised to see distress in his gray eyes.

She took a deep breath, strengthening her resolve to speak, when suddenly he blurted out, "It is no use. So much stands in our path that I cannot begin to enumerate the difficulties. You have been so kind in not pressing me when you had every right to demand to know why I have treated you so coldly since our shared embraces near Wentbridge— but I feel I must tell you all. Only, the truth is so distasteful—" he broke off, unable for a moment to continue, yet he did not look away from her.

She laid her hand on his sleeve, fingering the smooth fabric of his coat of blue superfine. "Edward, please tell me what is troubling you," she said. "It is breaking my heart that you will not speak to me, that you have not confided in me these three days past." He covered her hand with his own and pressed it very hard.

"I have lied to you," he said at last.

"Lied to me?" she asked, feeling the blood drain from her face. "I don't understand. When? About what? Whatever do you mean?"

"I think the moment I saw you I fell madly, deeply in love with you, Julianna. I have never known such extraordinary joy in all my life. Perhaps that must account for the fact that I could not seem to keep from *stealing* you away from Carlton." Here he paused, apparently struggling within himself. After a moment, he continued, "The truth is, Carlton did not know you were belowstairs when I went to gather my belongings together. I told him I had received word from a—a most beloved aunt who was dying and required my presence. You see, Carlton needed to marry you—to marry an heiress. He was deeply in debt. Do you wonder now that he was able to pass us on the road? I have little doubt once he learned that I had swept you away, he set off in immediate pursuit. There is so little that is noble in his character— he will have you to wife at any cost, even if you do not wish for it!"

"Oh, how horrid!" Julianna cried, pressing a hand to her cheek, unable to credit what he was saying.

"I know I deserve to hear your reproaches—"

"No, no!" she cried. "You have saved me from a monster. Why would I reproach you, when my first obligation must be to give you my most heartfelt thanks." She looked up at him and wanted to reassure him with a smile, but she was too overwhelmed by all that he had told her. Taking a deep breath, she said, "So you are telling me that the terrible *on-dits* I have heard of him are true, and that your previous efforts to uphold his character were untrue?" When he nodded, she continued. "What I don't understand is why you have been so loyal to him these many years and more when he is so very bad? Why have you remained his friend?"

Edward regarded her gravely. "I am, as you have said many times, a very loyal friend, and he wasn't always such a hopeless libertine. I believe he came into his fortune at too early an age, and his character has suffered for it. Whatever the case, I don't think until I met you I truly comprehended how ill-judged I have been to have continued befriending him even when I disapproved of his conduct."

Julianna was silent apace, a numbness stealing over her as she considered Carlton's wickedness. "So, he wanted my fortune," she said at last. "Then it is no wonder he was eager for the match. And to think he represented himself as having an annual income in excess of thirty thousand pounds! He lied, then, about needing to marry by his birthdate?"

"Precisely so."

Julianna felt a powerful rage pour over her. Carlton had lied to her and to her mother and father. "He is a gamester, then!" she stated angrily.

Edward nodded. "I had not been long in your company when I knew I could not permit you to wed him. To endure such a cold, unfeeling marriage." He turned bodily toward her and spoke rapidly. "You must believe me when I say that I never thought for a moment my strong, initial burst of sentiment for you would so quickly become the finest love I could ever have known. I meant only to take you to your father, but now I want so much more that I can hardly speak. Julianna, I want to be your husband, to share my life with you, but I know it is utterly impossible!"

"Don't say that!" Julianna cried. "It is not in the least *impossible*. I will not marry Carlton, if that is what you fear. I will not honor contracts agreed to deceitfully."

"You will have no choice, I'm afraid. Even your father will comprehend as much once we are arrived in London. Why, you would be banished from all of polite society were Carlton to expose you—us—this reckless flight of ours!"

"I don't care," Julianna said, lifting her chin. "I know that I have not had a great deal of experience, but these past few days in your company have been wondrous. I will never give you up, Edward! Never!"

Her impassioned speech seemed to give him pause. He appeared almost dumbstruck, his lips parted as though trying to prevent him from speaking. "You would never give me up?" he asked, searching her eyes.

"Never, Edward. I am in love with you and always shall be. What does an *entree* among the *beau monde* signify?"

"You do not know what you are saying," he said slowly.

"Yes, I do," she responded. "I know that for some, going about in society is everything. But I have never believed happiness can possibly come from such a paltry source. That is not to say I do not value my friends and acquaintances or the many finer aspects of art and music which the *haut* ton supports so vigorously. But the heart of my life has always been those whom I hold dearest—my family. And you must believe me when I say that I am fully persuaded my mother and father would come 'round to our marriage once they understood the depth of my regard for you, of my respect for you. Besides, what would you and I need London or Bath or Brighton for, when we could travel the oceans together?"

"What, indeed?" he murmured, the expression on his face one of bewilderment.

Julianna squeezed his arm and continued. "You spoke of impossibilities, but I see none. We have only to pass London by entirely. We—we could go to Paris, if you liked, and be married there, at the embassy. You have enough funds for the moment to see us safely aboard a packet, and I have enough for the rest of our lives. What do you say, Edward? What argument can you now present which could possibly stand in the path of our love?"

A deep frown furrowed his brow as he tenderly caressed her cheek. "Do you trust me so very much, Julianna, that having known me for only five days, you would be willing to elope with me to Paris?"

"I trust you with all my heart," she responded simply.

Lord Carlton looked down into Julianna's trusting, loving,

believing face and felt his heart and his conscience twist within him. How strange that she had proposed the very plan he had intended to place before her! How her green eyes radiated love and adoration as she entwined her arm in youthful simplicity about his own.

She loved him.

In his youth, had he ever loved so easily, so readily, so disinterestedly?

He patted the arm wrapped about his and told her he would give careful consideration to everything she had just said. For his reward, he received her head on his shoulder. She wore a soft, adorable hat of green silk, matched to a shade with her pelisse and muff. Her red curls danced beneath the brim of her hat in a lovely frame about her face. She did not seem to mind that the delicate fabric was being crushed against him.

He sighed heavily and set his gaze forward to watch the horses's flanks rise and fall with each galloping stride set on macadamized road. He atuned his hearing to the persistent powerful crunch of speeding hooves against rock, to the whir of the tall wheels, to the creaking of the body of the carriage as it drifted over excellent C-springs. His thoughts moved about restlessly, first hard, like the hooves, then swift, like the wheels, then lazy, like the drift of the coach. First to his desire to be that which he was gossiped to be—a rakehell—then to the swiftly flowing sensation of Julianna's love, then to strange desires that Paris never be reached. He had a sense that he was caught in a precarious niche in time, where his anger and subsequent actions had overlapped Julianna's guileless love. He couldn't think clearly, he couldn't really sort out his sentiments. All he knew was that of the moment he was dreadfully confused and what had begun as a journey designed to serve the Tabbies with their own sauce was transforming beneath him into a future he had never believed possible.

In quick stages, the village of Islington came into view. It was a small community of green sward, charmingly grouped

trees, cottages, and large, ivied houses of brick bearing pleasant porticoes. From the distance, Carlton could see the slender spire of St. Mary's Church.

The sight of the spire meant Islington. The established
coaching village meant London. London meant proceeding
with the elopement.

The multitudinous sounds of the road blended into a
murmur of accusations against the crime he was about to
commit. The wheels spun about in a whir of *guilty, guilty,
guilty.*

He glanced down at her hat again, the knowledge of what
her existence would be like after Paris—were he truly to take
her there—stealing into his brain in fiery rivulets. She would
have no life left to her in England once they returned from
France. No gentleman of honor would have her when it
became known her innocence had been robbed of her.

"Oh, my goodness gracious!" Jilly cried, slipping her hand
from about his arm and giving a clap of delight. Her exclamation had drawn him abruptly from his reveries.

Carlton had been so lost in his thoughts that he had not
noticed the carriage slowing to a stop. Glancing out the
window, he was surprised to find that a large flock of sheep
had started to meander across the high road, greatly to the
consternation of the driver of the Royal Mails on the approaching side.

Julianna laughed. "I have never heard such cursing
before!" she cried. "Except by the smithy in Redmere, when
a glowing shoe got away from him, flew into the air, then
landed on his shoulder." She paused for a moment before
continuing. "Do but look at the vapor rising from their
bodies. Papa once told me that some years ago, when he had
stayed the night in Islington, at the Peacock, I believe, he
rose well before dawn—in complete darkness—to begin his
journey north. But the early-morning hour had proved
foggy, and when a herd of bullock and sheep being driven to
market had surrounded his coach, the steam from the exertions of the horses and from the cattle rose to mingle with the

fog and created a maddening darkness which even the carriage lamps could not penetrate. He could do nothing but wait for an hour until the road was clear of animals and enough of the fog had abated for the postboy to see even two feet in front of him."

He glanced at the sheep in the road. "I can only be grateful, then, that it is not dark. What a lively flock, though. Listen to their bleatings! Why, I am almost put in mind of the ballroom at Lady Catterick's townhouse when the entire ton tries to dance all at once."

"How absurd you are," she responded, again taking his arm and snuggling her head against his shoulder.

Carlton smiled down at the green silk of her hat and the red curls peeping from beneath the narrow brim. He thought yet again that Julianna was so very different from every lady he had ever known. She had given herself to him—as Edward, of course—without the least promise of a handle to her name, or increased fortune to persuade her her love was true. He had never before considered the enormity of this truth—that her love for him was pure. If either of them should have had cause to doubt the legitimacy of the love of the other, all doubt would have to be on her part, since she was the one who ostensibly held the fortune and was a daughter of a peer. From her perspective, since he was pretending to be an impoverished Edward Fitzpaine, her love would have no reason to ring false, but his would have every reason to do just that.

Yet she trusted him.

And she gave no appearance of doubt. If anything—regardless of his own sullen behavior over the past one hundred and thirty miles—she had enough reason for a lifetime to doubt his affections. Still, she did not. She had believed everything he had told her—without the smallest hint that she mistrusted him.

He had an overwhelming awareness that he did not deserve such complete trust, not just because he had lied to her, but because from the first—even before he'd come to

York—his motives had been horrendously impure in every aspect of his relationship with her, beginning with his agreement to marry her in the first place. He had needed a bride to fulfill the conditions of his inheritance—he had to be married before his thirty-first birthday. What nobility in its truest sense had he brought to her—to a marriage with her? He could not even say that it had ever once occurred to him that his object, once he married her, would be to tend to her happiness. He had spoken correctly when he had—posing as Edward—related to her his endless stream of complaints about his forthcoming marriage, complaints which had begun, ironically, at the Peacock in Islington, a sennight earlier, and had only ended when he had watched her fly into the innyard of the Angel at Redmere.

As the sheep finally quit the road, and the horses jumped back into their collars, plunging the coach toward Islington, he recalled the magical sensations which had surrounded him the moment Julianna had appeared at the gates of the Angel in Redmere, and she had flown toward him on the hard snow.

His heart swelled within his breast at the memory. He closed his eyes, sighing deeply as he savored the images which flowed through his mind—of seeing her, of speaking with her, of kissing her for the first time.

"Julianna," he breathed.

"What is it, Edward?" she queried, gently giving his arm a squeeze. "Have you the headache?"

Lord Carlton opened his eyes with a mild start. He had not realized he had spoken her name aloud. He turned to look at her, and the same magic which had assailed him when he had first seen her astride her horse seemed to rush over him again. He fell into her green eyes as surely as if he had dived into a clear lake.

He loved her.

His vision blurred and sparkled before him, until her face came sharply into view. She was so exquisitely beautiful, and the creaminess of her complexion, the Grecian lines of her face, the delicate arch of her brows, the dreamy shade of her eyes were matched in an equal portion of spiritual beauty by her guileless, vivacious, honorable character.

Love flowed over him again and again. He was stunned by the truth of his feelings for her. Why had he not seen it before—that he truly did love her beyond measure?

He loved her.

Damn, he loved her with all his heart.

He understood then that he could never—regardless of how much he had longed to do so—take her to Paris.

Never.

Chapter Eighteen

At two o'clock in the afternoon, Lord Redmere sat in a straight-backed chair by the window in the parlour of the Peacock Inn, Islington's most famous hostelry. Behind him a dull march of travelers had been tramping in and out of the large, commodious chamber, partaking of refreshments in brief spurts of time as horses were changed on their private chaises. In one hand he held his fifth tankard of ale since his arrival at six o'clock that morning, and in his other, his palm swirled over and over the ivory-handled ball of his walking stick. He was waiting, his temper in shreds, for his wife to arrive in Islington as he again pondered the extraordinary tidings Lady Catterick had poured like hot coals over his head the evening before.

Good God, his wife and Fitzpaine! Impossible!

Of course, she was traveling with her maid, Polly. And that stupid coxcomb Captain Beck. Much difference *his* presence made to all the Tabbies who dined on the milk and meat of gossip. Even if he was not considered the least threat to his wife's virtue, Fitzpaine certainly would be thought as much—and unmarried in the bargain! What was his bird-witted wife thinking, to be traveling in the company of two bachelors, however harmless even one of them might be?

His fingers gripped the ivory ball and he slammed the stick down on the floor for the hundredth time. As had happened many times before, all chattering behind him ceased for an infinitessimal moment, only to continue in quieter tones. As before, his name was brought forward. Clearly, he was known by many, but woe to anyone who approached him in his current temper. Not that anyone had tried. After all, he was not precisely the friendliest creature on God's earth, at his soberest, and right now—damn, he sloshed his ale again!—he would gladly plant a facer on the next fellow who dared look at him cross-eyed!

Outside the inn, two dozen carriages, coaches, and wagons choked the High Street. But as he looked into the glass of the window, he was able to see his reflection and the melee of the Great North Road disappeared from his sight. He saw only himself, his features pulled into the mulish frown Millie detested so very much. He saw the thick black brows of his youth streaked with gray and his blue eyes clouded with anger. Peering closer, he could even see a far more dreaded spectre—his wretched loneliness.

It was no wonder she didn't love him anymore, he thought. After all, he had only himself to blame for the past year of unhappiness. And it was little wonder she had tumbled in love with Fitzpaine who was probably one of the most honorable gentleman of his acquaintance.

He sighed heavily, swirled his palm over the ivory ball of his walking stick, and took another pull from his tankard of ale.

Maybe if he told her the truth again, maybe if he persuaded Mrs. Garston to speak with her and refute the rumors, maybe if he begged her to forgive him, maybe if he—damn, what use would it be if she was in love with Fitzpaine?

No use at all!

The ale settled into his veins, easing away some of the dogged pain which afflicted his heart and had for the past twelvemonth. He didn't even know why he was in Islington, except that he would not permit Millicent to ruin herself by arriving in London with Fitzpaine sitting in her pocket. He would protect her or what was left of her tattered reputation from further exposure.

Good God! Traveling with two men.

She never had been much up to snuff, not by half. He had even warned her how it would be with Julianna and her marriage to Carlton.

He scowled, hearing the guard on the York Express—or maybe it was the Truth and Daylight—blast out the tune, "Oh, Dear, What Can the Matter Be?" Somehow Jilly had gotten caught up in all his difficulties with his wife. He knew—damn, he knew!—Jilly had agreed to marry Carlton because of Millie's unhappiness and subsequent persuasions. What he didn't understand was why Julianna had decided to elope with Carlton, instead of just marrying him at Marish Hall. That old bat Catterwick had tried to fob off some incredible tale of Carlton masquerading as Fitzpaine—but that wouldn't fadge. Anybody who'd ever seen the two men would know—

Lord Redmere gasped. Jilly hadn't seen either man! Could Lady Catterick be right? Then what was Carlton playing at?

He should have ignored Millicent's protests and joined her at Marish Hall anyway. He could have set things to rights before this whole escapade began.

He'd just been so curst hurt by his wife's belief he'd actually—but he wouldn't think of that. He would be angry all over again, and right now he wanted to meet his wife with some of his sense about him.

Another coach, the York Highflyer, was playing "When from Great Londonderry," or was that "The Flaxen-Headed Ploughboy?" Good Lord, he'd had too many tankards. He was about to take another swig anyway, when a soft, feminine voice called his name.

"Redmere?"

He looked over his shoulder, his vision blurred slightly. He narrowed his eyes and saw first a pretty dark blue silk muff trimmed with a sort of brown fur. He lifted his gaze upward, and saw a dark blue silk pelisse—quite elegant and costly, if he was any judge of females' clothing. Upward his eyes traveled, next seeing a narrow band of fur around the lady's throat. Above that, the creamiest skin appeared, then amused, rosy lips, a nose too sharp for his taste, yet quite familiar, brown eyes next, then shapely brows, a smooth forehead, and a fringe of dark brown curls, and another ribbon of fur wrapped around a blue silk poke bonnet.

"Yes?" he queried, still unable to bring all the lady's features into one sharp focus.

"My dear, how many of these have you imbibed since arriving?" the familiar voice queried.

He shook his head and leaned back, trying to arrange the bonnet, face, and pelisse into one person, but still couldn't achieve a satisfactory result. He was half-foxed and watched the lady settle into a chair beside him. He blinked hard two times, opened his eyes wide, and cried out, "You!"

Mrs. Garston glanced meaningfully to the many travelers crowded in the parlour and then back to Lord Redmere. "Of course it is I," she said sweetly. "I—I am going to visit my parents in Hertfordshire."

"How very nice for you," he responded, slurring his politeness.

"They are quite reclusive and rarely travel to London."

Lord Redmere nodded and took another pull on his tankard. "You were never my mistress, you know," he said, dropping his voice very low.

Mrs. Garston trilled her laughter. "Of course I was not," she whisperered conspiratorially in return.

"Then why did all of London believe you were?"

"Because, my lord, you flirted a great deal too much with me, and I am, after all, a widow. What else would you expect?"

He sighed and glanced out the window. "My wife is out there somewhere, I think. At least, Lady Catterick said she would be. I must stop her."

"Indeed?" Mrs. Garston queried. "Stop her? In what way? I don't take your meaning."

"She's traveling with Beck and Fitzpaine without a proper chaperone, only her maid."

"Oh, dear," Mrs. Garston responded kindly. "Any number of most improper conclusions could easily be construed from such a——a delicate arrangement."

"Precisely—I think. I wish you wouldn't talk so strangely. Just like a woman to mix up her words like that—*delicate arrangement*, indeed! Stupid coil, more to my thinking."

"Precisely," Mrs. Garston responded with a smile just at the corners of her mouth, which somewhere within Lord Redmere's foggy brain caused him to think the widow was laughing at him. Ordinarily, he would have taken umbrage at such a slight, but damn, she was a fine-looking woman, and he was in his altitudes. Maybe if Millie decided to take up with Mr. Fitzpaine, he might just——!

He must stop thinking such wicked thoughts.

He was so deuced lonely!

If only Millicent had believed he was innocent. But no matter how loudly he had protested, she never gave up her opinion that he had betrayed her with Mrs. Garston. Pretty thing, that, to have been condemned when innocent—and he was innocent. Even yet!

That was the rub. Her disbelief still rankled hard within him. He didn't care what the Tabbies said about him, or how many times they might have maligned his character to the whole world—but he couldn't forgive Millie that she had believed him guilty.

The trouble was, he missed his wife so very much. He felt like some part of him had died when she actually packed up all twenty of her bandboxes, all three of her monstrous portmanteaux, and five trunks, and disappeared on the Great North Road without so much as a goodbye.

The sight of her empty wardrobe had kept him in his cups for a full fortnight. A year later, they were still living under separate roofs.

Now he was here, at the Peacock, awaiting her arrival and ready to give her the worst dressing down of her life—so help him God!

Lady Redmere looked across the coach at Mr. Fitzpaine and smiled faintly. "We are nearly arrived at Islington, Edward," she said. "A minute more, and we will be caught in the traffic of the High Street. I could only wish we had been trapped by that flock of sheep as so many coaches behind us were, then we would not be so soon parted. Are you certain you must seek passage on the Mails?"

"I won't jeopardize your reputation further," he returned, his expression clouded. He reached a hand toward her, then drew back, his gaze slipping toward her maid to the right of him and a snoring Captain Beck beside her. "You are a most beloved friend," he added, watching her intensely, his blue eyes taking her breath away.

"Yes," she murmured. The cramped confines of the carriage permitted her to stretch her foot forward, quite surreptitiously, and press her ankle against his. She watched his chest rise with suppressed emotion as he held her gaze firmly and returned the pressure on her ankle.

Lady Redmere felt her heart quivering at the very sight of his love for her. The past three days had been a whirlwind of emotions that had fairly left her crumpling with love for the kind, strong, talented poet. He had composed sonnet after sonnet in her honor, and once Captain Beck fell asleep in the evenings, he had read them to her, extoling her beauty, her character, the richness of her red hair. Redmere had never made such delightfully sweet love to her. And the most wonderful part of all was that Mr. Fitzpaine had not even kissed her yet. Twice he had wanted to, and twice she had run away. But once arrived in London, and once Jilly's future was set on a proper course with or without that rogue Carlton, and once she confronted her husband one last time about his horrid affair with Mrs. Garston, she meant to let

Mr. Fitzpaine kiss her and flirt with her. She would take immeasurable delight in flaunting her new Cicisbeo beneath Redmere's nose. Mr. Fitzpaine could escort her to balls and soirées and to the opera, all to her heart's content. Most definitely, she would just happen to leave Fitzpaine's sonnets lying about—quite by accident, of course. Then let Redmere weep with regret that he had once offered Mrs. Garston a *carte blanche*.

Lady Redmere felt a wave of satisfaction flow over her at the thought of finally being able to serve Redmere with his own sauce—the brute! She knew Redmere; he would be furious. All her life she had been told to be careful with a man's pride, but what of her pride? How did her husband think she felt when it was bandied about all over London that he had set aside his beautiful wife and now shared his affections with a widow?

Lady Redmere gave herself a shake. If she continued to think about the affair, she would go mad. Instead, she blinked several times, and noting that Mr. Fitzpaine was watching her affectionately, she begged him to close his eyes and tell her to name the approaching coach. He did so immediately and she thought again how sweet it was to have a man obey her so very promptly.

Lady Catterick entered the parlour of the Peacock Inn with Mrs. Whenby and Mrs. Bulmer in tow. When she caught sight of Mrs. Garston sitting next to Lord Redmere, she held her friends back, one on each side, by throwing her arms wide. With her finger held to her lips, she silenced her astonished friends, then directed their attention toward the most interesting couple beside the window.

"Oh, my," Mrs. Whenby chirped quietly.

"Oh, my, my," Mrs. Bulmer boomed in a low voice.

All three ladies carefully backed out of the chamber.

Once in the taproom, Lady Catterick placed a hand on

each hip and faced her friends with a severe frown. "Which of you informed the Garston of our scandal?" she asked.

Mrs. Whenby and Mrs. Bulmer exchanged a glance of surprise and both began to protest their innocence immediately.

"We all took a vow not to involve *that woman!*" Mrs. Whenby cried, her voice sounding shrill. "And I assure you, Eliza, I would not for the world have broken our solemn agreement."

"Nor I," Mrs. Bulmer exclaimed, folding her arms across her bosom, an offended light in her eye.

Lady Catterick shook her head, nonplussed. "No one else can possibly have known of Julianna's flight. Goodness, it must be the hand of Fate, then. Imagine, Charlotte Garston, here, when a storm is about to break over Islington! Now that I think on it, I don't wonder but that it might be a very good thing she is come. After all, Lady Redmere will not like it above half and if Julianna had somehow come to learn Mrs. Garston's name had been linked with Carlton for the past several weeks—"

She let her hints drift toward her companions.

"Oh," Mrs. Whenby cooed.

"Oh, yes," Mrs. Bulmer stated.

"I still think it is very odd she is here," Mrs. Whenby added. "But where shall we go, now that the Garston has taken up a place beside Redmere?"

Lady Catterick smiled. "I think we ought to join our good friends," she responded nasally.

"Oh, do let us," Mrs. Whenby trilled.

"Oh, yes, do let us," Mrs. Bulmer agreed, her bosom rising with pleasure as she followed in Lady Catterick's wake and forced a pouting Mrs. Whenby to follow behind.

The coach was nearly upon Islington when Lord Carlton took Julianna in his arms. The discovery of his love for her had changed everything so abruptly, so dramatically, that he did not know precisely where to begin, save that he wanted to kiss her badly.

"Julianna," he breathed, pulling her close and having the delight of watching her lift her trusting, eager face to him. "You are so beautiful," he murmured, caressing her face with his hand and searching every feature with hungry eyes. "I love you more than you will ever know. I had no idea after five days I would have fallen so completely in love with you. The truth is, I had given up hope of knowing such fine sentiments."

"Oh, my darling Edward," she whispered, preventing him from speaking by appearing so adorable.

He meant to immediately correct her—to tell her at last that his name was Stephen, Lord Carlton—but first he wanted to kiss her, then he would tell her the truth. Slowly, he pressed his lips upon hers and felt her lean into him with a deep sigh.

He had not kissed her like this before. Always it seemed he was determined to force his passion upon her, but now he wanted to taste of her love for him. How soft her lips were against his, how sweet, how pleasant, like the warmth of the spring sun as winter slipped quickly into the year past . . .

He drew back from her slightly. "I love you, Jilly, so very much," he whispered, then kissed her again. He drifted his lips ever so slightly over hers and heard her sigh again as her hand slid around the collar of his coat and about his neck. She returned his kisses with a soft fluttering movement which caused a flush of pleasure to rise over him. He could not restrain kissing her very hard and pulling her tightly against him. He felt her hand slip into his hair as murmurs of delight cooed within her white throat.

He wished he could remain holding her in his arms forever, but the sounds of Islington broke over them, in a resounding of coach horns blaring, horses snorting, traces jingling.

He released her, and regardless of the busy traffic all about them, he knew he must now tell her the truth. Fear

froze his heart. Having acknowledged his love for her, he
now knew that to lose her love would rip his life apart
forever.

"Edward, what is wrong?" she asked, looking up at him,
her hand still laced through his black hair. "I can see by the
expression in your eyes you are sorely distressed."

He opened his mouth to speak, but something suddenly
caught her attention and her gaze became riveted beyond
the front window of the coach. When her complexion paled
ominously, he had a prescience of doom and knew, in a wave
of fright, he had erred gravely in playing out his charade.
Would she ever forgive him?

She seemed unable to speak for a long moment, her lips
quivering. She gestured toward the object of her gaze, and
finally said, "Who is that man? He looks very much like you,
except taller. And whatever is he doing with Mama?"

It had been only a few minutes since the *beau monde*'s most
famous hostesses had joined Lord Redmere and Mrs. Garston at his table by the window. But to the viscount, whose
head had begun to ache, he felt as though an hour had
passed by since they had taken up their seats around him.

At his best, he could scarcely abide the chattering, cluck-
ing, and caterwauling of ladies' conversation. But since he
had imbibed his sixth tankard, endured the dread of his
wife's arrival, and listened to Lady Catterick direct her horrid impertinences toward the widow Garston, the effort of
politely keeping his tongue had finally split his head into two
parts. In much pain, he rose unsteadily, intending to excuse
himself and seek the air outside. He straightened his burgundy silk waistcoat, tugged at the sleeves of his coat of blue
superfine, tweaked his limp, white shirtpoints, picked up his
ivory-handled walking stick, and cleared his throat, preparing to make his speech.

But at the very moment he opened his mouth, Mrs.

Whenby, who was staring out the window of the parlour, stopped him. "Redmere!" she cried out in her shrill, birdlike voice, her large blue eyes protruding ominously. "Is that not your wife in Mr. Fitzpaine's arms?"

Chapter Nineteen

Lord Carlton watched the scene unfold before his eyes, feeling as though he was trapped within a nightmare and completely unable to extricate himself.

Julianna gasped. "Why, that man is kissing her!" she exclaimed. "Oh, my goodness! Whoever could he be, but look—there is Papa—and in a towering passion, too! But why is he holding his head and stumbling about?"

Carlton blinked, his whole body stiff with tension. He held Julianna closely to him, watching with increased horror as Lady Catterick, Mrs. Whenby, and Mrs. Bulmer each emerged from the Peacock Inn, following in Redmere's wake.

The entire confrontation was taking place just north of the Peacock, and it was with no small wonder that Redmere immediately leapt upon Fitzpaine, attempting to plant him a facer. The commotion prompted any number of vehicles, including Carlton's, to stop abruptly.

Carlton felt dizzy with panic. And worse! If he did as his bride bade him, Julianna would learn the truth of his identity in a manner which would likely ruin him in her eyes forever. He drew her closer still, took her chin firmly in his hand, and tore her gaze away from the astounding spectacle not thirty feet from his carriage. "We must press on!" he cried, forcing her to look at him. His heart pounded more furiously in his chest than if had he been racing his horse across field after field in pursuit of a fox. "It would be disastrous to remain a moment longer. If we are discovered, all shall be lost." This much was true, he thought ironically.

The sight of her parent caught up in heated combat with a stranger pulled Julianna's gaze back to the tall gentleman struggling to keep Lord Redmere at bay. "Is—is that Carlton?" she queried.

Lord Carlton wanted to say yes, but he was done with his lies. "No," he responded flatly. "Please, Jilly. Come with me—to Paris, just as you suggested. Whatever difficulties your parents are experiencing, they are fully capable of sorting everything out. Please—to Paris and our future. Now!"

Julianna turned to him at last and searched his eyes. "You believe our case is so hopeless, then, that we cannot possibly lay the whole matter before my parents and see our dilemma resolved?"

"I do," he said, holding his breath, waiting for her to acquiesce.

She did not look back at the crowd now gathering about the flagways near Lady Redmere's coach.

"All right, then," she responded, appearing deeply troubled, a worried frown creasing her brow.

Lowering his window, he bade the postillion drive on. But traffic had so clogged the High Street that their progress was painfully slow and unfortunately offered a full view of the altercation. Carlton watched as Edward continued to step first this way, then that, in an effort to avoid Redmere's punishing left. The viscount was a solidly built man and had been known to incapacitate more than one of his opponents.

He sat beside Julianna, his arm still encircling her, and tried to offer what comfort he could, encouraging her to believe all would be well.

She said nothing, but he could sense in the stiffness of her form beside him that she was not at all reconciled to leaving Islington.

"Oh, Edward, suddenly I am frightened," she cried out,

her voice bordering on hysteria. "I—I don't want to elope, but I want to be with you more than anything." Tears of frustration sprang to her eyes and tumbled quickly down her cheeks.

As she wiped at her eyes with a kerchief withdrawn from her muff, the coach finally drew past the terrible spectacle. At last Lord Carlton released a suspended anxious breath, only to have Julianna cry out, "I'm sorry, Edward, I cannot!" She then quickly threw down the window and called to the postboy to stop the coach.

Carlton discovered they were now directly opposite the door of the Peacock Inn.

"Jilly, wait!" he cried, as she prepared to leave his coach. "There is something I must tell you first! It is of the utmost importance. Please, stay!"

But she had already pushed the door open and was leaping nimbly down onto the sidewalk. It seemed she had not heard him, for she turned back to him and said, "You must trust me a little, Edward! We will explain everything to my father. He will know how to get us out of this coil. He is very wise, I promise you."

Only then did he notice that standing at the entrance of the inn, not five feet away from Julianna, and looking at him with a mischievous smile on her lips, was none other than Charlotte Garston. He shook his head and murmured, "No," as a profound shock began descending over him.

Jilly, however, took no notice of the lady, but turned and began walking quickly up the street.

"Fitzpaine, do hurry!" she called back to him. "You can have no notion what is going forward. My papa has leaped upon that tall man again and knocked him down. Captain Beck is trying to pull Papa off the tall gentleman; even Mama is trying to do so. I can hear her shrieking even now. Do hurry!"

Before Carlton could stop his elusive bride, she had picked up the skirts of her green silk pelisse and was running toward the crowd of people gathered about her father and Mr. Fitzpaine.

"Fitzpaine?" Mrs. Garston queried with a lift of one impeccably arched brow once Julianna was out of earshot. "Then it is true. I had heard reports that you had stolen away your own bride under the pretenses of being your best friend. Quite original, I thought, but—" and here she gestured to the spectacle in progress a few yards north, before continuing, "—a bit awkward, don't you think?"

"Charlotte, I haven't time for your nonsense, but I do thank you for not revealing my identity just yet."

Since he immediately followed in Julianna's wake, Charlotte had to hurry to catch up to him. When she did, she took his arm. "She is bound to discover the truth now, however," Mrs. Garston said. "Though I could rely upon Fitzpaine to keep his peace and even Beck, those blackbirds sitting prettily by and savoring every scandalous demonstration of Lord Redmere's boxing abilities would be ever so happy, I fear, to kindly inform your little darling of your imposturing."

"I know," he said, his gaze diverted from Julianna for just a moment by the sight of Lady Catterick, Mrs. Whenby, and Mrs. Bulmer, all ecstatically watching the quite shocking proceedings.

"I might mention to you that Redmere is quite foxed of the moment," Mrs. Garston added. "He is all flurry with his fists, but if he has landed one square hit I shall be amazed. To my knowledge he imbibed at least a half dozen pints while awaiting the arrival of his adored wife."

"I see," he said, surveying the fracas with a critical eye. Since Julianna was already nodding toward Lady Catterick, Mrs. Whenby, and Mrs. Bulmer, he realized he had no hope whatsoever that she would long remain in ignorance of his identity. He decided, therefore, to come to the aid of both her father and Edward by intervening in their bout of fisticuffs. At the same time, he mentally decided to accept with equanimity in whatever manner Fate decided to introduce the truth to his bride. "Then I had best tend to Redmere, hadn't I?" he said.

With the aid of an oxlike spectator, Carlton disengaged Lord Redmere from off of Mr. Fitzpaine. Regardless of Redmere's condition, it required every ounce of strength they could muster to hold the peer back from Edward, as the latter regained his feet.

Lord Carlton was surprised by what he saw when Edward began dusting off the tails of his coat and the length of each sleeve. There was just such a set to his chin, just such a grinding of his teeth, that informed Carlton of the precise state of Edward's temper—he was fairly beside himself with rage.

So unlike Edward to be enraged!

But then, it was so unlike Edward to kiss a married lady— and that in plain view of the lady's husband!

Glancing toward Lady Redmere, he saw that a profound embarrassment had darkened her cheeks and anger had flared her nostrils. She glared at her husband, her vision blurred by tears that rolled down her pretty face. She swiped at them with quick jerks of fine, gloved hands. He wondered if she was even aware her daughter had arrived.

And Edward had kissed her!

What the devil had Edward Fitzpaine been thinking, to have kissed Lady Redmere at all, nonetheless on one of the busiest High Streets in the Kingdom?

"You are a brute, Redmere," his wife pronounced at last. "And always shall be!"

Ignoring the crowd, she turned back to her coach and realighted the muddy, travel-stained vehicle. She sat staring forward as more tears descended her cheeks, her hands now folded tightly upon her lap.

"And you are a ninnyhammer, Millicent!" he called back to her, straining to be released from Carltons' and the stranger's strong clasp. "Traveling alone with two unattached men, causing scandal in every village you passed through, and—and—" Suddenly he broke off, his eyes rolling back in his head, his legs growing limp as he slumped sideways and fell into Carlton.

"Let's get him into the inn," Carlton stated, catching him more fully under the arm. The stranger moved quickly into position, taking up Redmere's other arm and slinging it around his neck. Half-dragging Lord Redmere, the two men hauled the unconscious peer toward the Peacock.

"Carlton!" Lady Redmere's voice suddenly rang out. "However did you get here? And Jilly, my darling! I didn't even know you were here. When did you arrive? Did you see your father? Do come here! Come here at once, my pet! I was so worried!"

Lord Carlton sighed deeply, catching Julianna's surprised gaze just before he disappeared into the inn.

Julianna had heard her mother's voice call out Carlton's name, and she had quickly glanced first about the crowd, then toward Mr. Fitzpaine, but she was completely bemused. There was only one man present who was of sufficient breeding, and whom she did not know, who could possibly have been Carlton—the man her father was trying unsuccessfully to murder! But Mr. Fitzpaine had already told her the tall man now holding her gaze quite steadfastly was not Carlton.

Where, then, was her betrothed? She wondered if he had slipped behind one of the vehicles momentarily, but as she whirled about, visually searching the street and any nooks in which a man might have momentarily disappeared because of the press of the crowd, she found no one who might possibly meet with his lordship's description.

Only the tall man, who had kissed her mother not five minutes ago—and had so aroused her father's wrath—came close to bearing a ressemblance to Carlton's description.

Suddenly she knew something dreadful was wrong, though she didn't comprehend how she knew, or what it was. Yet she was fully convinced Mr. Fitzpaine had not lied to her when he had said that this man was not Lord Carlton. Perhaps because as he held her gaze quite firmly, she could see from a distance that his eyes were a very clear, quite attractive blue. By any description she had received of Lord Carlton, his eyes were sometimes hazel, sometimes gray, but never blue. On the other hand, Mr. Fitzpaine had been reputed as having *blue* eyes.

Blue eyes.

Truly, this man before her—especially because of the remarkable color of his eyes—more nearly fit the description of her darling Edward than Edward did himself. How extraordinary. He was quite tall and quite lean, and he had *blue eyes.*

Somewhere in the distant reaches of her mind, she knew her mother was begging her to join her in the coach. She knew as well that the crowd was dispersing at last. But her attention was positively riveted to the man who had been kissing her mother.

Who was he, and why had he been kissing her mother?

She sensed that in this man resided the key to the riddle of her intuition that all was not as it should be. Dazed by the strength of her premonition, she approached him, extending her hand to him. "Pray forgive my impertinence," she said quietly, "but since you seem somehow connected to at least one of my parents, I trust I may introduce myself without giving offense. I am Julianna Redmere."

"Yes, I know," he responded, taking her hand and bowing politely over it.

How well he moves, she thought distractedly, quite well mannered. Mama would like him for that, so different from Papa.

He continued, "I would know you anywhere because of your ressemblance to your mother. Though I have little doubt I will give you pain, I have no desire to continue a charade born in York and carried forward these many days by my misguided friend. I apprehend by your confusion that you are still under a terrible misapprehension. We—your mother, Captain Beck, and I—tried to find you along the road, to stop this horrendous elopement, but somehow we passed you by. I—" a terrible frown overtook his face, before he continued in a quieter voice, "I am Edward Fitzpaine. The man you have been traveling with, unless he has been wise enough to beg your forgiveness and reveal all to you, is your bridegroom—Lord Carlton."

Behind her, Julianna could hear the assembled gasps, sighs, and exclamations of Lady Catterick, Mrs. Whenby, and Mrs. Bulmer—one nasal, one shrill, one booming. It was like having magpies sitting upon her shoulders. She knew a profound desire to reach her hand up over her shoulder and brush them away.

She blinked once. Had she heard the man before her correctly? She couldn't have!

"You can't be Edward Fitzpaine," she said, giving a shake of her head and smiling faintly. "I mean, I suppose you could but it wouldn't make the least sense, you know. You see, I am in love with Edward, and you are not he."

She turned around and saw that the man she loved—or thought she loved—was returning from having settled her father in the inn. His expression was somber, and he did not smile when he met her gaze.

"Jilly, come here," Lady Redmere again called to her daughter.

Julianna turned to look at her mother, who had risen from her seat within the carriage and now filled the small door-way. She was beckoning for her to approach her carriage, waving toward her, but Jilly's feet felt frozen as they always did in those silly dreams where dragons attacked her in the hidden gills of the moors. In her dreams, she could not move, just as she could not move now.

"He was beyond cruel to have done this to you," Mr. Fitzpaine murmured. He lifted his hand as though wanting to lend her support, but Jilly backed away from him and made him stop in his tracks with brief pushing gestures of her hands.

"Pray leave me alone," she whispered. "I must think."

She heard the man she loved call her by name, sharply once, then tenderly. She knew both voices, they had become dear and familiar to her through the many miles of the journey south. She whirled around and watched the man she loved draw quickly near her. He tried to touch her, to take her arm, he said she should come into the inn, that they had much to discuss, and didn't she recall that he had said he had something he needed to say to her, but not here, and wouldn't she please come into the parlour of the Peacock?

But Jilly would have none of it as she wrenched her arm from his grasp and stepped away from him as though his touch would burn were she to permit him such a liberty again.

"Are—you—Carlton?" she managed at last, the truth beginning to crystallize in her mind. She could not quite bring his face into focus. Her eyes were blurred and burning with tears.

He nodded slowly.

"You—are—Carlton," she stated, confirming the truth by repeating it. "My—betrothed. The man who complained of marrying me the entire distance from Islington to York. Why? Why did you do this? I fell in love with you." She stopped herself and cried, "No, that is not entirely true, is it? I fell in love with Edward." She gestured wildly toward Mr. Fitzpaine and laughed a laugh which even to her own ears she could hear sounded hysterical.

"Julianna, please," he pleaded. "I made an enormous mistake."

"And what of Paris?" she cried. "Why did you tell me we had to go to Paris because otherwise *Carlton* would force me to marry him? What devilment were you brewing? I—I can only think you cherished within your wicked heart the vilest of purposes. You let me call you Edward! You let me kiss you like the stupid schoolgirl I am. Edward isn't even your name! Who are you? No, don't speak. I know who you are—a rake and a libertine, and I have been such a fool." Her voice caught on a sob. "Besides, your eyes are gray. Any fool could have seen that your eyes were gray and not in the least blue."

With that, she ran toward her mother's coach and mounted the steps quickly to fall hard upon her mama's bosom, a sob catching her throat.

Mr. Fitzpaine shut the door upon her, and though Jilly could hear Carlton protesting and calling after her, apparently Mr. Fitzpaine prevented him bodily. She heard him shout an order to the astonished postboy, commanding him to take the coach to the nearby Angel and have the horses changed there.

Lord Carlton stood beside his friend, watching his heart's desire escape into the dusty traffic of England's busiest coaching town, and for the first time in his life he knew too well what despair was. "How shall I ever win her back?" he queried.

"I haven't the least notion," Edward responded. "But this I will say—I should have stopped you in Redmere."

Carlton glanced at him and saw that Charlotte's conjecture was correct. Lord Redmere had done little more than effect a single glancing blow to Edward's right cheek which showed a strip of rough, pink flesh. "So tell me," he said, draping an arm about Edward's shoulders and ignoring the three fashionable Tabbies who eyed the two men with impertinent curiosity, "why did Lord Redmere see fit to attack you in public?"

Mr. Fitzpaine chuckled. "Besides being in his altitudes," he began, the expression on his face very much a reflection of precisely how Carlton felt, "he suspected the truth—that I have fallen in love with his wife and mean to take her to the Continent, if I can persuade her to let me."

Carlton stopped in his tracks. Glancing over his shoulder and ascertaining that the ladies behind him could not possibly hear him, he asked in a low voice, "What madness has possessed you? This is not the same man I left behind at the Angel in York."

"I had not before tumbled violently in love with a woman—any woman."

"She is married."

"I hope to persuade Redmere to divorce her."

"You would be more likely to see this town bereft of traffic over the next fifty years than to see Redmere relinquish his wife."

"I suppose you are right," Edward said. "But what of you? I cannot credit you did not come to your senses sooner than this."

"I didn't know I was in love with her until about half an hour ago," he responded. "Then I realized I'd been madly in love with her the entire time. What a complete sapskull I've been!"

"Indeed!" Edward returned.

"Well, you needn't be so quick to agree!"

Mr. Fitzpaine chuckled again, then sighed heavily. "What a coil," he remarked at last.

"Indeed."

Chapter Twenty

Jilly sat in an Empire chair by the window in her bedchamber, her hands folded and settled on her lap as they had been all morning. The room was decorated *en suite* in sky blue silk-damask—the drapes, the wing-backed chair, the shorter Empire chair of black lacquer in which she was sitting, the counterpane upon her tall four-postered bed of cherrywood, the fabric of her canopy drawn up into a rosette. A dressing table of satinwood, a generous wardrobe of burnished mahogany, and a writing table of cherrywood rested against walls painted a pale yellow and trimmed with white wood borders.

A beautiful chamber designed to promote rest and sleep.

If only she could sleep, but her dreams had been too vivid and too painful to do other than leave her exhausted by morning.

It was now past nuncheon and a tray of food, covered with a linen napkin, sat next to her. Vaguely, the aroma of fresh-baked bread, chicken, and cinnamon apples would remind her she still lived in the world, that she was in London, that she was residing in Berkeley Square, with both her parents, beneath a silent roof. But the smell of the excellent food— and all it brought to her—would disappear the moment her thoughts turned back to Carlton as they had almost perpetually since her arrival in the Metropolis three days earlier.

A terrible bout of sobbing had lasted for the first night, but had dwindled afterward to an occasional trickling of quiet tears whenever she was overcome by her memories of traveling with Carlton. A dampening of her usually vibrant spirits had followed, leaving her in a somber state of reflection in which most thankfully her parents had permitted her to remain undisturbed. She had needed this time to comprehend the enormity of Carlton's crime, as well as to grieve what was proving to be an almost unshakable attachment to him.

She sighed, staring out upon the city and the cloudy sky beyond. She had pushed back the white muslin underdrape to better view the world outside. March had disappeared and April had arrived since she'd been closeted in her room. She loved the month of April, knowing that daffodils would very soon be overrunning vast tracts of the Yorkshire countryside.

But she wasn't in Yorkshire, she was in London, her heart heavier than the storm which had passed through only the night before, bombarding her father's house with weighty raindrops. Rising from thousands of rooftops, smoke drifted from busy chimneys, combining with steam from the rain, and the dirty mist was already engulfing the city. Her mother always came home from London complaining how the soot had damaged her best gowns and bonnets. Even the buildings were pressed with the grainy residue. London fog—a perfect reflection of her heart.

Because of the heavy rainfall, however, the air was relatively clear this morning, and she could see for miles into the clouds above. Every once in a while the blue sky broke through, and then for a moment her heart would feel lighter, hopeful.

The trouble was, Julianna did not know what to do. Carlton had called each afternoon and had sent a lengthy note of apology and explanation. He had been a fool, his anger had been caused by the slanderous gossip she had been subjected to and which she had believed, but he should never have lied to her, deceived her; he loved her to the point of madness, and would she please, *please* forgive him? He had also sent several exquisite bouquets, which she had, in turn, given to the servants to enjoy in their garrets. She could not bear looking at such beauty and having the delicate roses, pansies, and lavender connected to such a vile creature as Lord Carlton.

Would she forgive him?

Today she could not.

Did she still love him? Did she want to run to him? Did she want to forgive him?

Yes, a thousand times, yes.

But she couldn't.

She swiped at unwelcome tears, as she had almost continually throughout the morning. They seeped uninvited from her eyes and down her cheeks reminding her yet again that her heart had been broken—nay, crushed—by the hand of an experienced rakehell. She still felt queasy when she thought of how completely Carlton had deceived her.

Lady Catterick had also called, along with her friends Mrs. Whenby and Mrs. Bulmer. Lady Redmere had received them, of course, but as with Carlton, Julianna had remained in her bedchamber. Their advice for Julianna was that she immediately begin going about in society, cutting a dash if she wished for it, in order to silence the multitude of wagging tongues who had quite mysteriously been fully informed of Carlton's mischief and the truly dreadful scene at Islington.

"Of course, Molly made all the difference," Lady Catterick assured Lady Redmere. "Your daughter's reputation was rescued solely by her presence. I will allow that Carlton showed sense in this instance. Only tell me, is she now become an actress by the name of Artemis Brown? I heard someone tell me of it, but I can't remember who."

Julianna smiled through her tears at thoughts of Molly. Carlton had bidden Milkmaid Molly pay her a final visit before launching her attack on Drury Lane. She thought it quite ironic that it was Molly who had found her dreams answered upon her arrival in London, and her own dreams shattered. She had received word the following day that one Artemis Brown had found employment—if nothing more than handing out playbills before each performance—at the famous theatre.

Another memory surfaced, one which followed Lady Catterick's visit.

Lady Redmere had frowned over her turtle soup that evening and posed the question, "But who was there who would have spread about the particulars of your elopement? Lady Catterick insists she said nothing and would have remained silent had word of your escapade not reached her through none other than Sally Jersey! Oh, I am come to hate the gossips, but who would have recounted that dreadful scene and Carlton's horrid conduct toward you? Who?"

Julianna had stared at her blankly, remembering in vivid detail everyone who was present—Carlton, Fitzpaine, her mother and father, of course, her mother's three friends, and another person, a woman. "There was a lady present, wearing a dark blue pelisse, I think. A very beautiful woman whom Carlton seemed to know."

Lady Redmere's hand flew to suddenly quivering lips and her eyes filled with tears. "The Garston," she breathed. "I remember it now. She was there! But how? Why?" She glanced first at Jilly in horror, and then at her husband. In spite of the presence of the butler, she ran from the room, the sound of her hurrying feet upon carpet runners heard clearly as she ran up the stairs. Even at that distance, the sound of her bedchamber door slamming shut rang in Julianna's ears.

The woman had been none other than Charlotte Garston—Carlton's reputed mistress.

Now, as she looked down at her hands, still clasped together on her lap, she watched teardrops splash upon each of her thumbs. Why had Charlotte Garston been at Islington? By arrangement with Lord Carlton? By her father's invitation?

These were questions to which she had no answers. But

THE ELUSIVE BRIDE   211

one thing she knew for certain—Charlotte Garston, with
designs upon Carlton, would have had sufficient reason to
spread the tale of the fiasco at the Peacock.

She wiped her thumbs each in turn with her kerchief, then
dabbed at her cheeks.

So Lady Catterick was willing to give her the *entree* among
the *beau monde* and thought she should cut a dash. What had
she said? That Carlton appeared to be making a cake of
himself, arriving at soirées and balls to which he had not
been invited, and inquiring after his *elusive bride*.

Julianna shuddered and covered her face with her kerchief. Lady Catterick had informed her mother of her nickname, a humiliating appellation given to her by the ton
when it came to be known—also quite mysteriously—that
she had jilted Carlton at the altar.

She laughed aloud, the tone to her laughter bordering on
hysterical. Was there anyone who had *not* been informed of
the whole of her adventures? She doubted it.

Well, if Lady Catterick thought she could get over rough
ground lightly by lifting her head high, by ignoring what was
being bandied about in every polite drawing room in all of
Mayfair, and by cutting a dash—all with her blessing!—then
she would do so.

Unclasping her hands, and letting each wrist rest upon the
arms of her chair, Julianna felt a marvelous peace descend
over her. Of course, her heart had been completely pulver-
ized like a dirty piece of laundry in the hands of a muscular
laundress, still her spirit was not in the least broken—perhaps not even perturbed.

"Storm in a teacup," she murmured, relegating Carlton's
brutal slaying of her heart to the dungeons of her soul.

With that, she rose from her chair, straightened her spine,
lifted her head, and proceeded toward her wardrobe. Once
there, she removed the prettiest of her gowns, then rang for
her maid.

But before her abigail arrived, she heard her father's
booming voice rise up through the floorboards of her bed-

chamber. Afterward, very faintly, she heard her mother's voice. The words were indistinct, but the quality was not.

Brangling again, she thought, as they had for three days—over Fitzpaine most likely, or Carlton, or both!

"Does he have to sit here while I am speaking with you?" Lord Redmere thundered, his finger pointed and wagging accusingly at Captain Beck.

Lady Redmere moved to stand behind her faithful supporter, who was sitting in a chair near the viscount's desk, and placed a hand on each of his shoulders. "He is here to protect me," she responded archly.

"Eh, what's that?" Captain Beck queried, straining to look up at her ladyship, his lazy brown eyes wide with sudden horror. "Don't like to mention it, Millie, but Redmere is known to have delivered a facer to the gentleman himself. Don't think I would be of much use to you."

"I'm sure you would acquit yourself to a nicety were I to call on you for assistance," she responded gently, giving his shoulder an encouraging pat.

Captain Beck sighed and shook his head, then slowly began leaning forward in his chair, his gaze directed toward Lord Redmere's feet.

"What are you staring at now, impudent puppy?" Lord Redmere bellowed, his hands upon each hip, his feet planted a foot apart. He stood in front of his desk and glared down at Beck's head.

Because Lord Redmere's Hessians were polished to a brilliant gloss, Captain Beck had leaned forward in his chair and was turning his head this way, then that, apparently in hopes he could catch his reflection in the viscount's boots.

"Good God!" Redmere responded with a snort. He then deliberately leaped forward with a small, jerky step and had the satisfaction of watching the captain recoil in fright.

"Oh, do stop tormenting him," Lady Redmere said, moving away from her Cicisbeo. "You avail yourself of every opportunity you can to make sport of Beck. I wish you would stop."

"I like to watch him jump," Lord Redmere countered, wearing a provoking smile. "After all, a man must have a little fun now and then, especially when his house is overrun with women and fops!"

"I have been thinking of removing myself and Jilly to a hotel," Lady Redmere presented tentatively.

"I shall help you pack your trunks, portmanteaux, and bandboxes, then," he retorted easily.

Lady Redmere pulled a face and moved to his desk, where he was standing. She had no intention, of course, of going to a hotel and adding to the scandal already surrounding herself and her daughter.

And Redmere knew as much.

She turned around, scanning the small chamber on the ground floor of the townhouse with a critical eye. The walls were covered in red silk-damask, as was the sofa in the Grecian style and the two Empire chairs opposite. Books in a glass case lined one wall of the study, and the desk was positioned opposite the single, long window. A pole, mounted horizontally above the window, with an eagle gracing the very center of the pole, had been draped with a length of yellow silk which hung elegantly to the floor on both sides of the glass and was held back by large red tassels.

Lady Redmere knew every inch of the fabric, had chosen the design for the sofa herself, had had the chairs especially made from sketches of her own making, and had had the desk sent down from Marish Hall for her husband's fortieth birthday some ten years earlier.

For a man of his years, she thought, as she turned her gaze upon him, he was still remarkably handsome. He had silvered brown hair in marked contrast to his light, clear blue eyes, and only faint lines touched his skin. She looked across the years, suddenly seeing her husband as he had been when she'd first met him in Bath, so many years ago.

Odd, that they had met in such a dull watering place as

Bath, but then, that was what had brought him to her attention in the first place. He had been like a fireworks display against the backdrop of the Upper Assembly Rooms. The whole of Bath society, including the assemblies, were presided over by a formidable set of dowdies, all holding to old traditions and a tiresome schedule for each day's activities which they adhered to strictly, as though their small lives depended upon ritual alone for sustenance.

She had been bored beyond belief, until Jack had walked in, looking like he had arrived on a lightning bolt. Even then, his voice had been thunderous. How the young ladies had quailed at his stares and abrupt compliments! But she had laughed and laughed in his company, knowing he had come to rescue her from a summer portent with so much social drudgery that within a fortnight she had kissed him a dozen times and had accepted his hand in marriage.

"Millicent," he said, taking a step near her and disturbing her dreamy reverie. "What are you thinking about that your eyes are shining as they have not in years?"

"Oh!" Lady Redmere cried, feeling a blush creep up her cheeks and wondering at her silliness. "Nothing of consequence—er, that is, Mr. Fitzpaine's delightful company, if you must know." She did not know why she lied to him, but she did not want him to know that any part of her still held him in affection.

"I see," he responded, clearly disappointed. "So that's the way of it, then."

Lady Redmere planted her gaze upon the *W* cut of his lapel and nodded.

"I trust you will be discreet, then," he said, a familiar, brutal edge to his voice.

At that, she lifted her gaze and met his squarely. "As discreet as you have been," she responded curtly. She watched his expression change abruptly, his nostrils flaring, and his lips turning a strange bluish hue against the sudden reddening cast to his complexion. Instinctively, she took a step backward.

"How dare you!" he cried. "The devil take it, Millicent, you always were as birdwitted as you were beautiful. Do you think I could have loved anyone when I was always so smitten with you even my friends—hang-it-all, I'm going to my club!"

With that he was gone, not turning back once to look at her or to see her hand outstretched to him as he drew the door shut behind him in a hard slam.

She remained where she was, leaning against his desk, her hands trembling as she placed them upon her cheeks. A terrible sob rose in her chest. How very much she wanted it to be true—that he had always been faithful to her. But she knew better. Everyone said he had pursued Mrs. Garston diligently until she had reluctantly become his mistress. Everyone—Lady Catterick, Mrs. Whenby, Mrs. Bulmer—everyone of consequence.

"I'm glad he's gone," Captain Beck said, interupting the unhappy train of her thoughts. "How have you borne his temper all these years, my poor Millie?"

"What temper?" she queried, absently, her gaze fixed to the door her husband had so recently slammed. "Oh, that. Well, that is just Redmere. He bellows like some men breathe or pick at their curls with chicken feathers. He means no harm by it, and indeed, he has never given me the least cause all these years to fear that he might do me injury—far from it. He has quite a tender heart, if you must know."

"What? Redmere?"

"Yes, Redmere. But he is something like a lake of fire, isn't he?"

"More like a volcano, if you ask me."

"Yes, that, too. I just wish I didn't love him so much."

Captain Beck did not respond to her last remark. When she finally tore her gaze from the study door, she found her Cicisbeo staring at the back of his pocketwatch and picking at his black curls with his featherless feather.

Seeing that her companion was absorbed in his task, Lady

Redmere felt for the missive in the pocket of her apricot-silk morning gown. Carefully, she removed the fine parchment, turning her back on the captain at the same time, and carefully spread it open on the desk now in front of her. The sonnet began with a dedication, *"To a lady who brings the sun forth on stormy days."*

She sighed, picking up the poem and pressing it to her bosom. Rounding the desk, she glanced nervously at the captain. When she saw that he was still fully engaged in his task, she let the paper fall by the chair in front of the desk. Looking down at it, she could see that it had fallen face-up, and even from that distance she was fully able to read Mr. Fitzpaine's signature.

A few minutes later, she informed Beck it was time for their daily excursion to Hookham's lending library.

She left the sonnet on the floor, where hopefully her husband would discover it before the servants.

Chapter Twenty-One

Three weeks had passed since her arrival in London.

Three long, extraordinary, exhilarating weeks.

Three exceedingly frustrating weeks.

Julianna brushed her fan against her cheek. The elegant creation—fashioned at no less an establishment than Madame Charbonneau, Lady Catterick's dressmakers—comprised several tips of small, white, soft ostrich feathers. She stood partially concealed behind a palm tree—one of many in Mrs. Whenby's ballroom, all collected at great expense in order to lend the chamber an exotic ambience.

Screens, which adorned the walls of the long chamber, had been painted by an artisan of no small talent to depict Oriental and Indian scenes. Chairs, which lined the same walls, were made of beechwood, but carved and painted to look like bamboo. Swags of bright fuschia and aqua, which had been draped across the walls in a sea of color or swagged at an angle across the white stucco ceiling, were of a fine, floating silk. The combined effect was mesmerizing, particularly since Mrs. Whenby had requested that her female guests lightly reflect the exotic theme by wearing turbans and that the gentlemen wear brightly colored silk sashes about their waists.

A costume ball, in part.

The effect was enchanting.

And Julianna had been entranced by the whole of it, not

less so because the full participation of the guests added to the general feel of excitement in the air. Beneath the glow of three fully lit chandeliers, the dancers whirled and turned to the elegant strains of the waltz until the yellows, blues, pinks, greens, and lavenders of the partial costumes formed into a living panorama of Eastern magic.

Her heart burned within her as the flow of color and the hint of other lands invaded her imagination. She closed her eyes and saw the ocean stretched out before her, she felt the ship rolling upon the waves, her hands clutching the railing, her face lifted to the sea-mist. Just once, she wanted to be in strange foreign places, to see people whose skin color was rich and dark, to smell the scent of heavy monsoon rains as they descended upon forests decadent with life. To hear animals she had never before seen roar and bellow in the distance, invisible to the eye, shrouded by jungle growth.

"I believe the first time I noticed Carlton was making a cake of himself," Lady Catterick's nasal voice whispered in fine tattlemongering fashion, "was at your *fête*, Henrietta, when he stood beside the columns in your entrance hall and watched Miss Redmere descend your staircase—he ignored every lady present and not once did he take his eyes from her."

Julianna was ripped from her reverie in quite the most startling manner possible. The mere mention of Carlton's name was enough to rivet her attention to the speaker, but the joining of his name with her own brought her crashing abruptly from the spell of her thoughts, her heart straining to hear more.

The spreading leaves of a large palm tree separated Julianna from Lady Catterick. Peering between the pointed fronds, she could see the back of Lady Catterick's orange silk and paisley turban, entwined with a thin chain of amber jewels. The black tips of her wig were visible on the back of her neck. On either side of her, in triumvirate fashion, Mrs. Whenby and Mrs. Bulmer attended the most fashionable of all London hostesses.

This much Jilly had learned since her arrival. None were more courted than these three ladies. Their pronouncements—besides those of the several patronesses of Almack's Assembly rooms—were heeded and bowed down to above all others. She thought that even if the Queen herself were to contradict these ladies, her opinions would be disregarded entirely in favor of Lady Catterick, Mrs. Whenby, and Mrs. Bulmer.

She remembered the incident to which her ladyship had been referring as if it had happened only the day before, instead of nearly three weeks earlier, when she had made her debut in society. She had begun her descent down the stairs, but after taking three steps, she noticed much to her chagrin that Lord Carlton was present. When he caught her gaze, he deliberately stepped away from the pillar he had been supporting, his gray eyes intent upon capturing her interest. He appeared quite magnificent in black and white evening dress, his neckcloth tied as always to perfection, his black hair combed in the loose manner that always reminded her of the *Corsair*, his features as handsome as ever—much too handsome to lend her comfort.

Her knees had trembled so. And even though she had determined to ignore him entirely—except for what civility decreed necessary—by the time she found herself halfway down the stairs, she had been drawn to meet his gaze by what she was certain had been the sheer strength of his will. She could not have kept from looking at him if she had wanted to. It was as though he was trying to speak to her mind through the force of his thoughts. A whispering had gone up all around the staircase, and she had only been snatched away from his gaze when she heard her nickname, *the elusive bride,* being bandied about.

All her former resentment returned to her.

Thank heavens dear Bartholomew Whenby—Mrs. Whenby's offspring—had been stationed at the bottom of the stairs, ready to rescue her from Carlton's presence. He whisked her away to the ballroom and immediately led her into a group forming for the quadrille.

She wished Lady Catterick's remark had not reminded her of that moment, yet strangely enough, she longed to hear more—more of Carlton. She pressed the soft feathers of her fan against her face as though in doing so she could press back the heat which was causing her cheeks to tingle with anticipation. She leaned into the palm tree, straining to hear more, and in doing so one prickly, tough leaf pushed her white silk turban slightly askew. The turban was alternately banded with dark green silk, and three feet of the white silk had been left free that she might loop it gracefully beneath her chin and over the opposite shoulder. She straightened her turban and gently readjusted the elegant loop.

"Speak," she commanded the ladies in front of her in an inaudible whisper. She longed to hear more, but would they oblige her?

"At a ball two nights later—the Duchess of York's, I believe," Mrs. Whenby chirped, "Carlton stood up with Miss Redmere twice but refused every partner presented to him in quite the rudest fashion. He then leaned against the wall, like a tiresome youth still in his salad days, and scowled at Julianna quite *à la Byron*. Really, it was entrancing! I only wonder how long our *elusive bride* will be able to withstand his assault."

There was that dreadful nickname again!

Julianna watched Mrs. Whenby's fan appear and begin a quick succession of flutters upon that lady's dark blue silk turban as though her speech had caused her some agitation. She then continued, "What an extraordinary man he is—so very handsome. If I were but a young girl again—oh dear, oh dear!—but *she* will never have him back. He certainly ruined her pride! Why is it no one ever thinks a woman has pride, that being proud of one's position or character or strength is purely a man's domain? I would never be able to forgive him for all that transpired from York to the Peacock!"

"Nor I!" Mrs. Bulmer agreed in her commanding voice.

Julianna remembered seeing Lord Carlton propping up the wall in the Duchess of York's ballroom, just as Mrs. Whenby had described. How very odd she had felt whirling by him in Horace Bulmer's arms, and seeing Carlton's expression so dark and somber, his gray eyes fixed upon her as though he saw no one but her. She had been entirely unable to listen to Horace's prattling about the fine pair he had purchased only that morning at Tattersall's. Even when she had torn her gaze from Carlton, and stared intently at an emerald stickpin tucked into the folds of Mr. Bulmer's neckcloth, all she could see before her was what had been burned into her mind's eye—Carlton's face, his pose as he folded his arms arrogantly over his chest, his gray eyes watching her, watching her, watching her.

Julianna's attention was drawn back to the present by Mrs. Bulmer's commanding voice, lowered to a hoarse whisper. "But did either of you, about a fortnight past, witness Carlton's folly at Vauxhall Gardens?"

"Of course!" her two friends chimed.

"Oh, my dears," she continued, her voice quite low. "I have never before witnessed any man go to such lengths in his pursuit of a lady. He all but forced her to dance with him, and his costume—so absurd, but not inappropriate, I thought. He was dressed as a jester, with bells on his hat and upon the toes of the most ridiculous green slippers I have ever seen. He didn't even wear a mask—well, at least his half-mask hardly kept his identity a secret. And he followed her about the paths even when my darling Horace led her toward the river for the fireworks display. Of course I can forgive him everything except for making terrible sport of my son, saying he looked like an ostrich with arms!"

Lady Catterick laughed outright and said, "You did not tell us he said so. How very droll, for he did resemble something of a large bird!"

"I see no humor in such an insult at all!"

"But you must admit," Mrs. Whenby said, "Horace did

not quite appear to advantage in a short white-and-gold tunic, his thin legs covered only in blue tights, and the ensemble topped by a narrow hat draped with three monstrous ostrich plumes. I never did quite comprehend the effect he intended to create. And his legs—like two walking-sticks! You ought to be very grateful Brummell brought pantaloons into fashion. I remember when I was a girl my mother used to warn me against giving any attention to a man who did not have a good leg. In her day, it was considered a mark of excellent breeding—"

"—And I always thought your mother had the queerest notions!" Mrs. Bulmer retorted. "A good leg, indeed. Now my mother spoke only of the necessity of avoiding young men with freckles—"

Mrs. Whenby gasped. "How dare you say that to me as though Bartholomew's freckles are of any significance whatsoever. Besides, he hasn't half as many since we began applying crushed strawberries at night—why are you laughing? Let me tell you—"

Julianna stopped listening. She certainly had no wish to hear the ladies brangling over their respective sons. Besides, their conversation had quite overset her. She could not help but recall to mind how truly absurd Carlton had appeared in a court jester's costume with only the barest half-mask to conceal his face. Even a half-wit could see who he was. She sighed. A masquerade at Vauxhall had seemed just the thing to give her spirits a lift. Instead, Carlton's persistence had worried her into a fevered state, so that by the time she had begged her mama to take her home, her head hurt her exceedingly. She had taken to her bed for two days, not even a visit from a surgeon relieving what she well knew to be a severe confusion of her heart and mind.

She had written Carlton a missive and begged him to leave her in peace. She reiterated her decision that she would never consent to renew their betrothal. How many times had he again offered his apologies to her since she had come out in London society? A dozen, a score? How many times had

he professed so great a love for her that he would do anything she required of him *except* leave her in peace? Twice he
had been on his knees before her. And every day he sent her
flowers, so many that her father's home smelled like mid-
summer in the sweetest of moorland dells.

But the worst episode of all had occurred at the museum
only the afternoon before. She knew Turner was displaying
a number of his magnificent watercolors, and she had longed
to see them. How Carlton had discovered her destination
she would never know, though she suspected he had bribed
either her father's butler or the housekeeper—both of whom
seemed inclined to approve of his suit.

She had been standing in front of a painting, *Hannibal
Crossing the Alps,* she thought, when he had come up behind
her and whispered his love for her in her ear. Perhaps it was
in part because she had been enraptured by the brilliance of
the painting before her, or because the pure physical sensation of having his breath on her ear sent waves of chills down
her side, but whatever the case, she had lost her balance and
fallen backward into him. He had caught her up in an
embrace, holding her fast for a long moment, as though she
had swooned into his arms. Only after a full minute did he
lead her to a chair in another chamber.

She could only stare at him for the longest time as he knelt
beside her, begging to know if she was well, if she required
her maid to seek a carriage, if he ought to escort her home
himself, and would she permit him the honor of seeing her
safely returned to her father?

She bit her lip, feeling tears burn her eyes at the memory.
She had whispered to him, "You said that once to me before,
or something very much like it. Will you never comprehend
that my love for you has died, that it perished in Islington
when I learned the truth? Why is it, my lord, that you refuse
to see that your conduct has incurred consequences you
cannot alter?"

"I will never believe that your love has died," he had said,
possessing himself of her hands and holding them fast. "I

most surely can comprehend that your trust in me, your faith in the goodness of my character, has been ruined, but not your love. I see your love in your eyes, Julianna."

"You are mistaken," she had responded dully. How dead she had felt inside at that moment. She remembered having added, "You would do well to seek the wife you require before it is too late. I know that you must be married by the end of April, but I cannot be the one to help you."

He had said nothing, but she had watched the impassioned light in his eyes dim and then disappear. As he left the gallery, he did not look back at her, and his usual brisk gait had dwindled to a slow, deliberate walk.

Perhaps he would begin to accept her refusal of his advances.

She gave herself a strong shake, trying to let the memories drain from her mind. Though the images disappeared, somehow the sentiments they had culled forth remained darkly within her.

She had been enjoying the company of at least a dozen fine men—some quite young, like Bartholomew Whenby, still in possesion of his youthful and forgivable freckles, and some older, like both Horace Bulmer and even Lady Catterick's eldest son and heir to an earldom, Edgar. Beyond these three, several fortune hunters had already—much to her amusement—offered for her hand in marriage. One, upon her refusal, had even said, "You *are* quite *elusive*, Miss Redmere."

Again, the train of her thoughts was interrupted by Lady Catterick's voice, "I only wonder that he has not yet completed his folly by seeking vouchers for Almack's."

"It is curious that he has not done so," Mrs. Whenby chirped.

"Why do you say that?" Mrs. Bulmer argued, "When he has refused for the past eight years to attend our assemblies because he can't bear to be bound by the least of society's chains, and never could be."

"I don't believe any of the patronesses would be inclined

to grant him vouchers," Lady Catterick said. "Not after it became known he had intended to elope to Paris with our poor Jilly. I only wonder how that part of his scheme got about. I certainly said nothing to anyone, and I am fully persuaded neither of you did as well! But who?"

The three ladies were silent apace, and Julianna found herself wondering the same. From first having come to learn that Mrs. Garston had been present in Islington on that fateful day three weeks ago, she had always considered it a possibility that the widow had been involved in the spreading of the gossip. But such was not Charlotte Garston's reputation. The widow was accounted a very discreet person by everyone.

The truth was, Charlotte had always believed that the whole of the gossip had been delivered to the waiting ears of the *haut* ton, in its entirety, by the ladies now standing on the other side of the palm tree—by Lady Catterick, Mrs. Whenby, and Mrs. Bulmer. But it would appear that they had agreed on a certain amount of restraint where her escapade was concerned—that is, the part which caused the strongest part of the scandal, Carlton's intention to take her to Paris. But if these ladies had honored their mutual agreement, and Mrs. Garston had been as discreet as she was reputed to be, who, then, had revealed the rest?

Mrs. Whenby queried softly, "Who would have been so completely without conscience as to have imparted the wickedest portion of Carlton's scheme?"

Julianna watched Lady Catterick and Mrs. Bulmer shake their heads slowly. She no longer believed a one of them was guilty.

Mrs. Whenby queried more softly still. "Does either of you suspect—"

"—Hush," Lady Catterick whispered in return. "Charlotte Garston may be many things, but she would never bring shame to herself by doing so. Never!"

"Who, then?" Mrs. Bulmer demanded to know. "Who would have been so cruel?"

All three ladies clucked their tongues.

"Oh, my!" Lady Catterick suddenly cried out. "Do look who is leading *the Garston* out!"

"Carlton!" her friends breathed.

Julianna pressed down the palm leaf in front of her, opening up her vista to a greater portion of the ballroom, and felt her heart collapse quite inexplicably within her. Well, she had told Carlton to find another wife. And here was one who would marry him in a trice, were he to speak the word. Of that she was fully convinced. After all, it was still generally believed she was his mistress. Though he had denied it—while posing as Edward Fitzpaine—his deceit had given her no reason to believe Charlotte Garston was not his fancy-piece.

"Since his return to London, I don't recall his having danced with the widow," Mrs. Whenby cried. "Do either of you?"

"No!" the remaining pair breathed.

"He means to marry her," Mrs. Bulmer stated baldly.

"I believe you are right," Lady Catterick agreed. "The terms of his inheritance have certainly crammed him into a corner. But whatever will become of Julianna? Oh, I see my dear Edgar is waving at me. You will excuse me, my dears, but I must speak with him."

Mrs. Whenby chirped, "And there is Bartholomew. Oh, dear, I *do* hope he does not mean to ask that dull creature to stand up with him again. I wonder if Miss Redmere has given away all her dances yet. You will excuse me, Hetty, won't you?"

But Henrietta Bulmer had already disappeared and was forcing her way across the busy ballroom floor, where a country dance was now forming. Her intended object was quite obviously her own son, Horace, the ostrich.

Julianna was not surprised, when, some five minutes later, all three gentlemen descended upon her and begged her to spare each a dance. Just as she was agreeing to a quadrille with Mr. Whenby, a country dance with Mr. Bulmer, and a waltz with the future earl of Catterick, Lord Carlton came within the range of her view. Mrs. Garston clung to his arm.

Julianna felt compelled to look at him, and received for her effort a polite nod of his head as he passed by.

She felt a terrible panic overtake her. Suddenly she was back on a sailing ship, caught in a whirlpool. The ship began spinning around and around. How dizzy she felt. How frightened!

The sensation passed only when Carlton and his widow were well out of sight. She returned her attention to the vapid flirtations of three men sent to do their mothers' bidding. A few minutes more, and the ostrich led her away.

Chapter Twenty-Two

Lord Redmere followed his daughter and young Mr. Bulmer into the ballroom. He watched her with considerable pride as she quite gracefully—and when had she become such an exquisite young woman?—gently tugged at the soft length of white silk from about her neck. He watched it slide forward off her shoulder to drape elegantly down the front of her white ballgown while she took up her place opposite her partner for the country dance.

She was a perfect vision in white, the purity of her gown enhanced by her red hair dangling in exotic long tresses from beneath her turban and fringed across her forehead in a riot of delicate curls which framed her beautiful face.

Was this his daughter? Was this the fearless young chit who had taken to the sea as though she had been born of it, like Venus herself? Was this the hoydenish young lady who had traversed the moors in the company of her quite brutish and platter-faced nurse, and with several of his hunting dogs at heel? When was it she had become as comfortable in a ballroom as she was either on the back of her horse or tramping across desolate moorland?

He clasped his hands behind his back and swelled his chest with pride.

Damn, but she was the image of her mother when he had first met her in Bath! For that reason it was easy for him to draw his mind back in time. He could see Millicent as she

was in that curst Assembly Room, in the dullest city ever
created on God's earth, surrounded by beaux, chatting politely first to one, then to another. He knew she had been
bored beyond speaking, though she'd betrayed it only in the
way her eyes would slide away from the young men while
they spoke to her of trivialities and her bosom would rise
faintly in the smallest of sighs. Lord, but they were all such
sapskulls that they could not see her complete disinterest in
what they perceived of as their clever sallies and flirtations.
A pack of harebrained gudgeons, the lot!

But he had seen her boredom, and the moment he could,
he assaulted her, forcing one of her beaux to relinquish his
claim upon her hand for a quadrille. And then, instead of
leading her onto the floor, he drew her into the octagonal
entrance hall of the Assembly Rooms, where he proceeded
to flirt quite outrageously with her. Damn, he even kissed
her!

And instead of being frightened of him, why, he'd never
heard a young lady laugh so much in all his life, giving him
answer for answer, for every bold and brash thing he said or
did. He tumbled in love with her right then, and he had
never stopped loving her for a minute since! Never!

He watched his daughter commence going down the
dance. Her mother had instructed her well. She danced
delightfully and was able at the same time to carry on a
reasonable conversation with even a blushing Mr. Bulmer.
Another fortnight, and he supposed Mr. Bulmer would be
begging a private audience with him. With thoughts of the
several silly pups he had already turned away from his door,
he could not help but wonder yet again how his family had
come to such a pass as this. Both his wife and his daughter
had been involved in one of the worst scandals of the season,
indeed, of the decade, he thought, but with thanks to Lady
Catterick, who had sponsored Julianna amidst a veritable
storm of gossip, the initial impact of his daughter's journey
from York to London in the company of Lord Carlton had

dissipated. Only a few aging dowagers, too high in the instep for his blood anyway, refused to acknowledge her.

His gaze drifted from his daughter and the now-stumbling Mr. Bulmer and chanced upon the form of his wife. He felt his heart leap within him because for just a moment he thought she might have been watching him. But since she gave no evidence of being aware of his presence, he thought it likely that his eyesight—which was not as it was a few years ago—might have been failing him.

Then he chanced to see her partner and anger flooded him all over again. Edward Fitzpaine! Dash it all! Their names were being linked together constantly, and as he looked at them, his fists balled up as though they had a will of their own. The tide of gossip now swelled one day out of two in the direction of his wife and Mr. Fitzpaine.

How dared he continue to make his wife the object of his attentions? Particularly when it was well known that Edward Fitzpaine did not dally in the petticoat line—not one whit— which made the *on-dits* all that much more infectious.

Mr. Fitzpaine, it would seem, had fallen in love.

He felt nervous suddenly as he watched Fitzpaine. It was one thing for a man to seek an illicit relationship with a married lady, one meant to be conducted in secrecy. Frequently, such relationships were so private that they were discovered only when they ended and one party or the other in a fit of pique exposed a longstanding affair which would shake the *haut* ton to its lascivious core.

But Fitzpaine clearly had no such designs.

That he was besotted with his wife even a baconbrained idiot could well see.

Divorce was even part and parcel of the rumors he had heard. Well, if Fitzpaine thought he would grant his wife a divorce, then he was as halfwitted as any moonling that had ever lived.

He had even found a sonnet of Fitzpaine's lying beside his desk and dedicated to his wife. What had the absurd title been? Something about *storms* and *sunshine*. And in the content of the poem, he had compared Millie's eyes to the jewels in heaven's gate.

Good God! The jewels in heaven's gate!

He couldn't abide poetry—it was all stuff and nonsense!

Why was it, then, that after handing the sonnet back to Millicent, after scoffing at her, and after watching her cheeks turn a dark, angry pink, he had swaggered off to his study and turned his hand at a couplet or two himself?

He had wadded up his several efforts, of course, and had imbibed more brandy than any man ought to, only to awaken at dawn to find himself slumped over his desk. He was behaving as absurdly as his wife.

When the country dance ended, he watched Mr. Fitzpaine bow elegantly over Millicent's hand and place a long, tender kiss upon her fingers. She seemed embarrassed, he thought, as he narrowed his eyes at the sight before him, trying to bring her face clearly into focus. Why, then, didn't she force him to release her hand? Instead, she stepped toward him and with a close, intimate movement slid her hand up his arm and took his elbow, holding it very tightly. She then looked up at him and smiled and the expression on her face caused Lord Redmere to feel as though a wave had just crashed through his brain, leaving a trail of gritty water pulling hard from behind as the tide swept back out to sea.

My God, he thought, his head reeling. *She fancies herself in love with him!*

An hour later, Julianna sat across from her parents as they left Grosvenor Square and headed back toward Berkeley Square. Her mother stared out one window of the traveling chariot, and her father stared out the other. Julianna found herself speaking as many inconsequentials as she could summon quickly to mind in an attempt to soften the blows of the silent battle going on between the two people on earth she loved most.

"Did I tell you, Mama, that Elizabeth was delivered safely

of a son? I received word only this morning. Her confinement took place Sunday last, I believe. She speaks of nothing but the most profound joy at the birth of her second child!"

"I am so happy for Elizabeth," her mother responded with the barest of smiles. "Such a deserving young woman."

So the attempt at introducing that subject ended.

The early morning hour swirled about the coach-and-pair in patches of dark mist and dark night, relieved only by the appearance and disappearance at fairly regular intervals of gas-lamps.

"How very modern London is become," Julianna offered again. "Imagine, gas-lamps!"

Her father grunted and yawned.

In the intermittent splashes of light as the carriage bumped over the cobbles, she could see that both her parents had taken on their most mulish expressions.

They are behaving like children, she thought, suddenly irate.

Her anger led her to speak again, and this time not of household news and city improvements. "Mr. Fitzpaine looked quite dashing tonight, I thought. He is such a gentleman, and his manners—I vow, Mama, there is not another man in England as well mannered as he."

Her pronouncement had exactly the effect she'd hoped for. Lady Redmere lifted her chin triumphantly and for the first time since entering the coach, turned to look at her husband. Lord Redmere's complexion had become a beautiful purple in hue. First he scowled fiercely at Julianna, then he turned the full force of his anger upon his wife.

"How grateful I am that our good daughter has kindly brought forward a *subject* I was reluctant to address. But since she has—"

"—Mr. Fitzpaine is *not* a subject," Lady Redmere countered, narrowing her eyes slightly and joining battle with all the deftness of twenty years of marriage. "Except to the crown. Otherwise, I would say he is a gentleman, in every possible connotation."

Even above the sound of the carriage rattling on its springs and axles and wheels and above the clip-clop, clip-clop of the tired horses plodding their way in the middle of the night toward their stables, Lord Redmere's teeth could be heard grinding together. It was to Julianna's ears like hearing his temper sizzling in a burning-hot pan. She lifted her feathered fan to cover her lips and smiled in pure amusement at the sight of her parents squabbling like little children.

Lord Redmere continued, "As I was saying, *my dear*, it is generally spoken of everywhere that your Mr. Fitzpaine, ever the gentleman, is making a complete cake of himself, fawning over you as though you were a schoolgirl instead of a matron of forty and a mere breath or two away from becoming a grandmama. I think he is the most ridiculous man I have ever known."

Lady Redmere was not impressed. "Indeed, and is that why, three years ago, you said to me that were he in possession of even a modest fortune he would make Jilly an agreeable husband?"

"I never said so!" he cried, horrified. But even in the darkness of the coach, Julianna could see that he was telling a whisker.

"Oh, yes, you did. We were at the opera, and Mr. Fitzpaine and Lord Carlton visited us. You said his manners were impeccable and he had perhaps the finest bow you'd ever witnessed."

"You are mistaken," he responded, folding his arms over his chest and scowling more heavily still. "But having given the matter a great deal of thought—particularly in light of our daughter's recent conduct—I must forbid you to continue this flirtation with a man ten years your junior. You are making a complete fool of yourself!"

"He is three-and-thirty, Jack, and I will flirt with Mr. Fitzpaine whether you forbid it or not. *You* can have no scruples upon the matter, and as for showing consideration for the family honor at this late hour, I can only suggest to you that you would have been a great deal better served to have curbed your own appetites last year when *Mrs. Garston* was fairly sitting in your pocket at every turn. Now perhaps you will comprehend a little with what impatience I witnessed your *flirtations* with her."

Lord Redmere opened his mouth to speak, then clamped his lips together as though he thought her remark made some sense. "You will never forgive me, will you? Even if I am innocent," he responded testily.

"Your conscience must determine my answer," was all she said.

When they arrived home, Julianna remained in the entrance hall as she watched her mother mount the stairs. Whatever was to become of her parents? she wondered yet again.

Her father entered the house last and took up a place at Julianna's elbow. When she heard him sigh, she turned to look at him and saw that he, too, was watching his wife ascend the stairs. In his eyes, Julianna saw an expression that took her completely by surprise. Her father was worried.

"I have made a terrible mull of it, haven't I, pet?" he said.

Julianna slipped her arm about his and said, "Perhaps you might try a little kindness. Mama is of just such a temperament that I know a little kindness with her can make a journey of miles."

"Kindess has never been my strong suit," he responded.

"I know," she said sympathetically, giving his arm a squeeze. "But only a very little is required, you know. And there is one thing more—you do know that whatever happens, I will always adore my papa."

At that he turned to look at her, his expression softening as he placed his hand over hers and gave it a squeeze. "I failed you, Jilly," he said. "I knew the betrothal was a terrible mistake at the time and that your mother was in such a state over my supposed infidelity that she could not see the error she was committing. I knew full well Carlton had no wish to marry you or anyone—at least, not at that time. He was forced to because of the terms of his inheritance. No man should marry unless he wishes very much for it. Will you ever forgive me for not putting a stop to the betrothal when I had the chance?"

"Of course," she replied quietly. "I just wish—oh, but it is such a dreadful coil! Papa, what do you make of Carlton? He used me so cruelly, yet he has apologized a score of times and—and—oh, the devil take it, I don't know what to think of him anymore!"

"You are fond of him, then?" he asked, frowning at her.

"Papa," she said, tears brimming in her eyes. "I tumbled very deeply in loved with a man named Edward—not with Lord Carlton. Yet it was Carlton. He deceived me so dreadfully—how can I ever trust him again?"

"I don't know," he responded gravely. "Not that I haven't given the whole extraordinary business a thorough going-over in my mind. I daresay none of us can quite comprehend what provoked Carlton to deceive you, to lie to you—in essence, to kidnap you. But life for Carlton has been quite different than for the majority of us—those with fortune and rank, I mean. Why, the trying terms of his inheritance alone would be enough to send most of us to Bedlam, but add to that the fact that he is devilishly handsome and generally agreeable in the drawing room, which I am not, and the truly astounding fact that he is worth every tuppence of thirty thousand pounds a year, and you've a man who's courted by society more for his assets than for his character. Good God, Julianna, when I think of his vast holdings and estates—well, sometimes I don't wonder if that is why I didn't make a push to end the betrothal. You don't know how many fine caps have been set for him. You've not been to his estates in Hampshire, or to his townhouse here, but let me tell you, there is nothing like his country house in all the south of England—artwork of every description, the gardens a triumph of design—Repton, you know. Add to all this a peerage, and he very soon became the greatest prize of them all. Every rejection of a lady prompted a new round of some of the most wretched gossip you could ever imagine hearing. To own the truth, I don't know any man who would not have been sadly affected by so much unwelcome attention for so many years."

Julianna sighed. "But why couldn't he have told me the truth initially, when I came to him at the Angel?"

Lord Redmere cocked his head slightly. "Look at it from his perspective, pet: how else would you expect a man of his stamp to conduct himself when you come to his inn, on the day of your wedding—with the intention of crying off!—and then divulge to the very same man all the gossip you had been hearing about him? I don't doubt that in the same circumstances I would have been instantly in the boughs and perhaps would have gone off half-cocked, just as he did!"

Julianna looked away from her father, trying to recall her initial conversation with Carlton. He had seemed piqued more than once while she explained her circumstances to him. She hadn't really thought what her arrival at the Angel Inn might have meant to him, but now she couldn't help but see the whole of it from a new vantage point.

Still, he had so wickedly deceived her.

Glancing back at her father, she proceeded down a different track entirely. "Did you want to marry Mama?" she asked.

He lifted his silvered brows. "Well, I suppose you will not credit it, after all that has transpired in the past twelvemonth, but I wanted to marry your mother more than life itself. She had become as indispensable to my happiness as breathing is to life. I still love her, Jilly. I have never stopped loving her."

"Then why won't you make amends?"

He dropped his gaze to stare harshly at the black-and-white tiles of the entrance hall. "She hurt me terribly," he confessed.

Julianna was stunned to hear him say as much. "I don't understand. Given the circumstances, I would think it more likely that it was you who hurt her."

He turned hard, blue eyes upon her and said, "Do you believe the gossip, too, then?"

Julianna was about to respond sincerely that indeed, she did, but something in his angry stare held a veiled meaning and she knew, without having to be told further, that her father was innocent. He had always been innocent.

The strangest of sensations flowed through her—of tremendous relief and happiness. She released his arm only to grab hold of him and hug him. "Papa!" she cried. "Oh, indeed, yes, you have made a terrible mull of it, silly man!"

He held her fast in return for a very long time. When at last he released her, Julianna could see that tears were in his eyes. "I did not expect to feel this way by having one of you believe me. My dear Jilly, thank you. Thank you ever so much!"

She hugged him again and together, arms slung about each other's waists, they began mounting the stairs.

"Carlton came to see me the day after your arrival here," he began quietly, reverting to their former subject.

"You never told me as much," she said, again surprised.

"It seemed pointless when you were so unhappy and he had used you so ill. I cannot excuse his conduct toward you, Julianna, but I feel I must ask you something."

"What?"

"Are you in love with him?"

"He is a monster."

He paused on the stairs and forced her for a moment to look at him. "Julianna, he made a terrible mistake. He did not eat his children."

"Papa!" she cried, laughing. "What a dreadful thing to say! All right, I suppose it is a bit harsh to say he is a monster. A beast, then."

"Much better," Lord Redmere responded facetiously, again drawing her up the stairs. "But tell me, did you not permit him to kiss you? He told me he had kissed you no fewer than three times on your journey together."

Julianna felt her cheeks burn. "I am ashamed to admit it is true," she confessed, deeply embarrassed. "I am only shocked he said as much to you. Oh, Papa, I wish I could undo the whole of it. I behaved so very foolishly—and he hurt me so badly. When I think of the many lies he told me, and of how scurrilous his motives were, I am sick at heart." A sob caught in her throat, and her father pulled her closer to him as they continued up the stairs.

"There, there. I did not mean to make you cry. Only, I have known you a very long time, and I am persuaded that you would never have permitted him to kiss you had you not fallen violently in love with him."

"I fell in love with a phantom—a Mr. Fitzpaine who did not exist—does not exist."

"Yet sometimes you watch him, Julianna, as though you are wishing away your every dream, your every hope of happiness. Make certain of your heart. Well, you must settle this in your own way, but remember that if he marries elsewhere, he is gone from you forever."

"I know, Papa. I know."

Once the landing was achieved, he walked her to her bedchamber door, where her maid awaited her. As the sleepy servant helped her undress in the dim glow of a single lit candle, Jilly found her mind in the worst confusion. She wished her father had not spoken highly of Carlton. She wanted to continue to despise him, but between his penitent behavior and her growing conviction he was not the monster she believed him to be, she found it was becoming increasingly difficult to hold Carlton in complete abhorrence.

When she was settled between the sheets, and the candle has blown out, Julianna tried to make sense of the full scope of her sentiments, tried to reason away her disquiet, but only one thought rose above the rest—Carlton had to marry within three days or he would lose his fortune, estates, and title forever. She knew Mrs. Garston was his choice, and howevermuch Julianna might have disapproved of her previous liaison with Carlton, she was an elegant, beautiful woman. She would reign over his world quite regally.

Why, then, did the thought of his marriage to Charlotte Garston leave her feeling as though *her* world was tumbling down about her ears?

Chapter Twenty-Three

"It is very kind of you to escort me home, Carlton," Mrs. Garston said, pulling her red satin cloak, lined with an exquisite sable fur, more closely about her shoulders. "But do I much mistake the matter when I say that you are fairly blue-deviled?"

Carlton turned from looking out the window of his town coach and only with the strongest of efforts refrained from sighing deeply. To say he was blue-deviled hardly came near to the sense of despair he felt. He knew every last bit of his future happiness was slipping away from him with each ticking of the clock.

Good God, he had only three days to marry or lose the life to which he had been bred. Every instinct within him forbade he let the viscountcy slip from him. He knew what he had to do regardless of Julianna's disposition toward him, and that knowledge forced him to shift toward Charlotte Garston and say, "You are a very intelligent woman and I have admired you for a long time. I can make no pretense to you where my sentiments lie, for even Edward has laughed at my folly. The state of my heart set completely aside, if my efforts fail, can you tell me the disposition of your own, if not heart, then willingness to align yourself with my estates?"

He watched a curious expression flit in a surprised roll over the widow's eyes as she cast her gaze to her lap. There she turned a bracelet of rubies thoughtfully about her gloved wrist. "I have so long waited to hear your addresses, my lord, that now receiving them and in so remarkable a manner, I find my mind to be a whirl of confusion. You cannot be unaware of my desires regarding marriage to you, but I believe until this moment—howevermuch I was aware that your pursuit of Miss Redmere was as dogged as it was intense—I don't believe I comprehended the depth of your love for her. May I inquire whether you still have hopes on that score?"

Only as she posed this question did she lift her worried gaze to look into his eyes.

"I will hope until I am given no choice but to set my hopes aside. This is a hard business, madame, and what I ask of you should not be asked of any lady. If you never speak to me again, I will surely understand."

She smiled faintly, and he thought she was nearly as pretty as Julianna. Slipping her hand into his, she gave it a firm squeeze and he had the answer he sought.

When his equipage drew before her home in Upper Brook Street, he said, "I intend to seek vouchers to Almack's."

He heard her gasp and watched as a strange, startled expression rippled briefly over her face. "Almack's!" she cried in apparent disbelief. "You? Your love for her must be great indeed, since you have not crossed the threshold in some eight years."

"It is," he responded.

Again she lowered her gaze, withdrawing her hand from his. In barely a whisper, she asked, "Will there be even a particle of love left for me, or would ours be merely a marriage of convenience?" He watched her swallow hard, her eyes still cast upon her lap.

"I will not lie to you. I don't know how well or how fully I would love you, but I tell you this, my life would be devoted to your happiness."

She smiled suddenly and quite brightly. He did not know precisely what to make of her quixotic shift in expression, but her words elucidated some of it. "A woman—loved or not—can ask for no greater gift from a husband. If your dear Miss Redmere does not find it in her heart to accept of your hand in marriage, I will most gladly give you mine. Goodnight, Carlton."

She hurried from the chaise at that, and he did not try to stay her. He felt unwell, sick at heart at the whole business. Why hadn't he been wise beforetimes, instead of permitting the terms of his inheritance to hedge him in so completely?

The following afternoon, Julianna sat in the gold and rose drawing room on the first floor of the Redmere townhouse and stared in disbelief at Lady Catterick, Mrs. Whenby, and Mrs. Bulmer. Her mother sat beside her, her mouth slightly agape, as she received the ladies' news unblinking. Julianna could see her mother was equally as stunned by the extraordinary tidings.

Lady Redmere finally took a deep breath. "You say he sought vouchers from Emily Cowper and means to attend the Assemblies tomorrow night?" she queried, utterly astonished.

"That's the way of it," Lady Catterick responded.

Mrs. Whenby chirped, "Indeed, and there is another rumor going about that he intends to marry the widow Garston."

Mrs. Bulmer's booming voice bounced off the wall behind Julianna and snuck around to her ears. "Almack's and the Garston. Incredible!"

"Indeed," Julianna whispered.

Lady Redmere looked at her daughter and finally blinked. "Did you know of this, Jilly?" she asked.

"No, how could I?" she responded, dumbfounded. "Only why do you stare at me as though I've grown whiskers or something?"

Ignoring the presence of London's busiest tattlemongers, she said, "Carlton must love you a great deal, my daughter."

Julianna laughed outright. "Because he is to attend Almack's? What an absurd notion! How can this be an indication of his love for me? Besides, I—I believe Mrs. Whenby has the right of it, he intends to marry Mrs. Garston. I believe he is merely attempting to please her. Everyone knows she adores the Assemblies."

Lady Catterick lifted a brow. "She dotes on London's many amusements," began in her superior, nasal voice. "She would live here year-round if the *beau monde* did not leave the Metropolis in June. There can be no two opinions on that head. The Garston must have London. But it is you Carlton loves, Julianna. And I caution you not to dismiss the significance of his having sought vouchers for Almack's—he once made a vow never to cross the portals again, and you know how seriously men take their vows."

Julianna pressed a hand to forehead, not because her head hurt, but because a wave of inexplicable tears had rushed to her eyes. She rose unsteadily and murmured, "Pray excuse me. I am not feeling well all of a sudden."

A murmur of heartfelt sympathy resounded behind her as she fled the drawing room.

Once in her bedchamber, Julianna let the pressures of the past four weeks sweep over in a powerful wave, pressures she had been keeping at bay until the moment Lady Catterick had spoken the words *"but it is you Carlton loves."*

She threw herself on her bed, sliding at least a foot on the sky blue silk of her counterpane. Stretching out flat on her stomach, she sobbed as she had the first day of her arrival. She hated Carlton for humiliating her so completely, but to think of him married by Thursday! Her heart ached dreadfully, and not until her face was puffy and red, her kerchief was drenched with tears, and her clock had sounded the hour twice did she at last stop crying and fall into a deep slumber.

* * *

Later that afternoon, when Lady Redmere found her daughter asleep upon her bed, she backed out of the room, closed the door softly behind her, and headed toward the stairs. She had for so long been absorbed in her own unhappiness that until she had actually heard her daughter sobbing, she did not fully appreciate the gravity of Jilly's situation.

Until that moment, she had not comprehended that her daughter was in love—deeply and forever—with a man who had made it all but impossible for her to give him that love.

The whole of the circumstance seemed quite familiar to her, and she realized it was a mirror-image of her quandary with Redmere. She descended the stairs in a slow, methodical manner, her hand sliding upon the slick, polished banister, her thoughts fixed upon her own love for her husband and the many wonderful years she had spent thoroughly enjoying his love. He had been right about one thing—she could not forgive him for his former entanglement with Charlotte Garston. Perhaps men never could quite understand how much it hurt a lady to think of her husband taking pleasure in the arms of another woman.

"Millicent," a man's quiet voice called to her.

She was so much inwardly trapped by her thoughts that she did not at first recognize Redmere's voice. When she turned toward the study, she saw him standing in the doorway, holding out his hand to her. "Will you spare me a moment, my dear?"

"Yes, of course," she responded calmly, her head still full of Julianna's difficulty.

She entered the chamber, and heard the door snap behind her. He begged her to sit down, but she shook her head, her thoughts still fixed on her daughter.

"As you wish," he said quietly.

At that, her mind seemed to clear, and she whirled around to stare at him. "As I wish?" she queried, facetiously. "Merciful heavens, Jack, are you not feeling well? I cannot recall in all these years together your ever having told me I may do as I wish." She laughed a little and added, "Or is your conscience troubling you so greatly that now you feel you must needs be polite to me?"

She watched his temper slide over his face like a waterfall across ancient rocks. She giggled and waved a negligent hand toward him. "How easily you rise to the fly. You always have, you know."

"Ah, Millie, what happened to us?"

Lady Redmere sank down into the soft cushions of the Grecian sofa covered in red silk-damask. "I think you know," she responded, letting her hand glide over the smooth fabric.

She looked out the window, not wanting to brangle yet again about the widow Garston. The conversation always proved as useless as it was unending. She expected to hear him begin railing at her yet again for always bringing the subject forward. Instead, she was surprised when he drew one of the Empire chairs to sit opposite and to face her squarely.

"I have no wish to speak of a woman who has been a friend to me for many years. Instead, I want to tell you that you are the only woman I have ever loved, or that I will ever love. I can't write poetry like Mr. Fitzpaine—though I did give it a try about a fortnight ago—"

"—You did?" she queried, her heart suddenly leaping in her breast. But the thought of Jack Redmere putting his hand to rhyme made her giggle. "You wrote a poem?"

He smiled and reached out a hand to her, letting two of his fingers just touch her knee. "The damned silliest non-sense you ever heard," he responded, laughing with her. He then grew somber and added, "Your eyes ought to be compared to the jewels in heaven's gate, though. Millie, have I not loved you well enough?"

"You have—you have," she responded, tears filling her eyes. "I was never unhappy, never! Only when—"

"Why can't you forget about Charlotte Garston? She is only a friend, that is all she has ever been or ever could be to me."

Lady Redmere touched his fingers, and biting her lip, said, "Tell me this, Jack, did you never—did you *enjoy* her kisses and her—her—" She could not finish the question and realized it was the first time she had ever asked him directly about his affair with her. If only he would tell her he hadn't touched her.

Lord Redmere looked down at the fingers touching his and slowly drew his hand away from her. He sat back in his chair and directed his gaze out the window, just as she had done earlier.

She felt crushed by his silence, and yet for a moment hoped he would relent and speak the truth to her. Instead, she watched in stages as his face grew taut with anger, and she knew the whole of it was hopeless when he crossed his arms over his chest.

She did not press him, but instead rose from the sofa and quit the chamber. As she crossed the entrance hall and prepared to remount the stairs in order to dress for dinner, her thoughts turned toward her daughter. She sighed deeply, sadly. Charlotte Garston had been the source of her pain and the sole reason she had not prompted Julianna to renew her betrothal to Carlton. After all, it was one thing for a man to have deceived his bride about his identity—an absurd prank which could eventually be forgiven him—but quite another for a man to carry on with his mistress up until the day of his nuptials.

No, she thought with a weighted heart, she could no more forgive Carlton for his liaison with the Garston than she could her own husband. Julianna was wise to continue to refuse the viscount.

And that was that!

Chapter Twenty-Four

Later that night, Lady Redmere took Captain Beck's hand and stepped down from her husband's traveling coach. Mrs. Bulmer's house was lined with waiting carriages and a dozen footmen were running up and down the flags, helping ladies to alight from their conveyances. A carpet had been laid out before the doorway, and the front of the house glowed with candlelight gleaming from every window. She could hear the faint melody of a country dance resounding from deep within the house, and the chatter and laughter of the *beau monde* at play floated into the night air all around her.

Lord Redmere followed behind her. He had been silent through dinner and the duration of the short journey from Berkeley Square to Mrs. Bulmer's home in Upper Brook Street. Captain Beck, unused to seeing Lord Redmere in so subdued a state, kept glancing askance at him, a worried frown between his brows.

"Is your husband bilious?" he inquired in a whisper to Lady Redmere, when they were but a few feet from the front door.

Lady Redmere laughed, then replied, "I suppose you might say he is."

"A purgative, I understand, works wonders, especially taken with the waters at Bath. Ought I to recommend such a cure to him?"

Lady Redmere leaned close to him and whispered, "Only if you wish to keep your head."

Captain Beck nodded wisely for a moment, then said, "Eh? What's that?"

Lady Redmere looked at him, thinking he was the most hopeless creature she had ever known. "Don't say anything to him," she responded, making her teasing remark accessible to his limited intelligence.

"I suppose I won't, then," he responded, with a blink of his lazy eyelids. "In quite a brown study, I should say, and no wonder! Just look at his neckcloth! He's still wearing an Osbaldton. Would make anyone bilious."

The thought of Redmere being overset because of his neckcloth caused Lady Redmere to take hold of Beck's arm and give him an affectionate squeeze.

"Have a care, Millie!" he cried, disengaging her arm and smoothing out the black superfine fabric. "My new man spent all day preparing this coat. I shouldn't like to have it rumpled before I've set foot in Bulmer's house."

"I do beg your pardon," she responded. How grateful she was to have Beck about her. He lived his entire existence on inconsequentials, and he never failed to lift her spirits by his absurdities.

Mrs. Bulmer's elegant curved staircase greeted her eyes the moment she crossed the threshold, the sight of which always served to please her. For all her inelegance of person and voice, Mrs. Bulmer had an eye for beauty unequaled. Her ball was a straightforward affair, a perfect reflection of her temperament. Every lady present sported her best jewels, her most elaborate gown, and her finest headwear, gloves, and slippers. The occasion was especially marked by the sparkle of diamonds, emeralds, and sapphires beneath a series of gloriously lit chandeliers present in every receiving room of the lofty townhouse.

After Lady Redmere ascended the stairs and greeted her host and hostess, she bid *adieu* to her husband, who was intent upon finding a game of whist in Bulmer's study. Turning Beck loose upon the yellow drawing room upstairs, he instantly found three aspiring dandies who tended to fawn over him. As she strolled by her companion, she heard him give his pronouncement, "Your pink coat, my dear Marcus, is completely *de trop*, but I approve of the vest. Bamboo leaves. Very clever."

Smiling, she began her own search of the rooms, looking for that one tall figure who would immediately bring joy to her heart.

She nodded here and there to her many acquaintances, most of whom inquired after Julianna. Her explanation that her daughter had succumbed to a most troublesome headache sufficed to satisfy the curious. To Ladies Catterick and Cowper she whispered the truth—her daughter was desperately unhappy and Carlton's cruelty to her had taken a hard toll.

Emily Cowper, the very soul of kindness, expressed her understanding. "What lady could tolerate so profound a deception? I know I could not. But the worst of it is, after all these years, Carlton—whom I adore—has finally fallen in love. I can't find it in my heart to blame your daughter for not forgiving him, but does she comprehend the depth of his love for her?"

Lady Redmere lifted her chin slightly. "I have always held you in the highest regard, Emily, but what difference would it make how much he loved her when not only did he deceive her and plot to rob her of her virtue, but even before the wedding, his—his conduct was truly atrocious!"

Lady Cowper frowned and tilted her head. "I don't take your meaning, Millicent. What conduct are you referring to? I know of nothing unpardonable, save a little unsavory and unfounded gossip, of which, I assure you, he is entirely innocent."

Lady Redmere found her patience wearing thin. "You do not believe that for a man to keep his mistress until the very last moment before his wedding is an unconscionable act?"

Lady Cowper opened her eyes wide with surprise. "His

what?" she queried in an astonished whisper. For a long moment her mouth remained opened. Her expression darkened suddenly and she took hold of Lady Redmere's wrist in an exceedingly hard grip. "You little simpleton!" she cried. "Are you referring to the most absurd gossip that was ever bandied from one lip to another? Charlotte Garston?"

"You are hurting me," Lady Redmere returned, trying to twist away from Lady Cowper.

"I won't let you go," she cried. Shifting her gaze to Lady Catterick, she added, "And as far as I am concerned, a great deal of trouble can be laid at your door, Eliza, and at Mrs. Whenby's and Mrs. Bulmer's. I know you never create the gossip, but I vow the semaphore system in the Army is nothing to the extraordinary manner in which every *crims. cons.* imaginable makes a swift and sure pathway about Mayfair before the cat could lick her ear. Pray leave us, Lady Catterick. I have a matter of great delicacy to put to Millie, and I will not have it go beyond my mouth and her ears."

Lady Catterick began to sputter. But since Lady Cowper dismissed her with a tut and a brisk snap of her fingers, Lady Catterick melted into the stream of guests crowding the drawing room.

"You needn't give me a dressing down, if that is what you intend to do," Lady Redmere cried. Lady Cowper did not immediately respond, though it was clear she wanted to. She waited instead for a string of young ladies to pass beyond the range of hearing. She then bade Lady Redmere remove to one of the windows overlooking the noisy street below.

"I have never been able to determine where the gossip originated regarding your husband and Mrs. Garston, or even regarding Carlton and the widow. I know that Lady Catterick and her friends were—as they always are—instrumental in seeing that news of this sort was transported quickly along, but their odd scruples are such that they tell only what is told to them. They would not make up lies. But I tell you this—I have known a great deal of men over the past decade or so, and I believe I have a perception which you do not, nor perhaps does your daughter, regarding the various natures of them all. I speak plainly to you, Millicent, because I have watched you behave like a little henwitted hare for over a year. The simple truth is, Charlotte Garston—for all her persistence—failed completely to attach either man to her side. Yes, she is beautiful, and utterly enchanting, as I have been told times out of mind by a score of enraptured men. But when a man loves as Redmere loves you, he is incapable of infidelity. And Carlton, contrary to the general conception of him, has never kept a mistress in his life, at least, not to my knowledge."

"Never?" she asked, stunned.

Lady Cowper shook her head. "He has too much delicacy of principle and common sense."

"And with all his *delicacy of principle* he eloped with my daughter! You've bats in your belfry, Emily Cowper. And I won't listen to another word!"

"Then you will be sad the remainder of your days, and so will your daughter. I bid you good evening, Lady Redmere."

She pulled a face as Lady Cowper disappeared through the doorway leading to the stairs. She felt like a little girl of six who had been reprimanded by her governess for getting her skirts muddied about the knees. She restrained a strong impulse to stamp her foot and pout and decided to remain by the window until she was calmer. Besides, she wanted to think about what she had just been told. Of course, it would be much simpler if she abhorred Emily Cowper, and could discount her recent revelations, but the truth was, she had always admired her and trusted in her opinions.

Now she was telling her that Redmere had not been in love with Charlotte Garston and had never taken her to be his mistress. Nor had Carlton!

Lady Redmere frowned and chewed slightly upon her lower lip. Why had she never doubted the gossip before? Why had she always believed Redmere guilty?

She sighed deeply. Because he had flirted with the widow almost as outrageously as he had flirted with her in Bath that first summer they had met. She recalled now that she had been out of her mind with jealousy a year ago, when she had seen Redmere leaning over Charlotte at some *fête* or other and making her laugh and smile. A sennight later, when she was told by a properly horrified Lady Catterick that Redmere was keeping Charlotte Garston, she had fled London on the instant and no persuasions or arguments on his part had prompted her to return. He had naturally denied an entanglement a hundred times at first, but she had never believed him. Never.

She felt queasy of a sudden, realizing she had chosen to disbelieve the man with whom she had lived for twenty years.

A henwitted hare, Emily had said.

What if Emily's belief in his innocence was true?

But how many times had she seen him—eyes dancing with pleasure—content in Charlotte's company? A score. She had begun to feel annoyed, hurt, cast-aside. And when the rumors started, she had believed them. She had never had the least doubt that the Garston had become her husband's mistress.

Until now. What if he had been faithful?

And what of Carlton? Had he been involved with the widow as well? Or was that, too, an unfortunate belief based upon unfounded gossip? What, then, did that mean where her daughter was concerned? Did Carlton deserve a second chance with her poor Jilly?

"Millicent," a familiar voice breathed into her ear.

She turned toward a man who could give her a proper answer. "Edward," she responded quietly.

"You are crying," he whispered, quickly removing a handkerchief from his coat pocket and dabbing at her cheeks. "Why are you so unhappy? Is it Redmere? Has he—hurt you?"

"Good heavens, no!" she responded, surprised to find Edward was right, that her cheeks were wet with tears. Wiping them away with her soft white gloves, she continued,

"Whyever would you think Redmere had hurt me? Because he barks instead of whispering softly into my ear, as you do? It is no such thing, I assure you."

"I will accept your word. I missed you today," he added, smiling down upon her, his blue eyes warm with affection. She felt her own heart strain toward him, wondering what it would be like to give her love to him, then regretted the unhappy thought. She was so confused about everything— about herself, her feelings, about Redmere, and especially about Edward Fitzpaine.

Setting aside her own troubles, she pursued her other concern—Carlton's guilt.

She took his arm and gently guided him into an ante-chamber which was momentarily bereft of occupants. She stopped him beside a black lacquered cabinet and bade him remain for a moment. Looking up at him, she queried, "Edward, I have never asked you about Carlton and—and Mrs. Garston. There were rumors that she was his mistress. I realize if he bade you keep his secrets you would be obliged to honor your friendship with him first, but it is of the utmost importance that I know the truth—was Mrs. Garston mis-tress to Lord Carlton?"

She took in a deep breath, waiting to hear his answer, and searched his blue eyes steadily and carefully. How would Emily Cowper judge whether a man was lying or not? She remembered hearing once that the eyes were the gateway to the soul. Edward's eyes were wondrously clear, guileless, intent.

"I break no vow to Carlton when I tell you she was not nor has she ever been his mistress. I believe she would have easily agreed to such an arrangement, but Carlton was not so inclined. Never has been, really, which only makes one won-der at the nature of gossip. I don't think anyone's character has been more thoroughly maligned than his. No, he never kept the Garston."

She let out a long breath of air. She believed him.

She had rejected Carlton as a husband for her daughter—

even after his abject apologies—because she had believed the gossips.

She now thought it likely that Emily Cowper had been right after all—that Charlotte Garston had not been her husband's mistress, either.

She again wondered why she had been so insistent on his guilt. Was it her pride?

"Why are you so distressed, Millicent? I don't think I've ever seen your brow knit with such grave concern. Are you thinking of Jilly?"

"Yes, in part. But also of—of Redmere."

Edward took her hand and led her to an Egyptian chaise longue and bade her sit down. Waiting until two young bucks had passed through the antechamber into the drawing room, he seated himself next to her and leaned close to her ear. "I have waited nearly a month now to say this to you," he began in a low, urgent voice. "I know this is not the proper place, but Millicent, I feel I must speak, to reveal my heart to you. Until now I have refrained from speaking, but my heart refuses to be silent a second longer. You cannot be unaware that I have fallen deeply in love with you." He took her chin in his hand and forced her to look at him, into his adoring blue eyes. "Millicent, more than life itself I want you to become my wife."

She opened her mouth to protest, stunned by what he had just said to her, but he quickly interjected, "No, please don't speak just yet. I must have my say. Though we were acquainted prior to the elopement, I had never considered the possibility of a union between us, even though I had always thought you an exquisite, charming woman. I daresay, until the elopement, we had never before exchanged much above a dozen words. I confess, however, that I was always intrigued by Redmere's obvious ardency for you—so incongruous with the general course of tonnish marriages. He seemed to dote on you, in his brusque manner, of course, that is, until spring last.

"And a few weeks ago, when I found you sitting so prettily

in Marish Hall, with your absurd Cicisbeo studying his re-flection in a nearby chest of drawers, suddenly I wanted that ardency for myself. I knew of your estrangement, of course. Who in London did not? And when I could see that you felt similarly—that you seemed to take pleasure in my com-pany—can you blame me for tumbling so very hard? And you have enjoyed certain sentiments toward me, haven't you?" He gave her hand a squeeze.

Lady Redmere looked into his blue eyes and remembered back to their flight along the Great North Road. She wished she was there now, enjoying his company without hin-drance, receiving his compliments and hints at warmer feel-ings with a joyous heart, playing at traveling games like children. "Of course I have," she responded softly, returning the pressure of his hand.

"Will you marry me, then?" he asked forthrightly.

Until this moment, Lady Redmere had not com-prehended the whole of her involvement with Mr. Fitzpaine. Until this very moment, she had merely been a leaf upon a swiftly moving stream and had been partaking of the ex-traordinary sensations of Edward's love and adoration of her without once giving the smallest thought to the future.

And not for a moment had she thought he would be intent upon matrimony. She was already married. Was he thinking she would ask Redmere to divorce her? But that was quite impossible, besides being absurd. Oh, dear Lord in heaven! That was precisely what he had been thinking—that she would ask Redmere for a divorce!

She felt her heart collapse within her and a terrible guilt flooded her mind, her soul, her very being.

What had she been doing in encouraging Mr. Fitzpaine's attentions? These several weeks and more he had been thinking *marriage*, and she had been thinking—well, she had not been thinking at all!

Did she ever think? she wondered suddenly. Or was she simply the henwitted hare Emily Cowper had told her she was? Yet she wasn't in the least indifferent to Edward, far from it. Were she not Jack's wife she would accept of his hand in marriage in a trice.

But she was married, and that was that.

She didn't know what to say.

Lord Redmere stood secreted on the other side of the ante-chamber, beside a doorway which led into a parlour where refreshments were being served. He had been looking for his wife for some time and would have entered the room promptly upon seeing her had she been seated upon the Egyptian sofa with anyone other than Edward Fitzpaine.

Whatever had possessed him to eavesdrop upon their conversation he would never know, and now he waited to hear what next his wife would say. He did not have to wait long.

"I think I tumbled in love with you as well, Edward," Lady Redmere said quietly, "the moment you advanced toward me in Redmere's study and bowed over my hand in your meticulous manner. How very kind and considerate your every word was—and has always been since that first day. Faith, but you are as much unlike Redmere as night is unlike day."

Night and day.

That was all Redmere heard.

Night and day.

His wife might as well have said *love and hate*, and he very well would have known which of them she loved and which she hated.

He moved away from the doorjamb and somehow made his way into the long gallery leading back to the stairs, the entrance hall, the front door. He could scarcely feel his legs beneath him as he moved swiftly forward. He knew only one thing: if he didn't very soon get a cold blast of April night air, he would very likely faint.

* * *

Edward looked down into the face he loved, and knew his suit was utterly hopeless. *Night and day.* Extremes. One loved, one loved a little more. He could see it in her eyes. He knew it by the way she had appeared stunned when he had mentioned marriage to her.

When she opened her mouth to continue, he pressed his fingers against her lips, and said, "But Redmere is the husband of your heart, isn't he?"

She nodded, tears brimming in her beautiful green eyes. "I never truly believed that I could possess you the way Redmere does. I think I longed for the love I've always known you felt for him, a love that has been denied me. Do you know, for instance, how many times during the past few weeks, when we would waltz or stroll about this or that townhouse, your gaze would search for Redmere in a room as quickly as a flock of birds rises in fright from a field? I had the firm impression you were hoping to make him jealous by encouraging my attentions. Now I know my impression was accurate."

"Oh, Edward, was it that obvious? I never meant—"

"—I know you did not. Yours was the heart full of innocence and childlikeness. And mine, full of false hopes and unfulfilled dreams. Yet I love you. I think I always shall. Should you ever need a friend, pray send for me. Know that I will always be, though the phrase is entirely overused, *at your service.*"

He watched her lower lip quiver and he pinched her chin. "You must go after him, you know. He heard our entire conversation up through your comparison of night and day."

"What do you mean?" she cried, turning around and staring at the various pieces of furniture as though expecting to find him hiding behind one or the other.

Mr. Fitzpaine shook his head. "He was about to enter the antechamber when he saw me. He then hid himself just beyond the doorway."

"And you said nothing?" she cried, aghast.

"I thought it might be useful for him to know my intentions and your heart, only I fear, though he learned the former, he is not fully conversed with the latter."

"I must go to him," she cried. "Oh, Edward, I am so very sorry. I shouldn't have toyed with your affections as I have. I never understood until now how wretchedly I have behaved."

"You were very unhappy and lonely," he said. "And I forgive all especially since it is not precisely the most sensible thing to do, to pursue a lady known to be deeply in love with her husband."

"Goodbye, Edward," she said, standing up. When he stood up beside her, she looked up into his face and all his feelings for her rushed over him in one blinding moment. He did not know what possessed him to do it, but he caught her up suddenly in his arms, and kissed her quite passionately for several seconds.

Lady Catterick, Mrs. Whenby, and Mrs. Bulmer all gasped in hushed unison.

"Oh, my!" Mrs. Whenby chirped.

"Goodness gracious!" Mrs. Bulmer bellowed.

"A scandal!" Lady Catterick breathed.

Half an hour later, Lady Redmere—in full disgrace—quit Mrs. Bulmer's townhouse on her husband's arm. He had approached her solemnly, his complexion ashen, his eyes cloudy with a sentiment she could not quite comprehend. He had informed her politely that he had heard of Mr. Fitzpaine's kiss and thought it best that they return to Berkeley Square.

The trouble was, he didn't seem in the least angry, a circumstance so novel that Lady Redmere hadn't the least notion how to go about speaking to him. She wanted to reassure him that the kiss meant nothing, but somehow the thought of confirming the terrible rumor which had prompted him to request she come home with him immediately was beyond her present abilities.

It seemed so strange to her suddenly that even though she knew Edward was only bidding her goodbye—albeit quite passionately—the entire *beau monde* was whispering behind fluttering fans and staring at her as though she had murdered someone.

When the carriage drew to a stop outside the townhouse, she placed her hand on her husband's arm and said, "Jack, there is something I must say to you."

He recoiled from her as though her touch was poisonous. "Pray, not this evening, Millie. I daresay I drained a few too many cups of champagne. I'm not feeling at all the thing. Tomorrow. We—we can settle all tomorrow."

She felt a terrible lump rise in her throat. She did not like the way he was speaking—so very controlled. She wanted him to bark and bellow like he usually did! Had he finally decided to get rid of her, now that she had completely disgraced herself by kissing Mr. Fitzpaine? Her heart seemed to shrink within her breast at the thought of it and tears sprang quickly to her eyes.

She did not want Redmere to turn her away from his door.

When he helped her alight from the carriage, she looked up at him beseechingly, but he refused to meet her gaze.

So it was, an hour later, with trembling limbs and a truly frightened heart, she slid between her sheets, curling her hand beneath her cheek. Only after another hour of distress did she finally fall into a fitful sleep.

Chapter Twenty-Five

On the following day, Julianna sat across from her mother, partaking of a nuncheon which consisted of thin slices of ham, roast beef, lobster sauce, potatoes, celery, raspberry tarts, apples, and cheese. The morning room in her father's townhouse had always been one of her favorites, since it was quite restfully decorated in soft apricot silks—upon the windows and walls and covering the chairs. Creamy white stuccowork graced the ceiling and the wall above the fireplace. In front of her, in the center of the cherrywood dining table, was a vase containing ferns and white roses. But neither the welcoming ambience of the chamber nor the array of excellent food had increased her flagging appetite, and only with the strongest of efforts had Julianna been able to force a slice of ham, a single bite of potato, a strip of celery, and some tea down her throat.

She was experiencing a fatigue like none she had ever known, in part, she was certain, because her sleep had been liberally laced with nightmares about carriages of all shapes and sizes careening wildly upon the Great North Road. Though a good night's rest would undoubtedly serve to restore her spirits, she knew a great deal of her lethargy must be laid at the door of her troubled heart.

She lifted a cup of tea to her lips and sipped slowly.

"Did you sleep well, my dear?" her mother asked.

Julianna glanced at her and saw to her surprise that bluish

shadows—very much like the ones she had witnessed beneath her own eyes only that morning—had given her mother a peaked appearance. She realized that she had been so absorbed in her own difficulties of the past few days she had failed to notice her parent's obvious unhappiness.

She answered her mother's question. "Wretchedly," she responded with a half-smile. "But not worse than you, I would imagine?"

At that, Lady Redmere darted a quick, scrutinizing glance toward her daughter and smiled faintly. "I wonder if we did not share the same dreams. Mine kept me turning throughout the night. I awoke tangled in the bedclothes."

Julianna smiled in return and settled her cup back upon its delicate saucer. "So did I," she said with a sigh. "But tell me, where is Papa? He always enjoys a hearty nuncheon. It is not at all like him to absent himself."

Lady Redmere lifted her own cup of tea to her lips, her hands trembling slightly. After swallowing her sip, she replied, "He—he left quite early."

"Indeed," Julianna responded, curious. "But where did he go?"

"I don't really know," Lady Redmere said, her gaze fixed blindly to a rose drooping over the side of the blue and orange vase. She returned her cup to its saucer and settled her hands on her lap. Julianna thought she looked desperately sad and had proof of her opinion when she watched a tear roll down her mother's cheek.

She rose from her chair immediately, some of her lethargy deserting her in the light of her mother's evident misery. She circled behind Lady Redmere's chair and lightly touched her back and then her arm, afterward kneeling beside her. "What is it? What has happened? Is he gone forever, do you think?"

Lady Redmere shook her head slowly from side to side. Her brow was wrinkled and her lips turned down in the manner of a child who has lost a favorite pet. "I don't think so. The truth is, something dreadful occurred last night and—and your papa has not given me an opportunity to explain what truly happened. I fear I have gone beyond the pale and he will never forgive me now!"

Julianna opened her eyes wide, a sensation of horror filling her heart. "Mama, you did not—that is—Mr. Fitzpaine. He loves you so, but you did not—I mean—"

Lady Redmere gasped. "No, of course not! How could you think! I would never—never! Oh, my goodness. Is it possible your father—but how could he think such an absurdity? He must know me after so many years!" At that her shoulders slumped forward and she covered her face with her hands. "I have been such a fool, Jilly! Such a wretched fool!"

Julianna did not know how to comfort her mother, but she remained beside her, on her knees, patting her shoulder.

After a moment, Lady Redmere removed her hands from over her face and swiped at her tears. She looked down at Julianna and smiled a very watery smile. "And you, my darling daughter! I have not attended to your trying situation at all. Emily Cowper informed me of something last night which I feel I must impart to you. It would seem that all the gossip we heard regarding Carlton and the Garston has not been entirely true. It would seem she was never his mistress, after all. I know we have not discussed this before, but because I was fully persuaded she had been his mistress, for that reason alone I never pushed for a reconciliation between you and Carlton. I realize only you can decide whether or not he is the husband for you, but I thought you ought to know Lady Cowper's opinion. And if anyone was conversant with the truth, it would be Emily—she has been a particular friend of Carlton's forever. Besides, even Mr. Fitzpaine has confirmed his innocence where Charlotte Garston is concerned."

Julianna felt oddly detached from news which should have brought some measure of comfort to her heart. Instead, she only felt more confused, unable to discern how to incorporate Carlton's innocence into the fabric of all that had transpired from York to Islington. So he was innocent of that crime—did his innocence, then, make up for all the rest? She didn't know what to think.

"Thank you for telling me, Mama," she responded quietly.

"You look so sad," Lady Redmere said, stroking her daughter's cheek lightly with her fingers. "I have been far too absorbed with my own difficulties to be of any use to you. I have not been a good mother to you."

"Mama," Julianna responded. "I am fully nineteen years of age. If I cannot solve my own problems, then I am completely hopeless and your attentiveness would be fully wasted upon me anyway. Besides, I have not precisely been a source of support for you, either."

"We are a pair, aren't we?" Lady Redmere returned, more tears beginning to flow down her cheeks. "But I am primarily to blame for your current distress. Had I not been such a goosecap and believed all the gossip about your father and the Garston, I daresay I would not have encouraged you quite so strenuously to accept of Carlton's hand in the first place. You would have had an ordinary Season, like all young ladies ought to, you would have fallen in love in quite the most harmless manner possible, and even now we might be celebrating your betrothal, instead of trying to overcome the terrible events of a month ago. My dearest, will you ever forgive me for being, as Emily Cowper so charmingly phrased it, a *henwitted hare?*"

Julianna leaned forward to slip her arms about her mother and gave her hug. Lady Redmere returned the embrace for a long moment until she was completely overcome. She sniffed loudly, pulled from Julianna's arms, and bade her daughter not to make the same terrible mistake she had made by believing all that she heard. Then, on a sob, she fled from the morning room.

Julianna remained kneeling on the planked floor, the hard wood hurting her knees. She didn't care. Several times in the course of the night, after awakening from a dream, she would try to make sense of the whole of her relationship with Lord Carlton, but couldn't. When a vision of him would rise before her and she would look yet again into his wondrous gray eyes, her heart would wash away every sound reasoning her mind might have presented a minute earlier and she would imagine herself tumbling into his arms.

But then the doubts would assail her—of his wretched conduct, of his liaison with Charlotte Garston, of his intention to take her to Paris, of his lies and deceit and false embraces. Then she would feel queasy with shame and humiliation, her love—yes, her love for Carlton—overshadowed by her deep mistrust of him.

Then thoughts of his repentant conduct would rise in a powerful swell, seeming to overtake her shame and mistrust. She would recall to mind the flowers, the apologies—spoken and written—his determined pursuit of her in stark contrast to the many and varied jokes made about him, and his professed undying love for her.

And tonight he would be at Almack's, or so she had been told.

Almack's.

She knew his intense dislike of the place—as did the entire *haut* ton—that the Assembly Rooms represented to him everything in polite society he abhorred. Almack's was referred to as the Marriage Mart, where no doubt he had been scrutinized, examined, and all but physically prodded by the matchmaking mamas who were perpetually seeking advantageous matches for their dowered daughters.

Carlton had refused vouchers year after year in protest.

Now he had begged them of Emily Cowper, had published abroad his intention of attending the Assemblies for the first time in eight years, had pursued Julianna so doggedly that she was certain the entire ton would attend this evening, if for no other reason than to witness what had been nicknamed *Carlton's Folly*.

Only what was she to do?

Thursday—the day after tomorrow—he must be married, or lose his inheritance forever.

Her heart was so pulled apart she could hardly think. More of her own tears again rose to cascade down her cheeks and plop unladylike upon the dark blue silk of her morning gown. She had cried so much in the last month that she made a vow to herself that once the whole dastardly business with Lord Carlton was safely behind her, she would never cry again! Not in her life had she been such a watering pot as she had been since her arrival at the Peacock in Islington over four weeks ago.

Rising from her knees in some disgust at her tears, frustration, and inability to ignore Carlton, she briskly strode from the chamber and headed toward her room. One thing she knew for certain—after tonight, all would be settled, one way or the other. And even if she must speak with Carlton—as she would undoubtedly be required, by the enormous scope of the occasion—at least she could give him her final answer and he could then find a woman, undoubtedly Mrs. Garston, to accept his hand in marriage. Her heart could at last bid him a final *adieu* and she could seek solace in the enjoyment of the remainder of the Season.

There, she told herself, nodding firmly as she mounted the stairs, *I can still be quite sensible, quite reasonable.* With a lighter heart she reached her bedchamber and pushed the door open quite purposefully. But after taking two steps into the chamber, she drew in an astonished breath.

"Oh, no!" she cried aloud. For there, sitting upon her round inlaid table by the window, was a beautifully carved, fully masted sailing ship. A missive leaned up against its side.

Against her will and her better judgment, she crossed the chamber and picked up the smooth letter. Turning it over, she found that it was sealed and that Carlton's seal was fully exposed in the hard pool of wax. She slowly tore the paper above the seal and spread out the sheet. Written upon the page was a single phrase which caused fresh tears to start to her eyes.

Come with me, Jilly, to every port of which you have dreamed and dreamed again.

It was signed, *Carlton.*

She drew her gaze from the pressing, pulling, persuasive words and ran her finger over the muslin sails, so carefully hemmed and attached to the tall poles stained a dark brown. The entire ship, from bottom to top, from the base of the wooden hull to the tip of the highest mast, was over two feet in height and fully three feet long. Oddly enough, its appearance in her bedchamber told her something she had suspected, but not quite comprehended fully—namely, that even the servants were inclined to look favorably upon Carlton's suit, regardless of the fact that the staff had been informed of the viscount's previous, quite heinous conduct. She might easily be able to dismiss the pressure of her friends to succumb to Carlton's addresses, but she could not quite so easily ignore the opinions of the servants. She was not certain why this would be so, but it seemed to her that Lord Redmere's faithful retainers had a greater eye to her happiness than her friends, whose interests and motives might be quite different from those of a set of people who had served her father since times out of mind.

For most of the afternoon, particularly given her mother's unhappy condition and her own distress, she was *not at home* to morning callers and remained exclusively in her bedchamber. During this time, she evaluated every aspect of her life and her parents' lives, of Carlton's character, both overheard and experienced, her heart, her wishes, her hopes, her expectations. She did not try to come to a conclusion. In fact, she realized she could not draw a conclusion until probably the moment she actually saw Carlton and spoke with him— perhaps for the last time—at Almack's.

At the same time, she prepared meticulously for the evening, having a small tear repaired in her gown of emerald silk, having every wrinkle removed from the underskirt of white satin, having a row of tiny pearls looped delicately at the hem of each puffed sleeve of tulle, bathing in perfumed water as she had been told was Beau Brummell's habit and which was—as she was wholly convinced—his best contribution to tonnish society, having her coppery curls dressed to perfection with the use of curling irons and her maid's incomparable skill.

When she finally descended the stairs to join her parents in the rose and gold drawing room before dinner, she was pleased that each expressed their approval of her careful chignon, of the pearls in her hair and the added pearls to her sleeves, of her green silk and white satin gown. But as she watched her father drift quickly into a silent state, with his arm propped upon the mantel, and as she watched her mother take up her place across from him in a tapestried chair and also slip into silence, her gaze cast upon her red silk slippers which she propped up onto a low footstool in front of her, she knew all was far from being well.

She seated herself opposite her mother on a sofa of rose silk-damask, but her every light attempt to draw one or the other into conversation failed miserably. Her remarks upon the weather, upon her mother's coiffure or the fastidiousness of her father's arrangement of his neckcloth drew nothing more from either than brief, fluttering smiles, nods of acknowledgment, or monosyllabic responses.

Fortunately, dinner was served fifteen minutes later, promptly at seven, and they could all busy themselves with filling their plates, chewing, drinking, and swallowing in silence.

Charlotte Garston stared at the remaining gowns in her wardrobe, pulled the tenth gown out, and threw it behind her, on the floor. She watched her abigail carefully pick up the gown, and as with the others, lay it out on the bed. She was not trying to be cruel, but since she was not in the habit of explaining her conduct to her servants, she could not bring herself to say that six months of careful effort was being put to the test tonight. She trembled with fear that every groat she had spent on her idiot spy was soon to go for nought.

In this one respect, she was particularly grateful her pursuit of Carlton was drawing to a close—her spy had been rather trying upon her purse, given the limits of her own funds. And he was such a dolt! She was glad to be rid of him and had told him that after tonight, she would no longer be in need of his services. He had been shocked, of course, since he had no other source of income, but she recommended he set up a little shop on New Bond Street and give boxing lessons. She had laughed very hard at this piece of humour, but poor James had not found it in the least amusing and had left her home a trifle blue-deviled.

She did not give a moment's consideration to his fate, however. After all, she had her own future to consider now. The best part was, she still had an excellent chance of securing Carlton to her side. He had made his intentions clear, and though she hoped she had given the appearance that she was saddened by the degree of his love for Julianna Redmere, it had required her every effort to keep from turning cartwheels in the street when he had asked her to marry him in the event his *elusive bride* refused to forgive him.

These thoughts brought her a measure of peace and calmed the panic which had risen time and again over the course of the day within her avaricious heart. Another thought lifted her spirits further—Julianna was far too young to forgive Carlton's atrocious conduct. She smiled and pulled the eleventh gown from her wardrobe and tossed it backward, where it landed at her maid's feet. She wouldn't forgive him, she wouldn't marry him, and all that Charlotte had sought—a handle to her name, a fortune, a place of consequence among the peeresses of the land—would be hers.

Finally, she found what she was looking for: the gown best suited for the evening. A rare creation of deep rose silk and tulle. Along with her diamonds—strictly paste, of course, but no one would know as much—with a single white ostrich feather to draw attention to her glorious brown hair, and with the extreme décolleté of her gown, she knew she would be the most desirable lady present.

Though she was nearly thirty, she knew that a young chit of nineteen was not in any manner her equal.

After dinner, Julianna took up her place beside her father within the confines of his traveling chariot. Captain Beck—who had arrived at eight o'clock—was seated opposite her. Lady Redmere sat opposite her husband, but rarely cast her eyes his direction.

Captain Beck also seemed strangely dispirited. He did not even try to steal a glance into Redmere's highly polished *chapeau bras* to determine the condition of his curls. Instead, he stared quite moodily out the window, his arms folded across his chest, his lazy brown eyes fixed upon nothing in particular, save the inscrutable thoughts that might be coursing of the moment through his brain.

Julianna was about to ask him if he was feeling well when Lady Redmere suddenly took her hand in hers. "Jilly," she said. "There is something you must know before our arrival at Almack's this evening. I would have mentioned it at nuncheon today, but as you recall, I was, er, a trifle out of sorts."

"Yes?" Julianna queried, watching her mother's gaze slide briefly toward Lord Redmere, then back again.

Lady Redmere took a deep breath, and still holding Julianna's hand, continued, "Last night, I permitted a very foolish thing to happen, but because it did, I became the object of a great deal of gossip. The fact is, Mr. Fitzpaine kissed me in plain view of *everyone*. And it was not a friendly kiss, nor a brotherly kiss, but an embrace which—which even a complete nodcock could see indicated his sentiments toward me."

"Oh, Mother!" Julianna cried, her eyes opening wide, her

hand pressed to her cheek. "And here you are, braving society's censure by attending me at Almack's?"

"I hope I am not so lost to all sense of my obligation toward you that I would set a parcel of meaningless scandal above your future."

"Meaningless scandal," Lord Redmere interjected. "I believe I've heard everything now and will confess no greater absurdity has ever passed your lips. How can you speak of kissing Edward Fitzpaine in plain view of Lady Catterick, Mrs. Whenby, and Mrs. Bulmer as a piece of meaningless scandal? At the very least they will expect me to call him out."

Lady Redmere swallowed hard and responded, "Pray do not, Jack. I am a deal too fond of him to have him killed by my—my—"

"—By your what? By your fool?"

"That is not what I meant to say!" she retorted.

"What did you mean to say, then? By your husband? By your avowed enemy? By the man you wished to humiliate, to disgrace, to torture by your unseemly conduct?"

Julianna watched her mother swallow hard again. She was clearly struggling to control herself. "I had wanted to speak with you very much last night, Jack, but you wouldn't listen to me then. And this morning you left before I had risen from my bed. Pray do not at this late hour provoke me into an argument which we cannot possibly reconcile. I do wish to say, however, that if I could, I would have undone that kiss. I never meant to hurt you or to bring another scandal down upon your head. I never meant for Edward to kiss me!"

Lord Redmere looked away from his wife, also clearly struggling not to succumb to the powerful feelings which raged about in his breast. He pressed his temple, wrinkled up his forehead and squeezed his eyes shut. "You are right, of course," he said at last, taking a deep breath. "I do apologize for trying to provoke you." He then shifted toward Julianna and said, "Your mother and I have much to discuss and resolve, and this is neither the time nor the place. But it would seem in our difficulties we have not been attending very well to your circumstances. I am fully aware that Carlton means to attend this evening? Do you know as much and can you bear the notoriety you will receive because he is breaking an eight-year vow in attending?"

Julianna nodded. "I know it will not be easy," she responded quietly. "But it cannot be helped. Because he must be married by tomorrow midnight, I am forced tonight to give him my final answer. He has not said as much, but I know he expects me to state clearly whether I will release him completely or accept of his hand."

Mother and father exchanged a long, portent glance, then turned back to her. Lord Redmere said, "You are the only one who can properly judge the man who can make you happy. Marriage at its best comes closest to heaven, at its worst—well, this last year I am sure has shown you all that it is at its worst. Choose wisely, my pet, if you can."

He looked as though he wanted to say more, but at that moment Captain Beck announced their arrival at Almack's.

Chapter Twenty-Six

Julianna found it faintly amusing that because her mother had been involved in a scandal the evening before, not only was she the object of many critical stares and whispers behind fluttering fans, but the whole of it provided Jilly a welcome respite from her own notoriety. For the present, the *haut* ton was far more interested in trying to determine whether, once Edward Fitzpaine arrived, Lord Redmere would strike him across the face with his glove than with her dilemma over whether she should surrender her heart and marry Lord Carlton in spite of every sensible, rational reasoning of her mind.

She was able, therefore, to follow behind her parents and to seek out with trembling heart the one face she most wanted to see above all others, and yet most hoped not to see. When she did not find Carlton among the dancers or spectators, she was surprised to find how overset she was. And worse, she could not determine whether her distress was from sheer disappointment at not seeing the man she loved, or from the anxious knowledge that she must give him an answer.

What if he did not attend the Assemblies after all? What if he had already decided to marry the Garston and was even now seeking a special license?

Her heart lurched at the thought and her mouth grew exceedingly dry.

As she lifted her pearl-strewn fan to her face and composed herself, she wondered just how much she truly did love the viscount. If only she could comprehend the whole of her sentiments without having to consider his conduct toward her. Instead, even the smallest wish to merely see Carlton again was quickly shaded with memories of how painful it had been to discover the truth of his identity.

She was not able to continue trying to adjust her thoughts for very long, since a minute later, she watched Lady Catterick, Mrs. Whenby, and Mrs. Bulmer each give their sons a push in her direction. She would have smiled at the absurdity of the ladies trying to coerce their offspring into falling in love with her, but after a month of enjoying the brilliance of her first London Season, she realized she was growing quite fatigued with the exertions a profound number of matchmaking mamas were directing toward her fortune. She had received several offers already, none of which had tempted her in the least, and since a full six weeks remained before the Season drew to a close in mid-June, she suspected she would very soon receive a dozen more.

She was not disappointed in her unhappy belief when Horace Bulmer, Edgar Catterick, and Bartholomew Whenby each in turn made an attempt to fulfill their respective mother's expectations. Mr. Bulmer offered for her quite awkwardly during a country dance. Mr. Catterick, choking on his cake while he partook of refreshments with her, begged her to make him the happiest of men. And Mr. Whenby, having drawn her too near the orchestra, fairly shouted the profound strength of his undying attachment to her. She did not fail to notice the relief each experienced when she gently refused their solicitous requests for her hand in marriage.

When the young men turned, one after the other, to eagerly pursue ladies quite obviously more to their liking, she recalled that Carlton had frequently alluded to this aspect of the Season in particular and tonnish society in general with disgust. She could well comprehend his sentiments now, since she had begun to feel more like a horse at auction than a young lady with feelings, opinions, and wishes of her own.

But where was Carlton?

An hour passed, and then another.

Where is he? she wondered. *What if he does not come at all? What if he is already married to Mrs. Garston?* She found her stomach grow queasy with fear.

She did not want him to marry Charlotte Garston.

The doors would close permanently for the evening at eleven, and already it was half-past ten.

When it became generally known, with confirmation by none other than Emily Cowper, that Edward Fitzpaine had left London and was even now making his way northwest on the mails to Cumberland, an initial groan of disappointment swept through the rooms. There would be no duel after all. It seemed to Julianna that a pall of dejected gloom settled over the crowd—how very much like the *beau monde* to be sad when bloodshed had been averted!

Julianna watched her father receive the news with wide-eyed surprise, staring at his wife in disbelief. Afterward he turned away from her as though too overcome to speak. When he took Princess Esterhazy's hints that he ought to beg one of the young Miss Cattericks to dance, any chance of immediate resolution with his wife ended. But then, she thought, it was unlikely that her parents would be able to resolve a year's worth of bickering in one night—on an Assembly Room floor, anyway.

Within fifteen minutes, Julianna found that all the gossip formerly directed toward her mother was now aimed fully at her. She could hear the whispers—always spoken loud enough to be overheard by the object of the gossip!—as she passed by various groups of ladies and gentlemen. The same question was on everyone's lips—where was Carlton?

Again coming to stand beside her mother, Julianna sipped a glass of lemonade, her heart again turning over in her breast at the awareness that Carlton was still absent from the Assembly.

She had just returned her empty cup to a passing servant when she noticed that a hum of gossip had begun to roll in a series of swells across the crowded dance floor. She saw that dozens of pairs of eyes were fixed upon the entrance to the Assembly Rooms, and she found she could not breathe.

Surely Carlton had arrived!

Quickly she moved away from her mother in order to better see if it was indeed true.

She was handily disappointed. Instead, much to her dismay, she saw that Charlotte Garston had breezed into the rooms. Because of her beauty, the elegance of her coiffure, and the dazzling effect of her gown of pink silk, she was soon beset with admirers. Was anyone else curious at her late arrival? As a throng of gentlemen—young and old alike—suddenly rose up about her, she knew that the widow had timed her entrance to a purpose.

Just as she was about to turn away from the spectacle of Mrs. Garston surrounded by beaux, her gaze became riveted to the doorway beyond. There, much in the shadow of all the attention being rained upon the beauty, stood Lord Carlton. She felt frozen by the mere sight of him, her feet locked into place, her lips parted, yet unable to emit the gasp she was feeling rise within her, her heart stilled within her breast.

He was looking directly at her.

Julianna's mind swept her back to the moment she had first seen Carlton at the Angel, in the village of Redmere, nearly five weeks ago. She would never forget seeing him standing in the snow-banked innyard, watching her as though she had been some unearthly vision. She could still feel how his gray eyes had seemed to speak to her, to some part of her soul so deep she did not even know it existed. She thought of the wooden ship sitting on her table in her bedchamber and of his letter inviting her to a life of adventure.

She wanted that life so very much!

She wanted him.

His expression now, as he watched her, was the same as

it had been the day she had met him—intense, vibrant, yearning. He was speaking to her as surely as if he had been letting his throat give voice to each thought that entered his mind, and she felt as she had on that first day, overcome with profound, inexplicable longings. She was completely immobilized. She could neither advance forward, nor retreat. She became convinced that had they been alone, he could have simply taken her in his arms and carried her away without the smallest protest passing her lips.

She watched him smile ever so faintly, his eyes a little sad. He took a step toward her, she could see that his intention was to approach her, but before he could advance further into the room somehow, Mrs. Garston detached herself from her bevy of worshippers and took up a station beside him. She wrapped her arm securely about his, standing on tiptoes to whisper something in his ear.

How audacious of her, when she must know the entire assemblage was directing its attention toward Carlton and toward her!

He frowned slightly, tearing his gaze from Julianna's to look down at the pretty bird on his arm. He tried to disengage Mrs. Garston, but she chirped loudly at him, laughing and teasing all the while, then fairly dragged him toward the Assembly Room floor.

She was forcing him to dance with her! To have refused would have been an unforgivable breach of manners and would have set three-score tongues instantly a-wagging.

Julianna watched for only a moment longer as the viscount acquiesced to Mrs. Garston's provocative persuasions. When Horace Bulmer begged her to go down the country dance with him, the spell which had kept her pinned to one spot broke immediately. She agreed readily, grateful to be doing anything except watching Carlton and the Garston together.

Mr. Bulmer proved to be a great deal more at ease in her company since she had refused his offer of marriage, and she found him an even more agreeable partner than before.

Several times she endeavored to attend politely to him. However, she found her gaze slipping toward Carlton and the widow.

How brightly she speaks to him, she thought, as once again she turned her attention the direction of Charlotte's exquisitely coiffed brown hair. Mrs. Garston was all sparkling smiles and attended to Carlton with a familiarity which Julianna thought quite improper until a logical conclusion followed.

Improper, perhaps. But not for a bride.

And with all the instincts of a woman full grown, she knew that he had reached an understanding with the widow.

Julianna missed her steps completely and caused poor Horace to stumble into her. She reverted her attention instantly to her partner and begged his pardon as the young man valiantly searched the couples about him for a hint as to what he ought to be doing. He quickly found his footing and drew her back into the steps.

"I am so sorry," Julianna cried.

Mr. Bulmer looked down at her, grinning, as the steps of the country dance brought them back together again. "You are quite forgiven, Miss Redmere," he said. "But maybe you'd best speak with Lord Carlton and settle matters before attempting to go down another dance."

She was so surprised at his forthrightness that she nearly missed her steps again, but he admonished her with a grin and a shake of his head.

"Maybe I'd better," she agreed. "But tell me, Mr. Bulmer, what do you know of my needing to settle matters with Lord Carlton?"

He blushed slightly as he responded, "Even a simpleton can see that you are head over ears in love with him."

"Even a simpleton?" she queried, feeling that she had been told in the tidiest manner possible the precise state of her heart.

"Yes, of course. I hadn't been in your company twice before I noticed that whenever his lordship but entered a room, your attention—however graciously you hid it any number of times—was all for where he was and with whom he was speaking and what he was wearing and how many times he turned to look at you and acknowledge you."

When the dance separated them momentarily, she let his words drive through her head several times. When they came back together, she asked, "Ought I to forgive him?"

Mr. Bulmer lifted his brows in a pondering expression. "Forgiving is the easy part, I've always thought. It's knowing what to do afterward that's a bit tricky."

"I believe he still wishes to marry me."

"Well, of course he does," Mr. Bulmer responded as a matter of fact. Oddly enough, she couldn't help but be pleased with the compliment beneath the way he said, *well, of course he does*. She thought it was one of the nicest things he had ever said to her.

"What would you advise, then, Mr. Horace Bulmer?"

"Choose for yourself, first, if you can. Beyond that, I have no answer."

"Choose for yourself?" she asked, unable to resist teasing him, "As you did when you offered for me?"

He laughed outright. "I knew you wouldn't have me. I was perfectly safe—er, not that I wouldn't have been deuced happy to have been leg-shackled to you—but the fact is—"

"—You needn't explain. I fully comprehended your predicament. I am only grateful for your sake that I did not somehow fancy myself in love with you and so spoil all your comfort."

"I hadn't a doubt on that score," he said, the music drawing to a close.

She walked from the dance floor, her arm upon his, and looking up at him, said, "You're a good man, and I do wish you every happiness."

"Thank you," he returned brightly. He then glanced over her head for just a moment and in a whisper added, "And good luck!"

With that he released her arm, turned her around, and gave her the gentlest push.

She gasped to find Carlton standing barely three feet from her.

"Will you dance with me, Jilly?" he asked, his gray eyes beseeching her intently.

"Yes, of course I will," she breathed, uncertain if she had spoken loudly enough to be heard. He smiled, faintly again, as he had when she had first seen him at the entrance to the rooms. He then offered his arm and led her out onto the floor.

Her heart began to beat so loudly in her ears that though she knew he was again speaking, she couldn't hear him. "I'm sorry," she whispered. "What did you say?"

"Are you all right?" he asked, turning her to look at him. "You're very pale."

"How else should I appear," she asked, "given the circumstances?"

He frowned slightly as he led her to a place on the floor in preparation for the waltz. Only vaguely was Julianna aware that all about her other couples were arranging themselves to make up the numbers. Her heart, her mind, her eyes were, for the moment, all for Carlton.

"I suppose you are right," he said, responding to her query. "I have put you in an intolerable situation. I am sorry for that, but I wanted you to know that you mean more to me than anything—even more than my silly vow not to attend Almack's. And Jilly, I am truly sorry for what I did." He placed an arm about her waist and took her hand in his. "But then, I have told you so already, haven't I?"

"Yes, a score of times," she responded, as the orchestra began the first beats of the music. "And I have accepted your apologies—"

"—But you haven't forgiven me."

She smiled, thinking of what Mr. Bulmer had just said to her. "Of course I've forgiven you," she responded.

"Jilly!" he whispered. "Tell me it's true?"

She looked up at him, tears barely touching her eyes. "Of

course I have forgiven you, Carlton, but beyond forgiveness, how do I trust you again? Perhaps, in time—"

"—I don't have time. You know that. Is there nothing I can say to convince you that I would undo the five days we were together if I could? Except, would I have come to know you as I have if we had been in London, or Bath, or Brighton, or at the Harrogate Assemblies? I imagine you would have been just another young lady among so many whose true character and love of adventure I could never have come to know. So I regret everything, yet nothing, only that you seem so immovable in your opinion that I am lost to all decency forever."

The first strains of the waltz resounded through the room and he gently led her into the rhythmic, swirling movements of the dance, guiding her expertly about the floor.

Something about the gentle turns and sways and peaks of the dance began to ease Julianna's tortured mind. She stopped struggling completely with all her confused thoughts and let Carlton draw her closer to him than he ought to. She permitted her slippered feet to follow his lead without hesitation, for the moment letting her heart go out to him as it had so many weeks ago.

He began speaking, and it was as though her mind was inside his own. "I love you," he began quietly, looking into her eyes. "Whatever you choose tonight, it will not change that love. I will always love you. But tonight you must choose. Tomorrow, I must marry. But I beg you will choose me, Julianna. Choose me, choose my love for you and my determination to spend the rest of my life if I must needs do so proving that you can trust me."

She averted her gaze, not wanting to think or to choose. She wanted for the moment to forget about the terrible dilemma that threatened to tear her mind asunder. She closed her eyes, hearing only the music, feeling only the touch of his hand upon hers, the strong feel of his arm about her as he waltzed her up and back, around and around.

Her mind was swimming now and free of the persistent

turmoil which would beset her yet again the moment she turned her attention fully toward him. She could feel him lean closer to her still, as he turned her about, up and back, around and around. His breath was on her cheek. He whispered to her. "What of the Orient? It would be a very, very long voyage, even a dangerous one. We could see the land Marco Polo discovered so many years ago. And what of the Japans? Even the Americas, if you wished for it. We could visit Fort Ross. A year, Jilly—at least a year to complete an entire voyage and visit the Russians at Fort Ross. Enough time to have a child together, a child born on the seas, or in a foreign land. Our child."

She sighed deeply. She thought of the ship he had sent to her home, of his invitation. She wanted this life with him very much. She wanted his love, to be loved by him, to love him fully. She wanted a child with him.

She opened her eyes and turned to look at him.

His gaze was fierce and insistent, demanding that she forgive him, love him, trust him.

She opened her mouth to speak, her heart completely mesmerized by his closeness, by his words, by his eyes.

Suddenly, someone rammed her hard from behind and she fell into Carlton. He lost his footing and only by some small miracle kept them both from toppling over. She cried out, and immediately, he was all concern. "Are you all right?"

"Yes, of course, but what happened?" She turned around and saw Mrs. Garston, partnered by Captain Beck, standing next to them.

"Oh, my dear, I do beg your pardon!" the Garston cried. "Beck, you foolish creature, I told you to take care, and here you nearly crushed our poor Miss Redmere!"

Captain Beck's complexion was a bright crimson from his jawline to his hairline. "Jilly, I am so sorry," he cried, swallowing hard. He glanced at her guiltily and quickly led his partner away.

Julianna felt quite strange. Somewhere in her mind, she

knew that Mrs. Garston had intentionally ended their waltz together, but she couldn't quite respond to this truth. She felt only a sudden, profound relief that the spell Carlton had cast over her was now completely broken. Their position at the outer rim of the dancers, made quitting the floor a simple matter and she begged Carlton to return her to her mother.

How very much the abrupt ending of the waltz seemed to have imitated to perfection the abrupt ending of her journey from York to Islington. She was brought fully back to reality. As she took up her place beside her mother, she held her hand firmly out to Lord Carlton. "I shall say goodbye now, my lord. I wish you every happiness."

He took her hand and his gray eyes became very angry for a moment. She met his hostile stare squarely.

"Don't be a fool, Jilly," he whispered in a tight voice. "Come with me. Come with me now!"

Almost, the strength of his will again persuaded her.

I loved Edward Fitzpaine, she thought sadly. *Or at least, the man who called himself Edward.*

Her mind was now fully decided. She withdrew her hand from his. Summoning her courage, she shook her head and responded, "I can't. Your deceit ruined my ability to love you well. In time, I hope you will be able to forgive me."

She heard a long, heavy sigh escape his lips. He did not move away from her for a tense moment, but continued to look down at her. Finally, he said, "As you wish," then turned and strode away. Immediately he sought out Mrs. Garston, and the expression of supreme joy which cascaded over her quite beautiful face confirmed Julianna's belief that Carlton had, indeed, already begged the widow to become his wife.

"Mother," she whispered. "Will you please take me home?"

Chapter Twenty-Seven

Later that night, after Lady Redmere saw her beloved daughter settled as comfortably as possible in her bed, she kissed her on the cheek, blew out the candle, and gently closed the door behind her. Once in the hallway, she kept her hand upon the brass door handle for a long moment, her gaze fixed to the pool of light on the carpet created by a wall sconce opposite Jilly's door. She wasn't certain why it was she felt as though some great evil had just occurred, but so she did.

Jilly had rejected Carlton.

And she shouldn't have.

She knew that now as clearly as she had known the night before, when Edward kissed her, that Redmere would always be the man she loved. Always, regardless of how many women he chose to flirt with.

She wondered if she ought to try to change Julianna's mind. Perhaps there would be enough time to seek an audience with Carlton early tomorrow morning, before he married Mrs. Garston. It might not be too late, unless, of course, he had eloped with the widow after leaving Almack's, in which case it wouldn't matter what steps she took now or in the morning. For that reason, she decided not to disturb her daughter.

After making her decision regarding what she would next do for Julianna, her thoughts took an abrupt turn.

Edward Fitzpaine was gone. Gone to the beautiful wilds of Cumberland and the Lake District. Gone to ease his heart, to forget about her, to pour his soul again into courting the Muse.

Lady Redmere found herself exceedingly grateful he had departed London so quietly. A duel could easily have been the result of the public kiss they had shared, and she would not have been in the least surprised if Redmere had called him out—even though the laws of the Kingdom expressly forbade dueling of any kind.

Still, he was gone.

A part of her would always love him, she thought sadly. But only a part of her. The whole of her being would always be given to Jack.

Redmere, she thought wistfully, finally releasing her hand from the door. But she didn't move far. She was too absorbed in her thoughts to do more than to keep her gaze fixed to the pool of light and clasp her hands in front of her.

She had not been unaware of the profound affect the knowledge of Edward's leaving had had upon her spouse. When Redmere had learned of his departure, the expression on his face had first been one of astonishment and then one of complete and utter relief—there could be no two opinions on that score. She knew her husband well, that his relief had nothing to do with the fact that he wouldn't have to challenge Edward to a duel, after all. But rather, his expression had indicated he had truly believed she could actually have left him in favor of Edward's suit.

It seemed strange to think of her husband fearing she would leave him.

The carriage ride home had been a quiet one, except that frequently she found Redmere's gaze fixed upon her, a slight frown between his brow as he watched her. Once he even smiled, afterward taking her hand and giving it a squeeze. He had said so much with his looks and his smile and that squeeze.

When they had arrived home, and were mounting the

stairs, Redmere had whispered in her ear that he wanted her to come to his chambers once she had seen her daughter safely abed.

He had not requested her company in a long time, and there was just such a look in his eye that she was now suddenly overcome with anticipation.

She lifted her gaze from the pool of light and made a purposeful progress to her husband's chambers two doors down the hall. She paused before his door, her heart racing, and with trembling fingers she lifted her hand to scratch lightly upon the coarsely grained wood.

She counted the seconds, waiting for the door to open. One, two, three, four, five.

The door opened with a swoosh. She felt a wave of warm air flow over her and could see at a glance that the room was in complete darkness, save for a brightly burning fire in the grate. The light against the furniture of her husband's bed-chamber—all heavily carved of mahogany—cast dramatic shadows all about the chamber.

He stood beside the door, a familiar intense look in his blue eyes as he watched her. Her knees began to tremble. He held her gaze steadily. She could hardly breathe. "Jack," she murmured, as she glided into the room on feet she could no longer feel.

He closed the door, caught her arm by the elbow and pulled her hard against his chest. He enveloped her in a crushing embrace. "Oh, my," she breathed again, her entire body tingling.

"Do you believe I am innocent?" he asked, glaring at her, scowling at her beneath his silver-streaked brows.

"I've been a complete simpleton," she whispered in return, admitting her guilt.

"But do you believe I am innocent?"

"Yes."

"Good," he responded, his gaze drifting over her face hungrily. "Then we can begin again just like the day *before* we were married."

Lady Redmere drew in a long, quavering breath, her eyes hazy with the memory of that wicked day. "We should never have—" she returned, tilting her head slightly and straining toward him. Why didn't he kiss her? She wanted him to kiss her so very much.

"I have no regrets about that day," he returned, searching her face. "I only regret having brought you so much misery by responding to Mrs. Garston's flirtations. It was a betrayal of my love for you. I am sorry for that, Millie, but for the last time I will tell you again—I never—"

She placed her fingers over his lips. "I know you did not," she breathed, and quickly replaced her fingers with her lips. She felt the length of her body melt completely into him, as he kissed her hard in return. It seemed to her that the whole matter was settled between them in the twinkling of an eye.

When he picked her up, carried her to his bed, and in the tidiest manner possible, tossed her on his pillows, all the tensions of the past year dissipated in the golden glow of his bedchamber. She took him into the full embrace of her arms, forgiving all, forgetting even more, and drawing the man she loved into her heart.

Julianna awoke the following morning with a dull ache stretched across the top of her head. The first thought which greeted her as she opened her eyes and stared up at the charming blue silk rosette in the center of the canopy over her bed was, *Where is Carlton now, I wonder?*

When she squeezed her eyes shut, trying to push the thought away, a terrible image filled her mind, that of Carlton kissing the widow Garston.

She groaned aloud, and because she could not tolerate the thought of seeing more images as horrible as that one, she catapulted herself from the bed, crossed the room to throw back the curtains, rang for her maid, and began pacing the room. With each passing minute, her agitation increased. When she looked at the sailing ship and saw Carlton's final missive to her lying flat upon the cold wood, her stomach rose up like an ocean swell and broke in a hard wave over her heart.

She grew sick with something very much like terror.

Her maid arrived rather sleepy-eyed, since it was still quite early. She undoubtedly had not expected her mistress to rise before ten o'clock nonetheless eight, as it was now. "I can't lie about in bed today," she explained. "You may return to your slumbers once you have dressed my hair."

"Of course, miss," her maid returned, eyeing her mistress sadly.

A half hour later, Julianna was dressed in a morning gown of white muslin embroidered about the bodice and hem with dark green acanthus leaves. A ruffle encircled the whole of the hem, as well as the high neckline and the long sleeves. She left her chambers intending to descend to the morning room and write a letter to Eliza. Perhaps her dear friend could soothe her broken heart with a strong dose of common sense.

But when she passed by her father's door, she heard a woman's giggle through the thick oak.

She stopped abruptly and pressed a quick hand over her mouth to keep from gasping. Her father had taken a woman to bed while his wife slept in her chambers? One of the maids? Impossible! How could he be so cruel?

The whole of it was so revolting, so terrible, that she immediately passed quickly beyond to her mother's chamber. She scratched on the door several times, wanting to warn her of what was afoot. When there was no answer, she opened the door slowly at first, not wanting to startle her sleeping parent, but when she saw that the bed was empty, she threw the door wide, staring in disbelief at the counterpane stretched tidly from corner to corner.

Her mother's bed had not been slept in!

Without the least qualm of conscience, she retraced her steps and pressed her ear to her father's door. She heard murmurs and more laughter, but this time it was her father's, and then another feminine giggle and another. "Oh," she breathed, startled, surprised, stunned. She could not mistake the precise tenor of that giggle, one she had known all her life.

Her mother's!

She could not credit her ears!

Her mother and father, together, sharing the same bed. Was it possible?

The answer came to her in a single heartbeat. Yes.

She pressed her forehead against the door and sighed very deeply, very thankfully.

"It is over," she whispered to herself.

A moment more and she backed away from the door, grateful that the year-long breach in her parents' otherwise loving marriage had been healed. Her heart felt lighter than it had during the course of that same twelvemonth and she resumed her original objective, tripping down the stairs, smiling until she reached the bottom step.

There she paused, her hand on the banister, a sudden insightful realization breaking in her mind like an ocean wave against rocks. The spray rose high in the air to fall in a hard rain over her indecisiveness of the past several weeks.

It was her mother's unhappiness that had held her back, prevented her from recognizing the extent of her love for Carlton, as well as both her complete willingness to forgive him and her desire to forget a mode of conduct he had wanted undone a thousand times. She was not certain why it was that she had so thoroughly confused her mother's difficulties with her own, but so it was. For many months her mama had warned her against loving a man too much because then she was sure to be hurt. And when she had gotten hurt as surely as she had been promised she would, her ability to permit her to love Carlton in light of his repentance, to override her sense of betrayal, had simply not existed.

Until now.

Only . . .

Oh, Lord, it might be too late!

What should she do now? What could she do?

She turned about and dashed up the stairs. She penned a quick missive to her parents, tugged a warm green pelisse from her wardrobe against the drizzly April morning, pulled down three bandboxes from the shelves of her wardrobe until the matching green bonnet was found, pulled half-boots over her leather slippers, and a minute later was hailing a hackney which had just deposited a fare across Berkeley Square.

Lord Carlton resided in Grosvenor Square, which in truth was not all that far from Berkeley, but her own desperation gave her the sensation that it might as well have been a hundred miles or more.

She bade the driver to 'spring 'em, but on damp cobbled stones, a horse could not career breakneck through the streets, by even the smallest stretch of the imagination, without risking grave injury.

She held her hand to her stomach, watching the gray buildings move all too slowly past her window. She found she was searching every carriage that rolled by, in case one might be inhabited by either Carlton or his bride.

What if they were already married? There would be nothing she could do. Yet even if they weren't actually wed, since Carlton had offered for Mrs. Garston, the marriage could not be overset unless the Garston would somehow be willing to step aside—which of course she would not!

But Julianna would not think of that just yet! She would go mad if she did.

Regardless of Carlton's present circumstances, Julianna knew she simply had to speak with him before he was married. She wanted him to know how much she loved him, that not only had she forgiven the past, but that she had come to understand the source of her reticence and that her refusal of his hand had not been a lack of trust in his character.

When at last his home was reached, she hurried to the door and begged admittance of an extremely astonished butler. He glanced up the square and down the square and after frowning for two seconds more, permitted her to cross the portal into the entrance hall.

Julianna had not meant to let her surroundings deter her even a second, but just as she opened her mouth to speak, her gaze fell upon a staircase spiraling widely to the left of the entrance hall. She was struck dumb by the sight of it. The banister and attendant rails were meticulously carved of fine old oak and polished to a glimmering shine. Her gaze was drawn upward to a domed ceiling, decorated in finely sculptured stucco of white, the flat portions painted a medium shade of blue. Her gaze dropped to the exquisite white marble floor, veined with shadings from deep gold to a delicate apricot. Across the entrance, in a cove, stood a Grecian statue of Apollo. Her father had told her of the magnificence of Carlton's possessions, but she had not in her smallest daydreams conceived of so much beauty.

She pressed a hand to her breast and glanced toward the butler, who was watching her curiously. "I didn't come here for this," she stated, fearing he would misconstrue her motives. Yet it was entirely absurd to try to justify herself to a servant. She ordered her thoughts and addressed her more immediate concern. "I do apologize for seeming—that is, pray tell me, is his lordship at home? It is very urgent. Will you tell him Miss Redmere desires to speak with him?"

The butler frowned heavily and seemed almost sad as he replied, "I am ever so sorry, miss, but Lord Carlton left a half hour ago—"

"—With Mrs. Garston?"

"He was fetching her."

Julianna felt as though the beautiful marble floor beneath her feet was opening up and swallowing her. She did not know she was swaying on her feet until she felt his hand under her arm and his other arm about her waist. "I can see I've given you a bit of a shock. Come, sit down for a moment."

"I—I must go. I must stop him."

"Indeed, I believe you are right, miss, but sit down for a moment. Let me give you a sip of sherry and then we'll see."

"I must go now!"

"Sit!" he commanded.

For some reason, Julianna did so, staring up at him in surprise as she dropped into a black lacquer Grecian chair near the statue of Apollo.

"That's better," he said. He then rang for a footman, and within a few seconds a rather out-of-breath servant appeared. He requested the sherry and whispered several more unintelligible instructions to the astonished footman. The servant left and a few minutes later another breathless footman appeared bearing a decanter of sherry and a glass, all settled elegantly on a fine silver tray. After the butler sent the servant away, he watched Julianna swallow a generous amount, then asked if she was feeling better.

Julianna took a deep breath and was surprised to find that indeed, the sherry had had a somewhat soothing affect upon her nerves. Her mind was not jumping about so much and she was able to breathe more normally. "Yes, much better, thank you. It is unforgivable in me to have come here I know, but—but I simply had to! I've made a mull of it, you see. And I had *so* hoped to find his lordship still at home!"

The butler gave every indication he knew both who she was and the dilemma which had kept her trapped for so many weeks. "I've known Carlton since he was in leading strings and because many of the particular offices where you were concerned were fulfilled through my efforts, I know of his hoped-for intentions toward you. I don't know if I can offer you much hope, but I have ordered his lordship's barouche brought 'round for you. I believe he would have wanted me to do as much. He is headed north, since Mrs. Garston's mother and father reside in Hertfordshire. It is my belief they were to be married by the vicar there. If you can reach Islington as quickly as possible, I believe you will have an excellent chance of intercepting them beforetimes."

"Thank you so much," she said. "For—for everything."

He smiled down at her, and as she returned the now empty glass to him, he whispered, "If you can, detach him from Mrs. Garston. She is—well, let us simply say her character is not such that will in the end bring his lordship a great deal of happiness."

An hour later, Julianna sat in the parlour of the Peacock Inn at Islington in an extreme state of agitation. She watched the road with very much the same level of concentration a cat might watch a mousehole. Her gaze never wavered once from the continual press of carriages, coaches, and wagons traveling both directions. She was sure from her inquiries that Lord Carlton's town coach had not passed through the village.

She had had little doubt she would arrive before him, since he had departed his townhouse only a half hour before her arrival there and by necessity had had to retrieve Mrs. Garston from her home at the other end of Mayfair before heading north.

So it was that she waited, fretted, felt faint and dizzy all at once, until his coach with its unmistakable crest came sharply into view. As the large wheels rolled by, slowly to avoid locking wheels with a burdensome wagon, she rose from her seat, struggling to keep from fainting. Her knees trembled, her heart beat wildly in her breast. Would he turn into the inn, or would he continue on?

She saw in the window of the coach a smiling Mrs. Garston. How happy she looked.

Julianna's spirits took a sharp downward turn. Even if she was able to tell him of her mistake, he was not free to marry her any longer. How strange to think that only a few hours had made the difference between a lifetime of happiness or one of utter misery! She knew in her heart of hearts she would never love again, not like this, not someone so perfectly designed for her as she now fully comprehended Carlton was.

When his coach did pass through the gates of the Peacock and it became evident that she would be speaking with him, all her anxiety disappeared and in its stead was a sadness so profound that she simply sank back into the straight-backed chair, folded her hands upon her lap, and waited.

If she was regarded with some curiosity by a large family situated near the door and intent upon consuming a vast breakfast before continuing their journey, she ignored them completely.

Her attention was all for the moment when Carlton would cross the threshold.

Chapter Twenty-Eight

Mrs. Garston held her breath as Carlton's carriage rolled through the gates of the Peacock and entered the busy inn-yard. She swallowed hard, trying not to panic, as she released the viscount's arm and began making a quick visual search of the maze of vehicles packed about the stables of the inn. She had not been entirely certain that the young lady she had seen in the parlour window of the Peacock was Julianna Redmere until she found what she was looking for—Carlton's crest on a barouche at the far end. The moment she recognized the crest she knew that her rival was present and also precisely what had happened—Julianna had awakened to discover her stupidity, she had gone impulsively to Carlton's townhouse to inform him of her change of heart, and upon finding her quarry absent, she had somehow persuaded that wretched butler of Carlton's to lend her the barouche.

How did she know Julianna had done as much? Because had she been in Miss Redmere's pretty slippers, she would have done exactly the same thing! Except, of course, that she would never have let Carlton slip through her fingers in the first place, but that was neither here nor there!

If only she had not been such a sapskull as to have insisted upon stopping at the Peacock. Carlton hadn't wanted to, he had wanted to press on. But she had had to pause and revel in her victory by celebrating on the very spot at which the viscount had ruined his chances of ever wedding his elusive bride.

And now the bride was here!

She fairly ground her teeth together at this sudden shift of events. Until the vows had been spoken, she could not be entirely easy. Yet what could Julianna possibly hope to accomplish now? Carlton had already agreed to marry her, and being a gentleman of honor, he would not jilt her. She breathed a little easier at this thought.

No, she was safe. Of that she was certain.

Still, it would cast a considerable pall over the wedding night to have Stephen's thoughts fixed on some sort of absurd farewell to his true love.

Laying a hand on Carlton's arm, she decided her first objective must be to get the viscount away from the Peacock before he had spoken to Julianna. "You know," she began in a lilting voice, "I suddenly find I am not in the least hungry after all. Why don't we continue on our way just as you suggested, once the horses are changed? You cannot imagine how anxious I am to see my parents."

"If you wish for it, my dear, of course we can," he responded softly.

Mrs. Garston looked up at him and refused to accept as significant the resigned quality to his voice. Marrying for love was not all it was reputed to be. She had done so and had discovered one could be made quite miserable when one married strictly for love. No, Carlton would soon come 'round. After all, she fully intended to make him a very agreeable wife.

She immediately pinched his cheek. "You are the dearest man who ever lived, and I am fortunate beyond words. Mama will be so pleased when we arrive. Did you know that she has always been half in love with you herself?"

He laughed, and she could see that some of the tight lines about his mouth and eyes softened as he smiled. She was further gratified when he took her hand and wrapped it about his arm.

No, Carlton would be content, eventually.

The horses were nearly changed and she was grateful that the relative angle of the coach permitted him only the smallest space through which to see the old barouche. A minute more, that was all she required, and they would be gone.

But a minute was proving too long, for as he glanced past the horses, he saw the vehicle and said with a laugh, "You don't see that very often."

"What is that, my dear?" she asked, her heart beginning to jump about in her breast.

"An old barouche like the one my mother kept. In fact, that carriage is just like hers, the black top and burgundy body and—" he paused. "Good God! That *is* my crest!" He jerked his head around suddenly, looking first through his side window and then through hers, searching for whoever might have taken or borrowed his coach.

"What the devil—?" he cried, half-laughing, half-bemused.

"Carlton," she said, opening a sentence she did not know how to finish. She wanted to tell him they should leave anyway, but that would sound utterly ridiculous.

"Yes?" he queried impatiently, as he continued to scan the coachyard.

But she could think of nothing sensible to say. She did not want to utter the words *"Your beloved Julianna is here."* Nor could she find any reasonable way of preventing him from learning the source of the mystery. So she finally swallowed her fear and suggested, "Perhaps you should inquire of the hostler whether he knows who occupied the coach when it arrived."

"A perfectly sensible suggestion," he responded, as he opened the door of his traveling coach. "I cannot imagine anyone actually stealing my coach, but one never knows."

Mrs. Garston followed after him. "I think I shall go inside and request a cup of tea and a little bread after all," she said, hoping she sounded perfectly natural. "And take your time solving this extraordinary mystery, and pray do not bother your head about me."

She watched him head toward his coach, a feeling rather like numbness invading her heart. She descended the coach and pulled off her gloves of soft yellow kid, sighing deeply. She turned toward the back entrance of the inn, walking stiffly, trying to keep her heartbeat even, trying to order her thoughts, trying to determine what she should say to Miss Redmere.

She tucked her gloves into the pocket of her pelisse. She smoothed out the creases from the front of her elegant pelisse of red Merino wool trimmed with ermine fur. She adjusted the soft red felt hat atop her head and fluffed the single white ostrich feather which graced the brim of her neat little hat. She always made certain her costume was correct when she engaged the enemy.

And Julianna was the enemy.

A few moments later, she pushed open the door of the parlour—how odd to think of a quite foxed Lord Redmere seated by the window so many weeks ago. In his place, she found his daughter, sitting erect and appearing quite lovely in a green pelisse and bonnet, designed to accent her red hair to perfection. She was obviously awaiting the arrival of Carlton, for she was turned toward the door. How very much she hated her in this moment.

She looked hard upon her, meeting her gaze coldly before advancing into the busy square chamber. She ignored the noisy family seated nearest the door, but crossed slowly, preparing for the attack.

When she was two feet in front of Julianna, she drew in a deep breath through flared nostrils. "How dare you!" she whispered beneath her breath, her back to the family. The chamber fairly buzzed with their activity and she knew she could not be heard above the noise.

Miss Redmere merely lifted a brow as she looked up at her. "I know I have no claim upon him now, but I must speak with him."

"You shall not speak with him alone."

"Of course not," Julianna replied coldly.

"You will never see him again, or chase after him in this truly obnoxious manner."

"When he is your husband, madame, I would not think of behaving so abominably. The entire notion of pursuing another woman's husband is repugnant to me in the extreme. You can have no notion!"

Mrs. Garston lifted a brow and smiled faintly. "So you've claws, then. Well, take care, Julianna Redmere, for I have battled with cats far more skilled than you. I warn you, if you do not do as I wish, you will only suffer in his eyes for it."

When she saw Julianna look past her, and watched as her expression changed to one of a truly wretched sort of mooncalf love, she knew Carlton had arrived. She schooled her features to one of surprise and turned slowly around. Catching the viscount's eye, she smiled and cried, "Do but look who I have found waiting here in Islington! It would seem there was something she forgot to say to you. I think it utterly charming that she has arrived to wish *us* well."

When Julianna rose to her feet, she took her arm and gave her a hard pinch. Afterward, she moved quickly toward Carlton to take his arm and hold him closely to her side.

Julianna refused to permit Mrs. Garston's theatrics to deter her the smallest bit. She did not take her gaze from Carlton for a second, but drank in the expression of longing in his eyes as he watched her, knowing that this last meeting must needs carry her through many years of unhappiness.

She felt relief rush through her as she realized how grateful she was that she would have this final moment with him, even if it was with his *bride* looking on and casting daggars at her with her eyes. "I know I shouldn't have come, Carlton," she began. "But I wanted to say something to you before you married Mrs. Garston. I know that you must marry her and indeed I did not come to persuade you otherwise, only I felt

I had to tell you that I was wrong last night to have rejected you. I know that now because—because I only came to understand just this morning why it was I could not acquiesce to your persistent courtship of the past several weeks. I—I can't precisely reveal the particulars to you, but I will say that the source of my unwillingness to forgive you completely was my fear that you and I should one day find ourselves as unhappy as my parents have been for the past twelvemonth. I have come to trust you and your character, I have forgiven you utterly for your misplaced desire to abduct me, and I want nothing more than to know you understand what I have said and will forgive me as well for my foolishness in not sooner separating my love and faith in you from my distress over my father and mother's brangling."

She was not certain precisely the effect her words had had upon Carlton. His face was almost masklike, except that he clenched his jaw tightly. He drew in a long breath and stretched out his free hand to her, since Mrs. Garston still clung tenaciously to his other arm. She took his hand and held it for a long moment, squeezing it so hard that had she not been squeezing his equally hard in return she might have cried out in pain.

"Of course I forgive you, and I do understand," he responded.

This is the last time I will ever touch him, she thought, gazing into his eyes and seeing in them her love returned in full.

"We really must be going," Mrs. Garston cooed into his ear.

Slowly, he released Jilly's hand, and his eyes seemed to glaze over with a blind sheen. He patted the widow's hand, and after bowing to Julianna, guided his bride toward the door.

Julianna watched him go, noticing in some amusement that every member of the shabby-genteel family of nine was staring at Carlton. She heard the matronly, heavily bosomed woman breathe out his name in some awe as she elbowed her thin husband hard in the ribs. He choked over his steaming coffee, then uttered a *"By Gawd, Annabelle, you're right again. 'Tis Carlton himself."* The children, ranging in age from about three to thirteen, were noisily teasing and provoking one another, pulling faces and hair, whichever seemed handiest.

She wondered if she would ever have a family and whether or not her children would be as wretchedly behaved as these before her.

She thought not, on either score. She doubted with all her heart that, having loved Carlton and having known the depth of his love for her, she would ever accept another man's hand in marriage.

Just as Carlton moved to open the door of the parlour for his bride, suddenly the door swung wide, nearly striking the viscount, and from the doorway the shrieking of a man in some pain could be heard. Lord Carlton and Mrs. Garston fairly jumped out of the way as Lady Redmere entered the chamber, pulling Captain Beck by the ear. "You're ruining my hair, Millicent! Pray stop. Besides, it *hurts!*"

Following behind Captain Beck, Lord Redmere strode firmly into the room and bade Carlton to please attend him for a moment—and Mrs. Garston, too, if she would not mind. Mrs. Garston's expression changed rapidly, her fine, rosy complexion dwindling to a chalky white. Julianna could not comprehend in the least what her parents meant by it, or why her mother was angry with Captain Beck.

Carlton kept Mrs. Garston's hand firmly about his arm as he moved back into the chamber, crossing the room to stand by the fireplace—the portion of the parlour farthest from the family by the door. He patted her hand reassuringly, thereby giving his silent promise, as a man of honor, that he would stand by his word and marry her.

"Mama! Papa!" Julianna cried. "You are preventing Lord Carlton from fulfilling his duty to Mrs. Garston! Whatever do you mean by it? Why are you here? What did Captain Beck do to deserve your wrath?"

"What did he do?" Lady Redmere cried. "You'll never

credit your ears, Jilly! Not for a moment. I didn't either. But never mind that. Jack, please get rid of these people! Who are they, anyway?"

She waved her hand toward the nine curious creatures across the room, all of whom were staring rudely at the commotion before them.

Julianna would have been amused at the spectacle they made, had she not been completely confused by her parents' sudden appearance. Her father turned to the thin man and issued a command. "Please get out! At once!"

The man's brows rose and he started to rise submissively from the table, apparently recognizing the sound of authority when he heard it. But the lady was not so kindly disposed, and responded, "I'll thank you very much, governor, not to raise your voice to me or my husband, or my darling children. We've a right to enjoy our breakfast before climbing aboard the Mails, as much as you've a right to be here, too. So just lower your voice and apologize!"

But Lord Redmere narrowed his eyes, and after scrutinizing the family several times over, pulled his purse from his pocket, crossed the room to stand before the table, and threw at least half its contents onto the covers. For a stunned moment, each member of the family stared at the money; then, as one, they pounced upon it with vigor, their voices rising into the air like a sudden caterwauling of excited geese, as they argued over the dispersal of the largess—that is, until *mother* appropriated every last groat. Then, with kindly condescension, the group filed from the public room.

When they were gone and Redmere had instructed the landlord that he required the parlour for a few minutes more, Lady Redmere, who still had Captain Beck by the ear, instructed her Cicisbeo, "Tell Carlton what you told me, and Redmere, not an hour ago! Tell him at once, or you shall never enjoy polite society again, for I shall personally see to your ruination!"

"All right! As you wish, only—" he glanced toward Mrs. Garston and swallowed nervously. Julianna followed his gaze and noticed that the Garston was still quite pale, her gaze darting nervously from Beck to Lady Redmere to Carlton.

Her gaze finally landed upon Beck. "If you say one more word, James," Mrs. Garston managed in a harsh whisper. "I shall—I shall—"

"What *shall* you do?" Lady Redmere queried, releasing Beck. "Do you know what I think would be a far better course at this juncture? I think you ought to tell your betrothed all about your nefarious activities, beginning with a certain campaign of yours of last year."

"This is all quite absurd!" Mrs. Garston retorted. Releasing Lord Carlton's arm and turning to face him, she addressed him firmly. "I refuse to listen to anything this family might have to say to me or to you. After all, it is perfectly clear to me that they want only one thing, to see you married to their daughter. Their ambition must outweigh the truth in any event and as for whatever it is Captain Beck wishes to say, what sensible person would dare to lend a jot of credence to his mindless sputterings?"

Lady Redmere opened her reticule and withdrew a letter from it. She flung it across the floor, and it landed at Carlton's feet.

Mrs. Garston looked at it, her brows raised in horror. She covered her mouth with her hand. Carlton watched her and thoughtfully gave consideration to the chaos about him. He then bent down and picked up the letter.

Mrs. Garston's hands trembled visibly as she watched her betrothed open the missive and read it through. When he was done, he looked first at Julianna's mother, and then at her father. But he posed his question at last to Mrs. Garston, turning to look down at her, his voice quiet. "You intended to destroy their marriage? You sought purposefully to undermine Redmere's love for his wife? Why?"

"You—you cannot possibly interpret the contents of that letter in so despicable a manner. I never intended anything of the sort!"

He placed his finger about mid-page on the thin sheet and read, *"I believe he is so far in my spell that a few weeks more and he will be seeking a divorce from M. which only Parliament can grant . . ."*

Julianna drew near her mother, inexplicably feeling frightened. Her mother slipped her arm about her waist and held her close. She looked at her father and saw that the expression on his face had become painfully tight. He was watching his wife, shaking his head and whispering, "I still can't believe it. I was such a fool!"

Lady Redmere looked from her husband to Captain Beck and asked, "And who was it, James, who began the rumor that my husband was keeping Mrs. Garston as his mistress?"

But Captain Beck was looking beyond Lady Redmere to a small looking-glass on the wall and was shifting his head about in a familiar circular motion. Just as he pulled his chicken feather from the pocket of his coat and would have begun plucking at his curls, Lady Redmere again caught him by the ear.

She forced him to attend to her. When he had heard her original question, and she had again tugged hard on his ear and threatened to dump a pitcher of water over his black curls if he did not speak the truth, he cried out, "I did! I did!"

"But why did you start the rumor?" she asked. "You must tell all of us why."

"She paid me, of course! Why else would I have done it?"

"Who? Who paid you?"

"Charlotte! I have been in her employ for over two years."

"And what of Jilly and Carlton? Did you put about that rumor, as well—that she was Carlton's mistress?"

"Yes! Yes! Pray let me go. You are hurting me!"

"If you weren't such a village idiot, James, I'd have you flogged! Now, tell Carlton the truth again—who told you, indeed, who paid you to spread about such wicked gossip about him."

He glanced at Mrs. Garston and said, "I am sorry, Charlotte, but, damn, I've grown fond of Millie and Julianna. I told you you'd gone too far the first time, and what came of it? Nothing. And last night, when you made me bump into Jilly, I wanted to crawl beneath one of the chairs and disappear. I don't mind accepting money for a little spying, but you're a very meanspirited woman and I won't be your friend anymore."

"This is all such nonsense!" Mrs. Garston cried.

She jerked the letter from Carlton's hands, and quickly turning around, tossed it into the fireplace. She then addressed herself exclusively to Carlton. "You cannot possibly believe all that is being said here, and as for that letter, it is quite ancient history. I admit I behaved badly, but not more so than you did when you tried to trick Julianna into eloping with you. I beg your forgiveness for the past, and knowing your character to be fine and generous, I am persuaded you will forgive me. And now, may we continue on to Hertfordshire?"

Julianna glanced at Carlton, wondering what he would say and do. How clever Mrs. Garston had been both to discount Captain Beck's confession and to refer slyly to his own guilt as though his conduct somehow made her behavior less heinous.

She watched the man she loved intently and could see that he strove to determine what he ought to do. She knew that all hung in the balance.

Carlton was a man of honor and Mrs. Garston was a member of the *haut* ton. He could not readily dismiss his betrothal to her without repercussions.

Julianna looked at Mrs. Garston and saw a triumphant expression in her eyes. She believed Carlton would still marry her. Perhaps she was right. If only there were something she could say or do!

Chapter Twenty-Nine

But Julianna did not want the man she loved leg-shackled to a lady whose character was suspect. For Carlton to live with a woman who had so set her cap for him that she would have done anything to win his hand in marriage. For Carlton to wed a woman who Julianna was certain would soon become a veritable fishwife once the vows were spoken.

Only look at how she arches one brow and lifts her chin as though daring anyone to challenge her, she thought.

In this moment Julianna despised Charlotte Garston.

No, the Garston was not for Lord Carlton.

In the awful silence of the chamber, Jilly suddenly heard her own voice speaking. "Carlton," she began, turning toward him, "I don't give a fig for what scandal might ensue if you break your engagement to a woman I am convinced is unworthy of you. If you choose to end your betrothal to her, I will most happily accept of your hand in marriage, even if it means I will never again be permitted to, to *attend Almack's.* The truth is, I have no interest in seeking the approval of a society which made it quite difficult for you and me to come together in the first place. Gossip has hounded both of us from the beginning. If you still wish for it, I have a sudden powerful longing to pay a morning visit upon the Russian commanding officer at Fort Ross."

He seemed thunderstruck for a long, long moment. But his astonished expression soon gave way to a grateful smile.

He then burst out laughing.

Mrs. Garston interjected, "I don't see what you find so amusing, or how Miss Redmere can possibly tempt you with a wish to see a fort. May I remind you that your commitment is to me? The announcement of our marriage has already been sent to the *Morning Post*."

"I am well aware of my obligations, Mrs. Garston, but however much you have *charmed* me, I find I cannot possibly refuse Miss Redmere's offer. I hereby end our betrothal."

"I don't understand!" she cried. "Of course the *beau monde* was completely *aux anges* when Czar Alexander paid England a visit, but I had no notion you wished to return the favor by journeying to Fort Ross. But if that is what prompts you to end our engagement, then I will of course be more than happy to accompany you there. Where is it, anyway? Near Moscow?"

"Hardly. At the farthest end of the American Colonies, the western shores. The Russians have a fur-trading interest there."

Mrs. Garston looked at him as though he had gone mad. "You wish to travel in a ship to America? Across the ocean?"

"And many other places—the Levant, India, China, the Japans! Do you not enjoy ocean travel? Perhaps I should have mentioned that once we were married I had every intention of taking you upon a long honeymoon to at least two score foreign lands."

"You have gone mad!" she cried, her hand upon her lips. She was turning white again.

He placed his hands behind his back and spoke with great expression. "There is nothing like the roll of a ship over wave upon wave, each swell cresting like thunder against the side of ship, then lifting the vessel up high only to drop it down again—"

"—Oh, pray stop," Lady Redmere interrupted. "We can all see your object, Carlton, and that it is having the effect you require upon Mrs. Garston, but I hasten to inform you that the mere mention of the word *sea* or *ship* affects me equally as badly. So, if you don't mind, I shall assist you in explaining everything to Mrs. Garston." She then turned to the widow and said, "If you decide to force Lord Carlton's hand, I wish to inform you that I have three other letters of yours, written to this simpleton you hired to inform you of my movements and later, Julianna's, which, if placed in, oh, let us say, Lady Catterick's capable hands, will undoubtedly ruin you in the eyes of society forever. Of course, if you are inclined, as my daughter apparently is, to take to the high seas with the man you love—Carlton, if you haven't already forgotten—then my threats will not matter in the least. Be advised, however, that if you do not immediately release him from a betrothal as avaricious as it is absurd, I will give these letters to Eliza Catterick—and I will be quick about it, make no mistake!"

Mrs. Garston looked from Lady Redmere to Lord Carlton and for a long moment seemed to withdraw into her own mind. No other emotion crossed her beautiful features than a rather sterile calculativeness.

Julianna waited breathlessly. She comprehended enough of Charlotte Garston's character now to know that the widow was as likely to reject her mother's offer as to accept it—though she strongly suspected that Carlton's threats of taking her to sea might tilt the scales against marriage to him.

Mrs. Garston finally came to her decision and spoke exclusively to Lord Carlton. "I could brave society's censure upon my conduct, even ostracization for a time, I might even possibly accustom myself to sailing around the world with you, but I strongly suspect that you would not at all like having your hand forced. I suppose I must seem the coldest fish ever, but I want you to know that whatever your opinion of me now, I would have done everything to have made you the best of wives."

Lord Carlton stepped toward her, clearly unmoved by this speech, and offered her his arm. "You may make use of my barouche, if you like."

"Thank you, I believe I shall."

With that, he escorted his bride from the parlour.

Captain Beck edged toward the door in their wake, but Lady Redmere crossed quickly to intercept him, catching him by the arm and pulling him back toward the fireplace. "Now, where did you think you were going?" she asked. "Silly man."

He opened his lazy brown eyes quite wide. "I—I don't know, precisely," he responded, swallowing nervously. "I suppose I thought to purchase a seat on the Mails and return to London."

"Captain Beck!" Julianna chided gently, drawing near him as well. "How could you have served my mother such an unhappy turn last year?"

He licked his lips. "I am a knave," he said. "I know that. I knew it finally when Charlotte bade me ram into you last night, Jilly. Even I could see by the way your face appeared—as though you had been transported by angels— that you meant to give your hand to Carlton."

Lady Redmere clicked her tongue at him. "But you saved us all in the end, and for that I shall be eternally grateful."

"You will?" he queried. "You do not mean to give me the cut direct?"

"On no account, but you must promise never to play at spying again."

"Upon my soul, I shall never cross you again."

Lord Redmere rolled his eyes. "You will, however, have to find another object for your attentions."

"Oh, I see. You do not want me about any longer."

"That's the way of it," Lord Redmere stated, then beneath his breath, "Idiot!"

Captain Beck shrugged. "I suppose I will have to accept Lady Catterick's kind offer, then. She has been trying to steal me away from Millie for the past year."

"She has?" Lady Redmere queried, surprised. "And what sort of bribery has she offered you?"

"Living quarters," he said baldly.

Julianna cried, "You are not serious? In London?"

"Yes, and in Bath, which she prefers to Brighton, and in Gloucestershire, through Christmas."

"Quite generous!" Lady Redmere said, patting his arm by way of congratulating him. "You are fortunate indeed. But I trust you will spend at least a fortnight each summer with us in Yorkshire."

"I would be honored."

Julianna then asked her mother, "How did you learn of Beck's treachery?"

"This morning, your father and I were discussing all that had transpired in the past year, and especially all that either of us knew of Charlotte Garston. I remembered that during the first two days of your elopement, Beck disappeared twice for no apparent reason—once in the study, when I was learning of your elopement from Mr. Fitzpaine, and later on our journey south, when we spent half an hour searching for him. When we found him, he complained of a drover's inn not being able to post a letter for him. I thought nothing of it until this morning, when I asked your father how it was the widow had been present in Islington at the very moment he was there. You see, I had always mistakenly believed he had asked her to join him, but he swore he had not. Of course, I already knew that Lady Catterick and her friends had not told Mrs. Garston about your elopement, so who, then, would have informed the widow? I began to consider the extraordinary circumstance of a lady so nearly connected by gossip to both Redmere and Carlton actually arriving just when she did. I could only conclude that some mischief had been afoot. Remembering how horridly James and the Garston had rammed you last night, well! When your father and I found your letter this morning, we decided to discover the truth and James, quite disillusioned with his employer anyway, did not disappoint us." She reached up and pinched the captain's cheek. "And he was truly repentant!"

"Just so," Beck replied on a firm nod.

"What a horrid creature Mrs. Garston is," Julianna said, shaking her head.

"Indeed, yes," Beck agreed. "But to her credit, I must say she is the only lady I have ever known who kept enough mirrors about. Never once in her house did I find it necessary to search for a shiny object by which I could adjust my curls."

Julianna exchanged a glance with her mother and both ladies laughed aloud. When Beck wished to know what they found so amusing, they laughed harder still.

After her chuckling had subsided, Julianna began to wonder where Carlton was. She was about to consider the possibility of going in search of him when she chanced to notice that her father, who was looking at something out the window, appeared as though he had been struck across the face. "Good God!" he muttered beneath his breath. "Who brought them here?"

"What is it?" Julianna cried, whirling about. "Oh! Oh, I see. Captain, what do you know of this?"

She watched Captain Beck turn a bright pink. "My new benefactress is quite exacting," he explained, swallowing hard. "Millie, I am sorry, but she is giving me a roof over my head and—and has already purchased a year's supply of macassar oil for me. There was nothing for it."

But Lady Redmere merely shook her head at him. "Wretched man," she said, smiling.

A few moments later, Lady Catterick, Mrs. Whenby, and Mrs. Bulmer entered the parlour. Lady Redmere called out to them, "You have just missed all the fun. Carlton is even now sending Mrs. Garston back to London."

"Indeed?" Lady Catterick queried, with a smile.

"Oh, my!" Mrs. Whenby chirped.

"How fortuitous!" Mrs. Bulmer boomed. "Are we then to offer Julianna our best wishes?"

Lady Redmere took up her place beside her daughter, and holding Jilly's hand, tightly responded, "Yes, you most certainly are."

"Ah," all three ladies returned happily.

Lady Redmere then carefully explained to society's finest hostesses and most accomplished gossips that since it was Carlton's wish to travel abroad extensively and since Mrs. Garston could not abide sailing vessels of any kind, it was concluded that Mrs. Garston would prefer not to marry the viscount after all.

The three ladies stared at one another for a long moment.

Lady Catterick broke the silence first. "Sounds like a hum," she cried.

Mrs. Whenby clucked her tongue. "Telling a whisker, Millicent?" she queried.

Mrs. Bulmer crossed her arms over her heavy bosom. "Pitching a bit of gammon, eh, my Lady Redmere?" she asked.

"The truth would be an ugly matter," Lady Redmere returned. "And I will not have the truth tarnish my daughter's wedding day."

"Nor would we," Lady Catterick said, addressing Lady Redmere. "Although I think it heinous of Mrs. Garston to have actually set Beck to spying on your household. I trust he told you as much?" Lady Redmere only blinked in response. "Good. I would imagine, then, that you informed the widow her deeds would be bandied about all of Mayfair if she did not relinquish Carlton?"

"But how did you know?" Lady Redmere cried, astonished at Lady Catterick's surprising knowledge of her very maneuver.

Lady Catterick tugged slightly upon her black wig and said, "It was a logical ploy and an effective one, I see."

As though to confirm her supposition, Lord Carlton returned, and after bowing to the ladies, delivered the happy news that Charlotte Garston was even now speeding back to London. He then announced that he had secured a private parlour for their comfort and had already sent one of the stableboys to request the services of the local vicar. Given the presence of Julianna's parents—and the intent of all—the clergyman could easily perform those rites so necessary to bringing about a happy conclusion of five weeks of miserable uncertainty and anguish.

When he saw his future father-in-law and mama-in-law, along with Captain Beck, Lady Catterick, Mrs. Whenby, and Mrs. Bulmer, led away to the parlour, he held Julianna back until the door closed on the last of them. He drew her to the door, and after securing it shut with his booted foot, took his *elusive bride* into his arms.

"There ought to be such an expression as the *twelfth hour*, since this entire episode seems well beyond the *eleventh,*" he said, smiling contentedly down at her.

Jilly looked up into his face, her heart so full of love for him that she could not speak.

"Jilly, my darling," he breathed, leaning so close to her she could feel his breath on her cheek. "Are you really here? Are you truly in my arms? Are we to be married, at last?"

"Yes, my love," she whispered in return, as he placed a gentle kiss upon her cheek.

His lips drifted slowly toward hers. She met his kiss and savored the sweetness of this first joining after so many weeks. She did not cling to him as she might have done, but instead reveled in the sensation of being gently embraced and tenderly kissed by the man she loved.

He drew back from her slightly and she found herself looking into serious gray eyes. "I love you," he murmured. "So very much. No matter what comes to us, Julianna, no matter what difficulties spring up in the trials of living out our lives together, I want you to hold to my love for you as I will in turn hold to the expression I see writ on your face even now, as I will trust to the memory of the look in your eyes when I saw you standing here a few moments ago, telling me you would forsake all of society's pleasures to travel the seas with me, as I will hold to the remembrance of how readily you fell into my arms at the Angel in Redmere so many weeks ago. Tell me you will always remember."

"I will always remember," she breathed. "Always."

He kissed her again, but his former gentleness was replaced by a possessiveness which she yielded to readily. She slipped an arm about his neck just as he encircled her waist with his arm and drew her tightly to him. Her thoughts began to swim lazily about in her mind, of how much she loved him, of how hard it had been over the past several weeks to keep from running to him when she would hold one of his letters in her hands, of how each of his bouquets had touched her woman's heart, of how he had attended Almack's in spite of his vow eight years earlier never to cross the portals again.

She loved him. She would always love him. Always.

When he drew back again, she said, "I fell in love with you the moment I rode into the innyard at the Angel. Did you know as much?"

"I knew only that I had begged of heaven to rescue me from marrying a young woman I had never before met and a moment later, you flew through the gates of the inn. I was convinced my prayers had been heard and answered."

Julianna, her arm still snuggled comfortably about his neck, giggled, "And it was me all the time."

"And it was you all the time."

"I love you, Carlton."

He sighed. "There is something most formal about that. Why don't you call me by my Christian name—Stephen."

She smiled up at him, relief, wonder and affection of the sweetest kind flooding her heart. "I love you, Stephen."

Again he kissed her, but this time forcefully, pausing only in his tender assaults to speak her name, to whisper his love into her hair, and to promise a long voyage upon the oceans of the world as soon as was reasonably possible.

Several minutes later, when the landlord begged admittance, only then did Carlton release her and lead her to the parlour, where they were greeted with uplifted glasses of champagne, smiles, and well-wishes. The vicar, quite out of breath but happy to be of service to his lordship, arrived soon after. Once he was apprised of the conditions of Carlton's inheritance, as well as the seriousness with which each party approached their marriage, he wasted no time in beginning the required ceremony.

All was proceeding tidily until the vicar caught sight of Captain Beck moving his head about in an awkward manner as he stared wide-eyed at a silver candlestick on the mantel behind the wedding party.

He broke off and whispered to Julianna, "Is he all right? Is it perchance the apoplexy? There is certainly an odd light in his eye!"

Julianna glanced at the captain and giggled. "He is perfectly well, I assure you," she responded in a low, conspiratorial voice. "It is his hair, you see. He can't abide a single strand out of place."

When Captain Beck withdrew his featherless quill from the pocket of his coat and began picking at his curls, the vicar breathed a sigh of relief. "Ah," he murmured knowingly. "I have some macassar oil I will recommend to him. Now, as I was saying, do you, Lord Carlton, take this woman. . . ."

About the Author

Valerie King lives with her family in Glendale, Arizona. She has written over ten regency novels for Zebra, including MY LADY VIXEN, CAPTIVATED HEARTS, A LADY'S GAMBIT, CUPID'S TOUCH, and LOVE MATCH. She is currently working on her next Zebra regency romance, MERRY, MERRY MISCHIEF, which will be published in December 1994. Valerie loves to hear from her readers and you may write to her c/o Zebra Books. Please include a self-addressed, stamped envelope if you wish a response.

ZEBRA REGENCIES
ARE
THE TALK OF THE TON!

A REFORMED RAKE   (4499, $3.99)
by Jeanne Savery

After governess Harriet Cole helped her young charge flee to France — and the designs of a despicable suitor, more trouble soon arrived in the person of a London rake. Sir Frederick Carrington insisted on providing safe escort back to England. Harriet deemed Carrington more dangerous than any band of brigands, but secretly relished matching wits with him. But after being taken in his arms for a tender kiss, she found herself wondering — *could* a lady find love with an irresistible rogue?

A SCANDALOUS PROPOSAL   (4504, $4.99)
by Teresa DesJardien

After only two weeks into the London season, Lady Pamela Premington has already received her first offer of marriage. If only it hadn't come from the *ton's* most notorious rake, Lord Marchmont. Pamela had already set her sights on the distinguished Lieutenant Penford, who had the heroism and honor that made him the ideal match. Now she had to keep from falling under the spell of the seductive Lord so she could pursue the man more worthy of her love. Or was he?

A LADY'S CHAMPION   (4535, $3.99)
by Janice Bennett

Miss Daphne, art mistress of the Selwood Academy for Young Ladies, greeted the notion of ghosts haunting the academy with skepticism. However, to avoid rumors frightening off students, she found herself turning to Mr. Adrian Carstairs, sent by her uncle to be her "protector" against the "ghosts." Although, Daphne would accept no interference in her life, she *would* accept aid in exposing any spectral spirits. What she never expected was for Adrian to expose the secret wishes of her hidden heart . . .

CHARITY'S GAMBIT   (4537, $3.99)
by Marcy Stewart

Charity Abercrombie reluctantly embarks on a London season in hopes of making a suitable match. However she cannot forget the mysterious Dominic Castille — and the kiss they shared — when he fell from a tree as she strolled through the woods. Charity does not know that the dark and dashing captain harbors a dangerous secret that will ensnare them both in its web — leaving Charity to risk certain ruin and losing the man she so passionately loves . . .

Available wherever paperbacks are sold, or order direct from the Publisher. Send cover price plus 50¢ per copy for mailing and handling to Penguin USA, P.O. Box 999, c/o Dept. 17109, Bergenfield, NJ 07621. Residents of New York and Tennessee must include sales tax. DO NOT SEND CASH.

TODAY'S HOTTEST READS
ARE TOMORROW'S SUPERSTARS

VICTORY'S WOMAN   (4484, $4.50)
by Gretchen Genet
Andrew—the carefree soldier who sought glory on the battlefield, and returned a shattered man . . . Niall—the legandary frontiersman and a former Shawnee captive, tormented by his past . . . Roger—the troubled youth, who would rise up to claim a shocking legacy . . . and Clarice—the passionate beauty bound by one man, and hopelessly in love with another. Set against the backdrop of the American revolution, three men fight for their heritage—and one woman is destined to change all their lives forever!

FORBIDDEN   (4488, $4.99)
by Jo Beverley
While fleeing from her brothers, who are attempting to sell her into a loveless marriage, Serena Riverton accepts a carriage ride from a stranger—who is the handsomest man she has ever seen. Lord Middlethorpe, himself, is actually contemplating marriage to a dull daughter of the aristocracy, when he encounters the breathtaking Serena. She arouses him as no woman ever has. And after a night of thrilling intimacy—a forbidden liaison—Serena must choose between a lady's place and a woman's passion!

WINDS OF DESTINY   (4489, $4.99)
by Victoria Thompson
Becky Tate is a half-breed outcast—branded by her Comanche heritage. Then she meets a rugged stranger who awakens her heart to the magic and mystery of passion. Hiding a desperate past, Texas Ranger Clint Masterson has ridden into cattle country to bring peace to a divided land. But a greater battle rages inside him when he dares to desire the beautiful Becky!

WILDEST HEART   (4456, $4.99)
by Virginia Brown
Maggie Malone had come to cattle country to forge her future as a healer. Now she was faced by Devon Conrad, an outlaw wounded body and soul by his shadowy past . . . whose eyes blazed with fury even as his burning caress sent her spiraling with desire. They came together in a Texas town about to explode in sin and scandal. Danger was their destiny—and there was nothing they wouldn't dare for love!

Available wherever paperbacks are sold, or order direct from the Publisher. Send cover price plus 50¢ per copy for mailing and handling to Penguin USA, P.O. Box 999, c/o Dept. 17109, Bergenfield, NJ 07621. Residents of New York and Tennessee must include sales tax. DO NOT SEND CASH.

DISCOVER DEANA JAMES!